PRAISE FOR DIANE A

'*Mosaic* flows like a novel, which once started is hard to put down. It is a compelling family history of extraordinary people against some of the most frightening events of our century. The depth of emotions evoked is stunning. I was thrilled and deeply moved.'
—Joseph Heller, author of *Catch 22*, on *Mosaic*

'Diane Armstrong's book is a source of delight to the reader. Written with fervour and talent, it will capture your attention and retain it to the last page.'
—Nobel Prizewinner Elie Wiesel on *Mosaic*

'A most remarkable book about one family's experience … a rich and compelling history…Just as AB Facey's *A Fortunate Life* and Sally Morgan's *My Place* have become part of the national literary heritage, so too has *Mosaic* earned its place in our social dialogue as part of our cultural tapestry.'
—*Daily Telegraph* on *Mosaic*

'Diane Armstrong's novel is a nuanced rendition of the moral conundrums individuals face in extremis. She concludes that "perhaps no sin is unforgivable, if you can understand the sinner". Among survivors, forgiveness and understanding are highly charged and hotly contested notions. Armstrong's novel is sincere contribution to that fraught discussion.'
—Louise Adler, *The Australian*, on *The Collaborator*

'Sometimes, if you are a writer, you read a book and experience a form of envy when you wish that you had been fortunate enough to uncover the story yourself. I had a little shard of that feeling in my heart when I read Diane

Armstrong's new novel ... the reader is in for a story that hinges on moral ambiguity—a satisfyingly rich and complex zone of shades of grey prompting questions about courage and personal responsibility.'
—Caroline Baum, Plus 61J Media, on *The Collaborator*

'[A] gripping story ... in which [Diane Armstrong] plumbs the depths of the human condition.'
—Amy Lees, Sunday Telegraph, on *The Collaborator*

'Guaranteed to hook you with its powerful and emotive journey back into a turbulent history, *The Collaborator* is a superb and compelling novel that comes highly recommended'
—*Canberra Weekly*

'Armstrong takes two apparently totally disconnected lives and weaves them together in an intricate historical design that enables her to tell touching human stories and also to explore serious philosophical issues such as the nature of goodness, evil, crime, guilt, forgiveness, and gratitude.'
—*Historical Novels Review* on *The Collaborator*

'Author Diane Armstrong re-knits savage history into a successful weave of heroism, betrayal, vengeance, and hope ... a well-researched, compassionate story that illuminates the complexity of the courageous, often impossible life choices made by individuals during—and because of—World War II.'
—*Washington Independent Review of Books* on *The Collaborator*

'I found myself replaying the scenes in the book like a film reel in my mind ... *Nocturne* is one of those novels that will leave

you reading into the night and will stay with you, like the notes of an unforgettable melody, long after you've read the last line.'
—*Australian Jewish News* on *Nocturne*

'A moving and poignant celebration of survival ...'
—*Booklist* on *Mosaic*

'A consummate writer at the top of her form ... remarkable for her narrative dexterity and emotional resonance. A bold adventure of a novel ... a fine fictional debut from a writer who's already made her mark.'
—Sara Dowse, *The Canberra Times*, on *Winter Journey*

'A cleverly crafted mystery ... a good story, well told. Armstrong's skill in weaving an elaborate fabric out of her characters and subject matter stand her in good stead ... the bleak wintry landscapes of the Polish countryside are vividly captured.'
—Andrew Riemer, *The Sydney Morning Herald*, on *Winter Journey*

'A complex and often heart-and-gut-wrenching novel. The book intelligently explores the need to confront and acknowledge evil before it can be exorcised. Armstrong's supremely confronting basic material is crucial to our understanding of ourselves as "warped timber" humanity.'
—Katharine England, *Adelaide Advertiser*, on *Winter Journey*

'The best and worst of the human spirit are dredged up in this profoundly moving, compelling and superbly written story.'
—Carol George, *Australian Women's Weekly*, on *Winter Journey*

'Like Geraldine Brooks, Diane Armstrong's historical research is expertly woven into the fabric of a fictional tale, providing an engrossing "action" of heroism and resilience which will appeal to both fans of fictional dramatic/romantic sagas, as well as lovers of insightful history'
—*Australian Bookseller & Publisher* on *Nocturne*

'Easy reading, racy … Diane Armstrong's *Nocturne* is in the category of blockbuster with extra heart. The stories of the role played by young women in the Warsaw revolt are extraordinary … Armstrong keeps us turning the pages and may well introduce a new readership to a story that must keep on being told.'
—*The Age* on *Nocturne*

'A gallant and gut-wrenching story. The accounts of the two uprisings … are dramatic and heart-breaking … superb reading.'
—*Australian Book Review* on *Nocturne*

'*Nocturne* had me captured from its opening chapters … it is an inspirational account of how ordinary people are forced to find strength and courage within themselves when the world around them falls apart.'
—*Vibewire* on *Nocturne*

'A stirring and powerful tapestry into which she has masterfully interwoven the story of her family with the enormity of the Holocaust, commuting fluently between the individual and the historical, the particular and the universal.'
—*Australian Jewish News* on *Mosaic*

'Her rich account of lives good and bad, love, joy, bravery, greed, and bitterness is a testament to the human spirit. Armstrong's stories will bring smiles and tears.'
—*Marie-Claire* on *Mosaic*

'It is no small achievement and it bristles with life … *Mosaic* is a work of many levels. But ultimately it succeeds because most of its characters demonstrate how the human spirit can soar way, way above adversity.'
—*The Sydney Morning Herald* on *Mosaic*

'A haunting Holocaust history that deserves shelf space alongside Primo Levi and Elie Wiesel. Diane Armstrong's work is a monumental accomplishment—both accessible enough and powerful enough to linger in our consciousness long after we have turned the last page.'
—Barnes & Noble on *Mosaic*

'*Mosaic* has the epic sweep and emotional depth of a nineteenth-century novel. Her skilful blending of vibrant individual voices across the generations makes this memoir a touching tribute to the healing powers of storytelling as well as to the unquenchable human spirit.'
—Amazon.com on *Mosaic* (one of Amazon's Top Ten memoirs 2001)

'A vivid, heartwarming family memoir. The plot and her characters move along in a fast-paced, tightly woven narrative.'
—*Publishers Weekly* on *Mosaic*

'Armstrong weaves in these individual tales with great skill. They flow in and out of the narrative in rhythm with the ship's slow movement from the old world to the new.'
—*The Age* on *The Voyage of Their Life*

'Armstrong's triumph in this history is to avoid judgment or argument…she allows readers to enter into the mindset of the refugees, to empathise with them'
—*Weekend Australian* on *The Voyage of Their Life*

'The characters become familiar and absorbing…almost unbearably moving'
—*Australian Book Review* on *The Voyage of Their Life*

'She is a natural sleuth…her writing is clear, incisive, yet imaginative'
—*The Sydney Morning Herald* on *The Voyage of Their Life*

'While it is a good read, *The Voyage of Their Life* is also an important historical document in that it gives humanity and dignity to the stories of dispossessed people arriving in post-war Australia.'
—*Wentworth Courier* on *The Voyage of Their Life*

'Diane Armstrong's study of the *Derna* is an important contribution to post-war Australian history. Her careful research combined with her excellent writing skills make this book essential reading for anyone interested in the development of Australian society.'
—Dr Suzanne Rutland, *Australian Historical Society Journal*, on *The Voyage of Their Life*

Diane Armstrong is a child Holocaust survivor who arrived in Australia from Poland in 1948. An award-winning journalist and bestselling author, she has written six previous books.

Her family memoir *Mosaic: A chronicle of five generations* was published in 1998 and was shortlisted for the Victorian Premier's Literary Award for Non-Fiction as well as the National Biography Award. It was published in the United States and Canada, and was selected as one of the year's best memoirs by Amazon.com. In 2001 *The Voyage of Their Life: The story of the SS Derna and its passengers* was shortlisted for the New South Wales Premier's Literary Award for Non-Fiction.

Her first novel, *Winter Journey*, was published in 2004 and shortlisted for the 2006 Commonwealth Writers' Prize. It has been published in the US, UK, Poland and Israel. Her second novel, *Nocturne*, was published in 2008 and won the Society of Women Writers Fiction Award. It was nominated for a major literary award in Poland. *Empire Day*, a novel set in postwar Sydney, was published in 2011, and *The Collaborator*, set in Hungary and Israel, was published in Australia, the United States and the United Kingdom in 2019.

Diane has a son and a daughter and three granddaughters. She lives in Sydney.

Also by Diane Armstrong

Non-fiction
Mosaic: A chronicle of five generations
*The Voyage of Their Life: The story of
the SS Derna and its passengers*

Fiction
Winter Journey
Nocturne
Empire Day
The Collaborator

Diane Armstrong

DANCING WITH THE ENEMY

Although this book is inspired by historical events, this is a work of fiction. Names, characters, places, and incidents are either the product of the author's imagination or are used fictitiously.

First Published 2022
First Australian Paperback Edition 2022
ISBN 9781867206545

DANCING WITH THE ENEMY
© 2022 by Diane Armstrong
Australian Copyright 2022
New Zealand Copyright 2022

Except for use in any review, the reproduction or utilisation of this work in whole or in part in any form by any electronic, mechanical or other means, now known or hereafter invented, including xerography, photocopying and recording, or in any information storage or retrieval system, is forbidden without the permission of the publisher.

This book is sold subject to the condition that it shall not, by way of trade or otherwise, be lent, resold, hired out or otherwise circulated without the prior consent of the publisher in any form of binding or cover other than that in which it is published and without a similar condition including this condition being imposed on the subsequent purchaser.

All rights reserved including the right of reproduction in whole or in part in any form.

This is a work of fiction. Names, characters, places, and incidents are either the product of the author's imagination or are used fictitiously, and any resemblance to actual persons, living or dead, business establishments, events, or locales is entirely coincidental.

Published by
HQ Fiction
An imprint of Harlequin Enterprises (Australia) Pty Limited (ABN 47 001 180 918),
a subsidiary of HarperCollins Publishers Australia Pty Limited (ABN 36 009 913 517)
Level 13, 201 Elizabeth St
SYDNEY NSW 2000
AUSTRALIA

® and ™ (apart from those relating to FSC®) are trademarks of Harlequin Enterprises (Australia) Pty Limited or its corporate affiliates. Trademarks indicated with ® are registered in Australia, New Zealand and in other countries.

A catalogue record for this book is available from the National Library of Australia
www.librariesaustralia.nla.gov.au

Printed and bound in Australia by McPherson's Printing Group

*For John Lewis, Peter Hassall and Bob le Sueur,
who lived through the Occupation of
Jersey and inspired this novel.*

CHAPTER ONE

Dr Jackson

St Helier, June 1940

It was a perfect June evening that began with hope and ended in despair. Every detail is tattooed on my brain, as if the movie of my life stopped midframe, frozen in time. It was twilight, that enchanting part of a summer's day when it feels as if the light will go on forever, as if night will never fall. Margaret and I had just finished tea in our new house on St Mark's Road and we were sitting by the French windows that opened onto our orchard, watching the blue haze of dusk begin to settle over the trees. A flurry of wings and a murmuration of swallows flew above the apple and pear trees in splendid unison. A moment later they were gone.

Margaret was knitting another matinee jacket with matching bootees in the palest lemon wool, her needles clicking away, while I sipped a glass of aged French Armagnac, a gift from a grateful patient to her even more grateful doctor. The cognac warmed and softened every part of my body and a rare sense of contentment flooded over me. We had bought our dream home, my practice was growing, and in two more months our family would be complete.

For the second time in my life I was seized by wild excitement. The first was when I held Margaret in my arms on our honeymoon. I could hardly believe that the girl whose delicate beauty had made my heart turn somersaults from the moment I first laid eyes on her was mine at last. The enchantment hadn't faded, and now I couldn't wait to meet our baby and look into its eyes. I'm certain she felt the same excitement, but she was more reserved, and said less. While she knitted, we discussed names as we did so often. She liked Vivien for a girl because she had recently seen *Gone with the Wind*. Her choice for a boy was James. 'Not Rhett or Ashley?' I teased.

As we waited for the BBC News on the wireless, I marvelled at how fast the tiny jacket grew under her nimble fingers. The last of the daylight filtered onto the polished timber floor and lit up Margaret's hair, which fell across her cheek as she bent to pick up the skein that had fallen from her small basket.

She sat up as soon as we heard the familiar fanfare that heralded the start of the news. We listened. A moment later, I put down my glass and she put down her knitting. Hardly breathing, we leaned towards the wireless so as not to miss a single word.

In a sepulchral voice, the announcer stated that the British government had decided that the Channel Islands were to be demilitarised.

Margaret looked at me in alarm. 'What does that mean?' she whispered.

'It means we are now on our own,' I said. 'Undefended, unprotected and betrayed.' Suddenly I remembered something my late mother once said: *Life fulfils and then betrays all your hopes.* In the space of that hour, I had experienced both.

It turned out that we'd been living in a fool's paradise on our peaceful little island, believing that our cocooned existence in Jersey would continue as usual, and that the war raging on the other side of the Channel didn't concern us. As if to reinforce our complacency, thousands of sun-hungry tourists from Britain continued to flock to our sandy beaches as they had always done.

Looking back, I think the world as we knew it had begun to crumble four years earlier, with the abdication of King Edward VIII. At the time, we saw it as a regrettable but isolated event, but in light of later developments, I think it indicated a general lowering of moral standards and foreshadowed a succession of unsettling events that threatened our comfortable lives.

Margaret applauded Edward's decision as a triumph of love over royal privilege, but I saw it as a dereliction of duty, and I suspected that it had as much to do with his distaste for royal responsibilities as with his inability to live without Mrs Simpson. And I felt sorry for his stuttering brother, who was now thrust onto a throne he didn't want.

For some reason, my attitude seemed to irritate Margaret, who became quite vehement in her criticism.

'You don't have a single romantic bone in your body,' she said. 'How can you put duty ahead of love?'

I replied that if everyone followed Edward's example and decided to abandon their duty, society would disintegrate, and I suggested that perhaps her condition had made her overemotional. This sparked a row, and we argued heatedly, not suspecting that the conflict between love and duty would soon be acted out in our own lives.

About eighteen months after the abdication, our country suffered another moral lapse, when Prime Minister Chamberlain travelled to Munich to appease a tyrant who seemed to believe he was entitled to trample over other countries with impunity. Mr Chamberlain came back waving that piece of paper and talking about nice Mr Hitler.

'Chamberlain's an idiot,' my father had fumed. Father was a retired army major who had fought in the Boer War, and later in the one they called the Great War, and he didn't mince words. 'You can't negotiate with bullies, and you certainly don't reward them. You whack them hard to teach them a lesson.'

As usual, he was right. Father, who never suffered from doubt, died in the spring last year, and I missed his dogmatic certitude. Encouraged by naïve politicians who averted their gaze, Hitler continued invading neighbouring countries until on 3 September our leaders finally opened their eyes and declared war.

So we entered 1940 at war with Germany. After that shock announcement, some patriotic Jerseymen enlisted in the British army, but then nothing happened, or so it appeared to us in Jersey. Although the British government had entered the war to support Poland's sovereignty, no British soldiers or fighter planes were sent to defend it from German tanks. War was being fought far away. We read about it, but it didn't affect us. In the meantime, merchant ships kept docking in our harbour, loading up tons of Jersey tomatoes and potatoes, the tourists kept coming to sunbake on our beaches, and life continued as usual.

But as the year progressed, it all changed. In May, the war exploded into our consciousness, first with the defeat of Belgium, Luxembourg and Holland, and then with the shocking defeat of France. We were appalled to see photographs of the swastika hanging from the Eiffel Tower.

Now the Germans were practically on our doorstep and we held our breath as we read about the plight of hundreds of thousands of British soldiers stranded on the beaches of Normandy. When they were rescued in the great evacuation of Dunkirk, we toasted the boats, the sailors, Mr Churchill, and our British refusal to surrender – unlike the French, whose capital had just been invaded without a single shot being fired. We vowed we would fight the Germans and we would never surrender.

All this time, we still felt protected by Britain. It was *blitzkrieg* in Europe, but we knew that Britain would never abandon us. Our connection went back almost a thousand years to William the Conqueror. The Channel Islands were the oldest part of the British Empire; that had to count for something.

Inside the Cock and Bottle, where I sometimes dropped in for a pint of our local Mary Ann ale, tempers flared as people argued about our future. Some predicted that as we were only a tiny speck in the English Channel, closer to France than to England, we were of no value to anyone and would be left alone. Just as well, as Britain was overstretched and didn't have the resources to defend us. The cynics maintained that Britain would throw us to the wolves if they thought it was expedient. Others shouted them down for being unpatriotic, but as I swallowed the last of the ale and wiped the foam off my lips, my stomach was churning. Mr Churchill had been warning parliament for years that Britain was dangerously unprepared for war. If push came to shove, what would they do?

And then, in that beautiful June twilight, we found out. Britain had decided we were expendable.

As soon as they announced a voluntary evacuation, the panic started, and our capital, St Helier, began to resemble an ant nest with people running in all directions, desperately trying to find out what it all meant and what they should do.

To add to our distress, we were only given twenty-four hours to decide whether to stay or go. Those who wished to leave had to register at once. How did they expect people to make such a major decision in such a short time? Some of the older Jerseyites decided to stay rather than become refugees in a strange place, but the dilemma weighed heavily on the rest of us. How much danger were we really in? Should we sacrifice our comfortable, familiar life for an uncertain existence elsewhere? Parents wondered if they should just send their children away. And if they decided to leave themselves, what if their elderly parents refused to go?

All over St Helier, in homes, pubs, hotels, tearooms, on street corners and over back fences, everyone was on edge. How could Britain abandon us like that? How could we defend ourselves if the Germans invaded? While some scoffed that there was nothing here to entice the Jerries except cows, tomatoes and potatoes, others argued that we were strategically important, an easy stepping stone to France. I felt apprehensive. Hitler had made no secret of his ambition to conquer England. What a feather in his cap the conquest of the Channel Islands would be.

I kept hearing heartbreaking stories from our neighbours. Mrs Bennett sobbed so much, she could hardly get the words out. 'We had all decided to leave, so I had our faithful old dog Sally put down. She was one of the family but we couldn't take her with us. She looked at me so reproachfully when I left her at the vet's, as if she knew I was abandoning her. I feel like a murderer.' She had to pause to wipe her eyes. 'We all rushed to the dock, but when we saw the coal boat we'd have to travel on, I knew I couldn't put my old parents on that, so we turned back. Now my children won't forgive me because I had our pet put down for nothing, and I gave away their bikes!'

In the panic to leave Jersey, long queues formed at the ticket office as people desperate to leave tried to get a berth on any vessel that would take them to England or Wales – mail boats, coal boats, barges, or cargo ships loaded up with potatoes. One patient told me her neighbour had been in such a hurry to rush to the ticket office that she had left a hot iron on her ironing board. Another swore she saw a woman rushing towards the dock without any luggage at all, just a Picasso under one arm and her fur coat in the other!

From the moment they announced voluntary evacuation, I knew that Margaret would have to leave. I couldn't risk her safety or that of our baby. But I knew I had to stay. Some doctors had already left, and I couldn't let down the pregnant women whose babies I had promised to deliver, to say nothing of the diabetic and cardiac patients who were counting on me to look after them. Knowing Margaret's quick temper, I dreaded telling her that I'd decided to stay, so I put off telling her as long as possible. But, I assured her, it would only be a brief separation. Just as soon as I had delivered the babies, and organised medical care for my other patients, I would join her. It would only be a matter of weeks before we were reunited.

At this point, I'd like to explain my special bond with my pregnant patients. For one thing, I'd promised to deliver these babies, and I've always regarded promises as sacred. For me, obstetrics is by far the best part of medical practice. There is nothing as exhilarating as delivering a baby, assisting at the miracle of birth, which is really the creation of a whole new world. This is the only part of medicine that doesn't deal with morbidity and sickness, but with affirmation of life and hope. The look of joy on the mothers' faces when they see their babies for the first time always brings tears to my eyes. This is the best reward for my long years of study and training.

Although I'd explained this to Margaret on numerous occasions, she was even angrier than I expected. Her face, usually so pretty and soft, was distorted, her lips taut, her eyes narrowed, glaring at me.

'You're taking the Hippocratic oath to ridiculous extremes!' She practically spat the words. 'It's all very well being noble, but what about your own baby? What about me?'

She was sobbing now, the tears running down her cheeks as she patted her large belly under the loose maternity smock. 'You can't abandon your patients, but you can abandon me.

You don't even care about our baby. How can you do this to us? What kind of man are you if you can't look after your own family?'

Shaken by her accusation, I suddenly remembered something Professor Ross had said on my first day of lectures at the medical school in Edinburgh.

'Jung once said that people become doctors for the right reasons but also for the wrong reasons,' he told us in his broad Scots accent. Then he raised his bushy eyebrows and surveyed us with a quizzical expression, as if waiting for us to decide which category we belonged to. We were expecting an inspirational pep talk, not a philosophical conundrum, and we glanced at each other, puzzled by this statement that made no sense.

But now, feeling guilty for choosing duty, I thought about Jung's words for the first time in years, and wondered whether I'd made my decision for the right or wrong reasons. My father had always impressed on me that it was actions, not words, that revealed a man's true character. He once said, 'One day you'll come to a crossroad that will test your moral fortitude, and the path you take then will affect the rest of your life.' Father didn't talk much, not even about the battle at Verdun where he had earned the Victoria Cross, and that's probably why his words made such an impact on me.

I knew that I was now standing at my moral crossroad, and if I took the easier path, I would let myself down. If I deserted my patients, I could never live with myself. I took comfort in the thought that our separation would be temporary and that we would be reunited in time for our baby's birth, and I hoped that would be the end of our conflict.

'It's only for a short time, darling,' I tried to reassure her on that last day, reaching for her hand, which she kept pulling away. 'You'll only be across the Channel, in England, and I'll phone you every day. Before you know it, we'll be together again.'

But she shook her head, and from the look in her eyes I sensed that she was staring into a different future from the one before my optimistic eyes.

The queue of passengers waiting to board the boats stretched for several blocks from the ticket office in Royal Square, all the way up to Gloucester Road. There must have been over a thousand evacuees, mostly women trying to cope with fractious toddlers clinging to their skirts as they wheeled perambulators and push chairs and dragged heavy suitcases along the ground on that blistering summer's day. The wharf resembled a chaotic car yard, with hundreds of vehicles scattered about, abandoned by people who were evacuating.

My heart ached as I watched Margaret step onto the mail boat with her valise, face averted, refusing to wave or even look back at me as I stood on the wharf, hoping that at the last minute she might relent and turn to smile or wave. As the boat pulled away from the crowd that had gathered to see their friends and relatives off, those left behind were crying. Someone started to sing – I think it was that popular Vera Lynn song, 'We'll Meet Again' – while I stood silent and alone in the heart-aching splendour of that summer's day, feeling my resolve dissipating in the foamy white wake of the steamer that was taking her away from me.

Although I'm not usually given to dwelling on my emotions, and introspection is not my style, writing this down has given me the opportunity to try and understand what has happened. It has also filled the long lonely evenings in between house calls when, with a comforting balloon of French Armagnac in one hand and my fountain pen in the other, I have tried to record the extraordinary situation in which we find ourselves.

It would never have occurred to me to keep a journal, but when, about a week after Margaret sailed away, I read the notice in the *Jersey Evening Post* that a government department was looking for people to keep a daily record of their experiences during the war, I surprised myself by signing up for what they quaintly called a Mass Observation Project.

I have no idea who, if anyone, will ever read this, but if they do, it might give them an insight into what it was like to live through this period of wartime history. It has occurred to me that like so many government initiatives, this one could well end up shoved into some dusty drawer, unseen and unread.

But signing up for something implies an obligation and a responsibility, and no matter what becomes of it, perhaps in years to come I will read what I once wrote and come face to face with the young, idealistic doctor I used to be. I wonder what I will think of him. Margaret and I might read this together, surrounded by our children. By then I will know if I've made the right choice.

In the midst of these ruminations, the deafening roar of aeroplanes flying shockingly low made me drop my pen and run to the window. I recognised the distinctive streamlined design of German Dorniers. A moment later I heard deafening explosions so terrifyingly close that the windows in my study rattled, the branches of the apple and pear trees swayed and shook, and the whole house vibrated.

In the distance, I saw thick black smoke rising from the direction of the harbour. What was going on? The only thing on the wharf was a convoy of trucks loaded up with potatoes from fields near Gorey. Why on earth would they attack us? Don't they know we are demilitarised?

I sank back in my chair and sat there trying to comprehend what I had seen. There was no question: we were at war.

I remember thinking, what will become of us?

And what will we become?

CHAPTER TWO

Xanthe

St Helier, April 2019

There's nothing like finding your workmate hanging lifeless from a hook to recalibrate your priorities in life. As Xanthe Maxwell drives along Jersey's country lanes she can still see Sumi's limp body and her discoloured face.

'Don't think about that now,' she tells herself, and blinks hard to shut out the memory. 'Focus on the scenery.' The lanes curve and climb, dip and wind, and every turn of the road reveals a heart-lifting vista of hedgerows frothy with white hawthorn, meadows scattered with bluebells, crocuses and primroses. She passes thickets of alder and ash, and aspens whose trembling leaves seem to be dancing. This is what she has come for, this is exactly what she needs, this serene simple beauty. 'Focus on this,' she tells herself. 'Only this.'

But her concentration soon wanders, and once again she relives the worst moment of her life. It's a scene that unspools in her mind like a horror movie she can't stop watching. It's six in the morning, and she has almost finished her night shift. She can hardly keep her eyes open as she heads down the corridor towards her room when she remembers that Sumi didn't answer the code blue message on the pager. When she rushed down to the ward in response to the urgent message, she found that the leukemia patient's vital signs were down, and he needed to be resuscitated. She can't wait to crash on her bed, and get a few hours' sleep before the dreaded pager beeps again, before the relentless daily grind starts all over again. But at the last minute she decides to find out why Sumi didn't answer the urgent call.

She knocks but there's no answer, and she assumes that Sumi is fast asleep. It's no wonder. They never get much sleep on their evening shift. When she tries to open the door, it feels strangely heavy, as if someone is pushing against it from inside. She is ready to cry from exhaustion, almost ready to give up, but one last time she puts her entire weight against the door. This time it opens.

The bed is empty, and hasn't been slept in, but Xanthe has the eerie sense that there is someone in the room. She turns and her hands fly to her mouth. It's Sumi, and she is hanging from a hook on the back of the door, her head lolling to the side, her face the colour of a bruise. Pinned to her scrubs is a note. It just says *Sorry*.

Xanthe's legs buckle and she sinks onto the bed. She can't scream and she can't cry. Somewhere someone is uttering the most visceral moans she has ever heard, but she doesn't recognise her own voice. She can't make sense of what she is looking at. Sumi was always happy and positive, keen to get ahead. She was the first to get to the wards in the mornings to check out the patients before the registrars' rounds, and she always knew the answers to their questions.

She didn't appear to have any problems, but now Xanthe is filled with guilt. Had she missed something? From their conversations, she knew that Sumi's parents were village farmers in South Korea who had sacrificed everything to raise enough money for her to study medicine in Australia. She was the first person in her family to have gone to university and, although it wasn't their custom to praise her, she knew they were quietly proud she had become a doctor. Sumi's success was the vindication of generations of struggle and hardship that went back to the time her grandparents had been persecuted during the Japanese occupation of Korea. Did she feel she had let them all down in some way? Was 'sorry' addressed to them?

If only Sumi had confided that she felt depressed, instead of always appearing so confident. Xanthe can still see her, so petite and energetic, her heavy black fringe above her bright eyes as she leaned towards the patients and spoke to them with such empathy. Sumi was everything that a doctor should be. She made Xanthe aware that her own compassion had become depleted by the daily struggle to keep going.

But she can understand why Sumi hadn't shared her black thoughts. Admitting weakness was unthinkable. Xanthe herself had been pushed closer and closer to the edge this year, exhausted beyond measure, stressed out by fear and anxiety, humiliated by the registrar's scathing comments whenever she made a mistake, and terrified in case she killed someone through tiredness, lack of sleep, or sheer incompetence. But she had never confided to anyone how desperate she felt. Everyone else was coping, so how could she expose her incompetence and insecurities? Obviously there had to be something wrong with her. She could imagine the supercilious registrar suggesting that maybe she was psychologically unfit to be a doctor. Perhaps she should try for a career in hairdressing.

Now, driving along the pretty lanes of an island on the other side of the world, Xanthe blinks hard to dismiss her demons, but they continue to haunt her. She knows, although she hasn't admitted it to anyone, how terrifyingly close she came to being undone that day at St Xavier's Hospital. She remembers the exact moment she knew she had to walk away from what had become a life of toxic anxiety.

They were standing around a patient's bed that morning, the consultant cardiologist, the registrar and a couple of students, when the consultant asked her to examine the patient. Minutes went by. Sweat beaded her forehead and her hands shook. She couldn't find his heartbeat. Obviously there had to be one; after all, the man was alive. Why couldn't she hear it?

They were still waiting for her answer. The registrar was sighing and drumming her fingers on her clipboard. From the ward sister's expression, it was clear that she was waiting for Xanthe to make a mistake. Xanthe listened again, wiping away the sweat. She swallowed. 'His heartbeat is very faint,' she said at last.

'I should think it would be very faint,' the consultant said in a scathing tone. 'His heart is on the other side of his chest!' At this, the sister gave a triumphant snort, while the others laughed. Xanthe felt the blood rush to her face, mortified that she hadn't recognised the rare condition called *situs inversus*. Not wasting the opportunity to belittle her, the registrar suggested she needed to spend a lot more time reading *Gray's Anatomy*. Sumi used to call it *Fifty Shades of Grays*, and recalling her mischievous comment, Xanthe saw her friend again, limp and lifeless, hanging from the hook on the door.

After that mortifying ward round, she fled to the terrace on the top floor of the hospital and stood at the railing looking down at the street six storeys below. Her head swam but she knew that the vertigo wasn't caused by the fear of falling but by the desire to fall. The urge to hurl herself down and end the hell that her life had become as an intern was almost overpowering. She closed her eyes. Only a few seconds and it would all be over. Her heart hammered in her chest. At that moment, her pager beeped and she opened her eyes and drew back from the edge. But she knew with startling clarity that she had to quit this job before she killed herself or a patient.

She decided to go to Jersey because she didn't know anything about it and no-one she knew had ever been there. Some distant relative, a great-aunt or great-grandmother called Nellie, had migrated to Australia from Jersey, but Xanthe wasn't searching for roots. She longed to be in a quiet, peaceful place where she might recover and reclaim her life.

Her reverie is interrupted as she comes to a roundabout at the base of a steep hill where a sign urges drivers to 'filter in turn'. The quaintness of this request makes her smile, and for the first time in days she feels her facial muscles relax. She breathes more easily as she turns towards St Helier, surprised there are so few cars on the road. Jersey resembles Brigadoon, she thinks. The ideal place to chill out and figure out what to do with her life.

She had put off telling her family. They were all doctors in love with their profession, and they expected her to feel the same. For as long as she could remember, Xanthe had listened enthralled to their stories, and even before she understood what the medical terms meant, she was enchanted by their exotic strangeness. By the time she was five, she knew about oxygen levels, diabetic comas, corneal transplants, pulmonary emboli and cardiac arrests. The words seemed to be a magic key to an exclusive world that she longed to join.

Medicine was all her grandfather, father and mother ever talked about – the rare cases they diagnosed, the operations they pioneered and the patients whose lives they saved. None of them, Xanthe included, ever doubted that she would become the fourth-generation medico in the family.

She never tired of hearing about her great-grandfather who travelled by horse and sulky along unpaved roads in a country town at the turn of the twentieth century, and performed emergency appendectomies on kitchen tables in farmhouses. Her father was an ophthalmologist renowned for his pro bono work in developing countries, restoring sight to those who would otherwise be unable to access such procedures. Her mother was a radiologist. There was a running joke between them: physicians were the clever doctors, surgeons were the skilful doctors, and radiologists were the antisocial doctors. Xanthe suspected that her mother had chosen that specialty because it minimised personal interaction.

She hadn't been home much during the year, explaining that she had very little time off. That was only partly true. The main reason was her dread of revealing how traumatic she found life in the hospital, and how anxiety was poisoning her existence.

She didn't expect sympathy from her parents. They'd be disappointed by her inability to cope, and their disappointment was the last thing she wanted to hear. She was disappointed enough with herself.

Eventually she'd had no choice but to visit them. When she arrived, they were having drinks on the verandah of their Hunters Hill home, a sandstone mansion over a hundred years old, on a street lined with liquidambars whose branches formed an arch over the roadway. She caught the end of a story her younger brother Oliver was telling.

'So the case was about a decapitated murder victim,' he was saying, 'and when the barrister asked about the victim's state of mind, the judge retorted that being headless, the victim's brain no longer functioned, so it probably belonged to a member of the legal profession!'

She joined in the laughter and glanced at her brother with a tinge of envy at his relaxed manner. Ollie had obviously chosen the right profession. Unlike her, he had never wanted to do medicine, which was just as well as he was needle-phobic and had once passed out when a nurse tried to insert a cannula in his vein.

He came over and gave her a hug. 'What's new, sis? How come you never reply to my texts?'

'Some days I hardly have time to go to the toilet,' she snapped.

He raised his eyebrows. 'I think you need a drink.'

'Hello stranger!' Her father boomed. 'To what do we owe this honour?'

'It's good to see you, Xan,' her mother said.

Sipping the Marlborough sauvignon blanc Oliver had poured into her glass, Xanthe gazed moodily at the row of terracotta pots their landscape gardener had arranged like a row of soldiers around the swimming pool. She waited for the right moment to drop her bombshell.

In a momentary lull in the conversation, she cleared her throat several times and said, 'This will probably come as a shock, but I've decided to quit my hospital job.'

There was a horrified silence and they all stared at her as if she had just confessed to murder. Oliver looked at her with concern. Her father was the first to speak. Putting down his wine glass, Alexander Maxwell sat forward in the cane armchair and made a dismissive gesture with his hand.

'You can't be serious. You can't possibly be thinking of throwing away a job in one of the top teaching hospitals in Sydney. Have you considered what this will do to your career? No-one will offer you a training position in your specialty at a teaching hospital. You'll end up as an unaccredited trainee in some third-rate hospital.'

Despite her exasperation, Xanthe marvelled at her father's enviable confidence in his own opinions. She saw her mother shoot him a warning glance, her usual response to his unfiltered pronouncements.

'I still remember how tough that first year was,' she said. 'And then there was that tragedy with your friend. No wonder you're upset, Xan. What about getting some counselling? Just don't do anything rash. Give yourself time.'

Oliver was watching her, waiting for her to respond.

Xanthe clenched her fists. Her parents hadn't even asked why she had taken such a drastic step. To infuriate her further, her mother, who was incapable of confronting any controversy, now changed the subject. Pointing to the new lounge suite she had bought, she asked Xanthe if she liked it. It was an angular Scandinavian design created for style rather than comfort.

'Minimalist,' Xanthe commented. Just like your emotions, she thought.

She had twisted her light brown hair on top of her head and secured it with a large clip, but two strands had escaped and fell over her face. Tucking them behind her ears, she said, 'I am serious, and I don't need counselling. And in case anyone is interested, I need to get away from the toxic culture at the hospital before it destroys me.'

'What you really need is resilience,' her father said. 'You millennials are hypersensitive. You have to be able to cope with difficulties if you're going to survive in this world.'

Xanthe was on the point of retorting that survival was actually the issue. Hers. Instead, she flared up. 'So is it our fault that we're sleep-deprived, humiliated and exhausted? You're blaming us for the problems of the system we work in.' She blinked away tears. 'I'm so exhausted that last week I prescribed penicillin to a patient who was allergic to it, and got yelled at by the sister in charge of the ward, and later by the registrar, in front of the patient who thought I was the nurse. Can you imagine how that felt? And it's like that all the time.'

Alexander Maxwell shrugged. 'In my day, the consultant was God, and we hung on his every word. We worked much longer hours than you do, with less supervision. I remember being on call for thirty-six hours straight in my first year as resident. But we all got through it. Nobody dreamed of complaining about being overworked, underpaid or bullied, and nobody quit,' he said pointedly. 'You are a generation of entitled wimps. You need toughening up.'

'So how come a pilot is only allowed to fly a certain number of hours for fear of endangering his passengers, but it's okay for us doctors to endanger patients' lives and make life-and-death decisions when we've had hardly any sleep?'

'Don't be melodramatic.'

'So I suppose Sumi was being melodramatic when she killed herself.'

'If she had a problem, she should have consulted someone about it.'

'Dad, can't you see? It's a catch 22, designed to stop us seeking help!' Xanthe was shouting now in frustration. 'If Sumi had consulted a psychiatrist, they might have reported her to the medical board as a danger to patients, and that would always be on her record. She might have even been deregistered.'

It was useless. She would never convince him. She knew him well enough to realise that he saw her decision as failure, and failure wasn't an option in this family. What was worse, in rejecting medicine, he probably felt she was also rejecting him.

She stormed out of the house, shaking, and had just got into her Mini Cooper when Oliver tapped on the window.

'Do whatever you need to do, sis,' he said. 'Don't take any notice of them. Just take care of yourself. And if you need me, just call.'

As she pulls over to let another driver pass her on the narrow Jersey lane, the memory of her brother's kind words brings tears to her eyes. She wishes she hadn't replayed that painful episode. She hasn't travelled all this way to keep dwelling on the past.

The lane is lined with granite farmhouses with names like Clos du Sable, Chalet des Arbres and Clos de la Mare. Intrigued, she wonders why they have French names. Then she remembers that the hotel she has booked for the night also has a charming French name: Pomme d'Or.

The lane has merged into St Saviour's Road, overlooking St Aubin's Bay. A short distance from the shore, an imposing grey stone edifice rises from the water like a fantasy castle. Although it's almost eight o'clock in the evening, it's still light, and she supposes this is what they call twilight in this part of the world.

Back in town, she parks her rented grey Nissan in the car park of the Pomme d'Or Hotel in Liberation Square. She has rented a house in St Mark's Road for a month, but there was some confusion about her arrival date, probably because she forgot the time difference when she booked and discovered when she arrived that the house wouldn't be available until the following day.

She sits on a bar stool at the highly polished timber counter and catches sight of her reflection in the mirror. She looks a mess. She had twisted her hair into a kind of bun, but several locks have escaped and are framing her face, which looks tired and pale. A boyfriend once said she had an interesting face, which probably meant he couldn't decide if she was attractive or plain. On this occasion, she feels plain. No lipstick, scuffed sneakers, black leggings and crumpled sloppy joe. She looks away and shrugs. She isn't trying to impress anyone.

The French barman raises his thick eyebrows when she asks for a Stoli. 'Vodka and orange?' he asks.

She shakes her head. 'Vodka. Neat.'

Now he's looking at her with interest, and she wonders if he's going to ask for her ID. It was her Russian boyfriend Dmitri who introduced her to his native spirit, and she had discovered that she liked this firewater whose explosive warmth made her feel deliciously light-headed. It was an express route to relaxation and sleep. Dmitri had long vanished, along with her other short-term relationships with men who couldn't cope with her constant tiredness and obsession with her work.

She downs the vodka, the way Dimitri taught her, head thrown back, one continuous swallow. More relaxed now, she looks out of the mullioned window. St Helier seems to be a busy coastal town with a large marina jammed with sailboats, superyachts and motorboats. The busiest part of Royal Square is the Cock and Bottle, where a noisy group of tourists is sitting outside. Boutique owners are locking their doors, jewellers are pulling down their shutters, and bank clerks are filing out of their offices, but tourists are still crowding around the money exchange kiosk, which remains open.

The noise in the bar is deafening. Groups of holidaymakers talk over one another, occasionally bursting into raucous laughter. At a small table in the corner of the bar, in an island of stillness, an old man is hunched over a pint of beer. Accustomed to observing people, she senses an invisible wall around him, which arouses her curiosity. Just then, one of the drinkers puts his glass on the counter, pushes his stool away from the bar and walks over to the corner table. She can't hear what he says, but she notices a spiral notebook in his hand. When the old man looks up and sees the man standing beside him, without saying a word, or giving the intruder a second glance, he rises abruptly, brushes past him and strides out of the bar.

Xanthe turns her attention to the bar menu. She doesn't feel like having dinner in the formal dining room with its heavy furniture and starched white tablecloths. Besides, she's not dressed for it. Instead, she orders something called Jersey Hotpot.

'I hope you have a cast-iron stomach.' The speaker is a stocky man with sparse reddish hair brushed straight back from his freckled face, revealing patches of pink scalp. He is sitting on the stool next to hers, nursing a scotch. She notes that unlike the other men in the bar, he is wearing a suit. Obviously not a tourist.

'You'd be better off having dinner inside,' he continues. 'The fish and steak are good. They also have fancy dishes with French names.' He looks at her with interest. 'I haven't seen you in here before. Holidaying?'

She hesitates and he says, 'Sorry, I shouldn't be so nosy. Goes with the territory I'm afraid.' He extends a large hand and gives hers a firm grasp. 'Detective Inspector Bill McAllister from Sussex. Originally from Glasgow, as you can probably tell.'

'Are you here on a case?'

He chuckles. 'They couldn't afford Bergerac, so they sent for me.'

Less uptight now that the vodka has done its job, she introduces herself and answers his questions. She glances towards the dining room. 'I think I'll take your advice and have dinner inside.'

Several minutes later, the waiter shows her to a table at the far end of the dining room. She looks around, surprised how ornate it is. There's a solid carved mahogany sideboard on one side of the room, and the chairs are upholstered with Regency stripes of cream and burgundy.

The dining room is almost empty, and across the room she sees that Bill McAllister is sitting a few tables away, also alone. It's ridiculous for them to sit at separate tables, she suddenly thinks, and besides, it might be interesting to talk to him. She walks over to his table and surprises herself by suggesting that he should join her, something she would never do in Sydney.

Over a bottle of local shiraz, he explains why he has come to Jersey.

'There's a case of incest in a village on the other side of the island. A teenage boy and his sister had a baby. From what I've heard, incest isn't that uncommon in some of the villages. I was up there today interviewing the two of them. To be honest with you, I canna see a problem. They're both happy, and the wee bairn is doing well, so you have to wonder why the law treats them as criminals.'

Her mind leaps to the genetic problems involved, but, she thinks as he refills her glass, he seems broad-minded for a policeman. Then she recalls the scene in the bar. He was there at the time, and a nosy cop like him might know something about the mystery man.

He nods. 'Aye. I saw that too. He's very intimidating, so people keep well away. The man who approached him is a reporter from a London paper. He's been trying to interview him for a few days now, but as you saw, he's not getting anywhere. Old Tom Gaskell obviously has an interesting story to tell, but from what I've heard, he will probably take it to the grave.'

He drains his glass, and turns his attention to her. 'And you, Xanthe, what do you do?'

She hesitates, wondering how to answer. Medicine is a topic she would prefer to avoid but he is studying her with shrewd eyes. 'I'm a medico,' she says, and looks down at the menu to forestall further discussion.

He shakes his head. 'Go on with you! You look far too young to be a doctor. My idea of a doctor is a kindly old gentleman in a white coat with a stethoscope around his neck, not a lassie like you.'

She smiles politely. Perhaps it was a mistake to suggest sitting together. She is thinking of making an excuse to leave when he says, 'I'm investigating another case as well. There's a home for unmarried mothers on the other side of the island. It's been abandoned for decades but they've recently found some wee charred bones in the garden, and there's talk it might be suspicious. That babies might have been buried there. I'm here with a forensic team to check it out.'

She sits forward. 'That sounds fascinating. I never thought of Jersey as a hotbed of crime.'

Now it's his turn to look surprised. 'You don't have to look very far,' he says. 'This hotel was the headquarters of the German Water Police during the Occupation.'

Her eyes widen. 'Germans here? When was that?'

He waits until the young Polish waiter has served their meal, filet mignon for him, Dover sole for her. 'They came in 1940 and stayed for the entire war. This was the only part of the UK that was occupied. Didn't you know?'

She is embarrassed by her ignorance. 'I had no idea.'

'You should go to the Occupation Museum while you're here,' he says. 'I think you'll find it interesting.'

Suddenly she feels that if she stays at the table any longer, she will fall asleep in her chair. Perhaps it's the two glasses of wine on top of the vodka on top of the long plane trip. She excuses herself and goes up to her room.

Just before she falls asleep, it occurs to her that perhaps beneath its flowered fields and idyllic country lanes, Jersey has a darker side.

CHAPTER THREE

Tom

St Helier, July 1940

It was war but it wasn't war. Not like any war he'd ever read about, anyway. Ever since he could read, Tom Gaskell had steeped himself in adventure magazines like *Hotspur*, *Rover* and *Wizard*, where heroes performed daring deeds in wartime, but to his disappointment, apart from occasional German planes that flew low over Jersey towards the end of June, practically nothing had changed. They had all been issued gas masks, and he had noticed that sandbags had been stacked around public buildings. Self-important air-raid wardens patrolled the streets late at night, telling people off for lights-out violations, but no-one took any of it seriously. In fact Tom and his friends Frank and Harry used the gas masks to make farting noises, to their parents' disgust. As far as Tom was concerned, the war could have been on Mars.

Riding his bicycle after school, he raced Frank to the top of the hill overlooking St Aubin's Bay, where they watched German planes flying over the port. As the slim fuselage of a plane swooped low over St Helier, he shouted, 'That's a Dornier Do 17. Do you reckon they've come to count the number of potatoes in the trucks down there?'

Frank gave him a mock punch, which he returned with interest. Frank was shorter than he was, but he was stronger than his compact build suggested. Their boisterous laughter resounded all over the grassy hill as they sped down the slope towards the slip at Havre des Pas to buy a penny ice-cream cone from Gino's red, white and blue cart by the water.

Tom was convinced that Jersey was the best place on earth, and that nothing would ever make him want to leave. He was relieved his parents had decided to stay, and felt sorry for his schoolfriends who had been forced to evacuate. Nothing could match the joy of exploring the cliffs and caves along the coast, climbing the rugged rocks above the bays, swimming, running, and cycling all over the island. He reckoned he knew every little cove, beach and clifftop.

There was another reason why Tom didn't want to leave, and her name was Milly. She had a smile that dimpled her pink cheeks, and eyes that were bluer than the sky on a summer's day. He was smitten the minute he saw her, struck dumb really, because he couldn't get a word out at the time. Just thinking about her aroused thrilling sensations in his body.

And he could tell from the way she looked back at him that she liked him too. He was only fourteen but he already knew there would never be another girl for him. For now, though, it was enough to know that she existed, and breathed the same air he did.

It wasn't until St Helier was bombed that he realised the war had really begun, and they were in the thick of it. He had been at Harry's place when they heard the roar of plane engines overhead, and they'd rushed to the windows. Flying above them were Junkers and Dorniers. Suddenly Tom pointed. Standing in the door of the plane, not very high above them, a gunner was firing and he seemed to be aiming straight at them. Harry's father yelled for them to come away from the window, and they jumped back.

'Reckon they're trying to scare us?' Tom whispered.

A few seconds later he had his answer. Deafening explosions and stuttering machine-gun fire came from the direction of the port. Harry lived at the top of Pier Road, overlooking the harbour, and, ignoring his father's order to stay put, both boys raced outside, mounted their bicycles, and pedalled at breakneck speed to the weighbridge to see what had happened. Already from a distance they could see that some of the fishing boats had been destroyed, and that shattered trucks lay on the dock, some of them on fire. A bossy air-raid warden shooed them away, but they cycled halfway up Pier Road and then came down to the harbour again by a different route and heard the warning bells of ambulances heading towards the port.

Down on the dock, the scene resembled a battlefield. Among the crumpled parts of blown-up trucks, burnt and wounded people lay on the ground with blood pooling around them. Some were screaming as ambulance men lifted them onto stretchers. Tom stared, horrified to see that one of the victims had one side of his face blown away and had only one eye left. He overheard an ambulance officer saying that the buggers had attacked La Rocque as well, while his colleague muttered something about shrapnel and bullets.

Transfixed by the scene, Tom couldn't move, and Harry was white as a ghost.

'You boys shouldn't be here,' someone said, and Tom looked around to see Dr Jackson.

'Did you see them, Dr Jackson?' Tom asked. He couldn't keep the excitement out of his voice. 'First there were three Heinkels, and then three Dorniers – the Do 17s they were. It's really war now, isn't it?' he said, then added, 'But why did they attack us?'

Dr Jackson didn't know either. This surprised Tom, who thought that Dr Jackson knew everything. He was their family doctor, one of the few adults who never talked down to him. Tom could tell the doctor anything. Dr Jackson would always put down his fountain pen, lean forward, and give him all his attention. He never interrupted or passed judgement. Tom had even told him about Milly, and Dr Jackson didn't dismiss it as an infatuation, as if it was a disease he would grow out of. He seemed to understand how he felt. Tom knew that Dr Jackson's wife had recently evacuated, and he wondered if that was why the doctor had that faraway look in his eyes whenever they talked about the war.

As Tom and Harry cycled away from the devastated harbour, they headed for Frank's house to talk about the attack. The three of them had been inseparable since junior school, and had shared adventures, scrapes and accidents. After Tom read Dumas's novel, they called themselves the Three Musketeers. They went over the incredible event that had taken place that evening, furious with the Germans, and bewildered by Britain's lack of action. How could they have allowed this to happen on their own territory?

But no matter how they looked at it, they couldn't come up with an explanation.

'It's just that they're Krauts. They wouldn't care that we've been demilitarised.' Tom shrugged, and they left it at that.

Even Frank's father, who usually had a lot to say about politics and politicians, all of it bad, couldn't explain the bombing. Before parting, the boys placed their right hands on top of one another, closed their eyes, and repeated their motto. As they intoned *All for one, and one for all*, they sensed that this might now acquire new significance.

Tom's cynical view of the Germans, which had been formed by reading adventure stories and fanned by his father's hostility, was soon reinforced by what followed. The Germans demanded that large white crosses be painted on the ground in St Helier's squares and ports, and that white flags be flown from all homes, offices and public buildings, as signs of surrender.

It was bad enough seeing the white crosses, but when Tom saw his mother hanging a large white towel out of their upstairs window, he was outraged. 'You're a coward,' he said.

'It's the law,' she shrugged. 'Let's see what kind of hero you turn out to be.'

In reply, Tom ran to the laundry, hung out a pair of unwashed underpants on his fishing rod and stuck it out of his window.

'That's what I think of the Krauts,' he muttered, feeling good about his display of rebellion. Out in the streets of St Helier, white sheets, towels, vests and tablecloths fluttered out of windows all over town, a depressing sign of their shameful capitulation.

Once the surrender was confirmed, more ignominy followed. Several days later, Luftwaffe planes landed on the tarmac and out stepped several crisply uniformed German officers, their black jackboots and silver insignia gleaming in the July sunlight. They were followed by a large contingent of troops who lined up on the tarmac. From the hill overlooking the airport, Tom, Frank and Harry watched the scene unfold, and what they saw shocked them into silence. Tom couldn't believe his eyes when he saw the Bailiff and the Attorney-General not only coming to meet the German invaders, but actually shaking their hands. Like a welcome party, he thought.

He cycled home as fast as he could to tell his parents what he had seen. 'They're here! They're here!' he yelled. His mother came out to see what he was shouting about.

'What's all the commotion? What are you making such a fuss about? You almost deafened me,' she said, holding her perfectly manicured white hands to her ears.

Everything was always about her, Tom thought, and he waited until his father emerged from his darkroom where he developed the photographs he had taken of visitors at the beach. Stanley Gaskell's expression grew sombre as he listened to Tom's account of the surrender.

'Bloody Krauts,' he muttered. He reflected for a few moments, then added, 'And bloody Brits. We sacrificed ten thousand men in the Great War to save one line of trenches in France, and we did it not just once, but over and over again, but they didn't even fire a single shot to defend us,' he said bitterly. 'And now the Krauts are at it again.'

He liked reminding Tom that they were descended from a long line of warriors, some of whom had fired crossbows at the battle of Agincourt, and he was outraged at what he saw as cowardice on the part of their leaders.

'Does that mean you wish they'd sacrifice ten thousand men now as well?' his mother commented, overhearing their conversation. Tom and his father exchanged glances. It was no use trying to reason with Alma. A neighbour who fell out with her once said that Alma drank vinegar for breakfast instead of tea, and Tom could see her point.

At least his father was usually on his side. Tom admired his father, who could build anything. Resourceful, too. He was a photographer and took advantage of the self-indulgence of tourists who couldn't resist having a record of their holiday. For those who took their own shots, he installed special boxes in hotel lobbies where guests could drop the films they'd exposed, so that he would develop them and return the prints the following day.

His father's pleasant manner was an asset in his business, but why this kind and affable man had married such a bad-tempered woman who was impossible to please, Tom couldn't fathom. People often commented on his mother's beauty and said she made heads turn, but Tom only knew that she made his head spin. Nothing he did ever pleased her. He suspected that his mother would have happily put him on a boat to England, not so much for his safety as for the relief of being rid of him, but luckily she had left it too late, and he'd literally missed the boat. In any case, he had already resolved that even if she'd bought him a ticket and pushed him onto a boat, he would have jumped overboard and swum back. He hadn't won swimming trophies for nothing.

In no time, the hated swastika was flying from the top of Fort Regent, its black tentacles looming over the town. Tom often cycled to the top of the fort on Mont de la Ville to gaze over St Helier. According to his teacher, a circle of prehistoric stones and megaliths had once stood on that site, but Tom was far more enthralled by an incident that had taken place here back in 1804, when the fort had caught fire. Inside were five thousand barrels of gunpowder that would have blown up the entire fort if three heroic men hadn't rushed in and risked their lives to put out the flames. Now, seeing the fort desecrated by the Nazis' crooked cross, Tom felt disgusted and ashamed.

His father's spirit had also taken a battering. 'The Krauts must be laughing their heads off back in Germany,' he remarked one evening. 'They couldn't have imagined in their wildest dreams that they'd get to invade part of Great Britain without a fight. Do you realise that we have the dubious honour of being the first British possession to ever fall into enemy hands? And if that wasn't bad enough, we surrendered not to a general but to one of Göring's officers. Without a single shot being fired!'

Tom's mother wasn't impressed. 'You men are so bloodthirsty. Surely surrendering is better than getting people killed.'

As usual, Tom and his father exchanged exasperated glances. Alma was too pragmatic. She didn't understand about honour and pride.

She turned her sharp gaze on her husband. 'Anyway, this might turn out to be an opportunity.'

Stanley stared at her. His usually quiet voice rose. 'Opportunity for what? For going into business making white flags and swastikas? Don't you understand? We've just been invaded. We are being occupied.'

Ignoring his outburst, Alma turned her attention to Tom. 'As for you, instead of wasting your time riding that bicycle and hanging around with those useless friends of yours, you'd better start learning German.'

Tom was horrified. Trust his mother to come out with some outrageous scheme. What would his friends think if they found out he was toadying up to their invaders by learning their language?

But before he could object, Alma added, 'You're not bad at languages, but French isn't going to help you these days. I'll take you to Professor Strauss tomorrow. Two hours a week, and you'll soon be speaking tolerable German. Might be able to help your father in his business.'

Tom looked helplessly at his father, who just sighed. 'You know your mother, once she makes up her mind about something, you might as well stop fighting and give in.'

Tom detected a note of admiration in his father's voice and wished, not for the first time, that Stanley had more backbone.

'Give in, like we did to the Germans I suppose,' he retorted. 'And speaking of giving in, did you know we're not allowed to listen to any radio stations except the ones the Krauts control?'

His mother tightened her vermillion lips. 'You'd better stop calling them Krauts from now on.'

Ever since the Germans had invaded, one restrictive order had followed another. All boats were confined to the inner harbour, all firearms, weapons and ammunition had to be handed in, and all orders had to be obeyed to the letter or else there would be serious consequences. Before they had time to absorb one lot of orders, new ones were posted in the Royal Square.

They were also published in the *Jersey Evening Post*. His father knew the editor, who had confided that the Germans checked every word before they allowed him to go to print and deleted anything they considered hostile. Now that they could only listen to German-approved radio stations, and read only German-approved articles, it was clear that from now on their main sources of information would be censored by their occupier.

The Kommandatur, as the German administration was called, had taken over their Town Hall, which they called the Rathaus, to the amusement of the locals who enjoyed emphasising the first syllable to get their own back for the swastika that fluttered over the building. But for Tom, the most galling of the new regulations was the one that affected the time. From now on, all clocks had to be moved forward by one hour, to be in sync with those in the Reich.

Now we really are part of Germany, Tom thought. If only he could find a way to avenge their humiliation.

CHAPTER FOUR

Dr Jackson

St Helier, July 1940

It's over a week since Margaret left, and I still haven't heard from her. Ever since the bombing, the telephone lines have been jammed, and my efforts to get through have been futile. To make matters worse, the telephonist has warned me that the lines might soon be cut altogether, and if that happens, contact will be impossible. I'm frantic. I want to hear her voice and make sure she arrived safely at her mother's place, but with the parlous state of our phone lines, she might as well be in Timbuktu. I haven't been able to sleep, and I've tried putting through a call every fifteen minutes throughout the night, but to no avail. I have never felt so anxious. The baby will be due soon, and not knowing what's happening, not being able to contact her, is the worst type of torture I can imagine.

I still feel torn about my decision to stay, but when I see the relief and gratitude on the faces of my patients, I realise I couldn't have made any other choice. Yesterday I delivered Mrs Thompson's bonny baby boy, quite a relief considering it was a breech birth, which meant I had to turn the baby several times, and then use forceps. It was touch and go at one stage, but all went well and her ecstatic smile as she held her baby validated my decision. At the same time, though, I felt depressed. Delivering other women's babies means I can't be with Margaret when our own baby is born. I try to keep my spirits up by consoling myself that she still has a week or so to go, and surely it can't be long before we're together again. As soon as I was sure Mrs Thompson and her baby were well, I rushed to the telephone to try and call England again, but I couldn't get through. I wonder if she has received my letters. I hope she doesn't think I've abandoned her.

And then this afternoon the unthinkable happened. They have cut our cable, so we can no longer communicate with the outside world. It's hard to believe that this could happen here in the twentieth century. It's barely a week since the Germans arrived, but from what I've already observed, anything is possible. They're an arrogant bunch who seem to think that wearing a German uniform entitles them to lord it over everyone else.

I was hurrying to have a pint of Mary Ann ale at the Cock and Bottle yesterday when one of these Luftwaffe types bailed me up and tried to engage me in conversation.

'I do not understand why we are at war,' he said in English. 'We Germans and you Englishmen are cousins, we should rule the world together!'

But if they think we're cousins, then they certainly have strange idea of kinship. From the moment they arrived, they've insisted that we have to step off the pavement whenever they're on it! Old Mrs Simpson showed them up the other day, though. She had a wicked grin on her face when she came to see me about her lacerated knees. She said that two Luftwaffe louts pushed her off the pavement the day before, and sent her sprawling on the road. They were laughing until she picked herself up and gave one of them a good kick in the shins. He howled with pain, and then grabbed her by the arm and marched her off to their headquarters at the Rathaus. They kept her there most of the day and threatened her with prison, but she told me it was worth it just to see the shock on his face.

I've noticed that the Aryan supermen are buying up everything in sight. Things can't be good in Germany, because they're grabbing whatever they see in the shops – cigarettes, liquor, perfume, silk stockings and jewellery. Food as well, lots of it. It makes me wonder how long our supplies will last.

They've already restricted the sale of petrol to essential vehicles. And speaking of vehicles, they requisitioned my pride and joy, the Kelly green Alvis tourer. It was an extravagance, but the model was called Doctor's Coupe, which was all I had needed to convince me to buy it. I was outraged at this daylight robbery and argued that as a doctor I had to have a car, but it didn't do any good. I've now bought a second-hand soft-top Austin 7. Of course it's not a patch on the Alvis, but at least it won't use up as much petrol and hopefully won't attract their thieving attention.

As the Germans seem to regard St Helier as one huge shopping emporium, I've started worrying about the future. What if they buy up all the liquor? As I have a weakness for good wines and spirits, I dropped in to see my wine merchant and discovered that much of his supply had already been depleted, but he still had some excellent French wines and champagnes secreted in his cellar. The prices he asked were exorbitant, but I convinced him that he might as well sell them to me at a considerably reduced price, because when the Jerries found them, they'd just confiscate the lot. I went away very pleased with my windfall, which included a few bottles of Pommery I'll keep to celebrate our victory. Surely that won't be very far off.

As soon as I got home, I started looking around for a place to conceal my haul. I pulled up the carpet and the floorboards in the dining room, stored the bottles in the space beneath, and replaced the carpet. I hope no-one will ever think of looking there. Encouraged by my success in the wine store, I headed for the tobacconist, remembering that in hard times, cigarettes can become a form of currency. I bought up as many packs of tobacco as I could afford, as well as boxes of cheroots. They're not just for me – you never know when these items might be useful.

I had a rare stroke of luck yesterday. As I was passing a bakehouse, and breathing in the irresistible yeasty aroma of fresh bread, I was shocked to see the baker shovelling good bread into his furnace. Turned out he had baked too much that day, so, unable to keep it or sell it, he'd decided to get rid of it. Apart from the fact that I am averse to waste of any kind, especially bread, I could see its future potential. I bought some sacks and filled them up with his stale loaves.

As soon as I got them home, I cut the bread into thick slices, and baked them into rusks which I packed into the sacks for future emergencies. The problem of course, was how to keep mice away. The driest, safest spot in the house was the roof space, so I fixed strong nails to the timber, and I hung the sacks up there. I knew they'd make good food for my chickens, and, if it ever came to it, I could soak them and eat them myself. Another precaution I took was to plant out lettuces, carrots, cabbages and beans in our large garden, past the orchard. All this activity has kept me busy during the long summer evenings and has helped to distract me from my anxiety about Margaret.

It occurs to me that my descriptions of stockpiling and planting are quite trivial in the scheme of things these days, but if anyone ever reads this journal, they will glean some information about everyday life in Nazi-occupied Jersey. Even though my food-gathering efforts are mundane and lack drama, I hope they might encourage people to have faith their ability to cope even in the most difficult circumstances.

And apropos of difficult circumstances, something rather strange happened several nights ago. I hesitate to describe it, but writing down the day's events relieves the loneliness I feel every evening when I come home to an empty house, and long for Margaret's warm body.

Anxiety about our personal situation, our lack of communication with the outside world, and the fear that perhaps this war won't end soon, makes it difficult for me to sleep. This is clearly a case of physician cure thyself! Here I am dispensing advice to my stressed patients, while my own angst is tearing me apart.

Coming back to the bizarre event of several nights ago, it's something I would not confide to anyone, for fear they might think I've become one of those irrational people who believe in ghosts, ouija boards, Madame Blavatsky and psychic phenomena. But writing it down might help me understand it.

So here it is. I had just gone to bed in the upstairs bedroom, and no sooner had I put out the light hoping to fall asleep, when the hair stood up on the back of my neck. I was convinced someone was in the room.

With some trepidation and a thumping heart, I switched on the light. I was alone and I wondered if I'd been hallucinating. But the moment I switched off the light, I again had the eerie sensation of an invisible presence.

I knew that before Margaret and I bought the house, a young woman had committed suicide in one of the bedrooms. Whether it was from unrequited love or endogenous depression, I wasn't told, and in any case, not being susceptible to ghost stories, it didn't bother me in the slightest. It obviously bothered other buyers, though, which was why we could afford to buy the house.

In the light of morning, the world was bright and normal again and I wondered whether I had imagined the whole thing. I've never believed in ghosts, poltergeists or any other supernatural phenomena, so the only explanation is that I can't explain it.

In my practice, I always find it difficult to admit to patients that I don't know the cause of their symptoms. It feels like a failure on my part. But perhaps sometimes we just have to accept that there are phenomena that defy logical explanation, and this strange nocturnal experience was an example of that. Whatever it was, it hasn't recurred, but if that dead girl had anything to do with it, I hope her poor soul rests in peace.

Speaking of disturbing sights, I had just visited Mr Fletcher, who has influenza, when I saw a group of Germans strolling along the street accompanied by some of our girls, dressed to the nines, arm in arm with them. It upsets me to see how quickly these girls have made friends with the occupiers, but the attraction is not hard to understand. These young Germans always look immaculate. Unlike our local lads, they have manicured nails and they smell of cologne. What's more, they shower the girls with gifts.

I can't stop thinking about something one of my patients said a few days ago. Mrs Goldman is a middle-aged woman who owns a music business. I have always admired her sensible approach to life, but on this occasion, her eyes were darting all over the place, and her hands were trembling.

'Doctor, I'm very worried,' she began. It seems that, being of the Jewish faith, she was exceedingly apprehensive about the Occupation. 'I have read reports about what the Nazis are doing in Poland, rounding up the Jews into ghettos, and I can't help wondering if they will do the same here,' she said.

I must admit I was astounded. It never occurred to me that our tiny Jewish population might be at risk. I assured her that our British system of justice would never permit the Nazis to persecute Jewish people, and that no-one on our island would agree to such discrimination. I think she left considerably relieved.

Another of my patients has also been on my mind. Young Tom Gaskell, a tall, well-built lad with blue eyes and fair hair who resembles the Aryan ideal far more than most of the soldiers I've seen here, has changed since the Occupation began. He was always a happy-go-lucky lad with so much energy that it seemed he was about to burst out of his skin. But lately he looks preoccupied, as if he's brooding. He told me that the day he saw the swastika flying from Fort Regent, he felt the impact of our humiliating surrender.

'I thought we British were brave. I can't stand the thought that we're really cowards,' he blurted.

I understood how he felt and let him talk. It's hard for idealistic youngsters to accept the situation, especially when they've been led to believe how courageous and invincible the British are. It wasn't easy for any of us, but it could be a lot worse, I told him, recalling what Mrs Goldman had told me about the Jews in Poland. We just had to get on with it as best we could, and trust that it wouldn't last too long. He didn't look convinced, and I can't blame him. But I'm glad he feels he can come and talk to me about things that worry him. From what I've seen of his mother, she's not the most understanding sort.

With typical Teutonic obsession with detail, German orders have kept coming thick and fast. They have now rationed bread, milk, sugar and meat, and even the use of fertilisers. It's hard to keep up with all their restrictions, regulations and rations. For some reason they have forbidden cyclists to ride two abreast. Even in quiet lanes where there is no traffic of any kind, a soldier often leaps out from behind a hedge and demands a fine or just confiscates the cyclist's bicycle. One young man who refused to hand over his money arrived at my surgery last week nursing a broken jaw.

But the order that most of us have found even more distressing than the rest, has been the one commanding us to hand in our wireless sets. Listening to the wireless, especially to the BBC News, has been a lifeline linking us to the rest of the world, and with that gone, we would be dreadfully isolated and have to rely solely on German propaganda. There was no way I was going to let them take my radio. So with a very solemn face I handed in my old set, which didn't even work, but kept my new one.

Like every infringement of their orders, keeping a wireless incurs severe punishment, and my patient Miss Spencer was sentenced to seven months in a German prison when they found hers, so I was aware of the risk I was taking in keeping mine. Especially when I heard that some people informed on their neighbours when they heard them listening to a clandestine set. People talk about the need to stick together against the enemy, but stooping to denounce neighbours shows how easily people give in to their meanest instincts.

So I had to find a secure hiding place for my wireless. Although I've never considered myself a handyman and always employed tradesmen to fix problems that arose in the house, I surprised myself with my ingenuity. I hammered a hole in the front of my bedroom chimney, built a timber shelf inside the cavity, and fixed the wireless on it, covering it with a plastic sheet. Making sure I could listen to the news without seeing the wireless was quite a complicated process but eventually I solved it. This involved using two leads; one had a plug that fitted a lamp socket, and the other a pair of earphones. These were on flexes that dropped down the chimney into an unused fireplace below. I built a shelf in there and placed the earphones and plug on it. From there, I was able to pull them down and connect them to a table lamp whenever I wanted to listen to the news. It also provided a safe hiding place for this journal. Then I bricked up the hole in the chimney, plastered it over, repapered it, and then hung a large painting over the mantelpiece.

Now that it's all in working condition, I'm delighted with the result. I can now listen safely to the news. The challenge is to keep the news to myself. It's hard not to be able to discuss the latest developments with friends, but unfortunately you can't trust anyone these days, not even Mrs Harrison, who comes in to clean three times a week. I don't want to end up in a German prison. Loose lips and all that.

Speaking of going to prison, two very brave young women who I happen to know have been daubing bright red V signs all over St Helier. The V sign, as everyone knows, is Britain's victory symbol, and of course it's anathema to the Germans, who regard it as treason.

'We've talked it over, and we decided we can't just sit back like everyone else and do nothing,' one of them told me. 'This is our way of resisting.'

They were young and wonderfully reckless, and I admired their courage, but I was worried. Day after day, the Germans painted over the V signs, but the next day the subversive signs were back. Eventually someone saw the women daubing the walls with their bucket of red paint, and turned them in. The fact that a local would inform on one of us, would collude with the enemy against a compatriot, was something I never thought I'd see among us British, but wartime cures us of many illusions. I believe that unless we stick together, the enemy has already defeated us. I'm upset to say that the Nazis sent those brave girls to a prison in France.

For several months we've had no communication with England and when I heard that the Red Cross was finally about to deliver letters from Britain, I was too excited to sleep. Our baby must have been born by now, and I prayed that all had gone well. The uncertainty and tension were unbearable, and if not for my practice, I don't know how I would have retained my sanity.

My hands shook, and my heart almost burst from my chest when I saw her handwriting on the envelope. I tore it open, and out fell a small black-and-white photograph with serrated edges. There was Margaret, prettier than ever, holding our tiny son, James. Everything blurred. I was choked with emotion. I studied the little face and longed to hold him so much that my arms ached with yearning.

Then I looked more closely at Margaret's face. She wasn't smiling. I tried to decipher her expression and recalled the way she looked at me when she was about to board the boat for England: as if she could see into the future, and was terrified of what she saw.

That's when I grasped the enormity of my decision, the high price I had paid, and would continue to pay, for choosing duty ahead of personal happiness. I wasn't present at my son's birth, I hadn't been able to look into his new face, and I had no idea whether I would see him crawl or take his first tottering steps, or hear his first lisping words. In Margaret's accusing eyes, I read that she held me responsible for abandoning her.

It was the moment I gave up the hope that had sustained me ever since we parted. The war would not end soon, and I would miss those wondrous months – possibly years – of my little son's life. He wouldn't know me, and Margaret would probably not want to know me. And there was nothing I could do about it. I was trapped.

CHAPTER FIVE

Xanthe

St Helier, April 2019

Xanthe sits on a brown leather chesterfield in the lobby of the Pomme d'Or Hotel, waiting for the real estate agent. On the dot of ten, the hotel door swings open and Jill Anderson strides in, brisk and businesslike in a black tailored suit and high heels. On their way to the house Xanthe has rented for a month, the agent keeps up a relentless flow of conversation, undeterred by her client's minimal responses. Jersey has become the flavour of the month, Jill says, and congratulates Xanthe on renting one of the most desirable properties in St Helier.

'So centrally located and comfortable,' she gushes. 'Modern yet full of character. With a large garden and an orchard. Where else would you get all that so close to town?'

It's a large building with a bow-fronted facade on St Mark's Road. 'Back in the 1940s, the owner turned part of the garden into a vegetable patch,' Jill says as she turns the key in the lock. 'They kept chickens, too, so with the eggs, apples, pears, beans and cabbages, they must have been pretty self-sufficient. Can't imagine anyone doing that now.'

As they enter the high-ceilinged lounge room, Jill says, 'The house stood empty for ages, but a few years ago the owner arrived from England, had it renovated, and let it. Makes you wonder why they didn't move into it themselves. Or sell it. Property like this is scarce these days, and it would have fetched a good price.'

From the French windows, Xanthe looks out on the emerald lawn of the level garden. Past the lawn, the orchard looks neglected. Small, wizened apples hang off the branches of the apple trees, and birds have feasted on the pears, which are scattered half-eaten on the ground. There's no trace of the vegetable patch the agent mentioned. She wonders why, on this island with such an abundance of fresh produce, anyone would go to the bother of planting their own vegetables. And why a house in such a good position close to the centre of St Helier would have been left empty for so many years.

After giving Xanthe a tour of the kitchen and laundry, and explaining how to use the washing machine, the agent gives instructions about the oven that Xanthe knows she will never use. Then Jill places her card on the benchtop and urges her to get in touch if she needs anything. Relieved to hear the front door close behind her, Xanthe goes upstairs.

Like the kitchen, the bathroom has been renovated, and the bedroom walls have been painted an inoffensive shade of cream. The rooms are bright and spacious, and she is pleased that they have left vestiges of their original character, like the old fireplaces in the lounge room and the bedroom.

Outside the sun is shining. Determined not to waste any time, Xanthe leaves her bag on the bed, gets into the grey Nissan she has rented, and heads for the Jersey War Tunnels to see the Occupation Museum that Bill McAllister recommended.

Driving with both windows open, her hair blowing in the breeze, she inhales deeply. The air is fresh, unlike the humid, polluted air in Sydney, and the light here falls differently. But as soon as she thinks of home, her mood darkens and she grits her teeth. I won't think about it, she reminds herself. For one month she will enjoy life on this delightful island. Here she wasn't a failure, a disappointment to her parents, or the butt of criticism from her superiors. Here she could slough off the mantle of failed doctor and reinvent herself as just another tourist in search of a relaxing holiday.

Driving the Nissan down St Mark's Road, past rows of Georgian houses and the granite church of St Mark's with its square tower, she follows Queen's Road down to the coast and skirts the wide curve of St Aubin's Bay. She pulls up to have a look at the granite castle whose round tower and battlements seem to float in the water just off the coast. According to the sign, this is Elizabeth Castle, and visitors are warned not to attempt walking out to it except at low tide. She makes a note of the kiosk near the shore that sells ferry tickets to the castle, but keeps driving.

Past the bay, she turns into a lane that leads inland. Suddenly she jams on the brakes. Looming in front of her is a medieval manor house whose turrets, arches and dormer windows resemble something out of gothic novels like *Dragonwyck*, *Jane Eyre* and *Rebecca* — books she loved as a teenager.

She checks the name. Manoir de Courcy. Unable to resist a closer look, she parks the car and walks up to the ornate wrought-iron gate, which swings open when she leans against it. She has already taken a few steps on the curved gravel driveway, lined with beds of daffodils whose golden heads seem perched on long straight necks, when she looks up and freezes.

The front door has just opened, and the man she assumes is the lord of this manor, in tweed jacket and riding boots, is striding towards her. Too late to turn back. Mortified, she feels like a schoolgirl caught sneaking out of school. She thinks she sounds like one, too, when she begins to stammer an apology.

'I'm so sorry, I didn't mean to trespass, but I've never seen such a magnificent manor house …'

He interrupts her with a smile and holds out his hand. 'I'm Edward de Courcy.' He says it as if it means something.

She introduces herself, and wonders how to extricate herself from this embarrassing situation.

He says, 'I detect an unfamiliar accent. You're not American or Canadian. Where are you from?'

She tells him and is starting to back away when he says, 'What a coincidence. I'm heading for the airport now to pick up someone from Melbourne who claims to be some sort of relative. I think he discovered we have a common antecedent on one of those ancestry sites. Seems everyone these days can trace their antecedents back to Jersey.'

She is about to tell him about her own connection through a woman called Nellie, but decides against it. It's pointless to mention a distant relative she isn't interested in.

He is surveying her as if he too is weighing something up. Then he says, 'I don't know anything about this Melbourne chap, or if we'll have much to talk about once we've established that his great-uncle three times removed was the bastard grandson of the fifth son of the second wife of a de Courcy back in the sixteenth century.'

Edward de Courcy is the image of an English aristocrat with his silver hair, ruddy complexion, and slightly supercilious manner with its hint of *noblesse oblige*, but she can't help laughing at his comment.

She is still figuring out how to make a graceful exit when he says, 'If you're not busy, Xanthe, why don't you come back in an hour or so and join us for a drink to celebrate this serendipitous encounter with your compatriot?'

She isn't interested in meeting another Australian, but the prospect of being invited inside this manor house is too exciting to resist.

An hour later, she raps the lion's head knocker on the massive timber door and is examining the elaborate heraldic crest above it when a plump woman in a black dress, lace-up shoes and a white apron opens the heavy door and ushers her into what looks like a baronial hall.

Xanthe gazes at the cathedral-like ceiling, uneven timber beams and oak-panelled walls. The windows are hung with wine-coloured velvet curtains with gold tassels, and the walls are hung with large portraits in ornate gilded frames.

It occurs to her that this scenario resembles the beginning of a gothic novel. Jaded medico arrives in a strange country and snoops inside the grounds of a chateau, when the lord of the manor catches her in the act and invites her inside. Of course in a gothic novel he would have been tall, dark and mysterious, and they'd have had a torrid love affair until she discovered he had a mad wife locked up in the attic, and a jealous housekeeper lurking around the shrubbery.

Disappointingly, however, Edward de Courcy is the antithesis of a fictional hero, without a psychotic housekeeper or crazy wife in sight. What's more, the motherly housekeeper who opened the door and is now offering them glasses of sherry from a crystal decanter on a silver tray is no Mrs Danvers. Instead of being locked up in the attic, his wife Emily is a vivacious woman with a mass of white hair and a merry laugh who wants to know about Xanthe's plans in Jersey.

Seated in an armchair facing their host, the guy from Melbourne stands up and introduces himself. His name is Daniel Miller, and from the conversation between him and their host, Xanthe figures out that he's an academic of some kind. He doesn't say much, but he doesn't appear to be as overawed by their surroundings as she is. She watches him while he is talking to their host and notes his cleft chin, a feature she has always found attractive.

Sipping her sherry, she turns her attention from Daniel to the portraits of bewigged men and bejewelled women whose elaborate hairstyles and intricate costumes seem to illustrate fashion through the ages. Following her gaze, Edward de Courcy waves his arm casually towards the portraits.

'The de Courcys arrived in Jersey with William the Conqueror, who, as you probably know, was the Duke of Normandy.' He lets that sink in while he sips his sherry. Looking from Xanthe to Daniel, he adds, 'You realise, of course, that this makes Jersey the oldest part of the British Empire.'

All this is new to Xanthe, but it explains the French place names she has noticed. Daniel is nodding, and she supposes he is better informed about history than she is. Then she remembers why he has come to Jersey and realises that of course he would have checked out the family history – the history of his own family – before leaving home.

'Ever since the Norman Conquest – 1066 you may recall – and down through the centuries,' their host continues, pointing to one of the earliest portraits, a woman garbed in a medieval conical hat with a long gauzy veil, 'the de Courcys have distinguished themselves in every major land and sea battle, crusade, revolution, revolt and rebellion that England has been involved in. John de Courcy was at Richard the Lionheart's side during the siege of Jerusalem, and Edward de Courcy fought beside Henry V at the Battle of Agincourt. I daresay you've heard of Sir Walter Raleigh? He was governor of Jersey during the reign of the first Elizabeth and built Elizabeth Castle, which he named in her honour. During the English Civil War, King Charles II took refuge here, in the home of George de Courcy.'

He waits for their reaction, and then, turning his gaze on his Melbourne relative, he says, 'During the English Civil War, George de Courcy supported Charles II, and after the Royalists had defeated Cromwell, the king rewarded

George with a large grant of land in the New World. And do you know what he called it?'

Xanthe shakes her head, slightly irritated. How could she possibly know? Daniel Miller, however, just waits. She suspects he knows.

'New Jersey!' Edward de Courcy cries triumphantly. 'Do you see? It's called New Jersey, in honour of our ancestor and our island!'

Edward de Courcy is justifiably proud of his heritage, and she is fascinated by this extraordinary family history. No wonder Daniel was eager to meet the last Jersey member of this illustrious family.

Emily de Courcy turns to her husband. 'You've bored these young people quite long enough with your stories, Edward,' she says, and turns to Xanthe. 'Do tell us something about yourself.'

'I've recently graduated in medicine,' she says carefully, 'and I'm taking a short break.'

Emily nods. 'A doctor! How marvellous! You young people are so lucky these days, to be able to travel overseas. When I was your age, we were fortunate to travel to England or Wales. I still remember the first time my parents took me on the ferry to Weymouth! It was such a treat!'

'Now you're boring them, my dear,' Edward points out.

Emily ignores his comment. Turning to Daniel, she asks, 'You said before that you were engaged in an academic project. I should very much like to know what it is.'

'I'm working on my PhD,' he replies. It seems to Xanthe that he's being cagey, but perhaps she is merely projecting her own reticence on him.

Emily forges ahead, undeterred. 'A PhD, how frightfully interesting. You must be very clever. May we know your subject?'

'The treatment of Jews in Jersey during the Occupation,' he says evenly.

The temperature in the room seems to drop several degrees, and the bonhomie has dissipated. Edward de Courcy walks over to the mahogany sideboard, picks up the crystal decanter and refills their glasses before returning to his armchair, and it seems to Xanthe that this is a ploy to give himself time to respond.

'You're going back to a time many of us would prefer to forget,' he says to Daniel, and Xanthe senses that beneath the quietly controlled words and suave manner, he is bristling. 'I do hope you haven't come here in search of sensational stories about Jews and collaborators. For the past few years, journalists and amateur historians have had a heyday publishing such stories, full of fabrications and exaggerations that malign decent people. Let me assure you there was no collaboration in Jersey during the war, and our leaders did all they could to protect the Jews.'

Xanthe is taken aback by Edward's vehemence. Why is he so hot under the collar, and why did he sound so defensive about collaboration, which Daniel hadn't even mentioned?

Emily looks from her husband to their guests, gives a bright smile, and tries to steer the subject into neutral waters, but Edward cuts across her conciliatory words, places his glass on the tray, and clears his throat.

'I'm afraid I must leave you, a business meeting, you know. But thank you for coming. I do hope to see you again.' And with that, he strides from the room.

Xanthe looks at Daniel but she can't read his expression. He is obviously a man who listens more than he talks. She figures he is probably one of those irritating men who keeps his thoughts so well concealed that you never know what he is thinking — a trait that contributed to the breakdown of her last relationship. She looks at him again. Surely he is as shocked as she is. After all, he has come all this way to meet a relative who has just rubbished his project and snubbed him.

Emily tries to keep up friendly chatter but she can't lighten the atmosphere. After thanking her for her hospitality, Xanthe and Daniel leave, and walk towards the gate in silence, their footsteps crunching on the gravel drive.

As soon as they are outside the gate, Xanthe says, 'I can't believe what just happened. He didn't even arrange to see you again. You must be shocked at his reaction.'

'Not at all,' he replies. 'I expected it.'

'But why? All this happened so long ago. After all, the war ended over seventy years ago.'

He shrugs. 'Wars never really end.'

'Well, I'd like to hear about your PhD,' she says.

For the first time he looks at her with interest. 'Really? If you have time tomorrow, I guarantee to bore you for several hours.'

'I'll take my chances,' she says.

The unexpected turn in the conversation at Manoir de Courcy reinforces Xanthe's decision to visit the museum that Bill McAllister mentioned. Perhaps it will help her understand the contentious issues Edward de Courcy raised.

At the end of a pretty country lane, behind a circular flowerbed planted with cornflowers and pansies, a stark red cross painted on a whitewashed granite wall indicates the Jersey War Tunnels. As she enters the long, dark passageway leading to the exhibits, she is transfixed by the spine-chilling sound of spades and hammers striking rock. According to the information on the wall, this tunnel is a hundred metres long, and was dug with picks and shovels by thousands of slave labourers during the Occupation.

The eerie sound effects and the cold air inside the thick granite walls make her shiver. How could they have hollowed out this solid rock using only picks and spades? Above a plaque that says most of them died of starvation or exhaustion, she sees names and nationalities scratched into the walls. The names are Russian, Polish and Spanish, interspersed by an occasional Star of David. As she continues walking towards the ticket office, she wonders why the Germans constructed tunnels here.

Intrigued, she walks on. Through a half-open door on her left, she sees a room where a long mess table is littered with plates, cups and unwashed beer glasses. Then she hears laughter and glasses being clinked in noisy toasts while drunken German voices sing 'Lili Marlene'. In the background there's the deafening sound of shells exploding. Although the room is deserted, the army jackets draped on the backs of some of the wooden chairs give the impression that the officers have just stepped out for a moment and will soon be back.

On the wall, an official notice from the German Kommandatur catches her eye. *A dance will be held on 5/4/41 at West Park Pavilion for the German soldiers, who will be pleased to welcome their friends as usual. Admission 6d. Curfew at midnight.*

Xanthe wonders about the girls who danced with the enemy. Why did they fraternise with the occupiers? What did their families and friends think of their behaviour?

As if in answer to her questions, signs beneath the photographs of handsome German soldiers ask visitors to consider what they would have done during the Occupation if polite German soldiers had stopped in the street to pat their dog or admire their baby, or if they said they were lonely, missed their families, and offered to buy their children an ice cream. They are polite and respectful, speak good English, and miss their homes and families. The sign asks, *Would you invite them home?*

Xanthe looks at the photos of the innocent-looking soldiers, and wonders how the locals did react. She also wonders what she would have done. Her thoughts turn to her unknown relative Nellie, who must have been a young girl at the time. Did she walk past the Germans and avert her gaze, or was she one of the good-time girls who attended the dances?

The signs make the German soldiers sound innocuous, almost as though they were victims of the war themselves, just like the locals. Then she reads the orders they posted in Royal Square. Cycling two abreast was a crime, ownership of more than one dog was forbidden, all fishing was prohibited, and in October 1940 a register of Jews was to be compiled and Jewish businesses were banned from trading and were to display a yellow printed notice: *Jüdisches geschäft*. That didn't sound so harmless. She thinks back to

Edward de Courcy's indignant comment and rereads that order. It looks as if the Nazis pursued their discriminatory racial laws in Jersey.

Under the glass of some display cases, she reads letters from informers denouncing their neighbours for owning a wireless, or for having more coal than regulations permitted. There are documents regarding people who have been deported to prisons in France, or concentration camps in Germany, for infringing an order or defying the occupiers, and gradually the dark nature of the Occupation reveals itself, with denunciations, punishments and deportations.

She reads the anti-Jewish order again. Was a list of Jews ever compiled? What did happen to the Jews of Jersey? Then she thinks about Daniel Miller. They have arranged to meet for coffee at the Royal Yacht Hotel the next day, and now she can't wait to find out more about his thesis.

CHAPTER SIX

Tom

St Helier, November 1940

The blare of trumpets, trombones, drums and glockenspiels resounded throughout St Helier, and crowds streamed towards the irresistible sound of the military band. Standing in the doorway of his father's photographic studio, Tom watched as German troops marched past in their steel helmets and polished jackboots, whose metal studs clicked on the tarmac. It was a victory parade to welcome the arrival of the new German commander, and it made Tom think back to the newsreel he had seen several months before, of the Nazis stomping along the Champs-Élysées. But this was far worse. This was a victory without a battle, without even a single gunshot, a triumph over their subservience. It made him feel like throwing up.

The parade wasn't the only thing he was watching. He was also aware that his father was darting in front of the crowd to get the best vantage point for his photographs. Since the Occupation had begun five months before, his mother had placed a sign in their shop window in German to entice soldiers to bring their films for him to develop. Her ploy had worked, and Stanley Gaskell had become the Germans' official photographer. Their shop was always full of soldiers bringing in their films, and asking for advice about cameras. They often wanted portraits taken, and thanks to the Occupation, his business thrived.

'They'll want photos of today's parade to send home,' his mother told Stanley that morning. 'Make sure you take close-ups of the band as well.' It seemed to Tom that she never stopped scheming and plotting, always finding ways to make more money. It meant that they were never short of anything, but the extent to which they depended on German customers for their growing prosperity embarrassed him.

Like his home, the whole island was being Germanised. From a vantage point above the harbour, he and Frank sat on their Raleigh bicycles watching barges, boats and ships piled up with cars, bicycles and yachts, as well as cows and potatoes, all bound for Germany.

'If they could lift the whole of Jersey out of the sea and transport it to Germany, they would,' he said.

'But they don't even need to, do they?' Frank retorted. 'Harry says that they come into his father's workshop and just help themselves to tyres, spare parts, spanners, screwdrivers, whatever they want.'

Harry, who helped his father in his mechanic's workshop after school, rarely joined them on their after-school excursions, but he was always eager to hear about their exploits.

Tom admired Harry, who was different from him and Frank. While he and Frank were mad about sport, impulsive and recklessly outspoken, Harry was quiet and preferred reading to outdoor activities. He always saw the best in everyone and was irritatingly honest and truthful, perhaps because he attended a Jesuit college, Tom supposed. People often commented on the contrast between the three of them, but Tom felt that their friend's considered, thoughtful nature created a balance in their triumvirate, so his words that morning had astonished them.

'The best way to help tyrants is to do nothing,' he'd said.

Tom and Frank had looked at each other and then at Harry. 'Where'd you get that from?' Frank asked.

Harry shrugged. 'Read it somewhere. Makes sense though, doesn't it?'

'Doing anything right now just gets you into trouble,' Frank said. 'Look what happened to those two girls who wrote that V sign all over the place.'

Tom was silent. He couldn't stop thinking about Harry's comment, which reverberated in his mind for a long time.

He was struggling with a problem at home. Although he was upset that his father's business relied on the occupiers, what made him seethe was the social contact that had started up between some of the German officers and his parents, especially his mother. Once a week, their home on Gloucester Road resounded with music, the clinking of glasses, and loud German laughter. Their regular guests were officers from the Water Police, who were stationed at the Pomme d'Or. In his opinion they had no sense of humour, so he couldn't understand why his mother laughed so much at their asinine jokes.

On those evenings, Alma seemed to be in her element. She put dance records on the turntable, Gilbert and Sullivan songs, Strauss waltzes, or Franz Lehar tunes, while his father dutifully did the rounds pouring schnapps or lager into their guests' bottomless glasses.

It upset Tom to see Stanley being a waiter. Tom thought his attempt to look interested in the conversation, despite being ignored, was demeaning. What was even more infuriating was the way the fat officer, Gunther Kohl, gazed at his mother with doglike adoration he didn't bother to conceal.

Sometimes during the party, Alma would grab Tom's arm and push him into the centre of the room to boast how well he spoke German. Tom glared at her while she put him through his German paces for the benefit of their guests. It was true that he had made good progress with Professor Strauss's tutelage, but he hated being paraded like a performing monkey in front of the hated invaders, who clapped him on the shoulder and praised his mother for her foresight in having him learn their language.

On these occasions Tom couldn't get away fast enough, and would retreat upstairs to his bedroom, where he would spend the rest of the night trying to block out the convivial sounds of the party and his mother's sparkling laugh.

'I suppose next you're going to enlist me in the Hitler Youth,' he said one evening after their guests had left and his father was gathering up the glasses.

With a scathing look, she hissed, 'If you're too stupid to know which side your bread is buttered on, keep your infantile opinions to yourself.'

'Why do you have those Krauts here?' he asked his father.

Stanley shrugged. 'Your mother says it's good for business.'

Tom stomped back upstairs and slammed his bedroom door.

Didn't his parents see what the Germans were doing to their island? Barely five months had passed since their arrival, and already most of the shops were bare. Food was now severely rationed to eight ounces of meat, two ounces of butter, four ounces of sugar and ten ounces of bread a week, on an island where everything had always been plentiful.

Clothing and other essential items were almost impossible to obtain except on the black market, where the prices were out of most people's reach. He wondered why their larder was never empty, and obtaining food and wine, as well as new dresses, handbags and shoes, didn't seem to be a problem for his mother.

Although the seas around Jersey were rough, with unpredictable tides and dangerous coastal storms, Tom noticed that the possibility of supplementing their meagre rations with mackerel, sole or flounder encouraged many locals to try their luck. Like everything on Jersey these days, this activity was strictly controlled by the Germans, but Tom, who loved fishing, decided to apply for a permit.

While waiting for his permit at Feldkommandatur 515, the headquarters of the German civil administration at Victoria College, Tom watched two German soldiers saunter past. Two Jersey girls were clinging to their uniformed arms, looking up flirtatiously into their faces and giggling. He clenched his fists and stifled an impulse to rush up to them and yell 'Traitors!' Because that's what they were. The locals called them Jerrybags, but to him they were traitors. He supposed they were the floozies who attended the dances the Germans held every week at West Park Pavilion, and danced with the enemy.

Probably slept with them, too. It infuriated but also excited him, thinking of those girls slipping off their knickers and letting the soldiers do whatever they wanted. He often wondered about sex and how he could find out more about it. He thought about Milly, who was even more innocent than he was, and often imagined the bliss of seeing each other naked and touching each other's bodies. Just thinking about it engorged him, and he relieved that inexorable urge in the safe darkness of his bedroom.

Cycling around the island, Tom was intrigued by the proliferation of machine guns mounted on either side of the harbour mouth, and the concrete gun emplacements being constructed along Albert Pier. Others were appearing along the shores of St Aubin's Bay. Why the enemy was bothering to construct these fortifications on an island they had virtually walked into unopposed, mystified him. It was something that he and his friends often discussed, but they never found an answer that made any sense.

When Tom's father developed the films the German soldiers brought in, Tom noticed that many of the photographs included images of these fortifications. Some even had close-ups of the latest German night-fighter planes at the airport.

Locals were forbidden from taking photos of these sites. In fact, they needed a permit to take any photographs at all, except of their families, but the soldiers often posed in front of the fortifications. Tom, who would help his father develop the films in the darkroom, was fascinated by photos of this war materiel, and without knowing why, he began to make copies of them and paste them in his album. It gave him a sense of satisfaction to flip through the pages and know that he had defied one of their hated orders. He kept the album in a locked drawer and only allowed Harry and Frank to look at the photos after swearing them to secrecy.

German orders kept coming thick and fast, each one more restrictive than the last, and all aimed at strangling all island activities. Fishing, boating and photography were strictly controlled and sporting clubs were banned. Tom could hardly restrain himself from asking their frequent visitors, the officers of the Water Police, why they felt threatened by the Jersey Cricket Club and the Ladies' Tennis Club, because those had also been banned. Tom's mother, aware of her son's dangerous opinions, kept a sharp eye on him on those evenings, and made sure that he never had an opportunity to bail up their guests with some provocative comment.

Despite all the restrictions, and the summary punishments meted out to those who flouted the regulations, Tom was horrified to hear some people praising the occupiers for their politeness and forbearance. 'They're not as bad as they're painted,' one woman commented while queuing up for her diminishing ration of meat.

Her friend nodded. 'One of them bought my Dennis an ice cream yesterday and said he looked just like his little Hans. They miss home. After all, it's not their fault they were sent here.' Another chimed in with a story about her children being given chocolate by the soldiers.

Tom overheard that conversation on the West Park slip, where he and Frank had cycled that afternoon. They were surprised to see a German news team getting ready to film a group of schoolchildren lured there by the promise of chocolate. Speaking English, the announcer asked those who liked chocolate to raise their arms. Naturally every arm shot up, and the camera whirred to photograph Jersey children enthusiastically giving what appeared to be a Nazi salute.

Tom turned to Frank. 'That weasel Goebbels will be ecstatic. I can imagine them showing this film all over Germany to show how we all love the Germans.'

Tom had heard about some of the Nazi atrocities in Europe when he and his parents had tuned in to the BBC in the evenings before all wirelesses were confiscated, and he shook his head at the gullibility of people here. How naïve they were, so easily taken in by a clicked-boot greeting, ice cream and chocolate. He was convinced that before long, the real nature of their occupiers would reveal itself. What he didn't suspect was that he would soon discover the true nature of his countrymen, and their leaders, as well.

That discovery wasn't long in coming. It arrived with the order to register the Jews. Tom knew that there were some Jews on Jersey, but as he didn't know any of them personally, he didn't give it much thought. In fact, a movie he saw one Saturday afternoon presented them in such a terrible light, that for a time he found it difficult to shake off the antipathy the film had created.

Going to the Forum, the newest and most magnificent of the three cinemas in St Helier, was one of the highlights of his week. He loved watching the floodlit Hammond organ rise from under the stage with the organist Mr O'Henry playing the melodies they all knew.

The words were printed on the screen, and everyone joined in the singing, creating a warm community spirit in the movie theatre.

On one particular afternoon, however, that spirit did not extend to the Jews. The film being shown, *Jew Suss,* depicted anti-Semitic stereotypes of Jews with hooked noses and devious plans. The evil Jewish character in the movie was about to abduct and rape the innocent fair-haired German maiden until, at the last moment, he was thwarted by the Aryan hero. The film ended with the Jew's demise, which was greeted with enthusiastic applause by the Germans and their girlfriends. Tom left the cinema in two minds. It was hard not to sympathise with the hero and heroine against the evil Jew, but at the same time he was aware that he was being manipulated by the Germans' racist propaganda. Looking around at the soldiers as the audience began to disperse, it struck him that hardly any of the Germans stationed in Jersey resembled this ideal Aryan type, and that in fact he matched it better than most of them.

He didn't give the movie any further thought until some days later when he passed Mrs Goldman's music shop and saw it boarded up. The German sign on the large shop window said it was a Jewish business and must be closed. It had never occurred to him that Mrs Goldman was Jewish. Several years ago, when he was learning to play the piano, he had gone there to buy the score for a couple of songs from *The Mikado* so he could learn to play the tunes.

He didn't have enough money, and Mrs Goldman had let him have it for less than the marked price. Whenever he walked past her shop, she waved to him. A widow, he thought she was.

Now, looking at the empty shop with the ugly sign across the window, he wondered how she was managing without any income, especially now that food was so scarce and prices on the black market were skyrocketing.

Mrs Goldman lived above the shop, and on impulse he knocked on the door. It took such a long time for her to answer that he was about to walk away when the door opened slightly and through the narrow crack he saw her. She seemed much older and more wrinkled, and she looked at him with worried eyes. Now he was face to face with her, he didn't know what to say and regretted the impulse that had led him to her door.

'Why did you come here?' she asked, and he noticed that she was craning her neck to see past him, as if to check whether someone else had come with him.

'I just wondered if you were all right,' he stammered.

At hearing those words, her face smoothed out, and she smiled. 'You're a good boy,' she said. 'Come in.'

Upstairs in the room that she used as a lounge room and office, with a small wooden desk at one end and a worn sofa at the other, she made room for him on a chair heaped with files, and disappeared into what he supposed was a kitchen. He heard dishes clattering, and a few minutes later she emerged with a teapot and two cups and saucers on a tray, as well as a plate with two shortbread biscuits.

With shaking hands, she poured their tea, and offered him a biscuit but didn't take one herself.

'I'm very worried,' she said. 'Now that they have handed the Germans a list of Jewish people in Jersey, who knows what will happen to us?'

'Who handed them a list?'

'The States,' she said. 'Whoever is in charge of these matters.'

That was the first time Tom had heard that their government had given the Germans a list of Jews. He was shocked. Mrs Goldman was a Jersey citizen.

'You were born here, you should be treated the same as everyone else,' he said, biting on his biscuit. Instead of being crunchy, it crumbled in his mouth and he realised it was stale. 'There must be some mistake. Why would our government let them close your business down?'

She seemed to be deep in thought. Then she sighed. 'I suppose they were just obeying orders,' she said.

CHAPTER SEVEN

Dr Jackson

St Helier, March 1941

If anyone in Jersey still harboured any illusions about the benevolence of our occupiers, the tragic case of Francois Scornet must have woken them up with a jolt. Everyone was buzzing with the news. Scornet and fifteen other French youths were caught by the Germans and brought here after trying to escape from Normandy to join the Free French in England. Why the other fifteen got prison sentences while poor Scornet was condemned to death, I have no idea, but mercy and justice are not the occupiers' strong suit.

Not long after the sentence was passed, I was driving along a steep road leading to the Jersey General Hospital to check on Mr le Guay, who had pneumonia, when a

German soldier standing in the middle of the road shouted *Halt!* I stopped and looked around but couldn't see anything. A few minutes later, however, I heard the grinding sound of a motor labouring up the hill and craned my neck to see who was in it. It was an open lorry, and in it was a young man who was manacled like a dangerous criminal and escorted by several soldiers.

That's when it dawned on me that this must be Francois Scornet, and they were driving the poor fellow to his execution. I noticed that he was very pale but looked defiant. What made the scene particularly gruesome was the pine coffin lying beside him in the lorry. I wished I could show my support and admiration for his courage in some way, but there was nothing I could do, so I relieved my feelings by sounding my horn, to the fury of the German soldier on duty, who gave me a threatening look and ordered me to get out of there, *schnell*.

I didn't see the execution, but next day a patient told me what had happened. Apparently they drove Scornet to the grounds of St Ouen Manor, stood him against an oak tree, and offered him a blindfold, which he refused. As the execution squad raised their rifles, ready to fire, he shouted '*Vive la France!*' A moment later, the volley resounded through the parkland and silenced his voice forever.

Since that day, I've been haunted by the sight of that brave young man riding to his death beside the coffin that would soon hold his body. When I think about it, that scene seems like a metaphor for our own precarious existence at the mercy of our occupiers. Perhaps, unseen and unacknowledged, our own coffins are riding in our shadow. That execution was obviously a warning to anyone foolhardy enough to try escaping from the prison our island has become.

The Germans flatter themselves that they have so much in common with the British, but as time goes on, I see more contrasts between us. For one thing, they have no sense of humour whatsoever, but what's more important, they lack that particularly British quality we call bloody-mindedness, a doggedness that makes us resent authority and question those who issue orders, while they seem to thrive on obeying orders to the letter.

Here's a good example. Last week I dropped in at the library to look for recipe books. I wanted to find out how to make the best use of my apples and pears when they were ready to pick. I only have to look around to realise that summer is still a few months away: our spring meadows are still carpeted with bluebells and primroses, and the wild apple and cherry trees on the cliffs are just beginning to show their delicate foliage, but with our food supplies dwindling day by day, I am thinking ahead to make sure I don't waste anything.

I feel I should point out that, unlike most of the locals, I'm not badly off for provisions. Apart from my own chickens, which keep me well supplied with eggs, and the carrots, beans and cabbages I've planted out, patients often bring me a piece of pork from a pig they have slaughtered, or a home-baked loaf of bread, instead of money. Speaking of money, have I mentioned that our new currency is the hated Reichsmark?

Less than a year ago, the idea of a food shortage here was unthinkable, but that was before the marauding Germans arrived and denuded our farms to send our food to

Germany. I've noticed that many of my patients have lost weight and their children have become sallow and skinny. I often take eggs and vegetables when I visit some of my patients, but I can't help thinking that instead of lamenting the shortages, more people should be turning their useless lawns into vegetable patches, as I have done.

Another problem is the shortage of petrol. We've actually had to resort to using a horse-drawn ambulance, something my grandfather might have seen in his lifetime, but I certainly never expected to see in mine. I've taken to doing my rounds on my old Raleigh bicycle by day so I can save the petrol for night visits. It makes me furious to think about our situation but I suppose everyone who suffers privations in wartime has the same feeling of outrage, injustice, and incomprehension: life used to be so good – how could this have happened to us?

Anyway, now that I've got that off my chest, I want to go back to the library and my search for a recipe book. Miss Murphy, who is the librarian, jumped up from her chair when she saw me come in. She has short brown hair that I suspect she cuts herself, fastening it either side of her forehead with a couple of bobby pins, and usually wears a baggy grey cardigan.

She is the type people tend to underestimate, but from what I've observed, beneath her mild, mousy exterior, she has a feisty nature that doesn't suffer fools.

In response to my query, she recommended a cookbook by a Mrs Beeton, and as she went off to fetch it, I noticed that on some of the shelves, which had once been tightly stacked, the books now leaned against each other at angles that suggested they were compensating for gaps.

'Bloody Krauts,' she said, following my glance. 'A group of them, full of self-importance, stomped in here the other day, saying they came from their department of culture. Culture my foot. Anyway, they demanded to see all the books that were either written by Jewish authors or dealt with Jewish topics. I told them in no uncertain terms that I had no idea which ones they might be, as I was only interested in the quality of the books, not the religion of those who wrote them. Of course they didn't like my answer, and started yelling at me, but I just stared at them, and when they realised that yelling wouldn't help, they divided themselves into groups, and started going through the books shelf by shelf with that relentless Teutonic thoroughness, consulting a list of banned authors they'd been given.'

Fascinated, I asked what happened next.

'After finding the offending volumes, they tossed them onto the floor as if they were rubbish. Dr Jackson, I'm not a religious woman, but as far as I'm concerned, mistreating books is as close to sacrilege as you can get, and I had to bite my tongue to stop myself from telling them that what they were doing was an example of barbarism, not culture. Finally they threw the books into sacks and drove off, probably to destroy them. Imagine that. A nation of supermen terrified of books written by or about Jews. I wouldn't have believed it if I hadn't seen it with my own eyes.'

Miss Murphy described this episode as another instance of the German obsession with obeying orders, but I saw it as something darker. To me it was a worrying example of their fanatical racism, and I wondered if this was just the beginning.

Miss Murphy's story made me think of Mrs Goldman, and how worried she had been during her last consultation, so a few days later, when I saw that disgraceful *Jüdisches geschäft* sign on the window of her music shop, I decided to look in on her, as I hadn't seen her for some time. But when I rapped on the door, there was no answer. That was strange. I knew that she was a widow with no children, and I couldn't figure out where she could have gone. I made a mental note to follow up on her, but I was run off my feet that week with an influenza outbreak, and all thoughts of Mrs Goldman went out of my mind.

Summer is finally here, and I've just realised that it's been months since I last wrote in this journal. I have been so busy looking after my patients that by the time I've finished my morning surgery, visited patients in hospital, and done house calls in the afternoon and often again at night, I'm so exhausted, I fall into bed.

Which is just as well, otherwise I'd be lying awake dwelling on my loneliness and sexual frustration. And wondering what's happening to Margaret and our baby.

These days my morning surgery is busier than ever, probably because the shortage of nourishing food has weakened people and made them more susceptible to infections. I also suspect, although this is something I can't prove and many doctors would dispute, that anxiety has contributed to the increase in illness.

I have always believed that plenty of fresh air and exercise are essential for good health, so whenever I have an hour or so to spare during these long golden days, I try to spend it outdoors.

My favourite spot is the woodland at Rozel Woods, where walking among the birches, limes and beech trees always lifts my spirits, especially at sunset when the paths are laced with light and shade, and the bark of the Scots pines glows with the warm colour of copper. Sometimes I catch sight of blackbirds, robins and wrens flitting from branch to branch. Once I even heard the eerie song of the blackcaps. At St Catherine's, another haunt of mine, I spied the long bill and speckled brown feathers of the short-toed tree creeper, and almost dropped my binoculars in excitement. Just listening to the bird calls and looking at the shimmering greenery lifts my spirits. Nature is a great healer. Its effect on me is almost spiritual. At least that's one thing the Germans haven't been able to steal from us.

Walking through the woods and along the clifftops where once Margaret and I hiked together helps to take my mind off the emptiness I feel whenever I think about her and my little boy. Jamie – that's what I call him in my thoughts – is ten months old now, such a delightful age. In spite of all our privations and restrictions, I envy parents who can hold their babies and witness the wonderful little milestones of their lives.

Not being able to hold Jamie and play with him, to see him crawl, take his first faltering steps, or hear his first words, torments me, and I try not to think about Margaret and her accusing glance in the one photograph she has sent me. The only thing that consoles me at those times is music. I take a record from its brown paper sleeve and put it on the gramophone, place the needle on the outside groove, close my eyes, and let the sublime melodies of Mozart fill my heart. I've always believed that music takes over when words fail.

If not for my nature walks, and the solace of music, my ever-increasing patient workload, the never-ending effort to keep ahead of the food shortages, and the obligation to continue recording my experiences in this journal, I don't know if I'd manage to get up in the morning.

Something happened a few days ago that has taken my mind off all my other preoccupations. I was on my way to visit one of my patients in St Lawrence, when I saw something that stopped me in my tracks.

A long column of men was shuffling along the road. I'm talking about several hundred men, in the most shocking condition I have ever seen – just skin and bones, with matted hair that hung down over their bearded faces, filthy rags on their feet instead of shoes, tattered clothes on their emaciated bodies. They looked like walking skeletons.

They were being herded by German soldiers who yelled at them and bashed them with rifle butts to make them walk faster. When several of these emaciated men collapsed on the ground, the guards set upon them, kicking and beating. Unable to watch this vicious behaviour, I jumped out of my car, but a soldier pointed a rifle at me and yelled that I'd better get back in the car fast, or else. *Raus* and *schnell* are the only two words most of them seem to know.

Where did these prisoners come from? What crimes had they committed to be treated like this? And what were they doing here? Horrified by this appalling scene, I lingered nearby to try and figure out what was going on, but the soldiers threatened to shoot me, so with a heavy heart I turned the car around and reached my patient by another route.

As it happened, Mrs Wilson died soon after I got there, a terrible death in which people drown in their own fluid. Perhaps one day they'll discover something that will cure pneumonia and save lives, but sulphonamides, the only medication we have at present, are woefully inadequate to treat this deadly lung infection.

That evening, depressed about my patient, who leaves a distraught husband and five small children, I stopped at the Cock and Bottle, hoping a glass of Mary Ann ale and some convivial company might lift my spirits. Two German soldiers were sitting at the other end of the counter, raising glasses of schnapps and shouting *Prost!* in drunken voices.

Recalling the nightmarish sight of that column of walking skeletons, I asked the barman if he knew anything about them. Charlie was the type who always knew what was going on, probably because he had a talent for eliciting information without appearing to ask questions, and also because his customers – locals as well as Germans – became less guarded and more garrulous with each pint of beer or glass of schnapps. Having spent a couple of years in Germany, Charlie could converse with them.

In response to my question, he nodded without replying but the movement of his head and the knowing look in his eyes indicated that I should wait until he was free to talk to me.

After pouring more schnapps into the Germans' glasses, exchanging some pleasantries with them, and greeting three noisy locals who had just sat down at the counter, he turned away to wash some dirty glasses, then picked up a tea towel, as if his life depended on making them sparkle. Watching the scene in the pub, where we locals and our German captors drank side by side, made me realise how enmeshed we all are, and how difficult it is to establish and maintain clear boundaries between us.

When Charlie spoke to me, his lips hardly moved, and his voice was so low that I had to sit forward to catch what he was saying. From time to time he glanced around to make sure no-one overheard.

'Slave labourers, mostly from Russia,' he murmured.

I knew from listening to the BBC News on my secret wireless that the Germans had recently invaded the Soviet Union. This was shocking news that I didn't dare to share with anyone for fear I'd be reported for having a wireless. Not long ago, a young woman reported her own father for having a wireless set, and he was sentenced to six months in prison. I don't know what was more shocking – the fact that someone would inform on their own parent, or that having a wireless could lead to deportation to some terrible prison camp from which they might never return.

Listening to my own wireless, I found out that within a few days, the German army had already cut a swathe through the Soviet Union. The news reports suggested that the attack took the Russians completely by surprise. As for their leader, Stalin, who had always appeared so shrewd, wily and aggressive, he was apparently holed up in his dacha at the time, so paralysed by fear that he could neither comprehend what was happening nor take decisive action to counter it.

Perhaps he had put his trust in the agreement that he and Hitler had signed before the war, and couldn't believe that Hitler had broken it and attacked.

The barman went over to serve his customers, and after refilling some glasses, he returned to continue our whispered conversation.

'I heard that the Germans captured these men in Russian villages, pushed them into sealed wagons, and transported them across the country for days in carriages that didn't even have toilets. They didn't give them any food on the journey, and hardly any water, so some died on the way and others went crazy. They didn't unlock those wagons until they got to France.' He shook his head while he kept drying the glasses. 'It doesn't bear thinking about.'

It was a shocking story but I knew it must be true, as he had heard it from the Germans themselves. Now I understood why those poor wretches were in such a pitiable state.

I drained my glass and ordered another. 'But why did they bring them here?' I asked.

He shrugged. 'From something one of the Germans said, it sounds as if they're planning to build fortifications in Jersey.'

That made me almost choke on my ale. 'Fortifications, here? Whatever for?' Before he could reply, I added, 'Surely they don't expect men in this condition to do any physical work? They can hardly stand up.'

He shrugged again. 'Don't know the answer to that one, but I'll try and find out,' he said, and turned away to serve his other customers.

Before I turn in tonight, I want to end on a positive note and mention someone who is doing an outstanding job in a very difficult situation. I'm referring to the matron of the Jersey Maternity Hospital, Miss Aoife O'Connor, a brilliant organiser and an indefatigable worker. Unlike so many women in her position who tend to throw their weight around, treat the junior nurses like dirt, and think they know more than the doctors, she has a beguiling softness about her. The junior nurses are devoted to her, and do whatever she asks without complaining, no matter how long it takes or how arduous it is.

In case you think I'm exaggerating, here's a good illustration. Despite all our care to avoid infection in the maternity hospital, we had a couple of cases of puerperal fever recently.

I remember from my lectures on public health that when women in labour were dying of this fever in the nineteenth century, it was a remarkably prescient obstetrician, Dr Ignacy Semmelweis, who proved that it was caused by poor hygiene in maternity hospitals. It's hard to believe nowadays, but the main offenders were doctors who failed to wash their hands before delivering babies.

Naturally we always took all necessary precautions to avoid infection in the Jersey Maternity Hospital, but some of the women who were about to give birth were quite debilitated, especially those who had other children and had to spend most of their time trying to find enough food for their family. Their anxiety and cramped living conditions made them especially susceptible to disease.

We were horrified when we identified an outbreak of puerperal fever, something I had never seen before. And to make matters worse, the Germans, who had taken over a large section of the hospital for their own soldiers, had also taken over the sterilising plant, leaving us with hardly any disinfectant.

Matron O'Connor didn't waste any time wringing her hands. 'We'll just have to do the disinfecting ourselves,' she said in her Irish brogue. I quailed at the prospect of making the entire hospital germ-free, but she rolled up her sleeves, arranged to move the maternity patients temporarily into smaller nursing homes, organised the nurses into groups, and set out a plan of action.

It was a daunting plan. She had every single bed dismantled, and directed nurses to scrub every part of each bed with soap and water and whatever disinfectant was available, and then to leave it all in the sun to dry out. Scaffolding was erected, and every inch of wall and ceiling in each ward was scrubbed. She ordered them to scrub the parquet floors three times. Every stick of furniture in the place was also washed down.

The amazing thing was that I didn't hear any of the nurses or their helpers grumble that they were tired, exploited or overworked. Every single patient recovered, and so far we haven't had any more infections. When I complimented Matron on her remarkable achievement, she just said that the credit should go to her hardworking nurses.

I can still see her standing there, pushing a russet curl back under the white veil, as she said with that mischievous smile of hers, 'Oh Dr Jackson, it's flattering me you are. You don't need to be thanking me for doing my duty!'

I was smiling all the way home.

CHAPTER EIGHT

Xanthe

St Helier, April 2019

Xanthe jolts awake, cold dread spreading through her body. It's her first night in the rented house and in the blackness that surrounds her, she feels there's someone in the bedroom. 'Don't be ridiculous,' she tells herself, but her heart is racing and her hand trembles as she switches on the bedside lamp, just to make sure. Of course there is no-one there, and she lets out a long breath, not realising she has been holding it in. 'Am I three years old?' she mutters to herself, trying to shake off the irrational fear. She supposes it was a figment of her overwrought mind, the result of the stress built up over the past few months. Thank God I'm in Jersey, she reminds herself.

When daylight streams into the bedroom, she opens her eyes, tired but relieved that everything feels normal once more. No ghosts. She glances at her watch, surprised how late it is, and springs out of bed. She has one hour to get to the Royal Yacht Hotel to meet Daniel Miller.

Inside the café, Xanthe is gazing at the black-and-white photos of historic sailing ships on the walls when he arrives. Daniel is wearing grey jeans and has a bag slung across a black T-shirt with a Ralph Lauren logo. He isn't wearing socks and his dark hair is fashionably dishevelled. It's a long time since she has paid so much attention to a man's appearance, and, glancing down at her flower-patterned leggings, she pulls at the loose white T-shirt, which has bunched up around her waist, and wonders what her clothing says about her.

He shakes her hand and places his bag on the vacant chair between them.

'So, how's your accommodation?' he asks.

'It's an old house with a big garden, a neglected orchard and an interesting past,' she says. While she speaks, she fiddles with her hair, hoping he doesn't notice that she's trying to twist it into a tidier knot at the back.

'Sounds like *The Secret Garden*. Did you find a mysterious little boy hiding behind the wall?'

At the mention of the house, she feels uneasy. It's as if the invisible ghost of the previous night has just brushed against her and settled on her shoulders. It reminds her of the feeling she had the night when she stepped into Sumi's room, just before she found her friend's lifeless body behind the door.

In the silence that follows, she tries to shake off that memory and calm her breathing.

'An interesting past?' Daniel is saying. 'How do you mean?'

Xanthe takes a deep breath. 'Apparently decades ago the owner planted a vegetable garden and kept chickens, but then for some reason the house stood empty for ages before the current owner had it renovated. The agent implied there was something mysterious about it, but that's all she said.'

The waitress, a young Italian girl with a thick plait down her back and a wide smile, hands them a menu. Without glancing at it, Daniel orders a pot of Irish breakfast tea, but Xanthe, who hasn't had breakfast, reads the entire menu twice before asking for eggs Benedict and a flat white.

The waitress frowns. 'Flat white? What is this?'

Xanthe explains, and the waitress beams. *'Allora, café latte!'*

Daniel looks amused. 'They obviously don't get many Australian tourists in here,' he says. 'Did you go to the Jersey War Tunnels yesterday?'

'It's an amazing museum,' she says. 'Those eerie sound effects made my skin crawl. It was like stepping back into the past. I had no idea what went on here during war. But of course you do.'

'I'm hoping to find out more while I'm here.'

This seems the right moment to ask about his thesis. 'What made you research the Jews of Jersey?'

He leans back in his chair, folds his arms, and narrows his eyes before replying. 'I've always wondered about the conditions that made the Holocaust possible. Could it happen anywhere? Did it have anything to do with nationality or personality? What systems were in place that enabled governments to carry out Nazi racial laws?'

She is listening intently. 'But why Jersey? There couldn't have been many Jews here.'

'That's exactly what makes studying the Holocaust here so important. You know what they say – the death of one person is a tragedy, but the death of millions is a statistic. If

I can examine what happened here, and how it happened, I might be able to understand the process through which this legalised killing machine was able to accomplish its goals.'

While he speaks, she notices that he spreads his hands as if to emphasise his words, as if pushing the air aside to make space for them.

This is the first time she has heard him speak at such length, and sound so animated, and she envies the passion he feels for the subject. Once she felt that passion for medicine, and she feels sad for its loss. She sighs and attempts to focus on his words when the waitress arrives with their food. Her chatter, along with the clatter of knives, forks, plates, cups and plates puts a temporary stop to their conversation.

As soon as the waitress walks away, Xanthe takes a sip of her coffee, pulls a face, and pushes the cup away.

Daniel is watching her. 'No good?'

'It's awful. All I can taste is hot milk.'

Daniel beckons to the waitress and asks her to bring a small jug of espresso coffee.

After tipping the espresso into her cup a few minutes later, Xanthe looks thoughtful as she bites into her eggs Benedict. She is still thinking about what he said about the Holocaust, and wonders if he's Jewish.

'Eggs Benedict OK?' From the bemused expression, she realises he is making fun of her. It occurs to her that he probably thinks she is one of those entitled young women who find fault with everything.

'Perfectly fine,' she says tartly. And can't resist adding, 'Thanks for asking.'

He looks as if he is trying not to laugh, which annoys her even more, especially as he is looking straight into her eyes, challenging her to see the humour in the situation. She has never liked being teased and looks back at him without smiling.

After a pause, he says, 'I gave you a very long answer to your question. It's just that once I start talking about it, I can't stop, and I forget that other people aren't as interested in it as I am. I hope I'm not boring you.'

No longer annoyed, she shakes her head. 'Not at all. It's a fascinating subject. But what made you decide to research this now?'

He pours himself tea from the pot and stirs two teaspoons of sugar into his cup. 'Luck, really. And synchronicity. The Jersey Archives have recently released wartime documents that haven't been available before. So for the first time we'll be able to find out exactly what happened here and which hands signed the papers.'

Xanthe thinks back to Edward de Courcy's reaction when Daniel mentioned his thesis. 'You'll be popular!'

Daniel nods. 'I know. I think I'm going to ruffle quite a few feathers. Especially as my relative Mr de Courcy is the Bailiff.'

'Bailiff? I thought that was someone in charge of a property.'

Daniel chuckles. 'Well, in a way it is, but the property in question is Jersey. The Bailiff is the highest official in the government.'

'I know you weren't surprised by his reaction,' she says slowly, 'but I don't understand why he got so shirty.'

Daniel hesitates for a few moments and looks out of the window. She takes advantage of the pause to look straight at him. He's not conventionally handsome but there's something about his gaze that hints at hidden depths, and reminds her of a French actor in a recent Netflix crime series whose name she has forgotten. And there's his sexy cleft chin.

He is looking at her, and she hopes he hasn't noticed that she has been appraising him. 'I could spend the rest of the day trying to answer that,' he says. 'But the short answer is that every country has its myths, its patriotic historical narrative, and resents efforts to question it. Does that make sense?'

She nods. 'So you're the new broom that's going to sweep uncomfortable truths out of their dark corners.'

'Exactly. And that's why my illustrious relative got so defensive.'

'Do you think he has something to hide?'

She has left most of her coffee, but Daniel pours himself more tea, which by now is almost black. 'Not necessarily. But as the Bailiff, he is deeply entrenched in every aspect of life on the island, so it's as if someone threatened to shake your family tree. Even if you didn't get on with all your relatives, you'd probably resent a stranger searching for skeletons in their closets.'

While she is digesting this, he looks straight into her eyes again with that compelling gaze and she looks down at her coffee cup. 'Xanthe.' It isn't the beginning of a sentence, it's a statement, and she waits.

'That's an unusual name. Greek, isn't it?'

She stifles a smile. So while she's been wondering if he is Jewish, he's been wondering if she's Greek. 'The name is Greek, but I'm not. My parents chose it because in Greek mythology Xanthe was the daughter of Asclepius, the god of medicine. He was represented by a serpent wrapped around a staff, and that's become the symbol for doctors ever since. Almost everyone in my family is a medico.'

'So was that your destiny from day one?'

She gives a wry smile. 'Pretty much. But I was a willing victim. There was never anything else I wanted to do.'

Suddenly everything blurs, and she is embarrassed by the tears welling up. I might as well have the words *failed doctor* tattooed on my forehead, she thinks as she dabs her eyes with her napkin.

'I've got something in my eye,' she mutters, but although he looks sympathetic, she can tell he isn't fooled, especially as the more she dabs, the faster the tears keep flowing. She can't understand it. She isn't given to weeping. She didn't cry when she found Sumi dead in her room, or when she was so depressed that the eternal unknown seemed a preferable option to the life she knew. She didn't even cry when she told her parents that she was quitting her job, or when she saw the look on their faces. But for some reason sitting in a Jersey hotel with a man she hardly knows, she feels so unexpectedly vulnerable that her tears are flowing and she knows that if he asks any questions or even pats her shoulder, she'll make a spectacle of herself, and break down in the café.

But he doesn't say anything. He unzips his bag and appears to be searching for something. She is grateful that he has given her time to compose herself without embarrassing her with questions or comments. When her eyes are dry, she looks up and sees that he is leafing through some documents.

'I have to go to the Archive Office,' he says, replacing the papers and zipping up his bag. 'They've promised to find some documents for me.' He looks at her for several moments before asking, 'Do you feel like having dinner with me tomorrow night?'

They shake hands and say goodbye, and as she walks out of the café, her heart is beating a little faster.

She strolls around Royal Square, past imposing bank buildings and the gilded statue of Queen Victoria, imperiously majestic on her pedestal, then pauses at the kiosk advertising charabanc rides. She is trying to figure out what these are, when she hears a man calling her name.

She turns and sees Bill McAllister walking beside a much older man who towers over him. Despite his advanced years, his companion holds himself ramrod straight, as if he has a two-metre pole lodged inside his spine.

'This is your lucky day,' Bill tells Xanthe. 'If there's anything you want to know about Jersey, Bob Blampied is your man!'

Bob gives her a firm handshake. The eyes gazing down at her under a shock of white hair look like two bright cornflowers in a ploughed field.

'That's supposing this lovely young lady wants to know anything,' Bob says.

'I certainly do,' she says. 'Are you a guide?'

The men exchange an amused glance. 'Among other things,' Bob says, and they burst out laughing like good friends sharing an in-joke.

'You couldn't have a better guide,' Bill says. 'Bob has a history that almost goes back to the Norman Conquest.'

'Longer!' Bob shouts, and they both roar with laughter again. Turning to Xanthe, he says, 'I'm over ninety, you know.'

She suppresses the urge to tell him that he doesn't look it. Bob seems to be the kind of person usually described as a local character, and the prospect of having a tour guide in his nineties intrigues her, specially one who seems so entertaining. 'Do you really take people on tours of the island?'

'Only special people,' Bob says with a gallant bow. 'Just say when.'

'How about tomorrow?'

'I'll be there at nine. Can you put up with an old codger for the whole day?'

'I can if you can,' she retorts with a laugh.

Back in her rented house that afternoon, she finally unpacks. She hangs up her clothes in the old mahogany wardrobe whose door squeaks whenever she opens and closes it. There are more drawers and shelves than she needs for the few clothes she has brought, and she is about to go downstairs when the large painting above the fireplace catches her eye.

It depicts an idyllic English rural scene in the style of Constable. Farm workers with pitchforks are loading hay onto a wagon beside a willow-lined stream, but it's not the painting that attracts her attention, but the fact that it tilts to one side. Crookedly hung paintings have always offended her love of symmetry, a trait that has either irritated or amused the people in her life.

She goes over to the painting and places her hands on either side of the gilded frame to correct the alignment, but it's heavier than she expected, and before she can straighten it, it crashes to the floor.

Cursing herself for being so clumsy, she bends down to make sure it hasn't been damaged. A corner of the frame that struck the floor has chipped off, but luckily the painting has landed face up and is intact. She breathes a sigh of relief and makes a note to buy some WD40 to oil the squeaky door of the wardrobe, and something to fix the corner of the frame.

When she stands up, her gaze is drawn to the area above the fireplace where the painting had hung. The plasterwork is rough and uneven, and the colour of the paint doesn't match the rest of the wall.

She wonders if the painting had been hung there to conceal the sloppy workmanship of the plasterer and painter. Curious, she palpates that part of the wall, and a bit of plaster crumbles in her hands.

'Now I've done it,' she mutters, and sinks onto the bed. 'I'd better go downstairs before I bloody wreck the place.' She turns to leave the bedroom, but something compels her to turn back and run her hands over that spot again, and this time she feels a hollow space behind the plaster, a cavity in the chimney.

Down in the kitchen, she makes herself a Nespresso, and as she sips it, she reflects on what she has seen. The rough plaster, the mismatched paint, the outsized painting covering the gap in the wall can't be accidental. They must add up to something more than the careless patching of sloppy work.

She runs upstairs and plunges her hand into the chimney cavity. She touches something solid, a box of some kind, perhaps. As she tries to push it out, she wonders if she will find jewellery or cash hidden inside. By tilting it on its side, she manages to drag it out along the base of the cavity.

Instead of buried treasure, she is looking at an old-fashioned radio encased in walnut, with shortwave stations marked on the dial. A pair of leads dangle from it, one attached to a pair of earphones. Disappointed, she wonders why anyone would go to so much trouble to hide an ancient radio. Some instinct prompts her to plunge her hand inside again. There is something else in there, and she holds her breath as she extracts it. This time she is even more astonished. It's a thick notebook, and as she flicks the pages, she sees they are filled with neat handwriting written in ink. The label on the brown paper cover says *Mass Observation Journal*.

CHAPTER NINE

Tom

St Helier, September 1941

The sound of a large vehicle screeching to a halt right outside the house startled Tom out of his sleep. He looked at his alarm clock. Three o'clock. A strange time for a vehicle to be on the street, especially during curfew. Rubbing his eyes, he stumbled towards the window. The street was dark and deserted except for the men unloading a ten-ton army truck. Looking across at the houses on the other side of the street, he noticed the curtains on upstairs windows being surreptitiously moved aside. So their neighbours had also been awakened by the noise, but the men downstairs were obviously unconcerned about being heard or seen. They shouted to each other as they continued unloading and carrying crates into his house, as if it was broad daylight. They didn't even bother lowering their voices. Pressing his face against the window, Tom recognised the portly officer who was barking orders to the men handling the crates. It was Gunther Kohl, his mother's admirer from the Water Police.

He ran downstairs and almost bumped into his mother, who was standing in the unlit hallway, observing the activity.

'What are they doing? What's going on?' he asked, craning to see past her.

She gave him one of her rapier stares. 'Get back to bed and mind your own business,' she snapped, positioning herself in a way that made it impossible for him to get past.

Tom stomped back to his room, determined to wait for the men to leave so he could snoop around and see what they had delivered. Finally the tailgate slammed shut, and he listened for the sound of the engine starting up, but instead of driving away, the men went back inside, and soon he heard the sound of glasses clinking and German voices laughing and shouting.

Occasionally he heard his mother's voice rippling above the others. An iron band was tightening around his chest, making it difficult to breathe. They were having a party, in his home, with his mother presiding over the celebration like a triumphant general praising the troops. His father was nowhere to be seen, but he hadn't done anything to put a stop to this revelry, Tom thought bitterly.

Then he remembered something his father had recently told him. It was impossible to obtain Agfa or Gevaert paper or rolls of film in St Helier. As most of his work consisted of photographing the Germans, Tom supposed that his mother had used her considerable powers of persuasion to convince the Feldkommandatur that these were essential items that had to be imported from France. She knew how important it was for the Germans to send home photos from Jersey, their first British conquest. That probably explained the unexpected delivery.

It was close to five o'clock and his eyes were closing when he heard the truck rev up and roar away. Wide awake now, he sprang out of bed and crept down to the living room, edging against the wall in case his mother was still up. She was nowhere to be seen, but what he saw made his jaw drop. He seemed to be in a warehouse, among dozens of wooden crates and boxes too numerous to count. Wooden crates of Normandy butter, cartons of Gauloises and Gitanes, and bottles of liqueurs. There were also old French wines. He could tell they were old by the layer of dust on the bottles and their old-fashioned labels. He stopped counting when he came to crates of smoked hams, boxes of chocolate and vials of French perfumes, enough to stock several large shops. A much smaller box contained Agfa film and photographic paper.

Tom sank to his knees on the patterned Axminster carpet, surveying this loot. It was like looking into a treasure trove, but he saw it as Pandora's box, its contents threatening to release evil all around them. No-one had seen such an array of luxury goods in the shops of St Helier since the Occupation had begun, and he felt guilty, as if seeing it made him complicit in what was obviously contraband.

He remembered the curtains moving in the houses opposite while the Germans were unloading. Now everyone would know that his parents were part of that despised group of locals who were profiteering from people's misery at a time when most were unable to afford even basic food. The situation had become so desperate that some people were resorting to barter, and just that day he had read a notice placed in the *Jersey Evening Post* by a woman who offered a pair of shoes in exchange for a pound of sugar.

Back in his room, he processed the significance of what he had seen stacked on the floor, spread over the mahogany sideboard, and piled up on the dining table. It didn't surprise him that his mother was involved. As far back as he could remember, money had always been her major preoccupation. No matter how much she had, it would never be enough. His father once explained that she had been very poor as a girl, but Tom dismissed that as a weak excuse. Stanley was so besotted that he always let her have her way. Although people often commented on how attractive his mother was, Tom only saw the calculating eyes and the practised smile. He couldn't understand why Stanley couldn't see through her, and it upset him that his father often took her side against him during their frequent clashes.

Next morning at breakfast, when Tom alluded to the new merchandise in their house, his mother's mouth became an angry straight line.

'I haven't heard you complaining about all the food I put on the table every day,' she said.

'But we have plenty of food without all this,' he protested.

'Well Mr High and Mighty, guess how it gets here,' his mother retorted.

His father remained silent until Tom's fixed gaze forced a response. 'Your mother is helping my business,' he said.

'I didn't realise you needed French liquor and perfumes in your work,' Tom said. Stanley didn't reply and Tom thought he looked uncomfortable, but perhaps he had imagined it.

Over the next few weeks, their home was gradually transformed into what reminded Tom of those tawdry saloons in American Wild West movies. On the nights when German officers came to play cards, drink, and sing their obnoxious songs, filling the whole house with the stink of Turkish cigarettes and the guttural sound of their voices, he took his secret revenge by casting Alma, arrayed in a tight-fitting low-cut gown, in the starring role as the bar hostess who consorted with the baddies. He would have liked to cast himself as the heroic sheriff who defeated the bandits, but he had to content himself with skulking up to his bedroom in disgust and slamming the door. His only show of resistance was refusing his mother's calls to come downstairs. He wouldn't give her the satisfaction of showing off how well he spoke German. Instead, lying in his bed, he concocted plots in which he had the starring role.

Saturday afternoons at the movies were the highlight of his week. He always met Frank and Harry outside the Forum, and they rushed for the back row, where, unseen, they uttered cat-calls, whoops and whistles, depending on the scene.

Whenever German propaganda newsreels were screened, they stamped, hoping to render the commentary inaudible, until they were silenced by threats from Germans and their toadies.

The previous Saturday, however, was different. Frank was in trouble and forbidden to go out, while Harry's father needed his help in the mechanic's workshop. Determined not to miss out on that week's movie, Tom went by himself. While waiting outside the ticket office, he turned to see if he knew anyone in the queue, and his heart flipped over.

There was Milly, further down in the queue. She had recently turned sixteen, just six months older than Tom, and he thought she was prettier than ever, with her blonde hair waving down to her shoulders like that American actress Veronica something-or-other. He liked what she was wearing, a blue and white gingham dress with a peter pan collar, a full skirt, and white bobby socks, and, best of all, she was alone. When he stepped up to the ticket office, on impulse he bought two tickets, waited for her to catch up, and surprised her by presenting her with a ticket with a hand that was embarrassingly moist.

He took a deep breath. 'Shall we sit together?' he asked. He tried to sound casual, but his voice gave him away.

She looked up at him with those amazing blue eyes. 'Well, since you bought the tickets ...' she said, but from her dimpled smile, he could tell she was teasing him.

Later, when Frank asked him about the movie, he couldn't give a coherent account of the story. Every few minutes, he stole glances at her, and when Mr O'Henry the organist finally disappeared beneath the floor with his Hammond organ and the cinema was plunged in darkness, Tom reached for Milly's hand. To his delight, she didn't pull it away. Her little hand was soft and warm, and he thought his heart would leap out of his chest with love.

He knew then that he wanted to spend the rest of his life with her, to have children with her. Such a thought had never occurred to him before, and its intensity startled him, but it felt right. He couldn't put it into words, but he knew he'd jump through fire for her.

As they were walking out of the movie theatre after the show, two youths barred his way. One of them planted himself in front of Tom, so close that Tom could smell his breath, and hissed, 'You must love the taste of shoe polish. What's it like licking the Jerries' boots?' Before Tom could gather his thoughts, his acne-scarred companion sneered, 'Poor Tom. Fancy having a Jerrybag for a mother!'

At this point, without thinking, Tom took a swing at the face in front of him and landed a punch that made the speaker reel. His companion joined the fray, and the three of them tussled on the ground, punching and kicking, while a curious crowd gathered around them.

There was ringing in Tom's ears and an excruciating pain in his ribs. He could hear Milly imploring them to stop, but he was past listening. And despite the pain, with each punch he landed, he felt a sense of triumph. After several minutes, some men stepped in and pulled them apart, and the two boys slunk away swearing.

'You were so brave, defending your mother like that,' Milly said, handing him her handkerchief to wipe away the blood under his nose and on his lip. It smelled of lavender water, and as he wrapped it around his bruised knuckles, Tom decided to keep it forever.

He revelled in Milly's admiration, but he knew he hadn't fought to defend his mother's reputation. He was venting the rage he felt at the shame she caused him with her carousing and black marketeering.

Especially when she used him as a delivery boy to provision people who could afford her exorbitant prices. He tried to stay out of the house as much as possible, but whenever she caught him and forced him to deliver her goods, he wished that the ground would open up and swallow him.

A week later, he was cycling with Frank and Harry when they paused on the hill overlooking West Slip. Dismounting from their bikes, they sat on the grass and as usual, they talked about the latest orders imposed by the hated Germans.

'I heard they've closed down all the Jewish businesses,' Harry said. 'How are those people supposed to survive?'

Tom wondered how Mrs Goldman was managing and felt a pang of guilt that he hadn't dropped in again to see if she needed help.

'Have you seen those prisoners they've brought here?' Frank was saying. 'Some of them look like skeletons. I wonder why they're here.'

'My dad reckons the Krauts want to turn Jersey into some kind of fortress, and the prisoners are supposed to build that stuff,' Harry replied.

'A fortress? Here? What for?' Frank asked.

Tom wasn't really listening. He was staring into the distance. 'I just wish I could get away.'

Harry waved his arms around the way he did when an idea appealed to him. 'That'd be fantastic, but what's the chance of that ever happening?'

Just then Frank nudged Tom and pointed.

Tom hadn't seen Milly since the idyllic interlude at the movies the previous week. Since that afternoon, he had replayed the scene a hundred times, from the moment he held her hand, to the look on her face when she had praised him for being brave. That memory had been wreaking havoc in his mind ever since, especially at night in bed, when his sexual fantasies invariably climaxed the same way. Breathing in the faint lavender scent of her handkerchief, he worked himself into a fever pitch of uncontrollable ecstasy.

Down at the Slip, Milly was strolling with her friend Dolly, whose superior tone always got on his nerves. He was deciding whether to go up to them when he saw two German soldiers crossing the promenade. They stopped in front of the girls and clicked their heels.

The taller one didn't take his eyes off Milly while he was talking. Tom expected her to turn away and continue walking, but she just stood there, her face upturned, and then he heard her laughing. He longed to go down and shout at the Kraut to go away and leave her alone, but he didn't dare, and felt ashamed of being so powerless.

To his relief, the soldiers walked away, but just as he mounted his bicycle to ride down to her, they returned, holding two ice-cream cones, which were beginning to drip in the afternoon sun. Tom watched as Milly and her friend accepted the ice-cream cones. With another click of their heels, the Germans bowed and walked away.

This time, Tom didn't hesitate. He freewheeled down the hill, and braked a few inches away from Milly who was licking her ice cream and giggling with Dolly.

'How come you're so friendly with the Krauts?' he demanded.

Milly's rose-petal complexion turned bright pink. 'They bought us an ice cream, that's all.'

'How do you know that's all? Now he'll think you're his girlfriend.' He tried to sound calm but couldn't control his anger.

Dolly was glaring at him. Pulling Milly's arm, she whispered loudly enough for him to hear, 'Let's go. You can do whatever you like. He doesn't own you.'

'I'm not talking to you,' Tom said. He felt miserable that their conversation was going so badly, but he couldn't see any way of salvaging the situation.

Milly wiped ice cream off her fingers with a white handkerchief embroidered with pink rosebuds, similar to the one he kept in his trouser pocket. She cleared her throat.

'They were very polite and said as it's a hot day, would we allow them to buy us an ice cream. One of them said I reminded him of his sister Liesl who he missed. What's wrong with that?'

Tom was lost for words. He thought of several answers and finally chose the worst one. 'You'll get a bad reputation, that's what. You know what they call girls who consort with Krauts.'

She stared at him with those sky-blue eyes and his head swam with love. Then she said, 'You've got no right to talk to me like that.' Taking Dolly's arm, she tilted her chin and said, 'Let's go,' and walked away without looking back.

Tom sat on his bicycle and wanted to kick himself. He wished he had kept quiet, but whenever he thought of that German soldier bending over Milly's hand and looking into her face, a wave of fury swept over him again. He couldn't stop thinking about Milly looking up at the Kraut with the dimpled smile that drove him crazy.

He slammed the front door behind him when he got home and already had his foot on the stairs when his mother called out from the dining room, 'Tom, come here a minute.'

She was holding out a large wicker basket covered with a lid. 'I want you to deliver this to Mrs Browning,' she said.

He shook his head. 'I'm not doing that anymore.'

Just then his father put his head around the door. 'As long as you live in this house, you'll do as your mother says.'

Tom didn't know which was worse, delivering the illegal merchandise for his mother, or being ordered by his father to do it.

He had always admired his father, but these days he felt increasingly disillusioned. He had lost respect for the spineless coward who looked the other way while his wife flirted shamelessly with the occupiers and conducted an illegal business with them.

Now, hearing his father threatening to throw him out of the house unless he continued making his mother's black-market deliveries, his anger boiled over. 'I wish I didn't have to live here,' he blurted out. 'I'm ashamed of both of you.'

His mother had her hands on her hips and was regarding him with a scornful expression, but his father looked shocked. As a parting shot, Tom added, 'I wouldn't be surprised if you were both charged with collaborating when this is over!' And without waiting for their response, he ran upstairs and slammed his bedroom door, his heart pounding at his audacity.

If only he could escape, from them and from this accursed island where collusion seemed to be the norm. Even the States seemed to go along with every order the Krauts imposed without any opposition, and every day they heard about people informing on friends and family members for owning wireless sets.

No wonder the Krauts looked so pleased with themselves. Jersey must seem like an island paradise. Surely not even in his wildest dreams did old Hitler envisage such an accommodating government with such acquiescent residents. This really had to be a model occupation. Tom thought about Milly's reaction to the German soldier and felt his blood pressure rising again.

During morning recess at school the next day, Frank slipped him a scrawled note. *Come over this afternoon. I've got something to tell you.*

Tom couldn't wait to find out what Frank was being so secretive about. The day dragged, and the lessons were more boring than ever, until finally the bell clanged. He jumped on his bike and cycled to Frank's house as fast as he could. Usually he stopped to chat with Frank's mother, who, unlike his own mother, was always interested in what he was doing, and even asked his opinion about things, but this time he rushed straight up to Frank's room.

Frank wasn't usually excitable, but from the speed with which he leaped up and closed the door, Tom could tell he was bursting with news.

In a hoarse whisper, he said, 'You'll never guess what happened. A chap called Dennis Vibert has escaped! He's in England!'

Tom's mind was whirring. If Frank had said Dennis Vibert had just landed on the moon, he couldn't have been more astonished. He had succeeded in a feat that until now had seemed impossible. Escaping risked death or deportation to a German camp. Tom didn't ask who Dennis Vibert was, or how Frank had found out about him. He only wanted to know one thing. 'How did he do it?'

Frank was almost jumping out of his skin with excitement. 'Wait till I tell you. He got hold of a boat, an eight-footer, and two outboard motors and …'

Tom was shaking his head. 'An eight-footer? Where from? And where did he get the petrol?'

'Don't know about the boat, but he siphoned the petrol out of a German lorry!'

'Sounds like a tall tale to me.'

'It's true!' Frank protested. 'Anyway, he nearly got caught by a German E-boat on the way. And then the seas got so choppy that he lost his spare engine, so he had to row the rest of the way.'

Tom was about to interrupt again, but Frank shook his head and kept talking. 'Just listen. He lost all his food and water too, but he just kept on rowing for two days. Then on the third day he got picked up by a British destroyer. He's safe in England!'

It sounded like one of the adventure stories in the boys' annual they used to read, but Frank couldn't be lying. Tom didn't ask how he knew. There was only one possible source of such information, and he knew better than to ask about something illegal.

Tom was silent. He was trying to process what Frank had said, and what it could mean for them. Somehow Dennis Vibert had managed to obtain a boat, petrol and a spare engine, and he had rowed across the Channel to England. And he had done it on his own.

Gripped by a sense of excitement he had never experienced before, Tom couldn't sit still. Could this be what he'd been waiting for? 'Quick, let's go and tell Harry,' he said.

CHAPTER TEN

Dr Jackson

St Helier, May 1942

Young Tom Gaskell turned up unexpectedly at my morning surgery last Tuesday, and when I asked why he wasn't at school, he claimed he wasn't feeling well. But as he had come alone, it occurred to me that he probably didn't want his parents to know about his visit. Some doctors refuse to see young people without their parents' consent, but Tom is a mature sixteen year old, and besides, from what I know of his parents, I can understand why he might be keeping things from them. I've heard people say that his mother is a black marketeer who entertains German officers in her home, apparently with the collusion of her husband, who runs a business that's almost completely dependent on the Germans.

Another despised group of locals are the men who have taken up employment with Organisation Todt, the German construction firm that is building those horrendous tunnels and emplacements all over the island. Knowing that their work is helping the Germans, and that their employers are mistreating their slave labourers, I used to concur with the contempt that has been levelled at them until Mr Edwards came to see me last week for an abscess on his back.

'My neighbours ostracise me for working for Organisation Todt, but what am I supposed to do, when they pay such good money? I can't let my kids go hungry and I can't feed them on what I'd earn anywhere else.'

I must say that whenever the subject of children comes up, I feel my chest tighten, thinking about Jamie.

As I lanced his abscess, I thought about the fine line between survival and collusion. I wonder what I would do in his place. Would I put principle ahead of Jamie's hunger? I doubt it. As a philosopher once said, to know all is to understand all.

But back to Tom. He was fidgeting in his chair, tapping his feet on the floor and clearing his throat, but when I questioned him, he looked away and sounded evasive.

I can sometimes put my finger on a patient's problem simply by watching them, and I owe this to one of the honorary physicians at the hospital where I did my clinical term. '*Observe, observe, observe,*' Dr McBride used to drum into us residents. 'Think of yourselves as Sherlock Holmes searching for vital clues. Non-verbal signs often reveal more than words.'

Watching Tom, I concluded that something was weighing on his mind. I have always had a good relationship with him, and I hoped he knew that anything he discussed with me would be confidential.

As he was finding it difficult to come to the point, I suggested that perhaps something was troubling him. As soon as I said that, his expression changed, and he sat forward in his chair. This time he looked straight at me.

'Have you heard about Dennis Vibert, Dr Jackson?' he asked.

That surprised me. Everyone knew about this man and his escape last year, but I was at a loss to understand why Tom had brought it up, and I said as much.

'It's the most exciting thing I've ever heard,' he said.

I heard more in his tone than mere boyish admiration, and I studied him for a while before saying, 'That man was extremely lucky. It could easily have ended in disaster.'

Tom's next words made me uneasy. 'He would have been lucky either way.'

I took that to mean that if he couldn't have liberty, he was better off dead, but before I had time to explore this dangerous idea, my secretary knocked on the door and in an urgent whisper told me that Mrs Normand had gone into labour.

As she was suffering from pre-eclampsia, a very dangerous condition for both mother and baby, the delivery was likely to be long and difficult, and I left hurriedly, promising Tom to continue our conversation as soon as possible.

I drove to the Jersey Maternity Hospital with a sense of foreboding, as much for Tom as for Mrs Normand, but for the next few hours, I put everything out of my mind and concentrated on delivering the baby safely, which, thank God, I did.

Exhausted, I was leaving the hospital when I heard Matron O'Connor's lilting voice calling my name. 'Dr Jackson, will you be having a minute for a cup of tea?'

I don't know if I mentioned that tea hasn't been available for some time, and the local substitute is a revolting brew made from dried sugar beets, which has as much in common with tea as an ant has with an elephant. As for coffee, I was desperate enough to experiment by roasting and then grinding a mixture of barley, acorns and dandelion leaves, but in the end, I gave up and resigned myself to drinking hot water flavoured with a slice of lemon and a nip of brandy.

So the prospect of sugar-beet tea was hardly enticing, but the opportunity to sit down for a few minutes with the delightful matron certainly was.

She beckoned me into her office, closed the door, reached into a cupboard behind her desk, and with a triumphant expression held up a small sachet of what looked like genuine tea leaves. Before I could ask where they came from, she placed a finger against her lips and whispered, 'A gift from a grateful patient.'

Closing my eyes, I breathed in the delicate herb-like scent of tea brewing in a teapot, and the tantalising memory of a time when tea was a drink we took for granted, not a rare luxury item and symbol of freedom. It was once described somewhat pompously as the drink that cheers but not inebriates, but feeling considerably cheered, I let a contented sigh escape as I sipped it.

Matron was watching me. 'It's grand to see you enjoying your tea,' she said.

I tried to make that cup of tea last as long as possible as we chatted about the endless problems of running a hospital at a time when even soap and disinfectant were in short supply, to say nothing of medicines, especially insulin for diabetics. 'I can make soap, but not insulin,' Matron said, and holding up a small grey cube, she explained that she produced soap by diluting caustic soda with water, and adding hot fat. 'If only I could add perfume, it would smell like French soap,' she laughed.

I was making a mental note to check if Margaret had left any perfume on her dressing table, when I felt Matron's eyes resting on me.

'I've heard that your wife was evacuated when she was about to have a baby,' she was saying. 'It was noble of you to stay behind.'

Praise usually embarrasses me, and I waved a deprecating hand, but seeing the admiration in her eyes wasn't unpleasant. I didn't disillusion her by admitting that had I realised that I would be trapped here alone, with no way of knowing how long the war would last, I wouldn't have been so noble.

But who could have imagined that in the twentieth century, so close to the English coast, we would be cut off from everything and everyone, as if we were living in some remote village in Africa?

Glancing at the calendar on her desk, I was startled to see that almost two years had passed since I last saw Margaret. At first, every day felt like a week, and every week felt like a year, but one becomes accustomed to everything, even loneliness and pain, and I have stopped counting the days.

Several months ago I finally received a letter from her through the Red Cross. She included a small photo of Jamie hugging a teddy bear, but from her few perfunctory words, I could see that she had no idea what we were going through here. Probably the newspapers in England weren't bothering to report our dire situation. I wondered if Mr Churchill ever felt ashamed of abandoning British territory to the Germans. Jamie looks like a chubby, bright little boy and I keep his framed photograph on my desk, and long for the day when I will be able to hold him and play with him. Then it strikes me – will he know who I am? I've sent several letters to Margaret via the Red Cross, but she hasn't replied. How long can she hold on to her resentment?

All this was going through my mind as Matron leaned over to pour me another cup of tea. Just then, the edge of her veil caught on the back of a nearby chair, and slipped back, revealing curls the colour of maple leaves in autumn.

She adjusted the veil and when she looked up, she laughed because I was staring at her. Embarrassed, I made an excuse about having to do a house call, and left, the taste of Matron's tea still hot on my tongue.

It was still light when I returned home. It had been a long day, and after the stress of the delivery, I was ready for a drink. In normal times, I always looked forward to relaxing with a dry martini or a gin and tonic at around six. Naturally these days neither of these are available, but, necessity being the mother of invention, I produced something resembling gin by adding juniper berries to some spirit I managed to distil from wine.

I'm mentioning this so that people who read this journal after the war will realise that we are all far more resourceful than we realise, and that adversity can inspire us to discover hidden talents.

After a comforting nip of 'gin' I lit one of the cheroots that I had bought at the start of the Occupation, and went upstairs to look for perfume. At the back of a drawer, I found a small vial of Margaret's favourite scent, Evening in Paris. When I squeezed the tasselled pump, no perfume sprayed out, but the smell lingered, which made me sink onto the bed and close my eyes, overcome by aching nostalgia. With a sigh, I sat up and looked at the bottle again. It struck me that by infusing it with a little of my spirit, I might increase the volume of the perfume, and give it to Matron O'Connor for her soap.

Feeling more cheerful, I went outside to water my vegetable garden. Seeing the carrots and beans starting to grow always boosted my spirits. The sun was setting, dappling the outer corners of the garden, and the horizon was like a watercolour painting with gauzy swirls of violet and rose against a radiant blue.

I found myself painting it in my head, and remembered that when we moved here, I had stored a palette and paint brushes in the attic, but only rarely used them. Of course there was little time for it now, but I promised myself that when the war was over, I would enjoy the pleasure of an activity totally unconnected with survival.

I lingered in the garden, breathing in the smell of the damp soil and observing the drops of water pearling on the plants. After rolling up the hose, I headed for the henhouse to feed my chickens, whose eggs have been a godsend not only for me, but for some of my patients as well.

One of the philosophers – I think it was Nietzsche – said that giving is basically selfish, as its purpose is to make the donor feel good. Well, Nietzsche was German, which in my opinion is all that needs to be said about that. Of course giving away some of my eggs to feed malnourished children does make me feel good, but that's a side benefit. I can't bear to think of children going hungry, and it's a relief to know that my little Jamie will be getting all the nourishment he needs living with Margaret's family in England. I wish I could do more for him, but I can't even send money. Every transaction here has to be in Reischmarks, which would be worthless over there.

By now the sun had already set, and the fading light cast a blueish haze over the garden as I crossed the lawn with a bowl of chickenfeed in my hands. I put the bowl on the ground to open the wire mesh door to the henhouse when I heard rustling behind me. Leaving the bowl on the ground, I walked around the garden, but saw nothing.

But when I returned to the henhouse, I saw a shadowy figure crouched over the bowl. A man in rags was stuffing the chickenfeed into his mouth as fast as he could. Horrified, I stared at this intruder, wondering how anyone could be reduced to this.

Engrossed in his meal, he wasn't aware of my presence until he turned, his wild eyes darting around as if to make sure that he hadn't been spotted. As soon as he saw me, he sprang up with a terrified expression. He was the thinnest, most wretched-looking human being I have ever seen. His eyes were huge in his gaunt face, his hair was long and matted, his bones protruded through his tattered shirt, and his feet were bound with filthy rags. Robinson Crusoe after years of being shipwrecked couldn't have looked more dreadfully unkempt.

I realised that he must be one of those skeletal prisoners I had seen that day while driving to visit a patient in St Lawrence, the slave labourers the Germans had brought here to build the tunnels, bunkers and emplacements that were appearing all over our island. Crazed with hunger, he must have escaped from the camp at Le Quevennais where, according to rumours that I'd heard, the Germans treated their slave labourers with shocking cruelty.

I'm ashamed to admit that I hesitated before indicating that he should come into the house, for fear of the stench, filth and disease he might bring inside, but another look at his condition and the beseeching look in his eyes, and I overcame my selfish impulse. To my amazement however, he shook his head and pointed to something in the garden that I couldn't see. Then in a low, urgent voice, he said a few words in a language I didn't understand, and a few moments later another skeletal figure emerged from behind the oak tree.

There were two of them!

I have never seen human beings devour food like they did, not once looking up from their plates, and shovelling eggs and bread into their mouths as if terrified that any moment it would be snatched from them. Watching this pitiful spectacle, I could only imagine the privation they had endured.

My first priority was to get them fed, cleaned up, and outfitted with new clothes. But what was I to do with them after that? Obviously I couldn't turn them out at night, after curfew, but what should I do the next day? The longer they stayed here, the more I was exposed to the risk of being reported. I felt sorry for them, I kept telling myself, but they weren't my responsibility. I had responsibilities of my own and I couldn't get involved helping prisoners evade their German captors.

My stomach was churning as much as my conscience as I tried to resolve the situation that had been foisted on me. I felt resentful that once again, something outside my control was dictating a course of action whose consequences might prove disastrous.

Keeping them here was impossible. Mrs Harrison, my cleaner, came in three days a week. She had been with me ever since Margaret and I bought the house, and I'd kept her on. She was a loyal, trustworthy woman, but I wouldn't be able to conceal the presence of two men from her, and these days it isn't fair to place anyone in a situation which involves keeping a dangerous secret. Besides, it would only take one thoughtless remark to a friend or relative to lead the Gestapo to my door.

Apart from Mrs Harrison, it wouldn't be long before neighbours suspected the presence of two strangers in the house, and unfortunately people often inform on their neighbours. According to the German orders posted all over the place, even feeding escapees was a punishable offence, so harbouring two of them would most likely result in my imprisonment or deportation.

So I was caught between Scylla and Charybdis, between endangering my life and blackening my soul. All my life I have abhorred vacillating. I've always felt that even a bad decision was better than no decision, but this paralysed me. Perhaps I was already dreading the decision I knew I would ultimately make.

First things first, I told myself as I tried to keep calm.

After burning their putrid garments, I searched in the wardrobe for old clothes. I've always liked to be smartly dressed, and to Margaret's disapproval, I used to discard clothes whenever they looked dated or tired.

My vanity now became a virtue, as I was able to clothe these men whose names, I discovered, were Igor and Sasha. Apart from the exchange of names, and the fact that they were Russian, we were unable to share any other information.

After getting them bathed and clothed, a more serious problem emerged: how to get rid of the lice with which they were infested. The nurses in the hospital knew how to eradicate lice, but I couldn't ask how they did it without revealing the problem. It crossed my mind to ask Matron O'Connor's advice, but I rejected that idea for fear of implicating her, so I consulted an old textbook of home remedies, which advised damping the hair and soaking it in a solution of carbolic for eight hours.

Before embarking on that treatment, I decided to add hairdressing to my other newly acquired skills. I sat Igor and Sasha down, cut their hair and shaved their beards. Clean-shaven, with short back and sides, and dressed in normal clothes, they no longer looked like escaped slave labourers. They kept nodding and saying something like *harasho*, which I took to mean very good. I had to admit I'd done a good job and felt rewarded by their smiles.

They were both quite young, and I thought about their mothers and the anguish they must feel, not knowing if their sons were alive or dead. It crossed my mind that if Jamie happened to be at the mercy of strangers, I would hope someone would show him some humanity. When I finally went to bed, leaving them snoring in one of the spare bedrooms, my head was pounding again. They couldn't stay here, and they couldn't stay together without arousing suspicion, especially as the Germans would already be searching for them.

So again I was forced to confront my choices. If they couldn't stay, and my conscience wouldn't allow me to turn them out to suffer a terrible fate, what should I do?

I kept turning over the alternatives in my mind until finally in the small hours of the morning, I fell into a restless sleep.

In the past, whenever I've had a vexing medical problem and couldn't arrive at a diagnosis, I've noticed that during sleep, my mind seemed to beaver away at the problem, because by morning, I would wake with a solution. And that's what happened in this case. As soon as I opened my eyes, I had a plan. I would create a network of people I trusted, who might be willing to shelter these escapees one night at a time. By moving them around constantly, to people in different parts of the island, we might prevent detection by the Germans and by neighbours. As soon as I was up, I started scribbling down a few names. At the top of my list was my patient Bob Blampied.

CHAPTER ELEVEN

Xanthe

St Helier, April 2019

Xanthe is so engrossed in Hugh Jackson's journal, so involved with his personal and professional dilemmas, that she feels she has stepped back in time to the war years. She is surprised by her sense of kinship with this man, a stranger who feels closer than many people she knows.

As she reads, she tries to imagine what it would be like to manage seriously ill patients when essential medication like insulin was scarce, when no antibiotics existed to treat serious infections, and soap and disinfectant were luxuries. And as for having to make house calls on bicycle because fuel was in short supply, that didn't bear thinking about.

Eager to find out more, she reads on, hardly looking up from the journal. She can't get over her good fortune in having found this hidden treasure and wonders why he concealed it rather than handing it in to the relevant authorities. He must have hoped it would be read, but did he imagine it would take over seventy years for someone to find it? Xanthe doesn't believe in karma, serendipity, or any of the New Age claptrap that masquerades as profound truth these days, but she can't ignore the fact that she, a doctor like Hugh, has discovered his journal.

She reflects on this coincidence, if that's what it is, as the morning light streams through the kitchen window, warming her eyelids as she closes her eyes against its dazzle. Everyone should read this journal, she thinks as she sips her coffee and waits for the toast to pop up. As a doctor, she finds it sobering to remember that there was a world before antibiotics, MRIs, ultrasounds and ECGs.

She thinks about her great-grandfather who performed emergency appendectomies on the rough-hewn tables of farmhouses. It had always been a popular family story held up by her parents to foster gratitude for the advantages they enjoyed. She had always admired his dedication and acumen, but now, thanks to the diary of a stranger, for the first time she can empathise with the heartache and anxiety of doctors who performed medical miracles in days gone by.

She rinses her mug and plate, stacks them on the draining board, and runs back upstairs. Still in her T-shirt and pyjama pants, she flops down in the bedroom armchair and picks up the journal, one hand propped against her cheek. A moment later she is back in the 1940s, with its restrictions, shortages and privations. She still finds it difficult to accept that this quiet, almost bland little island had gone through such a traumatic time.

Engrossed, she loses track of time, something that would never have happened in her Sydney life. She has already begun to divide her existence into then and now. 'Then' was a rigidly disciplined life in which time was the enemy. Even in her gap year after leaving school, while travelling around Europe with two girlfriends, she had filled every minute of every day with frenetic sightseeing, desperate not to miss a single gallery, museum or nightclub, all of which now form a kaleidoscope of jumbled memories. In Jersey, she is free to indulge herself, without measuring her life by exams to be passed, duties to be ticked off, or ward rounds to be endured. Now she feels her shackled spirit begin to pry loose from its bonds.

There are passages in the journal that make her feel like a voyeur peering through the windows of someone's life. At times it is painful to read how Hugh, which is how she thinks of him, lays bare his anguish, disappointment and loss. Personal disclosures make her uncomfortable. She has always avoided confiding in friends. If she couldn't keep her own secrets, why should she expect others to do so? She has never encouraged confidences either, unsure what was expected of her in return.

It strikes her that perhaps Hugh concealed the journal because he used it only to talk to himself on paper, to vent his thoughts and feelings. Perhaps the man whose profession obliged him to listen to the secrets of others could not bring himself to share his own. Maybe he never meant strange eyes to see the emotions he withheld from the world.

Xanthe puts down the journal and thinks back to the diary she kept in her teenage years. She recalls recording sizzling infatuations that invariably ended in crushing disillusionment, eagerly awaited events that never lived up to her hopes, and academic success that always fell short of her ambitions. Writing had been a purge rather than a revelation, and several years ago she had destroyed that embarrassing record of misguided adolescent hopes. Coming face to face with her teenage self made her squirm. Now she wonders what was it about the passionate outpourings of her turbulent heart that she hadn't been willing to confront.

Her thoughts return to Hugh, whose unintentional confidante she has now become. He couldn't have been much older than she is now, and yet he had made such painful choices, sacrificed his own happiness, and made the most of the traumatic consequences that ensued. She wonders how she would have reacted in his situation. She sighs. No way would she have had his strength. Or his resilience. That's a word that tightens her muscles. It reminds her of the situation she has come here to escape.

She reads on, eager to find out whether he and his wife will be reunited, and how his little boy will react when he meets the father he has never seen. And now, as she puts the journal aside for a moment, she thinks about Miss Murphy, the outspoken librarian, and about young Tom, who, like Hugh Jackson, have become so real to her.

Glancing out of the bedroom window, she sees a jaunty little red sportscar with its roof down, parked outside the house. It reminds her of Hugh's beloved Alvis, the car the Germans confiscated. It's a brand she has never heard of. A man in a peaked cap and navy windcheater is sitting at the wheel reading a newspaper. It takes her a few moments to realise that it's Bob Blampied, who has probably been waiting there for the past fifteen minutes. She springs up, and without stopping to brush her hair, she feverishly pulls on her leggings and lozenge-printed Zara top. Grabbing her puffer jacket and the black quilted Calvin Klein bag her mother gave her for her last birthday, she runs downstairs and out of the house, slamming the door behind her.

Bob folds the newspaper, and with a speed that belies his age, hurries to the other side of the car to open the door for her. She is amused by his old-world gallantry. As she fastens her seatbelt, she apologises for keeping him waiting.

He waves away her apologies with a smile that is engagingly mischievous. 'Not to worry! I have all the time in the world.'

As he removes his cap, his fine white hair falls across his forehead, and his eyes are a startling blue. 'Before we go, two questions. Do you mind having the roof down?'

'I love it.'

'Question two: is there anything in particular you'd like to see?'

'I've only been here a couple of days so anything you show me will be great. But if possible, I'd like to find out more about the Occupation. I was intrigued by the displays in the War Tunnels yesterday.'

He thinks for a moment and nods. 'Right. We'll start with the memorial to the slave labourers at Grouville.'

She is about to say that she has just been reading about the slave labourers but stops herself in time. Hugh must have had a reason for concealing his journal, and it would feel like a betrayal to discuss its contents.

As Bob negotiates the twists and turns in the roads with surprising speed, she keeps pushing her hair back from her eyes, but she likes the breeze on her face. Fifteen minutes later, they are skirting the broad sweep of sandy beach at Royal Bay. He offers to park so that she can look at the impressive beach, but she shakes her head. She has seen lots of beaches and would rather see the memorial he mentioned.

As they drive on, he says, 'We'll be there soon, but first there's something I'd like you to see.'

Several minutes later, they pull up near a sign that says La Hougue Bie. She looks at him questioningly but he gives a mysterious smile. They cross an expanse of lawn scattered with daisies, past nut-brown squirrels that dart along the grass and scamper up the trunks of birch trees. She tries to keep up with him as he strides towards a huge grass-covered mound that dominates the site.

They come to an opening in the man-made hill. 'You are standing in front of one of the most remarkable structures in all of Europe,' Bob says slowly, and pauses for his statement to sink in.

'This is a Neolithic burial site, a passage tomb that was built about 3500 BC, one thousand years before the pyramids. You can go inside, but be careful. You can't stand up in there, and it's dark, so just feel your way along until you come to the end of the passage. There are recesses along both sides where they used to bury their chieftains.'

Confined spaces make Xanthe feel panicky and trapped, but she doesn't want to miss out on this experience. Taking a very deep breath, she hunches over and steps through the small entrance. She treads slowly along the narrow passageway, sliding her hands along the gigantic slabs of stone on either side. They are surprisingly smooth to the touch, as though highly polished, and as she follows the passageway, she feels recesses on both sides and thinks about the chieftains buried there thousands of years ago. Her breath is shallow but she comforts herself with the thought that in a moment she will be outside again.

The passage ends in what seems to be a kind of altar. Xanthe is very still, no longer conscious of being in a confined space, and she allows herself to absorb the strangeness of this sacred site. She doesn't feel alone. It's as if, in this cathedral of stone, the breath of generations past emanates from the slabs of granite, reaching out and enveloping her. Overwhelmed by this sensation, she feels a link with the people who built this tribute to their chieftains and their gods so long ago.

She blinks as she emerges into the sunlight, where Bob is waiting for her. She doesn't speak, as if observing a brief silence in honour of the generations that have gone before them. He respects her silence in a tacit understanding of the impact of the experience.

After several minutes, he says, 'If you stand on this spot at dawn on March 21, which is the spring equinox, you'll see the sun gradually flooding the ground like a river of light until it hits the back wall,' he says. 'Bloody amazing, what those Neolithic people could do.'

Looking up, she sees a conical building sitting on top of the mound, like a hat planted on top of a squat body. She follows Bob along a steep, narrow path covered in daisies and buttercups until they reach the summit. Below them, fields and meadows are spread like a gigantic patchwork quilt in every shade of green and brown. In the distance, a misty coastline rises from the water. 'That's the coast of Normandy,' Bob says.

'I had no idea it was so close.'

Turning to look at the building on the hilltop, Bob says, 'That's Jerusalem Chapel. It was originally built in the twelfth century and became a pilgrimage site in the fifteenth century. Some of the pilgrims on their way to Jerusalem climbed all the way up here on their hands and knees.'

He chuckles. 'This was where the Dean of Jersey conned the pilgrims, who must have been a pretty gullible lot. He placed a statue of the Virgin in the chapel and told them that if they gave a generous donation, they would receive a sign. What they didn't know was that the wily clergyman had a small boy sitting behind the statue, and if the pilgrim's coin was big enough, the child would make the sign of the cross. Of course Dean Mabon claimed it as a miracle!'

Xanthe compares the piety of the pilgrims on the summit with the devotion of the Neolithic people beneath it. Although several thousand years separated them, the search for spiritual meaning remained constant.

From the base of the hill, they walk towards the German bunker that has become a memorial to the slave labourers. 'This bunker was originally supposed to be a command post if the Allies landed here,' Bob says.

She frowns, and he explains. 'Mr Churchill decided that we had no strategic value, but Hitler was obsessed with the Channel Islands. He was convinced that when the Allies invaded Europe, they would use these islands as a stepping stone, and that's why the Germans built massive fortifications all over Jersey. You might be surprised to hear that we were more heavily fortified than any part of the Normandy coast.'

On top of the bunker a bronze sculpture grabs her by the throat. It depicts a deformed man trying to claw his way out of the earth that threatens to swallow him up.

'That was sculpted by Maurice Blik, a survivor of the Bergen-Belsen concentration camp,' Bob says. 'He knew what it took to survive in inhuman conditions, and I think he conveyed it.'

By now they are inside. It is so dark and cold in there that she shivers, regretting leaving her puffer jacket in the car. On the walls are extracts from the testimony of some of the slave labourers. *The Germans killed starving prisoners for stealing potatoes in the fields*, one wrote. Another described the disposal of the dead: *Several bodies were placed in a single box and dumped in the harbour. That box was used over and over.*

'The boy who wrote that was fourteen years old,' Bob says, and his usually cheerful expression becomes sombre. 'When the Jerries couldn't get more work out of the poor buggers, they shipped them back to Germany, to one of their extermination camps. Some of them were only boys.'

She recalls Hugh's description of the escaped slave labourers he found in his garden stuffing chicken feed into their mouths, and his decision to form a network of people to shelter them.

Suddenly she recalls the unusual name at the top of his list. She looks at Bob again.

'You're one of the people who sheltered them, aren't you?'

He raises his white eyebrows. 'How on earth did you know that?'

'I googled you,' she says. It's true, she had looked him up last night to get a sense of what kind of guide she might be in for. Seeing his name in Hugh's journal had been a shock, as if he'd walked out of its pages. 'You were a hero during the Occupation.' She doesn't reveal that her curiosity about him was aroused by Hugh's journal.

He makes a disparaging motion with his left arm. 'Don't believe everything you read.'

'But it's true. You got an MBE from the government for what you did, as well as a medal from Russia for rescuing slave prisoners. And there's a photo taken of you in Red Square with Sasha's mother in the sixties.'

'I was just part of a network, but I wasn't any more heroic than the others,' he says slowly in his beautifully modulated voice. 'Hugh Jackson was in the thick of it. So were Brigid Murphy, Ethel Carter and the de Gruchys, among others.'

He stops talking and sighs. 'Sorry, I forgot you don't know any of those people.'

She is about to contradict him because she feels she does know them. Having to conceal what she knows from the man who has been so open with her makes her feel uncomfortable, but the secret contents of the journal are not hers to disclose.

He points to a quotation on the wall. *Remember the past, Live for the present, Hope for the future.*

'Abba Kovner wrote that,' Bob says. 'He was a Jewish resistance fighter who escaped from the Vilna Ghetto and joined a partisan group that fought the Nazis. After the war, he was consumed with revenge, but he realised that it would destroy him, and that the best revenge was living a fulfilled life. He became a great poet.'

She wonders if letting go of vengeance was a kind of forgiveness, and whether it was prompted by altruism or self-preservation.

'Where did these slave labourers come from?' she asks.

'Russia, Poland, Spain, France. Some were Jews.'

She recalls the Stars of David scratched into the granite walls of the Jersey War Tunnels. 'And the two I read about on the internet, where were they from?'

'One was Russian, the other was a Polish Jew.'

'That must have been so dangerous. How did you manage it?'

He shrugs and makes a dismissive gesture. 'I didn't do it on my own. There was a group of us.'

As they walk towards the car, she looks up at him, and does a swift calculation. 'You must have been very young at the time. How did you get involved?'

He looks at his watch. 'I'll tell you over lunch. Do you like crab sandwiches?'

The road north is unexpectedly rugged and the landscape is barren. Apart from slopes covered in blazing gorse, there is little vegetation and few houses.

Occasionally she hears the clatter of hooves and turns to see a rider wave as he gallops past. When she looks down, she feels dizzy. Savage cliffs plunge down to the dark water, which foams as it smashes against the base of the cliffs. The only sounds are the booming of the waves and the squawking of terns that roost in the cliffsides.

Bob parks the car and they walk towards picturesque ruins on the top of a headland.

'This is Grosnez Point, and you're looking at the ruins of a fourteenth-century castle,' Bob says, putting on his sunglasses against the glare. 'Philippe de Carteret defeated the French here in the sixteenth century.'

'Jersey is almost French but not quite English,' Xanthe says slowly, thinking about the proximity of the Norman coast, the French place names and the English history.

Bob slaps her on the back. 'You've got it in a nutshell,' he laughs.

As they continue driving, the scenery becomes even more spectacular until they are looking down on a beach that makes Xanthe catch her breath.

'Piemont Bay,' Bob says as they descend the steep road towards the café. 'Tides all around Jersey are treacherous, and you have to be careful not to get caught by them. If you come here one hour before the tide goes out, you can watch the beach gradually appearing before your eyes.'

Savage cliffs and treacherous tides reveal a surprisingly darker side of Jersey's landscape than its peaceful fields, lovely beaches and flower-spangled meadows would indicate, Xanthe thinks as the waiter shows them to a table at the Piemont Café.

The café is perfectly located to allow diners to feast their eyes on the view, and as they wait for their crab sandwiches, Bob sits back and places his sunglasses on the wooden table.

'I was nineteen when all hell broke loose in 1940,' he begins. 'I can still remember the moment when the bombing started. I was swimming and when I heard the explosions, I scrambled out of the water as fast as I could and sheltered behind some tamarisk bushes until it was over.

'At work, I was the lowest form of life, an office boy, but a few days later everything changed in a way I could never have imagined. As soon as they announced voluntary evacuation, our manager and his deputy fled to England, and when Colonel Wilson, our insurance boss in Southampton, put through a call to our manager, I had to tell him that both he and the deputy had gone.

'Colonel Wilson was a small man who insisted on being addressed by his title. God help you if you called him mister. He was a short man.' He pauses for a moment and chuckles. 'You know, I've come to the conclusion that tall men command respect naturally, and that's why small men are aggressive.'

Xanthe smiles. Bob is very tall. So is she.

'Colonel Wilson was furious,' he continues. '"Have you gone bonkers? Have you been drinking?" He was bellowing down the phone. "Are you trying to tell me that the British Government abandoned British territory without a shot being fired? I don't believe a word of this nonsense! Put me through at once!"

'He didn't seem to know anything about the demilitarisation or evacuation, but as I found out later, people in England didn't have a clue what had happened to us. There were still ads on the London Tube showing pretty girls lying on a beach and urging people to spend a bomb-free holiday in Jersey!

'So at nineteen, by default, I ended up in charge of our office. I had to hire a new secretary and I deliberately took on a young girl with no experience whatsoever. An experienced secretary would have terrified me, and I reckoned this new girl wouldn't realise that I had no idea what I was doing! She lasted about two years and then I employed another girl who didn't have any secretarial skills.' He has a faraway look in his eyes as he adds, 'Milly was the prettiest girl I've ever seen.'

Xanthe sits forward, intrigued that the memory of an infatuation more than seventy years before has the power to evoke such nostalgia. 'Sounds like a romance,' she suggests.

'Her heart was somewhere else, but that's another story,' he sighs.

Xanthe longs to hear more about it, but he returns to his wartime experiences.

When the waiter brings their crab sandwiches, she takes a bite and returns to the topic of the slave labourers. 'What did people think when they saw them?'

'I was shocked to the core. Until then, we tended to think that the horror stories we'd heard about the Germans were hugely exaggerated. It's probably what we wanted to believe. But now for the first time we could see what they were capable of. One day, at the old priory at Morville, I saw a young slave labourer attached to two trees by branches they'd wound tightly around his neck. The slightest movement would have strangled him. We heard that some of them had been thrown alive into wet concrete.

'The poor buggers used to scavenge for food in the fields or people's gardens at night, desperate for something to eat. You wouldn't believe it, but some of the locals reported them for digging up their vegetables.'

'So how did you get involved in helping them?'

'One evening Dr Jackson cycled over to my place in Victoria Street and said he had a problem. He and I had talked about the plight of the slave workers the week before when I came to see him about a medical problem, so he decided to sound me out. I told him I was in. He explained that we'd need enough people to move the escapees from one parish to another every night. One of our group was

Brigid Murphy, the librarian. I'd always thought of her as an old crank, but she was fearless. There were a few couples involved as well, people Dr Jackson knew and trusted, and we made sure no-one else knew we were sheltering the escapees.'

As they head back towards St Helier, Xanthe marvels that he showed such resourcefulness at such a young age. It occurs to her that crises don't create character; they reveal it.

CHAPTER TWELVE

Tom

St Helier, May 1942

If only she knew! Tom could hardly suppress a triumphant smile whenever he glanced at his mother over his breakfast of scrambled eggs. If only she knew that the night before he and his friends had made a decision that would change all their lives. For months now the idea had been teasing them, daring them to act. They had taken a solemn vow not to divulge their secret to anyone, not even their parents, and they'd sworn that no matter what obstacles stood in their way, nothing would stop them from planning to escape. But in a perverse way he wished his mother did know, so that he could boast about it. He longed to tell her that soon he'd get away from Jersey and from her. Would she be upset? Probably not.

Although Tom knew that it would take months before they were ready to escape, he was on such a high that he could hardly keep still. He couldn't wait to get away. Only the day before, a couple had stopped him on the Esplanade and hissed that when the war was over, they would charge his mother with collaboration. 'Just let me know when, and I'll be happy to back you up,' he'd retorted, and left them standing with their mouths open.

But by the time he, Frank and Harry met again to discuss their plans, the euphoria had subsided, and a fog of anxiety settled over them. Harry, the most cautious one of their trio, was the first to voice his concerns.

'How are we going to get hold of a boat? I mean the Krauts have made it almost impossible …' he began.

'I've figured that out,' Tom broke in. 'I'll get a fishing licence, so they won't suspect anything. You two will need to get one as well.'

He expected them to show more enthusiasm, but Harry was still frowning and even Frank was unusually subdued.

Pulling at the lobe of his left ear, as he usually did when he was thinking, Frank said, 'I reckon we're putting the cart before the horse. Where are we going to get the money to buy a boat?'

A despondent silence followed. Tom and Frank were still at school, and Harry wasn't paid for working in his father's business. They both looked at Tom, who knew what they were thinking.

'She doesn't give me any money,' he said. 'Reckons I get more than enough because she pays for my schooling.'

It was a misty afternoon in early autumn, and they were talking at the far end of Frank's garden, out of earshot of his mother and little brother. The days were becoming shorter, and as the sky darkened, swallows flew above the beech and alder trees. Frank was crushing a handful of fallen leaves, and while they mulled over their situation, the only sound they heard was the occasional cheeping of birds and the rustling of the leaves in Frank's hand.

Tom felt flat. It was like the time he'd hooked a big halibut and was reeling it in with all his might when, with a sudden lurch, it got away.

His mind was churning as he cycled home. Shops and offices had already closed, and people were cycling or walking home. Getting hold of petrol would be another problem, he thought moodily. There had to be some way of raising money without arousing suspicion. There had to be. But keeping anything secret was almost impossible in a community where everyone watched everyone else for any sign of illegal activity. That night he tossed and turned in bed, calculating the amount they would need to buy everything for the journey. It was far beyond the meagre sum the three of them had in their money boxes from delivery tips and birthdays. They might as well dream of going to the moon. But one thought kept hammering in his head. He couldn't give up. He had to find a way.

Next morning he woke with a clear mind and a plan that seemed foolproof. Several afternoons a week, his mother sent him to the Pomme d'Or after school to deliver bulging envelopes to Gunther Kohl, her protector at the Water Police. Tom had noticed that the hotel was always deserted at this time, with the Navy and Water Police staff on patrol duties in the harbour in the afternoons. Near Kohl's office was a flight of stairs that probably led to the bedrooms upstairs. Now he had the answer.

That afternoon the envelope was fatter than usual. When he handed it over, Kohl beamed, his face smooth and shiny as if basted with butter as he patted Tom's shoulder and complimented him on his German. Tom, who usually shrank from these displays of geniality, smiled back. It dawned on him that his friendly relationship with the head of the Water Police would now work to his advantage.

After receiving his envelope, Kohl always slid it into a drawer in his desk, locked his office, and then left the hotel. Usually Tom headed straight home, but this time he loitered around Royal Square and waited. When he saw Kohl striding towards the harbour, he sneaked back inside the hotel through the side door and flattened himself against the wall of the long corridor. His heart thrummed in his ears as he waited to make sure that no-one was around. If challenged, he would have trouble explaining why he was still there after Kohl had left.

On tiptoe he climbed the carpeted stairs, treading gingerly, one step at a time, as if balancing on a tightrope. He stood outside one of the rooms with his ear to the door but heard nothing from inside. He took a deep breath and was just stretching out his hand to try the door handle when a loud voice from the bottom of the stairs made him jump.

'Hey you! What are you doing here?'

His knees shook as he turned around. It was the cleaner, a local woman in a big apron with a scarf tied into a large knot on top of her head, holding a bucket, mop and broom. Her face was red and bloated, and her eyes were sunken in her puffy cheeks.

'I'm looking for Officer Kohl,' he said, trying to keep his voice steady.

Banging her bucket down on the floor, she stood there with her hands on her hips and eyed him suspiciously. 'Well, you're looking in the wrong place, sonny. I don't know what you're up to, but you've no right to be here.'

He cursed under his breath. Of all people, it had to be someone who had never seen him there before. He was trying to gather his wits to invent an excuse but she was already at the top of the stairs, fixing him with an accusing look that promised trouble.

Then she said, 'You're Mrs Gaskell's son, aren't you?'

His heart sank. Like many locals, she probably despised his mother, and would undoubtedly welcome the opportunity to embarrass her by dragging him to the police or, what was worse, telling Gunther Kohl she had found him snooping around the Pomme d'Or. He wouldn't be able to fob Kohl off with an excuse. Kohl would tell his mother, who wouldn't rest until she got the truth out of him. And their plan would end before it began.

All this was racing through his panicked mind as he returned the cleaner's stare with what he hoped was a nonchalant expression. Clearing his throat, he shifted from one foot to the other and muttered something about a message for Officer Kohl, while she surveyed him with eyes that made him think of raisins stuck in a lump of dough.

Then she said, 'As a matter of fact, I was going to drop in to see your mum after work today to get one of them bottles of French burgundy,' she was saying, and with a shrewd look she added, 'How about you save me the trouble and deliver it yourself?'

He breathed out again. So she was on the grog.

'Officer Kohl will be back tomorrow morning,' she was saying. 'I'm off now, love. So you'll come over this evening? Number 73, St Saviour's Road.'

Was it his imagination, or did she give him a knowing look? Either way, he sensed that they had reached an unspoken agreement. She wouldn't cause him any problems. But just in case, he made a mental note to put in a packet of Gauloises with the wine.

The cleaner trundled off downstairs without giving him another glance, and a few moments later he heard the side door slam behind her.

Tom looked at his watch. He had to hurry. In an hour the Navy and Water Police people would be back. One good thing about the Krauts, he thought, they were obsessively punctual. He tried the handle of the door again. To his relief, it opened. These Krauts obviously trusted each other. The room was spartan, with a bed, a small desk with a framed family photograph, and a large wooden cupboard against one wall.

He winced as the cupboard door creaked open. Then his eyes lit up. He was gazing at shelves stacked high with boxes of cigarettes and bottles of French wine and cognac. Slipping off his haversack, he stuffed a few boxes of Gitanes and Gauloises hurriedly into it and left, carefully closing the door behind him.

He proceeded to raid two other rooms, each time taking care not to disturb the neat piles. He ran downstairs and slipped out by the side door after glancing around to make sure no-one saw him.

From that day, he no longer objected to delivering his mother's envelopes to the Pomme d'Or. Surprised by his sudden willingness, she remarked it was good that he was finally coming to his senses. He used each errand to increase his stash of cigarettes and an occasional bottle of wine from the other rooms, but he never took so much that the theft would be noticed. French cigarettes were only available on the black market, and by undercutting his mother, he sold them quickly to his friends. He tried not to dwell on the irony of the situation, that his mother's illicit activities were working in his favour.

Emboldened by his success at the Pomme d'Or, he started to pilfer money from his mother's cash register whenever she left him in charge of the shop. He stifled his occasional twinges of conscience with the thought that what he was doing wasn't really wrong. After all, he was only taking stuff from the invaders who were stealing everything from them. Just evening up the score a bit. And as for stealing from his mother, that served her right. She was robbing everyone blind.

Frank concurred with this reasoning. As the pile of Reichsmarks grew, their goal moved a little closer, and they thumped each other on the back, but they agreed not to tell Harry the source of the money. He was so honest, he'd probably refuse to join them if he knew how their escape was being financed.

Four months later, Harry's eyes widened when they told him they'd collected enough money for a boat. With a meaningful glance at Frank, Tom muttered that his grandma and an uncle had chipped in for his birthday to help him buy a fishing boat.

But buying a boat proved more difficult than they had envisaged, as there were very few for sale. After they'd been looking for several weeks, Frank rushed in to Tom's place one Saturday and announced that he'd heard of a man in St Mark's Road who had a twelve-foot dinghy for sale.

But after checking it out, Tom came back looking glum. 'It's no good. It's been in dry dock for ages, and needs caulking and painting,' he said. 'We'd better keep looking.'

When another two months passed without finding a better boat, Tom came to a decision. 'I reckon we'd better buy that dinghy while it's still available.'

Frank was pulling at his earlobe. 'It's crazy to buy a boat in such awful condition,' he argued.

Harry settled the argument. 'We're running out of time,' he said. 'We decided to leave with the spring tides when the seas will be calmer. Well, it's nearly winter now, so if we don't buy that dinghy and get it fixed, we'll have to wait another year. And we still have to get hold of an outboard motor and petrol.'

After considerable haggling, the owner agreed to sell the dinghy together with the outboard motor and some petrol. It seemed that their biggest worries were over.

Tom decided to store the dinghy in his uncle's yard. Uncle Phil was his mother's brother, but he and Alma, who he often referred to as The Shrew, didn't get on and rarely talked to each other, so Tom was pretty sure he wouldn't tell her about the boat.

He'd told his uncle that he and his friends were planning to go on fishing trips, and as Uncle Phil wasn't a curious type, he didn't question it, although he did look askance when he saw the warped planks. 'You boys have quite a job ahead of you fixing those leaky timbers,' he commented in his laconic way.

It was a much bigger job than they had expected, and they spent every spare moment working on it. If they wondered about the dinghy's seaworthiness, they kept their doubts to themselves. Under Tom's direction, they stuffed oakum and putty in between the warped strakes to seal them, and then painted them with linseed oil. Each time they filled the boat with water to test it, they held their breath, hoping it had stopped leaking.

While Frank and Tom continued to work on the dinghy, Harry, who knew more about engines than they did, took the outboard motor apart, cleaned it and tuned it. When he pulled the starter rope and the engine fired, he beamed with pride. When the boat was finally waterproof and in working order, they cheered and did a celebratory war dance. It looked as if their worries were over.

Bit by bit, they collected compasses, life jackets and binoculars, and as they surveyed their growing pile of equipment, their sense of wonder at their own achievement grew. Their adventure was taking shape and their dreams would soon be realised.

One morning as Tom cycled to school, daydreaming about the look on his mother's face when she discovered that he was in England, he had an idea that made him stop in his tracks. He suddenly saw his chance to match the feats of the fictional heroes in the spy and adventure stories he loved to read. He would buy a map of Jersey, and while he and Frank were riding their bicycles around the island, he would pinpoint on the map the site of all the German emplacements, bunkers and fortifications. As soon as they reached England, they would hand over their map of Hitler's defences and provide Britain with invaluable military information.

'That's brilliant!' Frank said when Tom told him about his plan. But Harry, who didn't accompany them on their cycling expeditions, didn't share their enthusiasm. 'It's too risky,' he pointed out. 'What if the Krauts see what you're doing?'

Tom dismissed his objection. 'They won't suspect us.'

Shortly after that, Tom had another brainwave. The photo album! Over the past two years, he had collected prints of the photographs his father had developed showing German soldiers posing in front of tanks, night-fighter planes, troops and anti-aircraft guns. His album contained photos of practically every piece of German military ordnance on Jersey. What a windfall for the British that would be. And how they'd admire three Jersey schoolboys who had risked their lives to help the war effort.

Although they had sworn not to tell anyone about their plan, they realised they'd need outside help after all. They didn't know anything about navigation, and without help they wouldn't be able to plot their course across the Channel to England.

Harry suggested contacting a seaman he knew. Captain Beaumont used to skipper the tugboat in the harbour before being replaced by a German. He'd be the ideal person to help them, but it meant having to induct him into their secret.

When they arrived at Captain Beaumont's cottage, he was sitting at the window in his captain's cap, puffing a pipe as he gazed across at Piemont Bay. After Tom explained why they needed his help, they held their breath waiting for his response.

The captain was blunt. 'This is absolutely insane,' he said. 'Your dinghy isn't suitable for these treacherous waters, and you'll probably drown or be shot. The best you can hope for is a long stint in one of their concentration camps. Either get a boat twice the size of this one or forget all about escaping. I don't want to have anything to do with this.'

Then, seeing their crestfallen faces, he softened. 'I've told you what I think, but if you persist in going ahead with this dangerous scheme in spite of my advice, I'll try and help you, even though I'm dead against it.'

Tom was silent all the way home. He felt as if a bucket of icy water had been thrown over him. He wasn't familiar with the seas around Jersey, having only paddled a canoe around the inshore reefs. Suddenly he remembered stories he had heard over the years about unpredictable storms at sea and treacherous tides that had caused ships to capsize and men to drown. But he kept his brooding thoughts to himself. He wasn't going to be the one to chicken out.

While they were making their plans, the Germans imposed ever-increasing restrictions on every aspect of life, including owning livestock and fishing. Tom felt that their grip was tightening, and he was appalled by the collusion of the States, whose officials meekly adopted all the rules, and handed over lists of their Jewish residents. Thinking about Mrs Goldman, he felt guilty that he had become so engrossed in his escape plans that he hadn't given her a thought and feared that it was probably too late.

But the aspect of life that infuriated him the most was what was happening under his nose, at home, where the drunken parties with the Krauts continued, and his mother flirted blatantly with the officers, especially the head of the Water Police. Watching his father sitting in an armchair in an alcoholic haze, a balloon of French cognac in one hand and a cigar in the other while his wife carried on like one of those cheap French whores the Krauts were now importing to Jersey, enraged him even more. Distressed by his father's humiliation, he felt like snatching the cigar and cognac from his hands and yelling at him to act like a man.

The only person he would regret leaving behind was Milly. After his jealous outburst at the Slip, he had brooded about their argument over the German officers, but a few days later, when he'd calmed down, he apologised, and he thought she forgave him.

It was more than a year since that incident.

He hadn't seen much of her lately, partly because all his spare time was taken up with preparations for their escape, and also because she had left school at the end of the summer term and their paths rarely crossed. He heard she had landed an office job at an insurance firm, which surprised him, as she didn't have any secretarial experience, but he supposed that her pretty face had made up for her lack of typing and shorthand.

He was thinking about her one Saturday as he cycled along the Esplanade, enjoying the crisp freshness of the winter afternoon. He knew he couldn't leave Jersey without confiding in her despite their vow not to tell anyone. Surely if he swore her to secrecy, she wouldn't tell anyone. But what if she told her obnoxious friend Dolly, who disliked him and would probably blab?

The Esplanade was crowded with parents and children, some of whom were pulling their fathers' reluctant hands towards Gino's kiosk, enviously eyeing the lucky children whose parents could afford to buy an ice cream.

Tom was leaning against the stone wall licking a chocolate ice cream when his heart started racing. Milly had just appeared at the far end of the Esplanade.

She looked more grown up, older and more sophisticated. Instead of bobby socks she wore nylons, and her hair was parted in the centre and swept back from her heart-shaped face in marcelled waves. He preferred the way she used to look.

Without waiting to finish his ice cream, he tossed the cone into a rubbish bin and started striding towards her, relieved that Dolly was nowhere to be seen. He would tell Milly about his plans. If he couldn't trust her, who could he trust?

She stopped walking, looked around, consulted her wristwatch, and looked around again, as if expecting someone. He paused. Someone was hurrying towards her from the opposite direction and the blood drained from Tom's face. It was the same German soldier who had bought her an ice cream over a year ago. A moment later, their laughter floated in the air as he watched them walking away together.

CHAPTER THIRTEEN

Dr Jackson

St Helier, December 1942

It's just as well I had no idea what I was taking on when I decided to hide Igor and Sasha seven months ago, or I probably wouldn't have undertaken such a daunting task. The organisation involved made my head spin, and the risks were frightening. If it hadn't been for Bob Blampied, the whole scheme would have ended in disaster, not only for the escapees but for us as well.

The plan to move them from one house to another in different parts of the island every night made sense, but we hadn't taken the logistics into account. We knew we'd have to enlist enough reliable people willing to take the risk, but there was also the curfew and shortage of petrol to consider. Being a doctor, I had a good excuse for being out past curfew, but I couldn't use up my small ration of fuel for transporting the Russians every night. Apart from that, I was terrified in case a German patrol stopped and questioned me about the two men in my car.

As a precaution, I bundled the shorter one into the boot and covered the other with a dark blanket on the floor in the back. Even so, it made every trip an exercise in terror. And to make things worse, sometimes we didn't have enough available helpers to move both of them every night. It soon became clear that we'd have to split them up.

Identity cards posed another problem, one that seemed insuperable. Whenever we were stopped by the Germans, we had to produce proof of our identity, but it goes without saying that our charges didn't have documents. Naturally we insisted they stay indoors, which wasn't as simple as it sounds – they were energetic young men, and as soon as they regained their strength, they became restless. We had to keep reminding them of the dire consequences of being caught.

But even staying indoors posed a risk. As I've mentioned elsewhere in this journal, the war brought out the best in some people, but the opportunity to settle old scores or to curry favour with the occupiers brought out the worst in others.

So whoever was hiding them needed to have their wits about them in case a nosy neighbour appeared unannounced or a Gestapo agent, alerted by a suspicious shopkeeper, should bang on the door.

We all had contingency plans for such eventualities. While the fugitives ran to their hiding places, we would rush around to scoop up extra cups, items of clothing or dictionaries which might give away any sign of their presence.

As you might expect, recruiting helpers into our network was tricky and we had to tread very carefully when we sounded people out on their willingness to shelter escaped slave labourers. I was lucky in that I was able to gauge which of my patients might be sympathetic to our cause. I knew that Brigid Murphy, the feisty librarian, would be keen to be involved. So were the Rosses, the de Gruchys and the Coopers, who had farms around St Mary's parish.

But being sympathetic didn't necessarily mean being willing to risk imprisonment, and I approached prospective rescuers very cautiously.

Ethel Carter was a widow who lived in a neat little house on St Saviour's Road. She was pruning her rose bushes, a fragrant variety usually described as a tea rose, when I stopped to chat. As I am always in a hurry, she gave me a shrewd look and invited me inside.

As soon as I mentioned escaped slave labourers, her indignation at their plight encouraged me to proceed.

'Poor lads,' she said. 'If you ever need help, don't forget I have a spare room.'

Mrs Carter's husband had died of colon cancer many years before, and her only son Nigel had joined the British Army and was missing in battle somewhere in northern France.

When I told her about Igor and Sasha, she didn't hesitate. 'You can bring one of them here,' she said. 'As you know, I live on my own so I have room, and I'll enjoy having someone to look after.'

That evening I dropped Sasha at her house. I'd been wondering how they'd get on, given the difference in culture and language, but as soon as she opened the door, and Sasha gave her a bear hug, I stopped worrying.

When I dropped in to see them a few days later, Sasha was poring over a Russian–English dictionary. He jumped up as soon as he saw me. 'How. Do. You. Do. Dr Jackson,' he said, uttering one word at a time in a heavy accent.

Mrs Carter was beaming. 'I've been teaching Sasha a bit of English,' she said as she walked me to the door. 'He's a quick learner. Such a delightful chap. I'll be happy for him to stay here till the war is over.'

Naturally I was delighted that things were working out so well, but I felt I should point out the risk she was taking.

She looked me straight in the eye. 'Sasha is another mother's son. I don't know where my Nigel is, but if he's in trouble, I hope some French mother is looking after him.'

Something must have flown into my eyes just then because they started watering.

It was Bob Blampied who solved the vexing problem of the identity cards. A client of the insurance company where he worked happened to mention that her young brother had recently died of tuberculosis. Being the quick-thinking fellow he was, Bob asked if she still had her brother's identity card.

Luckily she hadn't handed it in, and he persuaded her that by letting him have it, she might save someone's life. But the ID card would only be useful if Sasha resembled the brother sufficiently to fool anyone who demanded to see it.

From the photograph on the ID card, we saw that its owner had a neatly trimmed moustache and smooth fair hair parted on the left. Otherwise he was an average-looking chap with no distinguishing features, which was just as well. We decided that when Sasha grew a moustache and cut his hair short, he would pass scrutiny.

It was about that time that I realised the Germans were taking Jewish people away. We didn't know where they were taking them, but from occasional items on the BBC News that I heard on my secret radio, I feared the worst. I can remember how shocked I was when I read about the assaults on Jewish people in 1938, and the burning of their synagogues by Hitler's thugs, but that was before the Occupation, when our *Jersey Evening Post* was still able to print the truth.

A wireless report I heard recently made my hair stand on end. Apparently a Polish diplomat had been smuggled into a place called the Warsaw Ghetto, and he described the horrific situation of the Jews who had been herded in there and were later deported on cattle trains to a camp where they were systematically murdered.

This diplomat, whose name I think was Jan Karski, was interviewed on air when he arrived in London, and sounded like someone who was haunted by his glimpse of hell.

This report makes me feel anxious about the fate of our local Jews, some of whom are my patients. Almost from the very beginning of the Occupation, the Germans have posted orders about the Jews, closing their businesses and demanding a list of their names. This astonishes me. As there aren't many Jews in Jersey that I know of, I can't understand the Germans' obsession with them.

Another thing I can't understand is why the States have acceded to their racist demands. Because without their cooperation, the Germans wouldn't have a clue who was Jewish and who wasn't.

Why didn't they just say there weren't any? Or simply ignore those orders? Unfortunately, from what I hear, our Aliens' Officer has gone to extraordinary lengths to investigate the heritage of people even suspected of being Jewish.

There's a reason why I'm getting so hot under the collar about this issue, and perhaps part of it is guilt. To be honest, I've never had much to do with Jewish people other than as patients. I know that they're not popular with some Jersey folk, but that could be due to religious prejudice. Deep down, I fear we are all tribal.

All I can say from personal experience is that I've found some of them to be charming, cultured and generous, while others have been less so, but that's the case with all groups. I should add that as patients they tend to question my advice more than others do. I don't have a problem with that, but I'm aware that some of my fellow practitioners do.

It's taking me time to come to the point, but this is a story that's difficult to tell. A couple of months ago, Lionel Stern turned up at my morning surgery. He was a retired antique dealer of about seventy whose company I always enjoyed.

He always had an amusing anecdote about his clients, but on that particular day he could hardly get a word out and looked as pale as a ghost. I was shocked by the change in him since his last visit. He was shaking so much that I rushed from behind my desk to take his arm and help him into the chair.

I hardly recognised the man with whom I once chatted about French clocks and Austrian porcelain. Many years ago he used to play the clarinet in the St Helier orchestra, and on one occasion he had presented me with a recording of Mozart's Clarinet Concerto, which he described in his flowery way as a celestial piece of music with intimations of paradise.

When I examined him, he had tachycardia, which wasn't surprising in light of his agitated state. I asked why he was so distressed.

'They're going to come for me,' he stammered.

I stared at him. Was he becoming paranoid?

'Who is coming for you, Mr Stern?' I asked gently.

'The Germans. They're going to put me in one of those cattle wagons and take me to a death camp. I think they've already taken Mrs Goldman.'

That's when I realised that he had been listening to the BBC as well. I tried to reassure him that Jersey wasn't Poland, that they couldn't do that here, but what he said about Mrs Goldman was worrying. As my assurances didn't convince him, I prescribed a sedative, and suggested he come back to see me in a week's time.

It occurred to me that someone should look in on him from time to time, but I was run off my feet what with the Russian fugitives and my patients, and to my shame, I forgot all about Mr Stern.

Two weeks had passed before I realised he hadn't come back to see me. I hoped that was because his spirits had lifted, but my gut feeling told me otherwise. Incidentally, I firmly believe that all our organs are connected, and that distress in one part of the body is capable of being communicated to another.

Anyway, that evening, after I'd transferred Igor to one of our safe houses, I pressed the buzzer at Mr Stern's house on

Bath Road. There was no reply and I buzzed again. I looked around, but as his neighbours on both sides had evacuated in 1940, there was no-one I could ask about his whereabouts.

I walked down the side passage that led to the back of the house and peered through the kitchen window. Although it was closed, I smelled gas. Standing on an upturned metal bucket I found in the passageway, I looked inside. The oven door was open and Mr Stern lay on the floor beside it. I could see he was dead. Beside him lay the brown paper sleeve of the Mozart Clarinet Concerto. I hope he felt he was entering heaven as he listened to its sublime melody for the last time.

There's no point going on about how wretched I felt. How could I have forgotten about the poor man when I saw how depressed he was? It struck me that Russian escapees who were strangers to me had elicited my care and assistance while I had ignored the plight of fellow residents I had known for years.

That night, I drank several glasses of Armagnac as I sat staring at my wood fire, thinking about Mr Stern and reproaching myself for my negligence.

I'm not one of those people who enjoys discussing personal issues with others. In fact, that would feel like admitting failure to solve my own problems. What would that say about me as a doctor?

I can't explain what made me gravitate to Matron O'Connor's office a few days later, after I'd visited a patient at the Maternity Hospital. Her door was ajar, and I stood there for a few minutes, watching her. She was looking out of the window with a pensive expression I found charming. As soon as she saw me, she sprang up with a welcoming smile. I know I was flattering myself but it felt as if I was the very person she wanted to see.

'Dr Jackson! It's a long time since I've seen you. Is it some tea you'll be wanting?'

While she bustled about taking out cups and saucers and filling the kettle with water, I wondered if she was teasing me. As she poured out the tea, the sweetly herbal scent of tea leaves filled my head and for the first time that week I began to relax. After taking a few sips I looked up and saw that she was studying me with those large eyes whose colour changed from dove grey to sage green depending on the light.

'I hope you don't mind me saying, but you looked that sad when you came in just now.'

It's been two years since anyone has cared enough to comment on my state of mind, and I was unsettled in a way that wasn't altogether unpleasant.

My eyes rested on her ring finger but I knew that in a hospital, the absence of a wedding band didn't signify the absence of a husband. To my embarrassment she caught my glance.

'I'm not married,' she laughed. 'No time for love!'

'But surely,' I began but stopped. It was too gauche to utter a cliché about an attractive woman like her not having someone special in her life.

She raised her eyebrows, challenging me to continue. 'Surely …?' she repeated.

My face was burning. I had to put an end to this awkward conversation, which was heading for more embarrassment.

'You were right,' I said. 'I was feeling down when I arrived. In fact I've been feeling that way for days.'

She nodded. 'Some days are like that. It's hard to keep being strong when so many people depend on you. That's the blessing and the burden of our profession.'

She hadn't asked why I felt low, and that deepened my regard for her. She understood. That was the first time in my adult life that I had revealed that I was vulnerable and that's when I knew that my instinct to trust her was justified.

CHAPTER FOURTEEN

Xanthe

St Helier, April 2019

A blessing and a burden. Hugh Jackson's words echo in Xanthe's head as she drives towards Royal Square in the early evening. The lanes she passes are lined with hedgerows covered in frothy white blossom, but right now she is preoccupied with thoughts that blot out the beauty all around her.

Once again she is struck by her connection with this man whose feelings so often mirror her own. Unlike him, however, she is more familiar with the burden of medicine than its blessing – the pressure to be in control, to know the answers in life-and-death situations, and to deny or conceal ignorance and uncertainty.

As she follows the curves of the road, she casts her mind back. Over the years, she has observed that pressure on her family in their need to appear omniscient and strong, to share the triumphs but sweep the failures into a shadowy corner, beyond the searchlight of doubt. For them, the blessing was the satisfaction of curing the sick, and having their expertise reinforced by gratitude; for her, it was knowing she had achieved her lifelong goal and met her family's expectations. But the burden has almost destroyed her. She sighs. These reflections are threatening to ruin an evening she has been looking forward to, and she tries to shake them off as she parks the Nissan outside the Trattoria Sorrento.

Daniel is already sitting at a table for two. He is looking out of the window, holding a pink aperitif that looks like Campari, and raises his arm in greeting when he sees her. As the maître d' ushers her to their table, she hears French and Italian spoken, but the loudest voices belong to a lively group with north of England accents.

Fishing nets are draped against the back wall, jars of scarlet capsicums and chilli peppers are lined up on a shelf, and on red and white checked tablecloths candles are stuck into raffia-covered bottles of chianti. In the background, a tenor is singing 'Come Back to Sorrento'.

'Just in case we miss the point,' she says as she sits down.

It's a warm evening, and Daniel has rolled up the sleeves of the casual jacket he is wearing over a white T-shirt. Trendy as usual, she thinks, as she smooths down the skirt of the turquoise Zimmermann outfit that her mother had persuaded her to buy before she left Sydney.

He is looking at her and self-consciously she flicks her hair back from her forehead. This evening she has left her hair down instead of twisting it into her usual knot, and the loose strands annoy her.

'You've done something different to your hair,' he says. 'I like it.'

She is flattered and irritated at the same time. It's not as if they're on a Tinder date. Her mouth twitches in an involuntary expression of annoyance.

Without missing a beat, he picks up on her reaction. 'Are you one of those women who find compliments politically incorrect?'

'Only when they're inappropriate.'

A smile flickers on the upturned corners of his mouth. 'So is my comment inappropriate?'

He is mocking her, and she feels foolish. Why did his well-meant comment irritate her? Was it something about him? She recalls that when they had met for brunch, he was amused by the fuss she made about the weak coffee. Maybe it's her.

Daniel motions for the waiter, who brings them large, leather-covered menus and calls her *signorina* in a fake Italian accent. She takes a deep breath and turns page after page listing *antipasti*, *primi*, *secondi*, *contorni* and *dolci*.

'Too much choice,' Daniel says as he closes his menu. 'I read somewhere that when you look at a menu, you should choose the first dish that takes your eye. I reckon that's not a bad idea.'

She can't help baiting him. 'Is that your recipe for life?' she asks. 'Avoiding choice?'

'On the contrary, when I see what I want, I don't waste time looking any further. What about you?'

His eyes are resting on her face. She senses that he is challenging her, and as she scans the menu, she wonders if he is talking about food.

Confused, she reminds herself that she agreed to meet him to hear about his research, not to arrange a rendezvous. So why is she so stroppy? Then it strikes her. It wasn't anything he'd said. It was Hugh Jackson's description of medicine as a burden that evoked the painful memories she has been trying to suppress. She wishes she could go out and come in again, to make a fresh start.

'Actually, I don't find it easy to make decisions,' she says, looking up from the menu and meeting his gaze. 'About anything.'

'But you decided to come to Jersey. On your own.'

She shrugs. 'The need to escape is a powerful motivator.'

Although she knows he can't possibly understand the desperation behind her words, she is relieved he doesn't question them.

'Life can be tough,' is all he says.

They place their orders. Xanthe takes a piece of bread from the straw basket on the table, and is tearing it into small bits when the waiter brings her eggplant parmigiana, and Daniel's cotolette Milanese, and they make small talk as they eat. He has always lived in Melbourne, is divorced, and shares a terrace in Fitzroy with two housemates, another lawyer and an IT guy. She wonders if he is in a relationship, but decides to steer clear of personal issues. She certainly doesn't want him to start asking about hers.

The English guy at the next table is shouting, 'Can't you see, we're controlled by the Brussels bureaucracy!' His companions look around with an embarrassed smile, and try to shush him, but he won't be silenced. 'The sooner we're out of the bloody EU the better!'

Xanthe takes the opportunity to steer their conversation to Brexit, relieved to find a neutral topic that won't push any buttons. When they have finished eating, and are sipping their complimentary glasses of limoncello, she leans forward.

'You've told me you chose your research topic because there weren't many Jews here during the Occupation, which makes it easier to trace what happened to them. I get that. But I've been wondering, is there a personal reason as well?'

He hesitates, and she supposes he is weighing up the urge to be frank with the potential cost of being honest. Or perhaps he is merely trying to find the words to express his feelings about something that might be deeply personal, and totally inappropriate to reveal in the course of a casual dinner with a stranger.

'There is,' he says slowly, 'and it's connected with the Holocaust, but probably not in the way you imagine.'

Intrigued, she places her liqueur glass on the table and tilts her head to one side. 'Do you feel like talking about it?'

At the far end of the restaurant, the barista is grinding coffee beans, and Daniel says, 'I'm going to order a short black. Are you brave enough to risk another flat white?'

She knows he is teasing her, and this time she laughs. 'I'm over flat whites. I'm going to have a macchiato.'

Small almond-flavoured biscotti arrive with their coffees. She bites into her biscuit, brushes the spray of crumbs off her top with a deprecating comment about being messy, and waits for him to speak.

'The Holocaust had a huge impact on my life,' he begins, 'but in a way that's probably different from the stories you've heard. I'm not descended from Holocaust survivors. You could actually say I'm descended from the perpetrators. My family name was Müller, with an umlaut over the u, and the family home was in a charming flower-filled German town called Mittelberg.'

Xanthe has seen countless movies set during the Holocaust. She had some Jewish friends at school, and she has even met a Holocaust survivor during an emotional high school visit to the Sydney Jewish Museum. But she has never come across anyone prepared to admit to being related to one of the perpetrators. As she fiddles with the linen napkin, she wonders how to react if it turns out he is related to one of Hitler's henchmen.

'My grandfather Hans Müller was a judge during the Third Reich,' Daniel begins. 'While I was growing up, he was always held up to me as a model of legal excellence and ethical behaviour, and it was always assumed that I would follow in his footsteps and study law.'

She nods. That's a scenario she recognises, the pressure but also the pleasure of continuing a family tradition.

His eyes rest on her. 'But they couldn't have predicted what my study of law would lead to, and how it would impact them.'

Xanthe sits still, anchored to her chair as she watches him.

'I'm sure you'll appreciate the irony. Because I admired my grandfather so much, I travelled to Germany to gather information about him for my Master's thesis. I was looking forward to vindicating a jurist who lived through that terrible period with his principles intact. But what I discovered was a huge disappointment. It made me realise that the legal profession during the war had a lot to answer for.'

She frowns. 'What do you mean?'

'There were hundreds of pernicious laws enacted during Hitler's regime, laws that restricted political freedoms and civil rights, and enabled the Nazis to dispossess, detain, deport and murder millions of Jews as well as dissidents, homosexuals and gypsies. Judges could have used their position to challenge the legitimacy of those laws, but the overwhelming majority – including my grandfather – never did. The documents I found showed that they not only upheld those laws, but they often interpreted them in ways that facilitated Hitler's agenda.'

Questions whirl in Xanthe's head, but she refrains from voicing them. She doesn't want to interrupt his train of thought.

'All lawyers have an unshakeable respect for the law. Any law,' he continues. 'Faced with the implementation of evil laws, the lawyers of the Third Reich concentrated on the laws, and ignored the evil.

'When people talk about those who were responsible for the Final Solution, they mention Hitler, Himmler, Eichmann and other high-profile Nazis, but I sometimes wonder about the role of the professional people, especially the lawyers. Without their acquiescence, would the Holocaust still have happened?'

He stops talking as the noise behind them intensifies. Voices are raised, chairs are scraped against the floor, and the English group make their way out of the restaurant, still arguing about Brexit.

Xanthe uses the pause to process his statement. 'That's huge,' she says after the door has closed behind them. 'So you're saying that the hands that signed the papers might have helped to put the guns in the hands of the murderers.'

He nods, and she thinks she sees a gleam of approval in his gaze.

'So when you examine the documents here, will you be looking to see how the Jersey lawyers acted with regard to the Nazi racial laws?'

'That's right. And I'll be looking at the behaviour of the administrative officers as well.'

They are the last diners in the restaurant, and the waiter is hovering to see if they want anything else. Xanthe finds it easier to think now the dining room is quiet, and she asks, 'How did your family react when they found out that you'd knocked your grandfather off his pedestal?'

'Not well. My father, Hans Müller's son, didn't want to know. He said I'd become part of what he called the Holocaust industry, blaming innocent Germans for Hitler's crimes. He argued that Hans had no choice. Which is the usual excuse, but it isn't valid. Anyway, that's what he chose to believe, and he never forgave me for sullying his father's reputation. My older sister sided with him so I don't see her anymore either.'

'And your mother?'

'She's an Aussie, and she never got on with the old man apparently. She said he was rigid and Germanic, so she was open to what I said. Unfortunately, the controversy about Hans didn't help their marriage, and they ended up divorcing a few years ago.'

'What about you?' she asks. 'Did you know your grandfather?'

'I did, but he died when I was eight. He used to take me for long walks. One day, when I complained I was too tired to keep walking, he told me that after the war the Russians deported him to Siberia, and when he was released, he walked thousands of kilometres, all the way back to Germany. That was the only time he ever alluded to his past. He took me for walks in the Melbourne Botanical Gardens and taught me the names of trees and plants, and told me stories about ancient Greeks and Romans. I loved spending time with him.'

'So it must have been hard when you realised he hadn't been the heroic figure you'd been led to believe.'

Daniel looks thoughtful. 'It took me a while to come to terms with it, but in time I came to understand that he was the product of the legal profession and the German culture at the time, both of which reinforced unwavering obedience and unquestioning enforcement of laws.'

'Do you know if he ever talked to your mother about the war?'

'She said he refused to talk about it, and if anyone asked, he changed the subject. I suppose he knew that people would have already made up their minds, and it was probably too complicated to explain to anyone who wasn't there and hadn't lived through it.'

Their conversation has moved into dark waters, and Xanthe tries to imagine what it might have been like to be part of the judiciary at a time when the law was used to support an evil agenda.

'Do you really believe he had a choice?' she asks. 'I mean, Hitler wasn't exactly tolerant when people refused to enforce his laws.'

Daniel seems to be considering her question. 'There's always a choice. Even the members of the *einsatzgruppen*, the killing squads, could have refused to gun down thousands of men, women and children. Raising objections about the legitimacy of those laws might not have made any difference, but it would be nice to know that he'd at least expressed dissent. But from the documents relating to his judgements that I read in Germany, it was obvious that, like most of his peers, he chose to rubberstamp rather than dissent.'

She wonders whether to take the risk and ask the question that has been on her mind ever since this conversation began, but she knows it won't let her rest. Taking a deep breath, she says, 'Have you ever wondered what you would have done in his place?'

He pauses, and she has braced herself for a retort, when he says, 'As a matter of fact, I have. Often. All I can say is that I hope I would have behaved with more principle, but hindsight is a great teacher. The trouble is, we have to live life forwards, and I don't think we can ever know how we would behave in any situation until it arises.'

For a moment, she feels the urge to confide in him about the toxic situation at the hospital that she had failed to denounce, but decides against it. 'Does that mean we don't know our own character until a crisis forces us to reveal it?'

'Probably.' He is surveying her with interest. 'You're very perceptive.' Then he adds, 'I hope I'm not being inappropriate!'

'No, but you're being sarcastic,' she says, laughing now. 'So how did you come to terms with your grandfather's behaviour?'

'This might sound odd, but eventually I decided that this research I've embarked on is his gift to me. I became so disillusioned with the practice of law that I was on the point of abandoning it, but then I decided to do my Masters and go into the academic side instead, and research the responsibility of lawyers during genocide. Not just during the Holocaust, but in Rwanda, Bosnia and Myanmar.

'This has given me the opportunity to do something meaningful with my law degree. Who knows, maybe in the end it will enable me to add something to our understanding of what makes events like the Holocaust possible.'

She envies him. It must be fulfilling to use your training to achieve something worthwhile. Reflecting on his words, she realises that he has trusted her sufficiently to share a deeply personal story. 'That's a great way to look at it,' she says, 'turning a negative into a positive.'

He makes that self-deprecating gesture with his hands, as though pushing away the air to make space for his next words. 'I'm sorry, I've been talking way too much about me. What about you? What's going on in your life?'

'Nothing nearly as interesting as in yours,' she says lightly, and adds, 'I still haven't figured out how to turn my negatives into positives.'

When the waiter places the bill on the table, she suggests splitting it.

He is smiling. 'Will it offend your feminist sensibility if I pay for dinner?'

Of the several replies that occur to her, she selects the one that implies they have a future. 'Not if I can pay next time.'

The square is quiet as they walk towards her car, except for shrieks of laughter that come from revellers drinking outside the Cock and Bottle.

She turns to him. 'I've been thinking about your relative Edward de Courcy. How does he fit in to your research plans? You must have had some reason for making contact, other than to get his back up.'

'Not only is he the current Bailiff, but his father was the Bailiff here during the war. So his father was the most powerful local figure at the time, and I believe the Germans deferred to him even during the Occupation.'

'Well, from his reaction it's obvious he won't help you. I imagine he'd like to put as many obstacles in your way as possible. Do you think it might have been better not to tell him why you were here?'

'I believe in being upfront. Anyway, he can't prevent me from getting hold of the documents that have been released. So tomorrow I'm going to spend the day at the Archive Office.'

Before getting into her car, she wonders how to end the evening. She feels she has painted herself into an awkward corner. What's the nature of their relationship? Are they friends, colleagues or casual acquaintances? A kiss would be too familiar, a handshake too businesslike. Maybe a casual comment like *Catch you later*, or *Let's keep in touch*?

While this is going through her mind, he is gazing at her.

'That outfit you're wearing is exactly the same colour as your eyes,' he says. Then he bends down and as his warm lips brush against her cheek, she breathes in the scent of his aftershave.

'I'm going to make sure you keep your word about paying for dinner next time,' he calls out as he walks off.

'You're on!' she replies.

The tantalising scent of his aftershave lingers in her mind for the rest of the evening. That night, she dreams she's in a courtroom. The judge is wearing a white wig and holds a gavel. He looks accusingly at her and she realises that she's the defendant, although it isn't clear what she has been charged with.

He is about to pronounce sentence, and although she doesn't hear what he says, from his furious expression and the way he bangs his gavel, she can tell that it will be severe. 'But you don't understand!' she is shouting. 'You can't judge me when you weren't even there.' She turns and sees that people in the packed courtroom are shaking their fists at her. Panic-stricken, she tries to run from the court but her feet are stuck to the floor and she can't wrest them away. There's no escape.

CHAPTER FIFTEEN

Tom

St Helier, April 1943

Whipped up by the wind, wild waves boomed and crashed onto the black rocks of the south Jersey shore. Watching anxiously from the shelter of the draughty wooden cabin, Tom couldn't stop shivering. They had spent all week observing the tides. Spring tides could rise up to thirty feet, and they knew they'd have to wait for the ebb, as rowing against the strong current would be impossible. But the tide was still rising and soon it would be too dark to launch the dinghy.

If only the tide would begin to ebb. 'Take it easy,' he told himself. 'Don't panic.' Wiping his clammy palms on his shorts, he glanced around, hoping the others couldn't tell how nervous he was. And how determined to carry out their plan. After all the decisions they'd made about the safest place, the best date and the most clement tides, the day had finally arrived, and he wasn't going to back out, no matter what.

It had taken them several weeks of cycling around the island to decide on the best location to launch the dinghy. In the end they had chosen Green Island, a rocky cove in the south-east. Frank, who couldn't swim, suspected that the jagged rocks around the bay would make the turbulent water even more dangerous, but Tom had insisted on Green Island. For one thing, he argued, there were no sentries or gun emplacements in the area, and for another, the Krauts hadn't planted the small beach with mines. Harry agreed. As there were already several small fishing boats moored in the bay, theirs wouldn't attract attention. Another boon was that behind the pine trees there were some abandoned fishermen's cabins where they'd be able to hide until it was time to set out.

For several weeks, they had cycled to Green Island on weekends, and spent hours pretending to search for crabs and eels among the rocks and seaweed so that the locals would get used to seeing them there and wouldn't become suspicious.

It was Frank who had suggested leaving on May Day. The Krauts would be celebrating in town with their usual parades and military bands, and wouldn't be likely to patrol remote bays, he pointed out. And by then the tides would be less treacherous.

Tom would have preferred to leave earlier, as he couldn't wait to get away. Apart from his disgust at his parents' behaviour, it was Milly's betrayal that had brought his fury to boiling point. He loved her so much that it hurt, but seeing her parading around with her Kraut boyfriend filled him with a rage he could scarcely control. If he hadn't been preoccupied with their plans, he might have done something he'd regret. The pain was so visceral he could imagine himself exploding and shattering into thousands of razor-sharp pieces. He tried not to imagine what she and her boyfriend were doing behind closed doors. First his mother and now Milly. The sooner he got away from Jersey the better.

Towards the end of April, they had returned to Captain Beaumont's cottage. Fixing them with a stern gaze, the old captain urged them to reconsider, but when he realised that his warnings were futile, he prepared a navigation chart with detailed instructions for their voyage to Weymouth.

According to the chart, they were to make their way to the tiny isles of Les Écréhous, wait there till it got dark, and continue on to Les Casquets west of Alderney the following day. On the third day they were to sail across to Weymouth on the south coast of England. He explained that they'd find plenty of hiding places among these tiny outcrops while waiting for the tide to ebb. Before they left, he warned them on no account to reveal his involvement in their escape, and to destroy the chart if they were in danger of being captured.

Examining the chart that evening in Frank's garden, they were exuberant. The experienced seaman had mapped out their route in so much detail that it seemed foolproof. They weren't surprised that he kept urging them to abort their plans. After all, he was an adult, wasn't he? They had to make sure no-one found the chart. Tom feared that wherever he hid it, his mother's eagle eyes would find it, and she wouldn't rest until she got the truth out of him. Frank shared a bedroom with his nosy little brother, which only left Harry, who offered to hide it under his mattress. 'My parents wouldn't dream of looking there,' he assured them.

At night, Tom would lie awake, smiling as he saw himself in England, being thanked by an admiring army officer for his invaluable photographs and the map that pinpointed all the German defences. Dennis Vibert's feat would fade into obscurity compared to theirs.

That afternoon, as they'd made their stealthy way towards the cabin for the last time, he had seen his companions exchange worried looks as they scanned the water. Frank was pulling his left earlobe. 'Maybe we should wait another day?' he asked.

Harry nodded. 'The tide is too high. Let's postpone it,' he urged.

But Tom was adamant. He knew that Frank and Harry had misgivings about leaving their families, but he had no such qualms. There was no going back. Not for him. He wasn't going to spend one more day under the German jackboots.

'And what if the tide is high tomorrow as well?' he countered. 'Are we going to keep putting it off? We've been hanging around here for a week, and so far no-one suspects anything, but the longer we wait here, the more likely someone will notice us, and report us to the Krauts. We've told our parents we're going fishing and we've got everything ready. I reckon it's now or never.'

Then he held out his hand and reminded them of their oath. 'All for one and one for all, remember?'

Impressed by Tom's unusual eloquence, Frank and Harry glanced at each other uneasily. He had thrown them a challenge, and, fired up by his words, they backed down.

Once again they went over their contingency plans in case of trouble. If the Krauts stopped them, they would say they were on a fishing trip, and in case of a mishap, they'd throw the map and charts overboard, and tell their parents they'd had a fishing accident.

Now, scanning the foaming waves from the cabin as the wind whistled through the broken windows, Tom prayed for a sign that the tide was beginning to ebb. There was no way they'd be able to row against that current, especially on such a dark, moonless night. He'd seen fishermen cut off by these unpredictable spring tides, forced to perch on the rocks until the sea ebbed. The pale spring light was fading, the wind had picked up, and the waves had become wilder. He wrapped a torn old blanket around him to stop his teeth from chattering as the wind tore through the cabin.

In the dying light, dark thoughts that he had suppressed now surfaced. What if they were caught, and the Jerries looked in his haversack and saw the maps he'd packed showing all the German gun emplacements? And the photographs he'd copied of their planes and weapons? What should they say if asked who drew up the navigation chart? And what if they saw his album with the incriminating photos of German fortifications? He put his hands in his pockets to stop them shaking. 'Stop worrying,' he told himself. None of this was going to happen because they had covered all the possibilities. They'd checked to make sure there were no German patrols on this deserted stretch of coast, so there was no risk of being caught. No-one knew where they were leaving from or when, except Captain Beaumont, and he wouldn't divulge their secret for fear of incriminating himself.

He checked his watch. It was close to 11 pm, and the others were watching him, waiting for a signal. The waves were still roiling against the rocks, but the water was ebbing fast.

A quick searching glance at his companions, a decisive nod, and they crept across the beach, their footsteps crunching on the pebbly shore. After dragging the dinghy onto the sand, they carried the outboard motor, oars, life jackets, gasoline cans, fishing tackle, milk and sandwiches, and placed them in the boat.

As soon as it was afloat, Frank jumped in, inserted the rowlocks, and pushed the oars into them, but when he tried to pull the bow into the waves, the surge was too powerful. Seeing him struggle with the oars, Harry leaped into the boat to help, and Tom climbed in too, but the savage waves tossed the dinghy around and they couldn't control it. Their bulky life jackets made it hard to row, so Tom suggested taking them off, and they flung them down, but although they put all their strength into rowing, the boat was heading straight for a massive rock.

Although they had agreed not to use the motor until they were out of earshot, Harry realised that without it, they had no hope of steering clear of the rock, and he tried several times to start the motor. Each receding wave was pushing them closer and closer to the rock, and still the motor wasn't starting, and Frank and Tom were yelling at him to hurry up. Just as the motor fired up, a huge wave broke over the boat and thrust them against the rock. A moment later, another wave swamped the motor, which cut out. As they watched helplessly, the boat listed to one side, filled with water, and pinned them against the rock. A moment later, another wave, much higher than the last, capsized the boat, and they all fell into the sea.

It happened so fast that there was no time to think, no time to even panic. Only one thing activated Tom's shocked brain – Frank couldn't swim. He looked frantically for the life jackets but they had vanished in the churning waves. If only he hadn't suggested taking them off. If only. But there was no time for recriminations – Frank was flailing around in the water, panic in his eyes. Tom grabbed hold of him. 'Hold on to me,' he shouted.

Frank, who was gasping and spluttering, grabbed the straps of Tom's haversack so tightly that they almost choked him.

'Just float, and I'll tow you to shore,' Tom yelled.

Tom was a good swimmer, but his heavy clothing and the strong ebb tide made it impossible to make much headway and in despair he saw that the current was taking them further and further from the shore.

He had to get help or they would both drown. Frantic, he kept calling out to Harry, but there was no reply. The night was black as tar, and he couldn't see anything around him. Guided by the sound of the waves breaking on the beach, Tom tried to head for the shore, wondering how long he could go on towing Frank, who was a lead weight.

Suddenly a huge wave tore Frank away. Thrashing around in the water, Tom called his name, but as soon as he managed to reach him, Frank grabbed him in a vice-like grip and pulled him underwater once again. He was coughing so much, he couldn't talk, and Frank kept grabbing hold and pulling him under. Tom knew that his own strength was ebbing. Several more times, he tried to keep Frank afloat, but to no avail, and each attempt ended with him being submerged in the icy depths. It was cold, so cold, and he was so tired. Chilled and exhausted, Tom kept trying to cough up the salt water he had swallowed, certain now that there was no hope, that he would surely drown.

In his exhausted state, his mind seemed to float outside his body and he had a vision of his parents looking at his limp body on the beach, and his mother crying, of Frank's mother thanking him for saving her son, and of Milly dressed in black, saying she had always loved him.

Just then, a monstrous wave wrenched Frank from his weakening grip, and the dire reality of his situation roused him from his dreamlike state. In the blackness, he kept yelling 'Frank!' but all he heard was the ominous crashing of the waves against the rock. With the last of his strength, Tom struck out for the shore alone.

He no longer wondered where Harry and Frank were, or what had happened to the life jackets, the chart, the maps and the album. He had become reduced to a single instinct, focussed on only one idea: to reach the deliverance of the shore. But as his arms lost power and his body was tossed by the waves, he knew there was no hope of rescue. There was no point struggling anymore.

At that moment of total resignation, a wave picked him up and carried him so close to the shore that to his amazement, he felt sand beneath his feet. Re-energised by the joy of survival, he found the strength to swim through the surf until he collapsed on the beach, rejoicing at his good fortune. He was alive.

His joy was short-lived. Where were the others? Scrambling to his feet, he called their names and ran back into the surf, shouting, but there was silence. Suddenly somewhere behind him, he heard Harry's voice.

'Tom? Are you okay? I got washed ashore. I've been waiting for you two.' He looked around. 'Where's Frank?'

Tom couldn't bring himself to answer. Several times he started to speak, but he choked up and kept shaking his head.

'Maybe he managed to get to a rock, and he's waiting there for us to come and get him?' Harry whispered, but his tone of voice belied his optimistic words.

Tom hung his head. There was no way Frank could have survived alone in that sea, but he suggested waiting on the beach just in case he turned up. Only an hour had passed since they had set out, but it felt like a hundred years ago. Tom slumped onto the sand, trying to grasp the enormity of what had happened. Frank couldn't have drowned, the boat couldn't have capsized, their dreams of escape couldn't have shattered so quickly.

As he sat there, his mind as numb as his body, he remembered the map he'd wrapped in a special pouch, the chart and the album. They were probably all at the bottom of the sea by now where no-one would find them.

But Frank. In some crazy part of his mind, he thought that maybe he had only imagined that Frank had been sucked down by the waves, that any moment he'd look up and see him grinning. *I bet you thought I'd drowned,* he'd say, pulling at his earlobe.

He must have dozed off, because suddenly he sat up, startled by the sound of cars that had come to a screeching halt above them.

Doors banged, and before he had time to jump to his feet and run, he was skewered by the powerful beams of a flashlight.

He blinked and started running but someone was yelling *'Halt! Hande hoch!'* and he knew his worst nightmare had just become reality.

Standing in front of him was Gunther Kohl, flanked by two of his Water Police associates.

Dazed, Tom raised his hands in the air and as he stared at the Germans, he tried to make sense of what was happening. What were they doing there? They never patrolled Green Island at midnight. How did they happen to be there at this particular moment?

Just then another car pulled up and two *feldgendarms* jumped out, and demanded to know what was going on.

'We were told that these young hooligans were planning to escape from here, and we came to stop them,' Kohl explained while the *feldgendarms* pointed their pistols at Tom and Harry.

Tom was so dazed that he was hardly aware that his arms were yanked behind him and handcuffed. There was only one thought in his mind. Someone had tipped the Krauts off. But who? The *feldgendarms* were still yelling as they dragged them towards the police car.

They were about to shove him into the back of the car when Kohl grabbed his shoulder.

'You need a good kick up the arse!' he hissed. 'But make no mistake, you'll certainly get what's coming to you now.

I just feel sorry for your poor mother. Look at all the trouble you've caused her. She was in tears when I left her!'

As the police car roared away, bearing them towards the police headquarters, Kohl's last words reverberated in Tom's head. *She was in tears when I left her.* Now he knew the bitter truth. It was his mother who had ratted on them.

CHAPTER SIXTEEN

Dr Jackson

St Helier, May 1943

When I glanced at the calendar this morning, I was startled to see that almost half the year has gone, and even more shocked to realise that I have neglected my journal for so long.

It has been a long and cold winter which brought with it more than the usual number of outbreaks of influenza and various respiratory ailments, some of which have necessitated admission to hospital. With the lack of fuel to keep warm, and the strict rationing and shortage of food, it's no wonder that those who can't afford to buy supplies on the black market go hungry and succumb to infections.

When I look at my patients, most of whom were well-dressed, rosy-cheeked and robust before the Occupation, I'm distressed to see how their health has deteriorated. It's eerie to see all the shops so empty, something I could never have imagined. Those who are handy with a needle and thread have managed to mend, turn, remake or refashion their clothes because new ones are not available. Shoes are a big problem. I've had to repair the soles of my shoes with pieces of ugly black rubber, and just this week I took some shirts to a seamstress so she could turn the collars, but I know this is trivial compared to the privations most people are dealing with. Just as a matter of interest, I've had to resort to making bicycle tyres from garden hoses as new tyres are more scarce than hens' teeth! As I've mentioned in previous entries, this situation has forced us all to improvise to a degree I never thought possible.

Keeping warm during power outages is another challenge. Although it hurt me to do it, I've had to cut down some of the trees in my garden and chop them into firewood. This, like almost everything else these days, is forbidden without official permission, which is usually denied, so I've gone ahead and done it anyway.

As I've shared my firewood with neighbours and needy patients, I don't suppose any of them will report me. When I get home on a cold night, it's wonderfully indulgent to sit by the blaze of my open fire sipping Armagnac and listening to the Mozart Clarinet Concerto, which transports me to another world. At such moments, my thoughts drift to happier times and I almost forget our humiliating and precarious situation at the mercy of the invaders.

Of course there are those among us who lack for nothing, women whose German lovers keep them well supplied with nylon stockings, ankle-strap shoes and French perfumes, but the less said about them the better. I suspect they are being watched by people who are silently keeping score and biding their time until they can wreak revenge.

In all fairness, however, not all the liaisons between local lasses and German soldiers are mercenary affairs. I've observed several instances of what appears to be genuine attachment. Although I detest the occupiers, and every time I see one of our policemen saluting them or obediently stepping off the pavement to let them pass, my stomach turns over, I have to admit that some of the soldiers are courteous young men who miss their homes, and are probably no different from our own soldiers. With most of our young men gone to fight with the British army, it's no wonder that some of our girls have been attracted to the Germans, who are polite and attentive. I gather that being sent here instead of being sent to fight on the Russian front is like winning the lottery, and most of them try to keep us on-side.

But although these young couples are discreet and avoid displaying their affection in public, in a small community like this it's hard to conceal liaisons with the enemy, especially from eyes sharpened by envy and malice.

I've been alerted to the extent of malice in our community by Mrs Latimer, who works at the post office. When she came to see me a few months ago about her varicose veins, she confided that whenever they receive anonymous letters addressed to German police headquarters, they steam them open. If it turns out their suspicions were correct, and the writer was informing on someone, they just tear the letter up and warn the intended victim.

'Doctor, you'd be amazed at the petty things people denounce their neighbours for,' she told me. 'Someone has more anthracite coal than they have, someone has a pig they haven't registered, a neighbour has been listening to a radio and so on.'

This shocked me. Disasters are supposed to unite people in common suffering, not turn them against each other. But I can understand the resentment people feel towards the black marketeers, and that brings me to a sensational event that took place recently, one I'm still reeling from. The whole island is buzzing with the news that my young patient Tom was captured by the Germans while trying to escape from Jersey in a boat.

As soon as I heard about it, I felt sick. The last time I saw him at my surgery, I could tell he had something on his mind but I remember being called away to the hospital for an urgent delivery before I had a chance to find out what it was, and to my shame, I didn't follow up on his visit. Perhaps he would have confided in me, and I might have been able to dissuade him from a course of action that was doomed to fail. It was only after I heard about the disaster that I recalled the admiring way he spoke about Dennis Vibert, the fellow who escaped to England, when he came to see me last year. It hadn't occurred to me that he might be planning to emulate him.

From the gossip around town, it sounds as if he and two friends had secretly got hold of a boat, which they launched from a particularly treacherous part of the coast.

When I think about it, I'm torn between admiration for their courage and horror at their foolhardiness, especially as one of the lads couldn't swim and drowned in the wild seas when the boat capsized. Apparently the lad's parents are blaming Tom for the tragedy.

As for Tom, he and his other friend are locked up in police cells at the moment, and no-one knows what their fate will be. As far as I know, nobody is allowed to visit them, not even their parents, which is very unusual, especially as they are so young. But the behaviour of our occupiers is impenetrable and their orders even more so.

Given that they're being held in isolation, I can't bear to think what will happen to them. The Germans regard attempting to escape as a serious crime which they punish severely. I can't stop thinking about Francois Scornet, the brave Frenchman they stood against a tree and shot for exactly the same crime.

There's one aspect of this catastrophe that puzzles me: their capture. From what I've managed to piece together about the events of that terrible night, it seems that the three lads kept their plans secret not only from their parents but from all their friends. One of my patients, old Miss Valland, who lives near Tom's uncle and loves to gossip, told me that they kept the boat on his land until they transferred it to Green Island, and not even he had any idea what they were planning. He thought they were going to use it for fishing, she told me, and went on to say that she had overheard Tom's mother screaming at her brother that if he believed that, then he was an even bigger fool than she'd given him credit for.

So that's what I can't understand. As they kept their plans so secret, how did the Germans know what they were planning, where they were, and what time they were about to sail?

There have been various rumours, but nothing that makes any sense. In the meantime, poor Tom is in gaol, incommunicado, awaiting his fate, probably terrified and overwhelmed with guilt about his friend who drowned.

If the town gossips are right, Tom's mother, who is one of the most active black marketeers in St Helier, is apparently excessively friendly with some of the members of the Water Police, so surely she will do all she can to pull strings on his behalf. But I recall that he came to see me that day without telling his parents, so their relationship may not be very close. Still, a mother is a mother. I don't know anything about his father, but from what I've observed about married couples, strong women invariably marry weak men who rarely summon up the strength to oppose them.

I know that if Jamie were in trouble, I would move heaven and earth to help him, but as things are at the moment, he is almost three years old, and apart from a businesslike note and a photograph on his birthday, I haven't had any contact with Margaret. I wonder if she has even told him about me.

And that brings me to the main reason I have been so remiss with my journal. For some time now, I have felt an increasing emotional disconnection from Margaret. Almost three years have passed with only grudging communication from her, and she has begun to recede from my thoughts, something I would never have suspected when we first parted on that sultry June day in 1940. I'm at a loss to understand why she persists in blaming me for being trapped here. You'd think I was personally responsible for the Occupation.

When I think about it, I don't even know if she is aware of our precarious situation or the restrictions and shortages we suffer at the hands of this ruthless regime.

These restrictions extend to all communication with the outside world, from which we are completely cut off. The only news we receive is from clandestine BBC broadcasts that we listen to at the risk of our lives, and from rare Red Cross letters. Margaret never replies to my letters, so it feels as if she and I are living on different planets.

This longwinded preamble sounds like an excuse, but it is leading to something I find awkward to write about, not only because I'm not comfortable describing emotions, but also because of the confusion I feel. And confusion is another emotion I'm not familiar with. I'm used to being the one in control who dispenses wise counsel to others about overcoming life's problems, not the one who is in need of advice. My father once said if you don't control pride, it will control you, and I'm wondering if my attitude is a sign of professional and personal pride. And if it is, will this confusion be a lesson in humility?

Anyway, enough explaining and reflecting.

As I was driving towards the Maternity Hospital a few weeks ago, I felt a lightness of heart I hadn't felt in a long time. It was a God-given spring day, with everything around me flowering and blossoming. Every turn in the road reminded me that, preoccupied with all our problems, I had forgotten how beautiful this island is.

It felt as if I were seeing it for the first time, the granite manor houses, the patchwork of potato fields, the hedgerows in full bloom, and the daffodils, primroses and bluebells sprinkled over the grass like a delicate floral pattern on emerald green silk. I could imagine painting it, and for the first time since the Occupation my fingers itched for my palette and paintbrush.

As soon as the stone hospital building came into view, I felt something akin to a mild electric jolt course through my body, and that's when I realised why I felt so excited, but also unsettled.

Perhaps I was building castles in the air without any foundation. After all, I knew nothing about Matron O'Connor. It's true that she always greeted me with a warm smile, and tried to detain me with cups of tea, but I couldn't assume that this indicated anything personal. Perhaps it was just her friendly manner.

All this was going through my mind and I was arguing with myself as I parked the Austin and walked towards the hospital portico. Should I nonchalantly knock on her door and ask if there was a chance of a cup of tea? Or maybe just hurry past and look the other way to prevent making a fool of myself? Surely such an appealing woman wasn't likely to be single. Even if she wasn't married, she might have a lover.

The thought of someone making love to her made my heart beat very fast and that's probably what propelled my legs towards her office before I even knew what I was doing or what I planned to say. I took a deep breath and knocked. Not too gently or assertively. A question mark rather than a statement or a demand.

She said, 'Come in,' but judging by her tone, she was distracted by something in her office, and immediately I regretted my decision. She was obviously busy and I didn't have a valid reason to see her. I stood there feeling very foolish, wondering if I could slip out before she looked up.

But at that moment she looked up, and a brilliant smile lit up her face.

'It's grand to see you,' she said, looking straight into my eyes. 'You look bothered. Are you all right?'

She continued to watch me with her steady gaze as I mumbled something about being concerned about my patient Mrs le Blanc.

Then I stopped talking because, not taking her eyes off me, she got up and came over to where I was standing, close enough for me to breathe in the scent of her hair.

'Oh, so that's why you came, is it? Because you're worried about Mrs le Blanc?' Her voice was low and teasing, and to my embarrassment I suddenly remembered that Mrs le Blanc had been discharged the previous week.

She was still standing close to me, still smiling up at me, and without thinking, I pulled her against me and kissed her soft lips and felt them part against mine. I was sixteen again, giddy with joy and desire.

'Aoife,' I whispered. It was the first time I called her by her name and I savoured the sound of it on my tongue. 'Aoife.'

As I held her against me, under her starched uniform I could feel the curves of her body, and for one insane moment, I felt like throwing caution to the wind and making love to her right there in her office.

She pulled away and adjusted her veil, casting a quick glance at the door. 'Not now,' she said. 'The hospital superintendent will be here soon. Come back this evening. I'm a terrible cook but I have a few praties and a bit of meat, so I'll make us Irish stew for dinner.'

I was at the door when she said, 'Oh, and don't forget to look in on Mrs le Blanc on your way out!'

I could still hear her laughing as I walked down the corridor, but this time I was laughing too.

The rest of that day I was in such a delicious agony of anticipation that time seemed to have stopped. I kept looking at my watch but it was three o'clock when I last checked, and what seemed like an hour later, it was only five past three.

After filling in most of that interminable afternoon with house calls, I took a basket of eggs and a bundle of firewood to the Clarkes, whose five children look peaky and malnourished. Thank goodness our Russian escapees have avoided recapture so far. Sasha is safe with Mrs Carter, and our round robin method of sheltering Igor in various homes has worked most of the time, although there were a few nights when we were short of volunteers, and he had to stay several nights in the same house, endangering his hosts as well as the rest of us.

On this particular evening, however, there was no problem, and I picked Igor up from Bob Blampied's house and dropped him at the Robinsons' farm. Finally, finally, it was time to see Aoife.

I had a bottle of Chateau Margaux I'd been saving for a special occasion and I put it in the car and wrapped it in a few sheets of the *Jersey Evening News*, which is so heavily censored it's best used in the lavatory. It reminded me of what Voltaire once wrote to a journalist he despised: *I am in the smallest room of the house and I have your article in front of me. Soon it will be behind me.*

Chuckling over his wit, I set off for the hospital. My excitement at the prospect of spending an evening with Aoife, and the thrill of discovering that she shared my feelings, led me to fantasise about how this evening might end. I was enjoying a delicious erotic daydream when a motorcycle pulled up alongside me, and a German *feldgendarm* motioned me to pull over.

Taking off his goggles, he wanted to know why I was breaking the law by driving after curfew. Calmly I showed him my identity card and explained that I was a doctor about to visit a patient in the hospital.

But instead of saying *sehr gut* and speeding off as they usually did, he pressed his nose against the window and peered suspiciously into the car. I held my breath. Then I saw him point.

'*Was ist das?*' he barked. He was pointing at the bottle, probably thinking it was a concealed weapon. 'Just some medicine for a patient,' I said casually. But the wretch wouldn't let it go at that and demanded to see it. There was nothing I could do to stop him. A moment later, he was tearing off the newspaper. '*Ah-ha!*' His eyes gleamed as he examined the label. 'Medicine for a patient, *ja?*'

I had to think quickly. I couldn't bear the thought of giving away my Chateau Margaux but my choices were limited. Either I offered him the wine, or he would haul me off to the police station, and that would be the end of my idyllic tete-a-tete as well as the wine. It might also mean the end of my freedom for several months. Of course there was also the possibility that he would accept the wine and still arrest me, but I decided to take my chances.

'Maybe you have a nice *fraulein* to share this wine with?' I suggested with a forced smile.

He grinned and nodded, and I cursed as he sped away with my precious wine in his sidecar.

That incident was a bucket of iced water over my overheated imagination. What was I thinking? I wasn't free to embark on an affair. I was a married man, a doctor in a community where I was respected. How would it look if people found out I was having an affair with the matron of the hospital? I decided I'd keep our arrangement for dinner, but leave straight afterwards.

After parking my little Austin in front of the hospital, I sat in the car for a few minutes, sadly contemplating the loss of my fantasy with Aoife. She would probably tease me about my sudden exit. *Oh, of course, you forgot you were married,* she would laugh. *That's a shame, so.*

But she knew I was married. In fact she had praised me for staying behind to look after my patients. She wouldn't laugh. She would understand.

I was almost at the entrance when I stopped walking. For three years I'd been living alone, abandoned by my wife who seemed determined to carry her vindictiveness to the grave. What kind of marriage was that? For three years I'd been dreaming of the day we could be reunited. Surely the war couldn't last much longer now that such a large part of the German army had been defeated at Stalingrad, according to the BBC News. But even if the war ended tomorrow, what could Margaret and I say to each other after all this time? What connection would we still have? Would she ever forgive me? Would I ever forgive her?

Aoife opened the door, and before I could say a word, she was in my arms, holding me tighter than I'd ever been held before. I don't know if her Irish stew was ruined, but we didn't eat dinner that evening. I felt as if I had been sleepwalking all my life, and had just woken up and seen the world burst into dazzling colour for the first time.

CHAPTER SEVENTEEN

Xanthe

St Helier, April 2019

It's morning, and from her bed Xanthe watches the scalloped leaves of the oak tree quivering in the breeze outside her window. Small robins are flying around, and she sees an occasional splash of red among the branches. The street is quiet, and the chirping of the birds is the only sound she can hear. It reminds her of the high-pitched chirping of the rainbow lorikeets among the umbrella trees in Hunters Hill. On the bedroom floor, shifting white lines of sunlight fall from between the slats of the venetian blind. Aside from the strange incident the night she arrived, she sleeps soundly here, and, feeling relaxed, she picks up Hugh Jackson's journal from the bedside table where she left it the previous night, rereads the last paragraph, and sighs. She is happy for Hugh, but envious, too. How wonderful it must be to feel that shared intimacy, and to know that your passion is reciprocated, to be willing to take risks and embrace the unknown.

It is something she has never experienced, and, looking back, she recalls too many nights when sex was ignited by too many vodkas. Too many nights when she was too tired, or too uptight, to let herself go. Too many guys who turned out to be boring, pretentious or demanding. Someone should explore the unequal balance between sex and power, she thinks, the pressure on women to be assertive and compliant at the same time. Although she is delighted by the honesty of Hugh's last entry, she is surprised that such a private man committed this intimate experience to paper, especially in a journal intended to be part of a war record.

She is still mulling this over when her phone rings. It's Oliver. 'Just checking in, sis,' he says, and she smiles at the sound of his voice, a little spark of Australia in St Helier. 'So how are things in Shangri-La?'

'I've met an interesting lawyer —' she begins.

'Hang on, that's a contradiction in terms right there,' he cuts in. Then he adds, 'I hope that's not the best thing that's happened?'

She tells him about Bob Blampied and the Neolithic mound that predates the pyramids, but she comes back to Daniel and his research.

'I'm seriously worried about you, Xan. You've travelled across the world and all you've come up with is a lawyer, a nonagenarian, and a pile of old rocks,' Oliver observes. 'I suppose next you'll find a talking dog.'

'Well, now that you mention it …' she replies, and they both laugh. She is still chuckling when the phone rings again. She thinks Oliver's forgotten to tell her something, but this time it's Daniel.

'I've bought two tickets for a symphony concert tonight. Feel like coming?'

'Thanks, but they'll be wasted on me. I'm not into classical music.'

'So what kind of music are you into?'

She senses a challenge and hesitates. Actually she prefers movies to music. Movies are engrossing and leave no space for thoughts. At the cinema she can lose herself. But during concerts her mind wanders along its usual thorny paths. Last year her parents had taken her to the Sydney Opera House see *South Pacific* for her birthday. She couldn't focus on the story, and the music became the background for the painful reel that kept playing inside her head about a patient she had misdiagnosed. The last singer she enjoyed was Adele at the Acer Arena, but that was because the anguished lyrics of disappointment and heartbreak the singer belted out resonated with her own mood. All things considered, she doubts if Daniel would be impressed by her taste in music.

'Jazz,' she says. 'I like jazz.' She hopes he won't ask what kind of jazz.

He doesn't. Instead, he says, 'Come anyway. It's a terrific program. Sabine Myer is playing the Mozart Clarinet Concerto.'

She has never heard of Sabine Myer but she recalls that this was the concerto that Hugh loved, the record his Jewish patient had given him. She remembers that because she cried when she came to the part where Hugh discovered that his patient had committed suicide while listening to that piece of music. She is curious to hear it.

'The second piece they're playing is Shostakovich's Leningrad Symphony,' Daniel says.

'That sounds heavy.'

There's a pause, and she supposes he is considering whether to give up or keep trying. Then he says, 'Why don't you come and see if you like it? You might be pleasantly surprised.'

As they take their seats in one of the horseshoe-shaped balconies that evening, Xanthe notices that the audience is smartly dressed. So is Daniel, who is wearing a crisp long-sleeved linen shirt, top button left open. She is wearing her turquoise Zimmermann outfit, the one he said matched her eyes, and she has left her hair loose, but he doesn't comment on her appearance. No wonder, after her prickly response last time, she thinks.

She looks around, surprised by the elegance of the Jersey Opera House with its ornate Victorian decor. The lights dim, and the soloist, a middle-aged woman in a long evening gown, walks onto the stage, greeted by enthusiastic applause.

'That's Sabine Meyer,' Daniel whispers. 'She's one of the best clarinettists in the world.'

Xanthe stifles a yawn and tries to look interested. He seems to know so much about music. She hopes she won't fall asleep.

The conductor raises his baton, the orchestra strikes up, and a few moments later she is transported to another level of existence. Now she understands why Lionel Stern wanted this to be the last sound he ever heard. All the beauty in the world, all the joy that has eluded her until that moment, is concentrated in this golden melody that swirls all around them. The concerto ends, the soloist bows to a rapturous ovation, and Daniel glances at Xanthe with a questioning look.

She is silent for a few moments. Then she says, 'That was exquisite. It sounded like a human voice expressing every possible mood.'

He smiles. 'I'm glad you decided to come.'

He leans so close that she can smell his aftershave, and whispers in her ear, 'At the risk of being inappropriate, can I say you look lovely?'

'Ouch,' she retorts, suppressing a smile.

It's interval, and there's an excited buzz in the foyer as patrons discuss the performance in animated voices. While she listens to their enthusiastic comments, Daniel joins the crowd milling around the bar, then pushes his way towards her holding two flutes of champagne. She would prefer to leave now while she is still bewitched by the concerto, but the gong sounds, and they follow the crowd back into the concert hall.

'Shostakovich lived in daily fear of being arrested by Stalin's secret police,' Daniel tells her as they take their seats. 'He used to leave a packed suitcase by the front door in case the secret police came for him during the night.'

So it's bound to be heavy, she thinks, and steels herself for an onslaught of anguish.

But from the first dramatic bars of the opening movement, she is transfixed by its raw emotion. This is terror, angst and trauma set to music. Her heart is beating fast, and without realising it, her nails leave deep crescents in her palms.

She has never heard anything like it, and the terrifying music reverberates in her head as they leave the concert hall.

'So, what do you think of Shostakovich?' he asks as they drive along Gloucester Road towards the town centre.

'I feel as if I've just lived through all that oppression and terror myself.'

Twenty minutes later, inside the busy bar of the Royal Yacht Hotel, she is still affected by the power of that symphony. Staring into her vodka and lemon, she says, 'If I put my life to music, that's exactly how it would sound.'

He looks surprised. 'How do you mean?'

She drains the vodka and sits back, her eyes fixed on something in the distance. 'Turmoil and tension. Everything unravelling. Fragile enough to snap any moment. That's how my life has been in the past year.'

He doesn't comment, but the way he sits forward and gives her his entire attention encourages her to continue. Perhaps it's his stillness and concentration, the way he doesn't take his eyes off her face, almost as though he has stopped breathing in suspense, and for the first time she opens up about her traumatic year.

She tells him about the relentless anxiety she felt during ward rounds, petrified of missing vital signs or prescribing the wrong medication in case she killed a patient. Her dread of being humiliated by her registrar and mocked by the sister in charge of the ward. About the terrible moment she walked into Sumi's room and saw her friend hanging from a hook in the door.

She pauses, and then describes the moment she stood on the hospital terrace, and considered jumping off because ending her life seemed an easier option than living it.

'All my life I wanted to be a doctor, but I ended up being a failure,' she says, and sighs. 'I don't suppose you know how that feels.'

He has listened in silence and when she stops talking, he reaches across the small table and takes her hand. She likes the feel of it, strong and warm and secure.

'So that's why the tears the other morning when we discussed your family. I had no idea you've been through such a rough time,' he says in a hoarse voice. 'You come across as so confident.'

She blows her nose and tries to smile. 'So now you've had a glimpse of the crumbling ruin behind the facade.'

He is studying her, and under his scrutiny she once again can't stop the tears falling. This is the second time she has cried in front of him, and she wonders what it is about him that dissolves her defences.

'Actually, I do know how failure feels,' he says slowly. 'After graduating, I struggled for a few years in a legal firm. Everyone told me how lucky I was to land a job in one of the biggest law firms in Melbourne, but I hated the culture of the place, the arrogance of the partners, and the trivial work I was doing. Charging people for every five minutes of my time made me feel like shit. I dreaded going to the office every day, but I thought there must be something wrong with me because everyone else seemed to be thriving. That place would have destroyed me if I hadn't done my Masters and found my niche in lecturing and researching.'

Her tears have stopped as she listens.

'That experience taught me that whether you're a success or a failure, you basically have the same problem,' he says, swirling the ice in his glass of Chivas Regal. 'Either way, you have to decide what to do next.'

The simple wisdom of this is a revelation. It had never occurred to her that instead of bashing herself up about the past, she should just focus on where to go from here.

'You've taken a huge step by getting out of your terrible situation and coming here to give yourself time to think,' he says. 'You're stronger than you imagine.'

It's a positive spin, and she appreciates it. 'I've always thought I was escaping rather than creating something new.' She tells him about her brother.

'Sounds as if you two are close,' he comments.

She nods. 'He called me this morning. Thought I sounded a lot calmer since coming here.'

'Do you have any idea why?' Something in the way Daniel says this, and raises his eyebrows, makes her wonder whether he is teasing her. Or flirting. Uncertain how to respond, she leaves his question dangling in the air and changes the subject.

'Tell me about your visit to the archives. Did you find anything important?'

'Two interesting documents so far. One had nothing to do with the Jews, but it made me realise that, as I suspected, the States' obedience to the laws superseded any moral or ethical considerations.'

'What was it about?'

'Apparently a local warden overheard a neighbour listening to an illegal radio, and he wasn't sure whether he should report it or not. In other words, should he obey the law or his conscience? So he asked the Attorney-General for his opinion. He was told that it was up to him, but if he did report it, the Attorney-General would be obliged to inform the Germans because that was the law.

'So what did he do?'

'He decided to go ahead and report the guy with the radio and the Attorney-General informed the Germans who sent the man to a prison in Germany where he died. But everyone behaved correctly according to the German orders. The law was the law, no matter what.'

Xanthe recalls parts of Hugh Jackson's diary in which he referred to the danger of listening to his clandestine radio. She had wondered if he was exaggerating, but now she understands why he had taken so much trouble to conceal it.

'What about the other document?' she asks.

'That one displays their attitude towards the Jews, which seemed quite different from their attitude to the rest of the population. According to the German orders of October 1940, all members of the British armed forces had to report to the Attorney-General's office, and all Jews were to be registered and their businesses marked with a *Jüdisches geschäft* sign. What happened was that the Bailiff tried to protect as many of the British army personnel as possible, but in the case of the Jews, he passed all the information over to the German authorities without comment. What I find illuminating is that he saw no conflict between his role as the representative of the British crown, and his actions in enforcing Nazi anti-Semitism.'

'But doesn't that conflict with your theory about abiding by the law no matter what? Because in spite of the German orders, they did their best to protect the British army people.'

'Yes, but their obedience was selective, wasn't it? Where one group was concerned, they tried to circumvent the order, but with the others, they just complied.'

It's getting late, and she nibbles the crisps from the bowl on the table while he orders another Chivas Regal. She decides against another vodka. The subject they're discussing is complex, and she wants to keep a clear head. She thinks about Hugh's patient Lionel Stern committing suicide for fear of being deported, and wonders what happened to Mrs Goldman, who had disappeared.

'So do you put this down to anti-Semitism? she asks.

'It's too soon to generalise. I need to do a lot more research. In fact, I'm going to have a chat with my recalcitrant relative about it. As his father was Bailiff at the time, he can probably shed some light on the prevailing attitudes.'

'After his reaction last time, I wonder if he'll even agree to see you.'

Daniel shrugs. 'I think he'll see me, if only to try and convince me I'm misguided.'

'I'd like to be a fly on the wall during that conversation,' she says.

'Then come with me. That will make the meeting more informal. And he might find it less threatening.'

As they get up to leave the bar, she sees Bill McAllister sitting at the little round table by the window where she saw the strange old man with the unforgiving expression during her first visit. Sitting with Bill, nursing a lager, is Bob Blampied, whose white hair is lit up by the lamp overhead.

Since she last saw Bob, she has read more of Hugh's journal, and there are questions she'd like to ask him about life during the Occupation, so when Bill invites her and Daniel to join them for a nightcap, she jumps at the chance.

'So you're still here?' she says to Bill, and, turning to Daniel explains that he is a detective from Sussex.

'Aye, still here. I canna think of a nicer place to be.'

She is curious about the incest case he was investigating when they met, and the children's bones found in the grounds of an institution where single mothers had their babies. But he may not want to discuss his work in public so instead, she tells Bob how much she enjoyed their day together.

'Bob is a tour guide extraordinaire,' she tells Daniel. Turning back to Bob, she says, 'If you can spare another day, I'd love to see more of Jersey.'

Bob is clearly delighted. 'Young lady, I'm entirely at your service whenever you wish,' he says, gallantly placing his hand over his heart and inclining his head towards her.

'You've obviously won two hearts there,' Daniel comments as they head towards his car.

Driving along the coast, with few cars on the road, the only sound she hears is the slapping of the waves against the shore. The granite silhouettes of gun emplacements loom ahead in the darkness, and she thinks about the long tunnels dug by the picks and shovels of the slave labourers. She plans to ask Bob about them when they meet.

'I often wonder what it must have been like to live here during the Occupation,' Daniel says. 'People here are so friendly and the place is so pretty and peaceful. It's hard to imagine people living in fear of their neighbours dobbing them in, and the Germans deporting them to concentration camps.'

Leaving the coast road, he turns inland and parks the car outside her place. 'So when are you going to meet your elderly beau again?'

'You sound jealous,' she says.

He turns towards her, placing his arm along the back of her seat. 'I am jealous. Can't you tell?'

He is teasing her again.

'Great evening, thanks,' she says.

She sounds uncertain, as if she has missed a vital cue somewhere along the way. But before she can slide out of her seat, he leans across. She supposes he'll brush her cheek as he did last time, but this time he kisses her lips hungrily, exploring the inside of her mouth with a passion that takes her by surprise. Her body is tingling with an urgency she hasn't felt for a long time.

'Why don't we go inside?' she says in a husky voice she hardly recognises.

As soon as she has opened the front door, his arms are around her, holding her so tightly she can hardly breathe, kissing her eyes, her cheeks, her neck. He cups her face tenderly in his hands and gazes at her with an exciting intensity.

Without saying a word, she takes his hand and leads him upstairs.

CHAPTER EIGHTEEN

Tom

St Helier, May 1943

The punch came from nowhere and slammed him into the wall of his cell. Without letting up, the burly guard kept bashing him, landing a barrage of blows that smashed into his face and body. With each blow, panting with exertion, the guard screamed, '*Schweinehund!* Just wait! You'll get what's coming to you!'

After a final vicious punch, he banged the door shut behind him, and the sound reverberated inside Tom's head like cymbals clashing. Dizzy and doubled up in pain on the floor of the cell, blood pouring from his nose, he was in despair. Alone for the first time, he went over the horrific events of that night. Poor Frank drowned, all their plans of escape ruined, and he and Harry imprisoned, awaiting their fate.

Of course he had always known that they risked being caught, but now that he was at the mercy of his German captors, he realised that he had been living in a fantasy world where danger was a distant and abstract notion, disconnected from the reality of treacherous tides and vicious guards. The terrible fate of Francois Scornet, blindfolded and shot, now loomed before him. How idyllic his former life looked from the confines of his prison cell and the bleakness of his future. He swallowed hard to stop the tears. He would have given anything to be home again, in the safety of his comfortable bedroom instead of lying in pain in this tiny cold cell, terrified of what lay ahead.

You've made your bed, so you have to lie in it, he could hear his mother saying. It was one of her favourite put-downs. But he did not want to think about his mother. Lying there in the dark, his mind wandered back to the moment when the dinghy capsized and Frank fell into the water. None of it seemed real. Frank couldn't be dead. He could see him now, laughing and joking as they raced down to the Slip, or arguing and pulling his left ear. How could he have drowned? It was hard to grasp that it all happened only a few hours ago. He could still see Frank's panic-stricken face as his friend clutched him and kept pulling him underwater. He could feel the numbing coldness of the sea as he struggled to keep Frank afloat. But had he tried hard enough?

Now the self-recrimination began again. How could he have suggested taking their life jackets off and then failed to put them back on, when they had brought them in case of this very eventuality, especially as Frank couldn't swim? His thoughts turned to Frank's parents, especially his kind mother, and he covered his face with his hands and let out a long groan. They must be distraught. What must they think of him?

Tom tried sitting up and was almost grateful for the physical pain that distracted him from his thoughts. He saw it all now with horrible clarity. The whole disaster, every bit of it, from choosing Green Island, buying the defective boat, bringing the incriminating maps and album, discarding the life jackets, Frank drowning and now their captivity. It was all his fault.

His thoughts turned to Harry, who was locked up in the adjoining cell. He had lied to him by omission. He hadn't told him how he had obtained the money for the dinghy because he'd known that Harry wouldn't approve. He'd kept him in the dark about bringing the album with the photographs of the military fortifications as well. Harry, who had such strong principles, had become the victim of his misguided optimism and duplicity. The least he could do was to take responsibility for it all and convince the Krauts that Harry was innocent. Maybe if he could persuade them to release Harry, it would ease his conscience.

Outside his cell, he heard the harsh metallic sound of bolts being pushed back, doors opening and slamming shut, iron buckets clanging, and guttural German voices yelling abuse. Bloody Krauts. They always yelled. Aching all over, he felt as though he'd been run over by a truck. His nose throbbed, and as he tried to stem the flow of blood with his sleeve, it felt strange, and he was sure it was broken. Every movement made him wince and moan. But he hadn't screamed while the brute was bashing him. At least he hadn't given the sadist the satisfaction of knowing how much pain he had inflicted.

That made him feel a little less helpless, even a bit more hopeful. Perhaps tomorrow his parents would come to the prison and intercede for him. Maybe if they explained that he and Harry got lost while on a fishing trip, they'd be released.

Then he stopped daydreaming. It was his mother who had betrayed him, and obviously his father hadn't stopped her.

But it was his father who was the biggest disappointment of his life. The hero he had idolised had feet of clay. So there was no point expecting help from either of them. The bitterness he felt was sharper than physical pain, and greater than the fear of what lay ahead.

It was hurtful, but not surprising, that his mother, whose behaviour was one of the main reasons he had been so desperate to escape, had informed on him to her cronies in the Water Police. She was responsible for his predicament. He clenched his fists.

'I'll never forgive her,' he muttered through swollen lips. 'Never.'

He must have dropped off to sleep because in his dream a huge wave was about to engulf him. He woke with a start, relieved until he looked up at the barred window and heard hateful German voices. It wasn't a nightmare; it was grim reality.

A moment later, his door was unlocked, and another guard burst in and ordered him to get up. He staggered to his feet and hobbled along the passageway to the washroom while the guard kept shouting *'Raus! Schnell!'* When he looked in the small cracked mirror above the metal basin, it took him a few seconds to realise that the image he saw was his own.

His bruised and swollen face was covered in dried blood like an amateur boxer beaten to a pulp by a champion.

With his hands shackled behind his back, he was taken downstairs and hustled into a waiting car. As they drove along the streets of St Helier, dawn was breaking and the sky was the colour of fairy floss. He stared straight ahead, relieved that it was too early for anyone he knew to see him bloodied and handcuffed inside a police car.

The car stopped at Victoria College, which was the headquarters of the Feldkommandatur and the Gestapo. Tom took a deep breath to try and steady his nerves. His handcuffs were removed, and he was pushed into an interrogation room where two officers in plain clothes sat behind a large oak table smoking French cigarettes. Gestapo, probably. He swallowed hard and hoped they couldn't tell how frightened he was.

The older of the two, a thin man with hollow cheeks, close-cropped iron grey hair and rimless spectacles, tamped out his cigarette in the metal ashtray, took off his glasses, and leaned forward. Without any preamble, he asked in English, 'Tell me who was behind your escape.'

Tom shook his head. 'But we weren't trying to escape,' he said, trying to look innocent. 'We were on a fishing trip.'

At this, the plump face of the younger officer distorted with fury. Pushing his chair back so fast that it fell onto the cement floor, he loomed over Tom with a menacing expression. 'Don't talk nonsense. If you lie to us, it will be worse for you. Tell us at once who planned this escape and who told you to take those photographs for the English.'

Tom's heart sank. So they had found the album. He had hoped it had been washed far away when the boat tipped over.

For several hours, they continued interrogating him, asking the same questions over and over. It was obvious that they didn't believe that three teenage boys could have concocted and carried out this plan without any help from adults, and that gave Tom a feeling of perverse pride. He had achieved something beyond their vision of what British boys could do.

But as the questioning continued, their tone became more threatening, and his bravado abandoned him.

'Stop wasting our time and admit that you were going to hand those photographs of German military fortifications and aeroplanes to the British. Tell us about the British army officers and spies who planned your escape,' the younger officer shouted.

By now the ashtray was overflowing with cigarette butts, and the overpowering smell of nicotine made Tom feel sick, but the scenario that the police agent had described reminded him of the adventure stories he used to read. In those stories the brave British hero always triumphed over the evil enemy, but confronted by these Gestapo agents, Tom wondered if his courage would last. The notion that he was in league with British military spies was so far-fetched that in spite of the danger he was in, he gave an involuntary laugh.

Once again the younger interrogator sprang from his chair. He grabbed Tom's collar so tightly that he almost lifted him from his seat, choking him.

'You'll be laughing on the other side of your face before long, because you're in big trouble,' he shouted. 'You've committed treason, and that's punishable by death. We have enough evidence to have you shot.'

Tom clenched his fists to conceal the trembling in his hands. Surely they wouldn't shoot him? But maybe they would. He had to get out of this situation, but how? While these thoughts were spinning in his head, his interrogators switched to German. They assumed he couldn't understand, but thanks to his mother's insistence on German lessons, Tom could follow their conversation. However, it struck him that it might be smarter to pretend he couldn't understand them.

It sounded as though the senior agent was inclined to believe his story but the younger one was convinced he was lying.

As soon as they turned their attention back to him, Tom said in a polite tone, 'I swear to you no-one else was involved. It was just the three of us going out fishing. And we never met any English spies.'

'You are still at school, so how come you had enough money to buy a boat?' the older man asked. 'Someone must have given you the money.'

'No-one did, I swear,' Tom replied. 'I love fishing, so I was saving my pocket money, and I earned the rest running errands for my mother.'

He was on the point of mentioning that his mother was a good friend of the chief Water Police officer, but at the last moment he refrained. They probably knew that already, and he felt it would be demeaning to use her shameful behaviour in his defence.

Although he kept insisting that it was a fishing trip, the interrogation went on relentlessly. They kept repeating the same questions to trip him up but he stuck to his guns, hoping that they would give up and release him.

At the end of that long day he was driven back to the prison. The next morning, and the one after that, he was driven back to the Feldkommandatur for further questioning. At the end of the third day, the senior detective took off his glasses, held them up to the light, wiped them with a spotless white handkerchief and put them back on.

Sitting back in his chair, he said, 'You don't seem to realise that you are in big trouble and all these lies are making things worse for you. We know all about the map you marked with our military installations, and the photographs you took of the fortresses and bunkers and emplacements. There could only be one reason for bringing those things with you on the boat, and it wasn't to help you catch fish.

'You're lucky that we are civilised people and don't shoot schoolboys, because what you did would warrant putting you in front of the firing squad. Did you stop to think about the worry you've caused your poor mother? I feel sorry for her, having an irresponsible son like you.'

Tom could see that there was no point insisting on the fishing trip any longer, and he was wondering how to answer their questions when the interrogation ended as abruptly as it had begun. Without another word, the agents stood up, grabbed his arms, and pushed him towards the door. As they headed outside, towards the waiting car, the older one said in a menacing tone, 'We'll get the truth out of you before long.'

While a guard handcuffed him and bundled him into the police car, the younger agent sneered, 'Pity you didn't wait a few weeks, because soon you'll be able to sail to England legally. In a matter of weeks, it will be part of the Reich!'

He could still hear them laughing as the car pulled away.

Back in his cell, Tom vacillated between hope and despair. He kept going over their questions, his answers, and their comments. They had said *We don't shoot schoolboys.* Perhaps that meant they would dismiss the whole escapade as a schoolboy prank and send him and Harry home. If only he hadn't brought that album. But he couldn't get the agent's threatening comment out of his mind.

He spent the next few days glued to the window that looked out onto a small yard where female prisoners exercised. He wondered whether Milly knew about his predicament, and whether she would come and visit him. But then he remembered her Kraut boyfriend. Even if she knew, she probably wouldn't care.

Some nights he managed to communicate in whispers with Harry in the adjoining cell.

'I don't understand why my parents haven't come to see me,' Harry whispered back. 'Maybe they've washed their hands of me.'

Knowing Harry's parents, Tom didn't believe that, but when he asked a guard why they hadn't had any family visits, he was punched in the stomach and told to shut up because he had no right to see anyone. He knew that even convicted prisoners were entitled to family visits once a week. There had to be some reason why he and Harry were being isolated, but no-one would tell them why.

'Listen,' Tom whispered, 'when they question you, just tell them you didn't know anything about the escape, that it was all my idea.'

Harry's reply was predictable. 'I'm not going to lie,' he said.

Several days later, they were both handcuffed and escorted from the prison by two *feldgendarms* in metal breastplates with pistols in their holsters.

They were pushed into a black car that drove along Gloucester Street, and then turned into the Esplanade. At the sight of the Esplanade, Tom's heart ached with memories of cycling, ice creams and Milly. For one crazy moment he thought perhaps they were going to be taken home. But at the weighbridge the car turned towards the dock where a cargo ship was berthed. They were ordered to climb down into the hold.

After an hour, the ship shuddered and the engines came to life. They were uncuffed and allowed to go up on deck but warned if they tried anything they'd be shot. They climbed up the iron ladder in time to see that they were rounding White Rock. Behind them, the spires and church towers of St Helier were becoming smaller, and their town was receding in the distance.

Tom turned to Harry, and his face was white. 'We must be on our way to France,' he said. He turned away so Harry couldn't see the fear in his eyes. When would he see his island again?

They disembarked at Granville in Normandy and, escorted by the two *feldgendarms*, they boarded a train for Paris. At the Gare Montparnasse, their escorts told them they had an urgent errand, but Tom knew from their conversation that they were going to a brothel. He and Harry were unshackled, given a bowl of tasteless soup, and left in the care of an armed German sailor.

When Tom told their guard that he needed to go to the toilet, the sailor pointed to a staircase at the far end of the platform, but to Tom's surprise, he made no move to accompany him.

Running down the stairs to the platform below, Tom found himself in the midst of a crowd rushing to and from the trains. The station was full of French civilians and German soldiers, but no-one gave him a second glance. Ahead of him was an exit sign and a large iron gate that led to Boulevard Montparnasse. He stopped. He could just go through that large iron gate and keep running. By the time the sailor realised he hadn't come back, he'd be far away. Free. He could speak French. Perhaps some kind person would help him? Somehow he'd survive till the war was over.

Then the fantasy vanished. With a sigh he turned on his heel and went back upstairs. He couldn't abandon Harry.

The two *feldgendarms* returned looking pleased with themselves. They handcuffed them again and dragged them down the stairs to a cobbled lane where a black Citroën was waiting.

The car sped through the outskirts of Paris and followed a sign to Domaine de Fresnes along an avenue lined with tall poplars. They drove through a massive gate and were handed over to a German army sergeant. Tom looked around. All he could see were barracks surrounding a massive central courtyard. They were in the huge military prison of Fresnes.

Harry saw Tom's expression. 'Buck up,' he said. 'Don't let them get you down. We'll get through this. Remember we're British!'

Tom managed a smile. If Harry could put on a brave face, he could too.

But later, inside a cell that was no bigger than a broom cupboard, without either toilet or window, fear overwhelmed him. Throughout the night he heard screams, the sound of blows, and guttural German curses. He knew that they had left their familiar life far behind and entered one of the circles of hell.

CHAPTER NINETEEN

Dr Jackson

St Helier, July 1943

I wrote my will yesterday.

This might sound dramatic, but I feel as though Damocles' sword is poised above my head. There's an outbreak of diphtheria in St Helier at the moment, so last week, when a woman telephoned to ask me to see her son who had a bad cough, I suspected diphtheria straight away. And as soon as I saw the child, my suspicions were confirmed. He was in a very bad way with a thready pulse and that dreadful hacking cough. He didn't look as if he'd last the night, but the panic-stricken mother was still insisting that it was just a cough, so I offered to look at his throat. I bent over him to demonstrate what I meant by opening wide, and at that precise moment he coughed right into my open mouth. The poor child was so far gone that there was nothing I could do for him, and he died that night. But considering the high rate of contagion, I expect I'll catch it now, and as Jersey's supply of anti-toxin is severely depleted, my odds of surviving are not favourable.

Contemplating how to dispose of my worldly goods has been a salutary experience. Taking an inventory, I realised that apart from the house, my second-hand Austin and my bicycle, I have little of value to bequeath. And with the dire shortage of petrol, the car is not a great asset.

It's not much to show for so many years of study and medical practice. When I think about it, the best indication of the state we are in is the fact that my most valuable assets are probably my Kilner jars of preserved chickens and bottled fruit, dried bread rusks, French wines and spirits, and the barrels of cider I made last autumn from my apples.

The house I will leave to Jamie, the bicycle to my friend Will de Gruchy, and I'll distribute the food among my patients, many of whom are suffering as a result of rationing. To give an example, while the Germans in their comfortable leather boots are gorging themselves on full cream milk and first-rate beef, housewives queue for hours in their wooden clogs — there are no shoes in the shops, and even if there were, they wouldn't be able to afford them — to get their small ration of skim milk and two ounces of scrawny French beef.

When I considered what I could leave my darling Aoife, I decided the best thing would be cash, so that she can purchase whatever she needs for herself or for the hospital and, as she has a very sweet tooth, I'll leave her my jars of honey.

Have I mentioned the honey? I don't really know what possessed me to buy a swarm of bees last summer from one of my patients, an elderly widow who lives near the Marais du Val. All my life I've been terrified of bees, having been stung so badly as a boy that for days I couldn't open my eyes and thought I was going to die. So I don't understand the crazy impulse that made me decide to buy the whole swarm.

As I tried to follow the apiarist's complicated instructions about buying hives and brood boxes lined with wax, I became thoroughly confused, and wondered what on earth I'd let myself into.

My heart was in my mouth while I was taking her swarm home in a hive, and I listened with trepidation to the frightening racket the bees made in the car. I didn't breathe out until I opened the hive and they flew out in search of elder, hawthorn and clover.

But in the end, my mad impulse was richly rewarded because these bees produced the best honey I've ever tasted. I ended up with over one hundred pounds of it, which is a welcome sweetener now that sugar has disappeared from our rations.

'You were very brave to take the swarm when you were so frightened of bees,' Aoife said when I gave her a jar the first time she came to my house for dinner. In the interests of honesty, I was about to explain it was madness rather than courage, but she was gazing at me with such admiration that I accepted the compliment with a smile.

Dinner that night was an enormous success. I'll never forget the look on her face when I brought out one of the chickens I'd preserved. But my attempt to provide a postprandial smoke was a dismal failure. It turned out that, like me, she enjoys smoking after dinner. Cigarettes are a rare luxury but someone had advised me to try dried blackberry leaves as a tobacco substitute.

Unfortunately the leaves emitted thick black smoke that tasted foul and made us both dizzy. But at least it gave us a good excuse to go to bed early.

It might seem that these experiments with bees and leaves are a bit of an adventure, but there is nothing exciting about having to live on two ounces of meat a week and scrounging to make the other meagre rations last until the next allocation. Although I prefer to describe successes rather than dwell on failures, I don't want to create the impression that life during the Occupation is a series of triumphs over adversity. It is a constant struggle.

I should add that my situation isn't typical because I am more fortunate than most people here. For one thing, I live alone, and for another, I anticipated the shortages and not only began to prepare provisions from the very start of the Occupation, but I also planted out vegetables and bottled my summer fruit. What's more, patients who own farms often supplement my rations with a piece of pork or beef, or a pat of butter.

But by far the luckiest aspect of my life is sharing it with Aoife.

'Do you ever feel guilty that we are so happy together when most people are suffering?' I asked her one night, propping myself up on an elbow to gaze at her, to convince myself, yet again, that she was really here, lying in my bed.

She shook her head, and her russet locks spread out on the pillow reminded me of a sensuous pre-Raphaelite painting.

'I grew up in Ireland, and I was brought up on guilt and hellfire, but I got over it. Life is a gift we only receive once, and we have to treasure every single minute while we still have it,' she said.

Just the same, there are times when I can't stop thinking of what lies ahead for us. We know that the war must end sooner or later, and, judging by the defeat of the German army in North Africa, which I was overjoyed to hear about recently on the BBC News, perhaps that will be sooner rather than later.

On a personal level, though, I wonder what will happen to me and Margaret. Our situation, living in marital limbo, can't continue forever. What if she returns to St Helier with Jamie? I don't suppose she'll want a reunion after the rift that has widened between us over so many years, but will she agree to a divorce?

Some women refuse to divorce unless their spouse admits to desertion or adultery, but a public admission of adultery would be embarrassing for me and for Aoife. She might lose her position at the hospital due to the scandal. And how will I feel when I see my boy for the first time? Will I have to make a choice that involves giving him up?

I know I want to be free to start a new life with Aoife. The joy I feel with her is so intense that I never want our lovemaking to end. I never knew it could be like this, that I was capable of feeling such passion and delight. Sometimes I feel such ecstasy that if I died in her arms, I would die happy. Compared with the way I feel about Aoife, everything I have experienced in the past is a pallid imitation.

But whenever I talk about the future, Aoife places a finger over my mouth and whispers. 'There is no future and no past. There is only now.'

I admire her philosophical attitude, but no matter how hard I try, I can't focus fully on the present. I have always sought answers. I have never felt comfortable with doubt, and now a dark corner of my mind dwells on an uncertain future.

But from what I see in my surgery every day, I realise that the only certainty we have is that the future is unpredictable. As a doctor, I feel helpless when I'm unable to provide the medications patients need. Just the other day Miss le Prevost was in tears as she begged me to do something for her diabetic mother, but we've run out of insulin, so there's nothing I can do. When I make house calls, distraught parents wring their hands because their children are hungry and they don't have enough food for them. Young girls are distraught because they have fallen in love with a German soldier and are terrified of what their parents will say.

That brings me to Betty, a street-smart nineteen year old who came to see me last week, her face partly covered by a scarf. When she removed it, I was shocked to see her black eye, split lip and swollen cheek.

'My dad,' she said before I had time to ask what happened. 'Someone told him I had a German boyfriend. He said I was a whore and belted me.' A venomous look came over her pretty face. 'But I got me own back. I went to the police and told them he had a pistol hidden in the attic.'

I was aghast. I didn't know what horrified me more, his violence or her vengeance.

'Did you realise what might happen?' I asked.

She shrugged. 'They'll probably send him to jail. That'll give him time to think about what he did to me.' Then she added, 'This wasn't the first time he beat me up. At least Otto is nice to me.'

I looked at Betty, sitting there with a defiant expression on her bruised face, and I was at a loss what to say.

'Do you love each other?' I asked at last.

She gave a sly smile. 'He gives me perfume and flowers, not like the local fellows.'

For all she knew, he might be married, and I was about to issue a kindly warning, but something about her made me stop and look at her more carefully. Unlike most of my patients, Betty had put on weight, and I wondered if she had told me the whole story.

'Do you think you might be pregnant?' I asked.

She looked down and pressed her lips together, and I knew the answer.

After telling her how to reduce the swelling on her face, I advised her to come back and see me in a month's time so I could monitor the pregnancy. After she left, I thought about her situation. What she had done in denouncing her father was reprehensible, but if he had a history of violence, perhaps she had been driven to it.

Sometimes it's hard to refrain from making judgements, but the more you know about people's lives, the harder it is to judge their actions. Betty would need all the support she could get in the coming months, and I decided that the most important thing was for her to know she could come and talk to me.

Looking after a baby in these times is very difficult and I don't envy new mothers, even when they don't have the added stress of German boyfriends and furious parents. Aoife has told me how hard it is to keep premature babies alive in hospital when power restrictions and fuel shortages mean that they only have candles for lighting and hot-water bottles to keep the babies warm. I'm amazed that despite those problems, very few babies have died, but that's due to the superb nursing at the hospital.

From my patients I know how tough life is for new mothers who have to get up on cold nights to feed or pacify babies in the dark, without being able to keep warm or heat up their food. You can't find a thermos flask for love or money.

I was still thinking about Betty the following morning when I left home to do my rounds. I was humming 'You Are My Sunshine' as I headed for the Jersey Maternity Hospital, which is always my first call of the day. At the hospital Aoife and I always maintain a professional demeanour, careful not to give ourselves away by our lingering glances. Clearing my throat, I said 'Good morning, matron. I came to see if I'm needed today.'

'Oh, you certainly are that,' she replied, with that mischievous sparkle in her eyes.

The sky looked bluer than usual and the sun shone more brightly as I continued my daily rounds. This time I was heading along the east road towards Gorey, one of my favourite places on the island.

The view of Mt Orgueil looming over the harbour never fails to make me catch my breath, and I'm always struck by the contrast between the grandeur of that medieval fortress and the rustic furrows of the ploughed potato fields rising steeply above the fishing village that faces the port.

But this time I hadn't come to have tea and scones in one of the charming little teashops in the village. I was hurrying to get to Trinity up in the north-east.

My motive for going to this distant part of the island wasn't connected with patients but with escaped slave labourers. I was heading for an old stone farmhouse that belonged to Mary and Will de Gruchy, who were part of our rescue network.

Sheltering escaped slave labourers has become more dangerous than ever, as the Germans spare no effort to track them down. But knowing the cruelty they face if they are caught has made us redouble our efforts to prevent them from falling into the brutal hands of the German overseers of Organisation Todt. It is horrible to know that on our island innocent people have been starved, beaten to a pulp, strung up by their thumbs, or stripped naked and doused with iced water, and we are helpless in the face of this barbarity.

Ever since Mrs Carter took Sasha under her wing, we have been able to shelter another escapee. Pierre was found emaciated and in rags, devouring raw potatoes on Will de Gruchy's farm. Distressed at his plight, Will brought him inside and gave him the first proper meal the starving man had had in months.

I've known the de Gruchys for many years. They're the kind of people who are often described as the salt of the earth, hardworking, warm-hearted and reliable. Will's wife Mary had sounded me out several weeks ago about my attitude to the slave labourers, and had offered to become part of our rescue network.

They liked Pierre, and as they had no children, and their farmhouse was fairly isolated, they decided to let him stay, as the risk of being exposed was negligible.

The only regular visitor to the farm was Mrs de la Mare, who came in twice a week to do the cleaning. 'She's been with us for years, she's like one of the family,' Mary assured me.

All had gone well apparently until the previous day when I had a phone call from Mary, who sounded unusually flustered. She rang to ask me to come over as soon as possible. I usually ride thirty to forty miles a day on my bicycle, so I wasn't looking forward to adding to my mileage by visiting their remote farm on what didn't appear to be a medical issue, but Mary wasn't prone to needless panic, so that morning as soon as I had attended to my other patients, I cycled over.

Will met me at the farmhouse door. He spoke unusually fast and sounded agitated. It turned out that when they discovered that their trusted cleaner had stolen some money from them, she threatened to tell the police that they were harbouring an escaped slave labourer.

'I don't give in to blackmail,' Will told me. 'I warned her that if she said a word about Pierre, I'd charge her with theft, and I sacked her there and then.'

I advised them to move Pierre to another safe house as soon as possible, and to destroy his clothes and every sign that he'd ever been there, but I had a feeling that they hadn't heard the last of it.

As soon as I got home, I telephoned Bob Blampied. I didn't trust the telephone exchange, and just in case someone was listening in, I told him that my cat had just had a litter of kittens and I needed a home for one of them. He understood and promised to make inquiries.

It's been at least a week since my last entry, but I have been so busy that by the time I return home, I'm too exhausted to write. So I'll continue where I left off. The day after my visit to the de Gruchy farm, as I was having my usual breakfast of hot water and lemon sweetened with honey, and one of my dried rusks with a boiled egg, my telephone rang. It was Will de Gruchy, and he seemed to be speaking through clenched teeth.

'Please come as soon as possible. Mary is desperately ill. Be sure to bring your doctor's bag.' With that he hung up.

I didn't think there was anything wrong with Mary, who had seemed perfectly well the day before, but from Will's tone and strange final comment, I knew something serious had happened. It's not often that a patient reminds a doctor to bring his bag.

As I hurriedly pulled on my trousers, I noticed that I would have to punch another hole in my belt which wasn't surprising, considering all that cycling and my diminished diet.

Their farm is picturesquely situated at the foot of Les Platons, the loftiest point on our island, but I was too preoccupied to appreciate the view, and kept cycling until I reached the farmhouse.

No wonder Will had sounded panic-stricken. Parked outside were two Opel police cars. As I had feared, Mrs de la Mare had denounced them. The front door had been left unlocked and, as I walked in, my heart was hammering in my ears and I wondered how I could possibly help.

Downstairs, two policemen gave me a suspicious look, but seeing my doctor's bag, they waved me through and continued rifling through drawers, throwing the contents of cupboards onto the floor, and poking at the back of shelves. I couldn't help wondering why someone searching for a fugitive would be rifling through drawers, but I suppose they were searching for incriminating items. I held my breath, hoping they wouldn't find Will's hidden radio.

'Doctor, thank goodness you're here! Come upstairs, Mary has taken a turn for the worse,' Will was shouting from the top of the stairs. I ran up two at a time, and saw Mary lying in bed, propped up on a large pillow while a German *feldgendarm* was checking every coathanger.

She certainly didn't look well, but at that moment I didn't feel too well myself, and as for Will, his face had a greenish tinge.

'How's your cough today?' I asked, giving her a meaningful look.

She got the message and uttered a hacking cough. This wasn't difficult as she was a heavy smoker. I had warned her for years about the dire consequences of smoking, but on this occasion, her cough was a godsend. I took out my stethoscope and made worried noises. She coughed again, so loudly that the police officer turned around.

'I'm afraid it's very serious,' I said to Will with as much gravitas as I could muster. 'I think she's got diphtheria. Make sure no-one comes anywhere near her, because it's terribly contagious.'

At this, the *feldgendarm* went downstairs and whispered something to his colleagues, and a few moments later the front door banged behind them.

After the police cars had roared away, Mary slid out of bed and almost collapsed in Will's arms. When she had recovered, she pulled out the pillow she had been lying on, and showed me the radio hidden inside the pillowslip.

As I set off for home, I couldn't stop thinking about Mary and Will's fate had the policemen found the radio. The Germans dealt severely with people who broke their rules, like young Tom and his friend who were caught trying to escape from Green Island. I've heard that not even their parents have been permitted to visit them, which is very odd, as they are such young lads.

No-one seems to have a clue what happened to them, whether they are still on Jersey, or whether they have been sent to France or Germany. It must be nerve-wracking for their families not to know what has happened to them.

I'm very relieved to say that, despite my fears, I didn't contract diphtheria. But I've left my will inside my favourite book, *The Citadel*.

One never knows.

CHAPTER TWENTY

Xanthe

St Helier, April 2019

Before she is fully awake, Xanthe stretches out her arm to feel the other side of the bed but the crumpled sheet is cold and empty. Daniel has gone. Was the tenderness and passion of the previous night merely a dream? Did she really hear him repeat her name in a breathless way no-one had ever done before? And did she quiver in his arms as she joyously lost control and knew that for most of her life, she had been faking it?

Her searching hand touches paper. A handwritten note, hurriedly scrawled. Her head still on the pillow, she reads it. *Sorry, had to go. You were sound asleep, didn't want to wake you. I'll pick you up at twelve. Can't wait to see you.* Then a PS: *I kissed thee ere I left thee, no way but this, that after a night of love to leave you with a kiss!*

She laughs aloud. So he's poetic as well. Like her, he must have studied *Othello* for his HSC. It's already ten o'clock, and over a big leisurely breakfast – thankfully unlike Hugh's spartan meal of dried rusks and hot water she has muesli, scrambled eggs, toast and Nespresso – she reaches for her phone to google *The Citadel*. She has never heard of Hugh's favourite book. The Wikipedia entry states that AJ Cronin was a doctor whose autobiographical novel *The Citadel* was an international bestseller when it was published in 1937. So he was a doctor too. A chain of medicos stretching across nearly a hundred years.

At last it's twelve o'clock, and she runs outside as soon as she hears Daniel's car pull up. He jumps out and wraps his arms around her. 'Let's go back to bed,' he murmurs, nuzzling her ear.

She wonders if he's joking, but she can feel his body harden against her, and a moment later they are running up the stairs two at a time, throwing off their clothes and falling onto the bed, all reference to *Othello* forgotten.

'I couldn't focus on the documents this morning. Couldn't wait to get you into bed again,' he says, gazing at her.

'The earth moved for me too.' She smiles. 'And I loved your *Othello* paraphrase.'

'I thought of quoting *Romeo and Juliet*, but I didn't want to risk bad karma. You know how they ended up.'

'What about *A Midsummer Night's Dream*?' she suggests

'You want to be compared to Bottom the Weaver? Or maybe the Ass?'

They burst out laughing and fall back into bed. When they finally get up, they shower together, and he soaps her body so sensually that she feels like making love again.

As they sit at the kitchen table waiting for the coffee to percolate, she says, 'You mentioned once that you were divorced. Someone from Melbourne?'

What she really wants to know is how long they were together, and what went wrong.

He is stirring the sugar far longer than necessary, and she waits.

Eventually he sums it up. 'We met too young, lived together too long, and married too late. She was the one who wanted to get married, but I already knew it wouldn't work.'

'Even though you were living together?'

'I suppose it became a habit. It wasn't that we didn't get on, but I sensed something was missing. We were more like good mates than lovers. When we split, a great weight dropped off my shoulders, but she was devastated.'

'She obviously didn't think of you as a chum.'

'No. And you? What's your story?'

She shrugs. 'Not much to tell. Too involved in study, too exhausted at work.'

'But you must have had boyfriends over the years?'

She thinks back. They have now all faded into insignificance, the ebullient Russian entrepreneur who introduced her to vodka and wanted to control her life, the arrogant Aussie journo who always let her down, the A&E registrar who was always trying to change something about her …

'You want to hear my litany of failed relationships and unsuitable blokes?'

'What do you think of long-distance relationships?'

She knows where this is heading. 'I had one of those too. It worked for a time until I discovered that distance confers a gloss on relationships that proximity destroys.'

'That sounds cynical.'

She hears disappointment in his tone but before she can amplify her comment, he changes the subject. 'Shall we go out?'

'I'd like to drive to Gorey,' she says. Hugh's account of his visit to the de Gruchy farmhouse has piqued her interest in that part of Jersey.

He glances at his watch. 'I've arranged to see Edward de Courcy at three, and it's almost two now. That's if you still want to come?'

'Of course I do. Maybe we'll have time to go to Gorey later.'

As they drive towards the manor house, along narrow winding country lanes in dazzling sunlight, it feels as if they are driving through a botanical garden lined with tall shrubs and white-flowering hedgerows, where blackbirds caw as they wing among the branches of oaks and maples.

'Speaking of relatives,' Daniel says as they approach Manoir de Courcy, 'have you tried to trace that ancestor of yours?'

She shakes her head. 'I can't see the point. My mother only mentioned Nellie once, in passing, and apart from her first name, I don't know anything about her, or how she was related to us. Obviously it was a very distant connection.'

'Still, why not follow it up while you're here?'

'You're the historian, not me,' she says, as Daniel parks the car outside Manoir de Courcy.

She feels the same heart-beating excitement when she walks through the gate and along the daffodil-lined drive, as she did the first time. Once again she catches her breath when the white-aproned maid ushers them inside the imposing baronial hall that resembles a historical portrait gallery.

But as soon as they enter Edward de Courcy's study, she feels a coolness in the air. With a perfunctory greeting and brusque gesture, Edward motions for them to sit down on the other side of his large oak desk. She glances at the leather-bound volumes with gilt titles stacked on the bookshelves lining the walls and wonders if, like his ancestors, they also arrived with William the Conqueror.

Edward is wearing a tweed jacket. His trousers are tucked into his long countryman's boots, suggesting that he is about to inspect his property or go hunting.

'I hope you're enjoying your holiday,' he says, and without waiting for her response, he turns to Daniel and asks, 'Well, what dirt have you managed to dig up on us so far?'

She is surprised at his bluntness, but Daniel doesn't react. 'That's not my aim. All I'm trying to do is find out what actually took place.'

'That's exactly what that journalist told me last year, oozing with false sincerity, but she had a hidden agenda. She maligned us and ended up stirring up a hornet's nest just so she could write a sensational article. Made out we were a den of anti-Semitic collaborators. I want to stress that we were under enemy occupation and everything was done in order to protect the population.'

'Maybe not the entire population,' Daniel comments.

As Edward leans forward, Xanthe notices that his bald head is covered in brown age spots, and she wonders how old he is. He sounds defensive, as if he personally was under attack, though he must have been very young at the time.

He holds up a hand, which is also splashed with age spots. 'Before I answer any questions, I want you to assure me that I won't be misquoted or quoted out of context in this so-called thesis of yours.'

Daniel points to the mobile he has placed between them on the desk. 'That's why I've brought this, so I can record what you say, exactly as you say it. I realise that this is a sensitive subject, and I appreciate your help.' Then with a trace of resentment he adds, 'But you don't have to worry. I'm not in the habit of misquoting sources.'

Edward grunts and nods. 'All right. Fire away.'

'It seems to me that there was a huge discrepancy between the States' attitude to the Jews and their attitude to some other groups in Jersey, and I wonder if you can explain that.'

'Well, it might seem that way to you, but it certainly wasn't the case.'

'I'm basing that on a document I came across,' Daniel continues. 'Your father was the Bailiff at the time, the most powerful member of the Jersey government, but although he tried to protect British army personnel from deportation, he seems to have acceded to the deportation of the Jews without making any effort on their behalf.'

Xanthe notices that Edward is tapping his foot on the floor, and with an irritation he can barely manage to conceal, he says, 'Look here, there were about twelve Jews living in Jersey at the time. As you know, we were occupied. Were we supposed to put the entire population at risk by opposing German orders?'

'So did it all hinge on numbers? Even though these twelve were also Jersey citizens? Not because they belonged to a different religious group?'

Edward bangs his fist on the desk, all pretence of urbanity gone. 'There you go again, accusing us of anti-Semitism just because we didn't want to risk our delicate equilibrium.'

'You mean your model occupation. Isn't that what a historian once called it?' Daniel suggests.

'Call it whatever you like, but it was a delicate balance that we didn't dare to upset for fear of the consequences.'

'I get that, but the consequences for those twelve Jersey citizens were appalling. They had their businesses closed, so they couldn't earn a living, their belongings were confiscated, and they lived in abject terror until they were deported to concentration camps where some of them died.'

Xanthe thinks back to the story of Lionel Stern's suicide, and she misses Edward's next words.

'Perhaps you're not aware that my father did oppose one of the German orders,' she hears him saying when she tunes in again. 'You should know that he objected to the demand that the Jews wear a yellow star on their clothing whenever they went outside. And as a result of his intervention, they dropped that demand,' he says. He looks pleased with himself, as if he has won the argument.

'I am aware of it, and good on him for doing that. But having succeeded in making his opinion heard, have you ever wondered why he didn't go on to oppose the other anti-Jewish orders? They too might have been rescinded if the most powerful man on the island had insisted.'

Edward makes a dismissive gesture. 'You weren't here, so you can't judge our situation. We were fortunate that the States were given a measure of autonomy, but we didn't want to push the Germans too far.'

Xanthe notes that he talks as if he were responsible for his father's actions.

'So the Jews were to be sacrificed on the altar of a balance that had to be maintained to keep the Germans onside,' Daniel says. 'Although of course we can't know what would have happened had your father objected to other orders instead of acquiescing to them. Like the appropriation of Jewish businesses, which left people with no means of earning a living.'

Edward suddenly makes a conversational detour. 'Did you know that we have erected a memorial to the Jewish slave labourers? And that one of our States' members is a Jewish gentleman?'

Daniel nods. 'And I believe he has written an account of what happened to the Jews here during the Occupation.'

After a brief pause, he adds, 'Did your father ever talk to you about what happened to the Jews? Did he ever express regret at the way things turned out?'

'My father was very proud of his role in steering our island through that terrible time with minimal deportations and deaths. In June 1940, the British government washed their hands of us. After demilitarising us, they urged my father to do his best, and wished him the best of British luck. I think that in the circumstances, he did a magnificent job for which all the people of Jersey should be extremely grateful. After the war, he received a congratulatory message from His Majesty King George VI.'

'The leaders of some European nations, like Denmark for instance, refused to give up their Jewish citizens,' Daniel points out. 'Their king even pinned a yellow star to his own jacket. Do you not think it was possible for the States to protect the Jewish citizens? After all, without their help, the Germans wouldn't have known who was Jewish and who wasn't.'

Edward seems taken aback by this question, and Xanthe wonders if it had ever occurred to him before. His eyes have lost their belligerent gleam, and for the first time he seems to be considering Daniel's comment.

He gazes out of the mullioned window, and after a long pause, he says, 'It's easy to know the answers in hindsight, but when you are in the midst of a perilous situation, you do the best you can as you see it at the time. You weren't here.'

Daniel and Xanthe walk out of Manoir de Courcy and blink against the dazzle of sunlight in the forecourt.

'We knew he'd be defensive and try to protect his father, but I do think he had a point,' Xanthe says as they drive away.

'That depends on your definition of human rights and morality, and whether you think that small groups should have fewer rights than larger ones. I'm about to get hold of some documents that relate to the actions of their top legal official, the Attorney-General, and the Aliens Officer who investigated and defined who was and wasn't a Jew.'

She glances at her watch. 'I keep forgetting that the days here are so long. It will be light for hours yet, so we still have time to go to Gorey.'

'What's the attraction?'

'I'd like to find the de Gruchy farmhouse.'

'The what?'

She realises why he looks puzzled, and decides to tell him about the journal she found in the house. It's a relief to share her secret discovery, and she tells him about Hugh's life, and his dedication to his patients.

'A journal written during the Occupation? By a doctor who lived through it? What a find. I suppose you'll donate it to the historical society?'

Now she regrets having told him about it. Her connection with Hugh Jackson has become so close that it feels as if he has been confiding in her, telling her about the secret life that he concealed from others, and talking about him feels like a betrayal.

She has regarded it as a personal rather than historical record, and she is shocked at the possibility of strange eyes reading it. What would Hugh think? After all, he must have had a reason for secreting his journal instead of handing it over to the relevant government body after the war.

He obviously didn't want it to be read, yet he hadn't destroyed it. Perhaps some of the information was too sensitive and might incriminate people who were still alive. But even if that was the case, over seventy years have elapsed, and she suspects it's her duty to hand this historical journal over to the custodians of the island's past.

'I'm still reading it,' she says. She knows she is being evasive, but she can't bring herself to release her proprietary hold on the journal. Not yet. Not until she is clear what she should do.

She notices him glancing at her from time to time, as if poised on the edge of a question he hesitates to ask for fear of disturbing an unspoken balance. Then he says, 'Have you ever wondered why you are so involved with this diary?'

Xanthe bristles. 'Of course I have. It's like listening to a voice from the past, describing the problems of that time. Why?'

'I wonder if it's more than that. Maybe you feel a professional and personal connection with this doctor that might help you solve your own dilemmas.'

'I think you're reading too much into it.' But she feels irritated, the way she always does when someone presses a button she has managed to conceal from herself.

As they follow the winding road northwards, they round a sharp bend and she sits forward. 'Stop!' she shouts. 'There's someone lying on the road.' Even before he has come to a complete halt, she has already jumped out of the car and is crouching over a man who isn't moving.

He doesn't respond when she asks his name. She puts her ear to his chest and picks up his limp arm. 'Shit,' she mutters. 'No pulse.' She checks his mouth to make sure his airway isn't obstructed by vomit and places her fingers against his neck to check his carotid artery. He isn't breathing.

She turns to Daniel. 'Quick, call the ambulance, and tell them it's urgent. He's in cardiac arrest so they need to bring a defibrillator.'

While she's talking, she's pumping the man's chest, putting her entire weight behind her strong, rapid movements. 'If I can't get him breathing he won't have a hope.'

Several minutes later, they hear the welcome shriek of an ambulance. Metallic doors slam, and two paramedics come running towards them holding the defibrillator. She steps back to give them room. She and Daniel watch anxiously as the man's chest jerks hideously with each jolt of electric current.

With a curt nod in her direction, the paramedics lift the man onto a stretcher, and slide it into the back of the ambulance. 'We've got a heartbeat. We'll take him to the hospital in St Helier. Good you were on the scene and knew what to do. Another minute and he wouldn't have made it.'

'I thought you were going to crack the poor guy's ribs, the way you were pummelling him,' Daniel says as they watch the ambulance speed away.

'Sometimes you do crack their ribs,' she says as they get back into his car. 'It makes a horrible crunching sound.'

'I think you need a drink. Or at least a cup of tea,' he suggests. 'We'll go to Gorey another day.'

The little teashop in the next village has trellised roses beside the front door, white lace curtains, and pots of scarlet geraniums on the windowsills. They choose a table by the bay window, and order a Devonshire tea.

He studies her. 'You were in your element back there. It was touch and go, but you were totally in control.'

'Well, I've done an A&E term, so I knew what to do.'

'It wasn't just that you knew what to do. It was like you were doing what you were always meant to do.'

The waitress brings a tray with cups and saucers of rose-patterned china, bowls of home-made raspberry jam and thick cream, a silver teapot, and a plate of freshly baked scones whose warm aroma pervades the teashop. While Xanthe spreads jam and cream on her scone, Daniel's eyes don't leave her face.

She puts down her scone, sighs, and looks away. 'That's part of the problem. What I was always meant to do almost destroyed me.'

'So have you thought about what you'll do when you go home? Can you imagine doing anything other than medicine?'

Xanthe sighs. 'I want to get away from it, but I don't know if I can. All my life I've wanted to help people, to make them better, but I've only made myself worse.'

As the waitress pours scalding tea into their cups, a plume of steam rises from the pot and curls towards the beamed ceiling. Wiping a rim of cream from her mouth, Xanthe says, 'In a way, I'm a bit like you, the victim of familial expectations, only you've found your niche within them.'

They are sipping tea in companionable silence when something strikes her and she puts down her cup. 'You once said that wars never end. It's the same with family history, isn't it? Look at Edward de Courcy, who feels obliged to defend his father's position during the Occupation, even though he couldn't have known anything about it at the time. But he still carries the moral responsibility. And your research is a direct result of your grandfather's actions – or lack of them – during the Third Reich. I have Jewish friends in Sydney whose lives are defined by the Holocaust, even though they weren't alive at the time. How do we escape the weight of family history?'

He reaches across the table and takes her hand. 'Perhaps there's no escape. It will always shape us, one way or another. All we can do is find some kind of accommodation. A coming to terms. Finding a balance.'

By the time they drive back to St Helier, the shadows have lengthened across the viridescence of the lawns, and somewhere in the darkened woods a nightingale is singing.

CHAPTER TWENTY-ONE

Tom

France, July 1943

Tom had his first glimpse of the Eiffel Tower from the back of a prison vehicle – not the ideal way to appreciate the beauty of Paris or its famous landmark, he reflected bitterly. He was being driven handcuffed to Gestapo headquarters. The destination made him feel so queasy that every time the car swerved he thought he would vomit his breakfast of black bread.

From the back of the black Citroën, the city looked drab and worn out, not at all what he had expected, and the Nazi flag flying triumphantly from the iconic tower made him clench his fists. Like the swastika planted on top of Fort Regent, it was further proof that the bloody Krauts were taking over the world.

Dropping his eyes from the hateful flag, he turned his attention to the street. German soldiers were wandering around, talking and laughing as if they owned the place. But despite their obvious presence, and the grimy miasma hanging over the city, Parisians were sitting at small round tables outside pavement cafés, the women in pert little hats and jackets with padded shoulders, drinking coffee and reading newspapers as if nothing had changed. Perhaps they were trying to blot out their ignominious fate while smoking their Gauloises, whose smoke greyed the air above their heads. He remembered the biting smell of those cigarettes. They were the ones his mother used to sell on the black market in St Helier.

He fixed his eyes on the scenes outside the car, hoping that the soldier escorting him wouldn't see him blinking away the tears that suddenly made everything blur. Scenes of his life at home, which he had left behind, perhaps forever, unspooled in his mind. Those wonderfully carefree days he had shared with Frank and Harry, cycling around Jersey, joking, and racing down to the Slip to buy ice creams from the Italian kiosk. It all seemed a thousand years ago, on another planet. Even running errands for his mother to deliver her black-market goods, which had once seemed so shameful, was now cloaked in the nostalgic glow of lost freedom.

As the car crossed the bridges of the Seine, not even the sight of the two square towers of Notre Dame cathedral boosted his spirits. It was just an ancient stone building. Something the prison guard had told him while getting him ready for his transfer that morning was still on his mind.

Ever since his arrest five or six weeks ago – he had lost count – he had racked his brains over the lack of contact with home. Neither he nor Harry had received any visitors while they were held in St Helier, and they hadn't received any mail in Fresnes. He knew that all prisoners were entitled to letters, so why weren't they receiving any? In the past, whenever he'd asked, the usual reply was a savage punch followed by a bellowed order to shut up, but that morning the guard had answered: 'You are under special investigation and not entitled to have letters, visits, food parcels or exercise.'

The guard's expression was almost sympathetic, and he'd even patted Tom's shoulder. Emboldened by the only sign of human feeling he had experienced since being arrested, Tom had pushed his luck to ask why, but with a shrug the guard had muttered, 'There are no whys in here,' and walked out of the cell, leaving Tom more despondent and frustrated than before. For some reason, he and Harry were being treated like lepers.

The Citroën pulled up on the Rue des Saussaies in front of a forbidding brick building with the hideous Nazi banner fluttering from the flagpole. Tom's heart pounded with dread.

He was pushed up several flights of stairs into a large room where two Gestapo agents, one in a beige trenchcoat and the other in a black leather jacket, sat behind a large table. The one in the trenchcoat had a face that reminded Tom of a weasel, while the other had the powerful build of a boxer. Leather coat sat forward.

'Who helped you to escape?' he yelled, spraying saliva across the table. 'Their names. Quick.'

Tom almost felt relieved. So these interrogators were just going to ask the same questions as the other lot.

Keeping his voice steady and polite, he said, 'I've already told the others who questioned me. Nobody helped us. We did it by ourselves.'

The weasel had a threatening expression in his colourless eyes as he stared at Tom.

'So who prepared this?' He held up Captain Beaumont's chart.

Tom swallowed hard. 'I don't know. Maybe it was Frank.' In his haste to clear himself, the shameful words were out before he had time to realise what he had said, but after all, he rationalised, nothing he said could hurt poor Frank.

'*English schweinehund*, you are lying again.' Leather Coat banged his beefy hand on the table, almost knocking the lamp over. 'You'd better start telling the truth because you are charged with espionage and you know how we deal with spies!'

The terror Tom felt was now replaced by indignation. He was sick of being bullied and accused of lying and spying. His father had always instilled into him that bullies were basically cowards who would back down when confronted.

'I'm not a spy,' he blurted, all attempt at calmness gone. 'But if I really am guilty of espionage, then show me the proof.'

'So, you want to see proof?' Leather Coat hissed. 'I'll show you proof.' With surprising agility, he sprang out of his chair, and before Tom knew what was happening he was being dragged into an adjoining room that was empty except for a freestanding bath full of water. The two agents yanked his arms behind him, tied them with a thick cord and thrust his head underwater. Being a strong swimmer, Tom was able to hold his breath for some time, but when they didn't relax their hold, his lungs were bursting.

He thrashed around trying to free himself, but the more he struggled, the harder they pushed, until he couldn't hold his breath any longer.

If only he'd drowned at Green Island and saved himself all this suffering. Was this divine retribution for letting Frank drown? He couldn't hold on any longer. At the very last moment, they released their grip. Gasping and spluttering, he raised his head out of the water and thought his heart was going to explode as he desperately tried to suck air into his lungs.

'Had enough? Are you going to tell us the truth now?' the weasel demanded.

While submerged, Tom had been ready to tell them anything they wanted to hear, but suddenly he knew he wasn't going to give in. With a rough gesture, Leather Coat pushed his head underwater again. Panic-stricken, Tom knew that this time there would be no last-minute reprieve, that any second he would drown, but again at the very last moment they pulled him out, coughing and choking, unable to catch his breath.

They hauled him back into the interrogation room, and threw him into the chair, gasping, shivering and soaked to the skin. Leather Coat held out a typewritten sheet in German. 'Sign your statement,' he ordered.

'I didn't give you a statement, so I'm not going to sign it,' Tom said, amazed at his own defiance.

At this, the thin agent sprang up and, with a look of fury on his face, grabbed him by the throat and yelled a stream of abuse in German while he kept squeezing, harder and harder, blocking Tom's windpipe. 'Ah, so, not going to sign, *ja*?' he shouted.

The more Tom tried to pry the agent's hands away, the tighter his grip became. Tom felt light-headed and knew he was losing consciousness. There was no point struggling anymore. Then he heard the other one bark, 'Enough!', and the murderous hands slid off his throat.

Tom's chest was still heaving when Leather Coat slid the paper towards him and translated it. It was an accurate account of the interrogation.

'We've been very lenient with you, but if you know what is good for you, stop trying our patience, and sign this,' he said.

Still gasping for air and rubbing his bruised neck, Tom picked up the pen and signed the statement.

Back in the prison in Fresnes, he felt relieved to be back in his cell where no-one was trying to drown or choke him, but he didn't delude himself that his ordeal was over. Night after night, the prison resounded with terrifying screams that reverberated through the corridors and made the hairs on the back of his neck stand up. Most terrible of all were the screams of the women that made it impossible to sleep or entertain any hope for the future.

He knew that many of his fellow prisoners were members of the French Resistance who were being tortured to reveal the names of their colleagues. Bloodied and broken, they were dragged out to the courtyard, often shouting '*Vive La France*' or singing the Marseillaise, before a sickening volley of shots echoed throughout the prison.

Left in his cell for the next few days, Tom reflected on the French. They were so brave, yet their country had let them down, surrendering so fast. Then he thought about the way his own island had been occupied without even one shot being fired in its defence, and he gave up trying to understand the decisions of leaders and the character of nations. Perhaps the only thing that mattered was the calibre of individuals.

He felt ashamed of having tried to blame Frank, of letting himself down during his interrogation. Harry would never have done that. He wondered whether his friend had been interrogated, and how long they'd be kept in this prison.

The answer came several days later when a guard escorted him from his cell to the main hall where a large group of prisoners had already gathered.

Harry was among them, and Tom couldn't wait to talk to him, but before they could communicate, a roll call was conducted and they were counted and recounted. It seemed that counting prisoners was a favourite German pastime.

When the guards were finally satisfied that the numbers tallied, they were all herded into an armoured cell-truck where a row of armed German soldiers pointed their rifles at them. If anyone had told Tom that in such a situation it was possible to feel a surge of happiness, he wouldn't have believed it, but now, sitting beside Harry, he felt calmer than he had felt since his capture. Wherever they were going, at least they'd be together.

He noticed that his friend's face was bruised. In a low voice, Harry explained that, like Tom, he had also been interrogated, beaten and almost drowned at Rue des Saussaies, but he said that he had stuck to the story that they had only been fishing, signed a piece of paper they'd pushed in front of him, and had been sent back to the jail.

'We must never forget we're British,' he whispered to Tom. 'We mustn't give in.'

At the sound of their voices, and the mention of the word 'British', some of their French fellow prisoners glared at them.

'They think they're superior, but they've forgotten that they surrendered after only a few weeks,' Tom whispered. Harry nodded. At least Britain would go on fighting. The British would never surrender. That's what Mr Churchill had said, and they believed him.

The truck lurched and bumped for about an hour until it pulled up outside a busy railway station, where they were ordered out and counted once again. Tom looked around. They had arrived at the Gare de l'Est. That meant that they would be travelling east, but where?

All around them, French travellers with tense faces were rushing towards platforms or hurrying out of the station, keeping their heads down and quickening their steps whenever they passed prisoners being counted by harsh German voices. Tom wished someone would stop to ask who they were, or where they were from, or at least offer a word of commiseration, but they hurried past, averting their faces.

Defying the order to be silent, Tom leaned towards one of the French prisoners.

'Do you know where they're taking us?'

'Allemagne.'

Germany! Tom felt as if he'd been punched. He was being deported to a foreign country that was even further from home than France was, to the dreaded Nazi homeland, a place beyond just laws and humane treatment, where their captors would be able to do whatever they liked and no-one would be able to protect him or intercede for him. He would be completely at their mercy. They could shoot him, torture him or imprison him forever, and no-one would ever know his fate because, as the guard had told him, no-one knew where he was, and no-one would never find out because he wasn't entitled to any contact.

Harry was clearly entertaining similar thoughts. As soon as they had climbed into the tiny armoured compartment of their train, he said, 'Tom, promise you'll stay alive and get back to Jersey, so you can tell my parents what happened to me.'

Tom stared at his friend, wondering what had prompted that pessimistic comment. Why did he think he wouldn't make it?

'Don't talk tommyrot, Harry. Of course I'll get back. So will you.'

'But promise me,' Harry insisted.

Tom nodded. 'Okay, I promise. But you'll be able to tell them yourself.'

As the train continued its endless journey, cramped in their tiny compartment, they peered through the small grille, hoping to see a place name they recognised, but they were all unfamiliar.

'I should have paid more attention in geography classes,' Tom said in an attempt to lighten their mood, but his comment didn't bring a smile to Harry's face, and, looking at his friend, Tom felt uneasy.

Listening to the conversations of their French fellow prisoners, Tom's apprehension increased. Some described brutal scenes in French towns where innocent hostages were rounded up and shot in the market square in reprisal for sabotage by the Maquis, the Resistance fighters.

They rounded up teenagers as well, and one of prisoners said that his young brother had been herded into a village church that was set alight with over a hundred men, women and children inside.

Some of the Resistance men spoke bitterly about their countrymen who had betrayed them, and swore revenge when the war was over. They promised they'd deal with the sluts who consorted with Germans while they were risking their lives to free their country.

Tom thought about Milly and her German boyfriend, and his mother who had betrayed him. Like his French companions, he longed for revenge, but how could life return to normal if vengeance prevailed? He recalled something his history teacher had once said: *An eye for an eye makes everyone blind.* But what was the alternative? How could they return and live among those who had helped the enemy? Noble sentiments were all very well, but surely his mother had to pay for her betrayal.

As he listened to these accounts of German atrocities, he realised that they had been living in a fool's paradise in Jersey, where the Germans had managed to conceal their iron fists in velvet gloves. Many of the locals, his parents included, praised the occupiers for their good manners and adherence to the laws, but Tom suddenly remembered the skeletal slave labourers the Germans were forcing to build their wretched tunnels and bunkers.

Most people chose to put the inhuman treatment of the slaves out of their minds because it was easier to avert your eyes than confront an uncomfortable situation and do something about it. He'd heard rumours that some locals were hiding escaped slave labourers, but most of the residents, himself included, had ignored their plight because it had nothing to do with them. They didn't know, and didn't really want to know, who these spectral creatures were, or why they had been deported to Jersey. Perhaps they'd committed a crime. In any case, it didn't affect him. He wasn't one of them. He had ignored people who were victimised, and now that he was in a similar situation, why was he surprised that passers-by at the Gare de l'Est walked past without showing any interest or compassion?

The train ground to a shuddering halt, interrupting his brooding thoughts. Tom heard dogs barking and guttural voices yelling. According to the large sign on the platform, they were in a town called Trier. They had crossed the border and arrived in Germany. The doors of the compartments clanged open, and as usual the guards started screaming at them to get out on the double. *'Raus!'* they yelled. *'Los! Schneller!'*

Blinded by the powerful beams of searchlights, they were surrounded by uniformed local policemen in full regalia, their large silver shakos embossed with silver eagles that gleamed in the light. Some carried submachine guns.

After being counted and recounted, they were marched out of the station. It was a foggy night, and apart from church spires, Tom couldn't identify any buildings along the way. Walking on a cobbled road lined with tall poplars, they reached a large gate and were led through an archway into what was obviously a prison.

After a sleepless and anxious night spent in an overcrowded, stinking cell where the sole toilet overflowed, they were given watery soup and marched outside for the usual counting ritual.

Roll call over, escorted by the police once again, they were marched back to the railway station and pushed onto the waiting train. From his compartment, Tom gazed longingly at pine forests, vineyards and flower-decked villages where women in kerchiefs bent over the fields.

Despite the anxiety that gnawed at him, he was surprised how quickly the beauty of the countryside boosted his spirits. Wherever they were going, perhaps things wouldn't be too bad. Perhaps he and Harry would be sent to work in the vineyards or in the forests.

After a brief journey, the train stopped at a small station and out of the window Tom saw prisoners loading farm carts with coal and wood. He stared. They were all as emaciated as the slave labourers in Jersey.

As soon as they lined up on the platform, one of the prisoners sidled up to Tom and whispered in French, 'If you brought any food with you, eat it now because they'll confiscate it as soon as you get to the camp.'

Tom had already wolfed down the black bread and chunk of sausage he'd received that morning, but Harry reached into his pocket and held out a piece of bread to the prisoner, whose eyes lit up. But before he could take it, a guard rushed up, snatched the bread away, knocked the man down and kicked him, and yelled at Harry to mind his own business.

It wasn't an auspicious beginning, but as they marched towards the camp along a country road lined with fir trees, the clean air and fresh scent of the pines filled Tom with optimism. That optimism evaporated as soon as he saw the barbed wire surrounding the camp. According to the wooden sign, they were entering SS Sonderlager Reinsfeld. He knew that this meant it was a special camp, and for a brief moment he entertained the hope that it was special because the inmates would be allowed to work outdoors. He didn't know the significance of the letters SS other than that they stood for *Schutzstaffel*, which had something to do with security.

They were lined up in a courtyard and counted again, but this time the tension around them was palpable, like the frightening stillness that preceded a hurricane. No-one moved or spoke, but the SS officers occasionally turned in the direction of a building that looked like the administration block.

They were obviously waiting for someone important to emerge, and for some reason Tom was trembling so hard he couldn't stop. Then a door opened and a nuggetty man with powerful shoulders strode towards them holding a large club. Like a coiled spring, he exuded dangerous energy and the air around him vibrated with malice. When he reached their group, he stopped, raised the club, and smashed it into the head of one of the French prisoners, who reeled and collapsed on the ground.

'That's how I deal with people who don't look straight ahead at roll call!' he shouted.

Tom stopped fantasising about picking grapes or sawing trees. He knew then that Sonderlager Reinsfeld was another name for hell, and he had just come face to face with the devil.

CHAPTER TWENTY-TWO

Dr Jackson

St Helier, September 1943

We had just finished dinner, and I was pouring Aoife some Armagnac when she leaned across the table, took my hand, and, not taking her eyes off my face, began singing a song I'd never heard before. It was an Irish air called 'Down by the Salley Gardens', and the simple beauty of the tune and its haunting lyrics entranced me. Spellbound by her low, melodious voice and the poignant story of love lost, I was intrigued. Why had she chosen to sing this? I supposed it evoked memories for her, the way poems and songs do when we hear them in childhood and respond to tantalising emotions we have yet to experience.

Once again, I realised how little I knew about her, and how little I cared about her past. As she had once pointed out, the only thing that mattered was the present, and what we shared right now. The past was over, the future was imponderable. When she had finished singing, she squeezed my hand while I stayed motionless, as if in a dream. Then, although it was a warm evening, I shivered as if someone had walked over my grave.

'I wonder what caused that,' I said.

'Ah, 'tis the little people!' she laughed, and added, 'Or the magic of Yeats, maybe.'

I left it at that, because we had finished the Armagnac and I could hardly wait to take her upstairs so that we could create some magic of our own.

Several days have passed since then, and I have re-read the previous sentence several times, uncertain whether to delete it. Ever since Aoife and I became lovers, there have been times when this journal of war experiences intended for posterity has crossed the line from the historical to the personal. What started off as part of a Mass Observation project has become a record of my intimate feelings, one that I certainly would not want others to read. And yet these emotions are an integral part of my war experience and omitting them would not feel honest. I must admit that unloading everything on paper at the end of the day has been therapeutic. Compulsive, too, which surprises me, as I have never been given to analysing my feelings. I'm like the woman who once said she doesn't know what she thinks until she hears what she says.

So perhaps I should continue writing it all down, without censoring anything, and when the war ends, which surely it must before long, I will go over the entire journal and then decide what to omit. Who knows, perhaps one day I'll write a novel that illuminates a doctor's dilemmas, like Cronin did.

I was still under the spell of Aoife's song the following morning, and I think I was humming it under my breath when my first patient walked in. Before sitting down, Brigid Murphy glanced around several times as if to ensure that no-one had followed her.

She wasn't afraid of confronting Germans. When they recently questioned her about escaped slave labourers, she told them indignantly to concentrate on catching criminals instead of harassing a law-abiding woman, so her nervous demeanour that morning was totally out of character.

When she was satisfied that we were alone, and no-one could overhear our conversation, she drew her chair closer to my desk, leaned forward, and spoke in a conspiratorial whisper.

'Yesterday afternoon, I overheard two women talking in the library yesterday about a woman in St Helier who was hiding an escaped slave labourer in her home,' she began. *It's a disgrace, her keeping him there and putting us all in danger like that,* one of them said. *Something should be done about it.* She didn't mention any names, but from the way her eyes narrowed when she spoke, and the knowing look in her companion's eyes, I could tell they both knew who it was. Of course I did too. The woman doing all the talking is a nasty piece of work who is likely to make trouble, so I thought you should know as soon as possible.'

I had no doubt that the woman they had been discussing was Mrs Carter, who still had Sasha living with her. Whenever I dropped in to visit them, I could see how splendidly things were working out. It was as if Sasha was the son she had lost, and she was the mother he missed, but on reflection I have to admit that not many of the mothers and sons I come across live together in such harmony.

So the possibility that someone in our community might consider informing on this wonderful woman, and exposing an innocent young man to the cruelty of Organisation Todt, made me angry. What's more, it worried me. I knew that this ideal arrangement would have to end, as we couldn't risk leaving Sasha there any longer and exposing them both to such danger.

That afternoon, I dropped in to see Mrs Carter, who was giving Sasha an English lesson, and it was a pleasure to see the progress he had made. Instead of the few hesitant words spoken in a thick accent when I first placed him there, he greeted me in reasonably fluent English. Mrs Carter beamed like a proud teacher when I praised his English, but I hadn't come to pay them compliments.

Without beating around the bush, I explained that Sasha would have to move to another safe place as soon as possible. They were both extremely upset, but I told them there was no choice. I warned Mrs Carter to destroy every sign that Sasha had ever been there, and conceal any indication that more than one person had been living in the house, such as crumpled bedclothes in the spare bedroom or used cups in the sink.

Mrs Carter, who was usually very ladylike, let loose with a string of words I didn't think she knew, and cursed anyone malicious enough to inform on her Sasha. 'They're Satan's children and should burn in the fires of hell forever,' she said.

Although Sasha probably couldn't understand everything we said, he was a bright chap, and her expression and tone of voice would have made up for any words he lacked.

I drove away heavy-hearted, trying to comprehend the motives of people who denounced their neighbours. After all, hiding escaped slave labourers endangered only the people who sheltered them, no-one else. As I have come to realise, war brings out the best and the worst in us, and it's a pity that some people allow the worst to triumph.

As soon as I returned to my surgery, I contacted Bob Blampied. 'You told me you knew someone who wanted a cat. I've got one here. Could you come over and pick it up from my surgery this afternoon?'

'Not to worry, I'll be there in an hour or so,' he said in his cheerful way, and, in case anyone was listening in at the exchange, he added, 'I know a woman who wants one.'

He's a surprising fellow. Despite his youth, he is a tower of strength, dedicated and reliable. Without the car he has at his disposal thanks to his position at the insurance firm, I don't know how we'd manage to move the fugitives from house to house.

I heaved a sigh of relief when he contacted me that evening to say he'd found a home for the cat. Unfortunately, from now on we will have to arrange for Sasha to move to a different house every night, a distressing situation for Sasha and Mrs Carter, who will miss each other. But I know that they have both been enriched by their relationship, and Sasha has experienced human kindness for the first time in several years.

That evening when I went outside to feed the chickens, my gaze was drawn to an ant nest in the yard. Looked at superficially, ants seem to meander aimlessly in all directions, but from what I've read, there is nothing random or chaotic in the ant world. Each one has a designated role to fulfil, a kind of ant caste system, from which they never deviate.

In that world, the insects cooperate to ensure the survival of the entire community. Reflecting on the case of Mrs Carter, I was sad to think that among us were people whose commitment to their countrymen was so weak that they were willing to endanger them, and to jeopardise the moral integrity of our island by collaborating with the enemy out of self-interest, envy and greed.

While I'm on the subject of insects, I've just remembered an animal story, this time about pigs. It's a good example of the ingenuity of our residents who try to circumvent the restrictive orders of the occupiers.

I can't recall if I have mentioned that farmers are forced to register all their livestock. In the beginning, the Germans ordered that most of the farm animals had to be offered up for public sale, but they permitted farmers to retain a few for their own use.

As time has passed, however, they have tightened the screws, reduced the number farmers can keep for themselves, and enforced their regulations with frequent inspections.

I know from my patients Fred and Hazel Lowry that every litter of pigs has to be notified, and each piglet is then tattooed and registered. As all this has made it difficult for farmers to survive economically, some of them have found ingenious ways of overcoming this regulation. They either conceal their animals in barns that have been divided in half, or cover the pigpens under a bale of hay so that they can carry on their risky traffic.

In order to put a stop to this, the Germans have organised spot-checks on pig farms to catch out the law-breakers.

'I had killed an illegal pig and hung it in the barn when our neighbour's son raced in to warn us that an inspector had just arrived at their farm, and would soon come to ours,' Fred told me.

'We were petrified. Where could we hide such a large, unwieldy animal with the inspector about to descend on us any minute?'

It appears that with disaster looming, at the last moment his wife Hazel came up with a solution. She and Fred ran down to the barn, grabbed hold of the pig, wrapped it quickly in several sheets, and hauled it upstairs to the spare bedroom. They laid it on the bed and covered it with a white sheet, tucking it in securely to make sure that no part of the animal poked out. Once the pig was lying in state, Hazel lowered the blinds, placed a candlestick on the bedside table, and lit the candle. At the last moment, she whisked the family Bible off the shelf, placed it beside the candlestick, and left sachets of lavender on the coverlet.

They had hardly finished creating this dramatic scenario when the Germans stomped into the house. Hazel met them at the door in tears. A death in the family, she explained, trembling in obvious distress. She wasn't playacting – she was terrified.

While she and Fred exchanged agonised glances, the Germans went through every room in the farmhouse with Teutonic thoroughness. They moved armchairs, lifted tables, and looked under couches as if expecting to see a pig hiding there.

After they had finished downstairs, they proceeded up the stairs to the bedrooms. With hands that shook so much she could hardly open the door to the spare bedroom, Hazel started sobbing. Pushing her aside, the soldier surveyed the dimly lit room.

He cast his glance at the body under the sheet, the flickering candle and the Bible, and with an embarrassed expression backed out of the bedroom, muttering apologies. A few moments later the front door closed behind the Germans.

Hazel was shaking with laughter when she told me this macabre story. 'You should have seen the look on that German's face!' she said.

As for me, I didn't know how to react. The Germans are literally taking the food from our mouths, so naturally I was delighted that they had been outwitted, but at the same time I had qualms about fabricating the death of a loved one using a pig and a Bible. But this illustrates the situation we live in, where we have to use our wits to survive as best we can.

Speaking of survival, I often wonder what has become of young Tom Gaskell. Months have passed, and still no-one knows where he is. It's as if he has fallen off the edge of the world. It's such a tragic story. The parents of the poor lad who drowned are distraught. I heard that his father went grey overnight. And the parents of the other boy are at their wits' end trying to find out where he's been taken, but their letters have gone unanswered, and their pleas for information from the Kommandatur have not yielded any results.

I would have thought that with her German connections, Tom's mother would have been able to find out where her son was, but someone told me that her protector at the Water Police had been recalled to Germany, so as far as I know, she is also in the dark as to his whereabouts.

I was thinking about Tom as I drove away from the Lowry farm yesterday. I had gone there because Fred had offered to siphon some petrol into my tank, which of course is against the law. Petrol, like everything else these days, is rationed, but as doctors are only allowed three-quarters of a gallon per week, that's insufficient for all my night calls.

The previous week, when I ran out of petrol, I had to do a house call at night on my bicycle. Suddenly a furious salivating dog rushed out of a driveway, making me swerve. When I fell off the bike, the wretched creature sank its fangs into my leg and ripped my trousers. This was extremely vexing as it is impossible to buy new clothes, and mine were becoming threadbare, to say nothing of the risk of contracting rabies. So I was determined not to risk that again, and when Fred suggested selling me some petrol, I jumped at his offer. Petrol is like gold these days, but a lot more useful.

That night the rain was pelting down, and, faced with the choice of opening the car window and getting soaked, or keeping it closed and continually wiping the steam off the windscreen with my hand, I opted for the latter.

Visibility was very poor, and as I was sitting forward, craning to see the road through my fogged-up windscreen as I drove home, I didn't see the car parked on the curve of the road, and before I knew it, I heard a bang. I had crashed into it. Swearing, I got out to inspect the damage.

Thankfully there was none, and, wet through, I was about to get back into the Austin when a police car pulled up beside me and two officers jumped out, demanding to know why I had broken the curfew.

I explained that I was a doctor returning from a house call and assured them that there was no problem, but as luck would have it, I had just filled my tank illegally, and one of them decided to check that I hadn't exceeded my ration of petrol for the week.

I had to think quickly. If they found that the tank was full, I'd have to pay a heavy fine, Fred would be imprisoned for selling it, and I'd probably have the Austin impounded. In a feeble attempt to play for time, I made a few inane comments about the rain while looking around in the unlikely hope of deliverance.

That's when I noticed that I had parked my car on a blind curve in the road.

'This road is dangerously narrow,' I said. 'I'd better move the car before it causes an accident.'

'Ja, sehr gut,' one of them said, nodding.

When I moved the car, I parked with two wheels partly in the gutter, so that it tilted to one side. When the officer plunged his metal measuring rod into the roadside part of the tank, the petrol level there was much lower on account of the tilt, and to my relief they got back into their car and drove away.

Several weeks have passed since my last entry but I've figured out why I've been so remiss. Ever since I started musing about the ultimate fate of this journal, and wondering what to delete when the time comes, I've lost my spontaneity. It feels as if I have a critic looking over my shoulder to check what I write. This is as inhibiting as trying to have a sincere conversation with someone you mistrust, when you have to watch every word you utter.

But when I don't write in the journal, I feel something is missing. Patients I've treated who have lost a limb tell me that they continue to feel pain where that arm or leg used to be. It's called a phantom limb. So perhaps that's what I'm feeling – a phantom hand that longs to pick up a pen!

But there's another factor that's inhibiting me from recording the day's events. The last conversation I had with Aoife has unsettled me.

I've noticed that she never talks about her life before we met. I never pry, but once, when I referred to her career before becoming matron at the Jersey Maternity Hospital, she kissed me and said firmly that there was no before, because she was reborn when we met. She said it in the teasing way she dismisses all references to her past.

It feels as if there's an invisible but clearly defined line in her life that I am not allowed to cross. She is entitled to her privacy, but I can't deny that her lack of trust bothers me. I don't keep any secrets from her, and I wish she felt she could be open with me.

We were sitting on my sofa that evening, her head on my lap, and I was stroking her flame-coloured hair while I told her a little about my childhood here on Jersey. How I loved exploring the coves, climbing on the rocks and searching for birds' nests in the woods. But when I asked about her schooldays in Ireland, her reply shocked me.

'I never talk about that, so please don't ask,' she said, and changed the subject.

So to avoid that minefield, I told her I'd always wanted to be a doctor, and asked whether she had always wanted to be a nurse.

At that, she sprang up and said, 'I'm tired, I think I'll be getting back now.' Before I could ask her to explain why she was so upset, she was gone. Bewildered, I sat on the sofa going over our conversation and her unexpected reaction to questions that hadn't seemed intrusive.

What had I said to upset her? Was I being too possessive? Should I step back a little and give her more space? Perhaps it had nothing to do with me, and she was overworked and at breaking point on account of the strain of trying to run a hospital with ever-decreasing medications and ever-increasing problems?

Churned up and distressed, I put the Mozart Clarinet Concerto on the gramophone. When that was finished, I played the Beethoven Violin Concerto and closed my eyes while I listened to it, trying to imagine how a man who was deaf and disappointed in love had managed to compose such life-affirming music.

But as I discover every single day, the human mind is unfathomable. Take my patient Mrs Browning. I knew she was co-habiting with a German soldier while her husband, who had joined the British armed forces, was fighting somewhere in North Africa, but she amazed me this morning by confiding that every night, before getting into bed with her lover, she kneels on the floor and prays for her husband to come home safely. 'Reinhard doesn't mind,' she told me. 'He understands.'

I can't judge her. We all need to be loved and understood.

That of course turned my thoughts to Aoife and her disturbing reaction to a simple question. I lay awake for a long time but instead of the melody of the Beethoven concerto, the lyrics of 'Down by the Salley Gardens' resounded in my head.

CHAPTER TWENTY-THREE

Xanthe

St Helier, April 2019

Why do people risk their lives to help others? That's the question going through Xanthe's mind as she sits beside Bob Blampied in his vintage sports car. He has the hood down as usual, and she regrets not pulling her hair into a ponytail because the spring breeze is blowing it all over her face and into her eyes. Pushing her hair back, she glances at Bob. With a jaunty peaked cap over his fine white hair, and big sunglasses, no-one would take him for a man over ninety.

At the end of Longueville Road, Bob waves his arm in the direction of the coast.

'Whenever I pass St Aubin's Bay, I can still see the Germans rolling out miles of barbed wire along here in 1940. We had German soldiers swarming all over the place – twenty-seven thousand of them in a place this size, can you imagine?' He shakes his head as if he still has trouble believing it. 'It was all so long ago, but the funny thing is that I remember it more vividly than things that happened yesterday. I suppose that's what old age does to you.'

He parks the car by the waterfront and they watch the foam-crested waves fountain against the granite sea wall. Turning towards her, he says, 'Did you know that the ratio of soldiers to civilians here was higher than anywhere else in Europe? That's because Hitler thought Churchill was going to use our islands as a stepping stone in the Allied invasion of Europe. They thought they'd bomb England to smithereens, bring Britain to her knees in no time, and turn Jersey into a holiday resort for German soldiers.' Then he adds, 'Which it already was.'

He releases the handbrake, but before turning on the engine, he says, 'I haven't asked you where you'd like to go today, young lady.'

'No special requests. Happy to leave it to you.'

She means it. It's a privilege to spend time with this remarkable man who lived here throughout the Occupation. She still can't believe her luck that a man who seems to have stepped out of the pages of Hugh's journal is driving her around Jersey and sharing his stories with her. It's almost as good as having Hugh as a guide.

Hugh's journal has plunged her headlong into the past. As if, like Alice, she has fallen through a rabbit hole and landed in a more vibrant and interesting world.

'You mentioned a Dr Jackson who was part of your network,' she says casually. 'What was he like?'

From Bob's nostalgic expression, it seems that her question evokes a flood of memories. 'He was the one who formed our rescue network. A real dynamo, he was. Nothing was too much trouble for him. And so selfless. You know, he stayed in Jersey to look after his patients when he could have evacuated with his wife.'

Xanthe feels a surge of excitement as she waits to hear more about Hugh, especially about aspects of his life she doesn't know, but just then the driver on the other side of the parking area pulls out without looking and is heading straight for Bob's rear fender. Bob hits the horn just in time to avert the crash, muttering about bloody hopeless drivers.

'Sorry about that,' he says.

She hopes to resume their conversation about Hugh Jackson, but Bob's attention has been distracted.

'You need eyes in the back of your head these days. Now, back to the important issue of the day: where are we going to have lunch? Do you like seafood?'

'I love it.'

Backing the car very carefully out of the parking space, he says, 'I know just the place. They have crabs this big!' For an instant her heart stands still as he takes his hands off the wheel to demonstrate.

As they drive along the west coast, past St Brelade, she observes Bob's obvious enjoyment as he drives his sportscar along the winding country lanes.

Her eyes linger on the evocative place names of the farms and manor houses they pass – Le Marais, Le Clos de L'Arsenal, Les Peupliers – and she asks Bob if his surname is also of Norman French origin.

He shakes his head. 'My Blampied ancestors were among the Huguenots who fled to Jersey after the massacre of

St Bartholomew's Day. That was during the persecution of the Huguenots by the Catholics in the sixteenth century.'

He points to a Martello tower along the road and sighs. 'Wars, rebellions, religious persecutions. Nothing ever changes. Despite what Santayana wrote about the importance of remembering history, no-one ever seems to learn from it.'

His comment about religious persecution seems a good introduction to a discussion about the way the Jews were treated on the island during the Occupation, but she is suddenly distracted by the view unrolling before them – the superb sweep of St Ouen Bay, whose glorious beach seems to stretch forever. On their right, an impressive round tower overlooks the sea.

'La Rocco Tower,' he says. 'It was built during the Napoleonic wars to protect the bay from French attack. Then during the Second World War, Hitler was convinced the Allies would land right here, so the Germans fortified it.'

She is gazing at him with admiration. 'You know a lot of history.'

'My mother used to say that if you live long enough, you can't help picking up a huge amount of information and a little bit of wisdom along the way,' he chuckles. 'Well, I've certainly lived long enough to pick up a bit of the former. Not sure about the latter.'

Then he adds, 'I've always been fascinated by history. That's why I've joined our local historical society.'

He's being modest again. Xanthe knows from Wikipedia that he's the president of the Jersey Historical Association, which makes her feel guilty for concealing an important record of life during the Occupation.

She hasn't lied, but she hasn't been truthful either, and she comforts herself with the thought that her deceit is temporary. When she has finished reading the journal, she probably will donate it to the historical society. For now, she feels as though Hugh has entrusted her with his diary, and she must guard his secrets.

When they reach L'Étacq at the northern part of the beach, Bob parks the car, and they pass a grassy area facing the sea where people are sitting on wooden benches as they gaze at the turbulent surf.

'Let's go into the *vivier*,' Bob says.

'*Vivier?*'

'Bunker. This fishery is inside a German bunker.'

They descend into a cavernous hall with thick cement walls. Jovial fishmongers are bantering with customers who are eyeing the fish and crustaceans swimming in the large tanks. Behind them, some red-faced cooks in white caps are lowering Jersey Royal potatoes into sizzling oil in wire baskets while others are boiling crustaceans and frying fish fillets. Xanthe watches this incongruous scene with a sense of unreality, a fish shop located inside a grim wartime structure erected to conceal troops and weapons.

'You'll never get seafood as fresh as this,' Bob says, steering her towards a fishmonger who is holding up the biggest crab she has ever seen.

'Good to see you, Bob,' the fishmonger says, resting curious eyes on Xanthe. 'Brought your girlfriend today, eh?' Turning to Xanthe, he says, 'You'd better watch him! A regular Casanova, he is. Different girl every day!'

'How are the new fishing regulations affecting you?' Bob asks.

The fishmonger sighs. 'The bloody EU trawlers are fishing in our waters and people who wouldn't know one end of a fish from the other are passing laws that affect the whole industry. Isn't that always the way? Those who can, do, and the others go into parliament and make life difficult for the rest of us.'

A few minutes later, she and Bob are sitting outside, tucking into their crab and Jersey Royals. This is the most succulent crab she has ever tasted, and with each bite she makes blissful sounds, like the presenters of TV food shows when they sample the chef's gourmet dish.

Sunbeams are silvering the crests of the waves that roll endlessly along the wide beach in front of them, providing a mesmerising soundtrack of booming surf. Gazing at the magnificent landscape, Xanthe washes her crab down with lager, and wonders if this is the right time to bring up the question she wants to ask, when Bob leans towards her with a conspiratorial smile.

'Tell me, what really made you come to Jersey?' he asks. 'Did you leave a heartbroken beau back in Sydney?'

'Nothing like that.' She pauses. 'I don't really know why. It's a mixture of things. Wanting to get away, mostly.'

To her relief, he doesn't ask what she is getting away from. He just studies her with his steady gaze, and nods as if he understands, as if it's the most natural thing in the world for a young Australian doctor to run away from her hospital job and her family to a tiny island on the other side of the world where she doesn't know anyone.

She is on the point of mentioning her distant Jersey relative, but as she has no intention of following up that connection, she decides against it. Instead, she returns to the topic he sidestepped earlier when he deflected her compliment about being heroic.

'Last time we met, you told me you were only nineteen when the Occupation started. I'd love to know why you decided to help those escaped slave labourers. You must have known the risk you were taking. How come you did it?'

Bob is staring out to sea, but from the faraway look in his eyes, she senses that he isn't seeing the Atlantic waves but scrolling back to the past. 'You know, I hardly recognise that young whippersnapper now. Young people don't weigh up consequences like old fogeys do. They think they're invincible. It's all action and very little thought. I suppose I was aware of the risks, but there was the excitement, too. An adventure. I wasn't just helping the prisoners, I was defying the Germans as well. Doing my bit to resist.'

This still doesn't answer the underlying question that has been on her mind all day. 'You hear about cases where there's a fire,' she says, 'and lots of people are standing around, horrified, but only one person charges into the burning house, in spite of the flames. Or a surfer is being attacked by a shark, and of all the people on the beach who watch the attack, only one dives in to fight off the shark. What makes people forget their own danger to try and rescue strangers? What made you do what you did?'

He counters her question with another. 'What made you decide to become a doctor?'

She shakes her head. 'Various things. But I wasn't risking my life to do it,' she begins, and then stops as it occurs to her that it almost did cost her life.

'But there was something in you that made your choice inevitable. And there was something in me that made it unthinkable for me to stand by, see people being mistreated, and do nothing. I don't know what that something was, but I couldn't ignore it. Later you try to analyse your actions, and come up with all kinds of possible motives, like your conscience, your subconscious, Christian morality, patriotic duty, or the categorical imperative to do the right thing. One theory might be correct, or maybe all of them are, but you'll never really know. That's irrelevant anyway because at the time you don't stop to think and weigh things up. You act on impulse. When you think about it later, you might be astounded by the risk you took. Perhaps the power of the soul is stronger than the urge to survive.'

He looks at her and raises his white eyebrows in mock horror. 'We're getting into deep philosophical waters here.'

Xanthe drains the last of her lager and wipes her mouth on a thin paper serviette. The answers to these questions obviously lie in the imponderable depths of the human psyche. She thinks about Daniel, as she has so often throughout the day, and wonders what he has found out at the Jersey Archives.

'What do you think of the way the Jersey authorities dealt with the situation here during the Occupation?'

Bob considers her question for some time before replying. 'They made some mistakes, no doubt about it. But it's easy to be wise after the event, isn't it? If only we could live our lives all over again with the benefit of hindsight. I think what people don't understand is, they were damned if they did, and damned if they didn't.'

'Isn't that the excuse given on behalf of all collaborationist governments, like Vichy and Norway?'

He gives her an approving nod. 'You know your World War II history. But our situation was different. We were a tiny island, with no mountains, nowhere to hide. There was a lot of fraternisation, which was inevitable given our close proximity with the Germans, but that's not the same as collaboration. And in my opinion, the States behaved superbly in what was a very tricky situation.'

She is about to challenge him with a question about the Jews who were betrayed, dispossessed and deported, but he is looking at his watch. 'I'm afraid we must drive back. I am being interviewed by the BBC this afternoon for a program to coincide with Liberation Day.'

'Liberation Day?'

'May 9. If you're still here, I think you'll find it interesting. And it might answer some of your questions.'

Back in the house an hour later, Xanthe keeps glancing at the time. She is impatient for Daniel to call, impatient to be in his arms and hear his passionate voice murmuring how much he wants her. She inserts a coffee pod into the Nespresso machine and while the aroma of coffee fills the kitchen, marvels at the coincidence, synchronicity, serendipity or whatever it is that has brought her and Daniel together. What were the chances of falling in love with another Australian on a tiny island on the other side of the world? Perhaps this is what they call kismet, something she has always scoffed at. But whatever you call it, it's a miracle, and she can't stop smiling.

Upstairs in the bedroom, she opens Hugh's journal, curious to find out more about his relationship with Aoife, but a moment later she puts it down and thinks about Bob's question. She knows why she wanted to become a doctor. The issue is not why she did medicine, but whether she wants to give it up.

Back in Sydney, she knew she had to get away from the hospital and everything connected with it before it destroyed her. But now she is no longer sure. Hugh's experiences have stirred something dormant, reawakened her excitement about being a physician. He has made her think about her own shortcomings. In staying at his post and not abandoning his patients, he seemed to reproach her for being self-indulgent. Despite the enormous personal price he paid, and the problems he faced, he continued to take care of his patients. And he didn't do it from a sense of duty, but because it was wired so firmly into his DNA that it was impossible for him to do otherwise. She is convinced his ego wouldn't have been fragile enough to be deterred by the toxic culture of a hospital, or the arrogance of registrars and specialists. Maybe not even by a colleague's suicide. So perhaps the question she should consider is simply whether she is willing to revive her lifelong dream of healing people. She thinks back to her discussion with Bob about risk. Would she be one of the bystanders, or the one who dashed into the flames?

Her mind returns to the scene on the road where she worked on the unconscious man, and she recalls the elation she felt when his heart started beating again.

Daniel had commented that she was born to do this, and that's what she had always believed, but her mission had been obliterated by humiliation, stress and anxiety. By her wounded ego. Did she really want to abandon what she had always believed was her vocation?

She is so deep in thought that when her phone buzzes, she jumps. It's Daniel, and he suggests meeting for a drink at the Cock and Bottle in thirty minutes.

She is the first to arrive at the pub and orders a Stoli on the rocks while she waits for him. It's pleasant to sit outside on this mild spring evening, a breeze ruffling her hair, which brushes her shoulders. She has left it loose, the way he likes it. The banks, offices and shops have closed, and people are hurrying home after work.

She has just emptied her glass and is considering whether to have another when she looks up and sees Daniel coming towards her. He places his bag on a chair, leans over and kisses her, a long lingering kiss that promises further pleasures.

'I've been looking forward to this all day,' she says when she finally breaks away.

'The vodka, you mean?' He says it with a straight face.

'Of course,' she teases back.

'Another?' he asks. She shakes her head, and he goes inside to order his Campari and soda.

'So what did you find out today?' she asks when he comes back with his drink.

He pauses before replying. 'I know this sounds dramatic, but I've come to the conclusion that the Jersey authorities became part of the structure that made the Holocaust possible. Like the lawyers in Germany, the Jersey lawyers became part of that killing machine simply by doing their job. And they didn't seem to realise that they were breaking their professional code of conduct.'

Xanthe frowns. This is getting complicated. She wants that second vodka after all. 'How do you mean?'

'Well, lawyers aren't supposed to divulge the names of their clients or their clients' businesses, but many of them did. They not only identified Jews, and compiled lists of their assets, but they handed them over to the Germans simply because they were required to by law.'

He is warming to his subject, and she sits forward to concentrate. 'I read a letter from a law firm about one of their clients. They couldn't tell if she was Jewish or not, but they informed the authorities about her, just in case. The fact that this law was immoral, evil and pathological didn't seem to affect their judgement. It was the law, and that was all that mattered.'

He pauses to shake the ice cubes in his Campari before continuing, and she notices that he is speaking more rapidly than usual.

'Sorry if I'm giving you too much information,' he says. 'Long story short, the lawyers here unquestioningly accepted the creation of Jews as a distinct legal category. Anti-Semitism became part of the normal legal system of Jersey, and anti-Jewish laws became ordinary laws to be implemented like any others. So Jews became a legal category, singled out and identified through normal legal and administrative processes. And no-one acknowledged what was happening.'

'I had no idea it was like that here during the war,' she says.

'It was like that in most occupied countries, but the interesting thing for me is that it did happen here, despite the myth of British moral superiority.'

Xanthe is silent, trying to reconcile what Daniel has told her with what Bob and the other members of the rescue network had done. 'But there were many people at the time who risked their lives to shelter escaped slave labourers,' she argues. 'You can't lump them in with the lawyers and public servants.'

'There are always exceptions, like the people who rush into burning buildings.'

As soon as he says this, she feels a jolt. It isn't just that he is unknowingly echoing her conversation with Bob. It strikes her for the first time that she had rushed out of a burning building herself.

'I think I've been trying to run away from myself,' she says slowly.

He reaches across the table, cups her face gently with his warm hands, and looks into her eyes. 'Maybe you've been running towards yourself,' he says.

CHAPTER TWENTY-FOUR

Tom

Germany, July 1943

Tom stood frozen to the spot, arms rigid by his sides, almost afraid to blink in case he attracted the attention of Kapo Mintz, who was smashing his club into anyone who wasn't looking straight ahead. When he heard the sickening thwack of the club on the heads and backs of his fellow prisoners, his heart pounded and his legs shook. Around him, several prisoners were already collapsed on the ground, groaning as blows continued raining down on their bodies. Mintz continued wielding his club with maniacal glee.

Standing at the back, just looking on, were guards with Death's Head insignia on their caps, and lapels embossed with the letters SS. The French prisoners had warned Tom that the SS camp guards were thugs, recruited from the dregs of the German population. From their cold, hard expressions, he realised he couldn't expect any human feeling from them.

Panting and sweating from his exertions, Mintz interrupted his bashing spree for a moment to shout, 'You are all filthy terrorists, and I'll discipline you if it's the last thing I do. From now on, you have no names, only numbers, and I'll deal with anyone who hasn't memorised theirs by tomorrow morning.'

Tom had no doubt of the fate that awaited him if he failed to remember his number and he started repeating it over and over in his head.

Mintz, who must have realised that none of them were German, now repeated his threats in French.

The tense silence that followed his announcement was broken by an apologetic English voice. 'Sorry, I don't understand.'

Tom held his breath. It was Harry.

Like an enraged beast, Mintz hurled himself at Harry and started bashing him with his cudgel. When Harry tried to protect his head with his hands, Mintz struck his groin. Harry screamed in pain. Tom was in turmoil. He couldn't stand by and do nothing, but he knew that intervening would unleash Mintz's fury on himself. The *kapo* continued bashing Harry, who tottered and fell, but Mintz kept kicking him as he lay on the ground.

Although he was terrified of becoming the next victim of Mintz's savagery, Tom heard himself speak before he even knew what he was going to say.

'Excuse me, sir, he is English and doesn't understand French or German,' he said in a voice he hardly recognised as his own.

Mintz's eyes bulged and he strode towards Tom, his cudgel raised. Tom held his breath and waited for the blow to land, but with a shrug, the *kapo* turned away. Tom put his arms around his friend and hauled him to his feet.

But Mintz hadn't finished with them yet. 'Form one line, and start running around the *appellplatz*, fast,' he yelled. Suddenly the SS men were among them, armed with pick-axe shafts, screaming '*Los! Los! Schnell! Schneller!*' They bashed the prisoners who couldn't keep up, and when that didn't speed them up, they kicked them mercilessly with their jackboots.

Tom looked anxiously at Harry, who was gasping but managed to keep going at the demonic pace the SS set. Although some of the prisoners crumpled onto the ground, the SS men continued kicking them and yelling for them to get up, while Kapo Mintz ran around shouting obscenities about good-for-nothing French criminals and promising to teach them good German discipline. The fact that by then some of the men were unconscious didn't stop the mindless brutality.

Despite his terror and exhaustion, and the pain in his chest, Tom managed to keep up the punishing pace around the perimeter of the yard. As he ran, too exhausted to continue but too terrified to stop, it seemed to him that this surreal scene resembled a painting of hell he had once seen in an art book. Like the satanic creatures in the painting, their guards were relishing their sadistic sport, and it seemed to Tom that Kapo Mintz was trying to outdo his SS masters, perhaps to prove that he could match their cruelty.

Bored with this activity, Mintz ordered the exhausted prisoners to do push-ups, and brought his club down on anyone who stopped. Before long, hardly anyone was able to raise their chest off the ground. This was the signal for the SS to run amok with their weapons, threatening to shoot anyone who didn't move.

Totally spent, Tom lay on the ground waiting for the bullet to shatter his skull, but then Mintz came up with a new idea, which he proceeded to demonstrate. They were to squat, jump like frogs, and squat again all around the exercise yard, until he permitted them to stop. His SS masters found this entertainment hilarious, inspiring Mintz to new heights of brutality.

'Now you're real French frogs!' he yelled, delighted with his wit.

But by now even threats of being shot had no effect on the prisoners, most of whom could no longer move. Tom's muscles were cramping and he was in such agony that he collapsed on the ground, beyond caring what ensued. If they shot him this torment would end. He marvelled that Harry was still on his feet, although he moved like an automaton.

Finally even Mintz and the SS could see that their fun was over, but before allowing them to return to their barracks, Mintz shouted that this was just a gentle prelude to life in the camp. He then issued instructions that they had to obey or suffer the consequences.

The list seemed endless, and Tom found it difficult to take it all in as his head was spinning and his whole body throbbed with pain. Walking was forbidden: no matter where they were going, they had to run. Whenever they passed a guard they had to remove their hats, slap them against their thighs, and snap their heads sharply to the left or right to salute them, probably to reinforce their slave-like status in the camp.

Finally they were dismissed from the exercise yard and were sent to the barber shop. After having their hair shorn, they were issued razor blades and ordered to shave their body hair. But as there was no hot water or shaving soap, and the blades were blunt, this was excruciating. The blades scraped and cut sensitive parts of their bodies, and soon blood was running down Tom's thighs. For the SS looking on, however, this was another source of amusement. Despite the pain, Tom couldn't help wondering at the mentality of these men.

The showers offered them another opportunity for entertainment. The water was alternately scalding and ice-cold, but anyone who tried to escape was immediately beaten back by the SS.

The humiliation continued during the medical inspection when they had to parade naked in front of the camp doctor, an obese leering brute who brandished a long thin cane with which he whipped them while making obscene comments about their anatomy. As they were marched off from the doctor they were handed ill-fitting prison uniforms and wooden clogs.

After another interminable roll call with its inevitable counting and recounting, they were finally allowed to go into the quarantine hut, where they were to remain for a week.

Tom sank onto his hard wooden bunk, shell-shocked. *This can't be happening*, he kept thinking. *It can't be real.* He should be at school, learning physics and chemistry, playing sport, riding his bicycle, even delivering his mother's black-market goods, instead of being brutalised by these monsters.

He thought back to the Occupation that he had found so unbearable and wondered how it was possible that the Germans who had behaved in a relatively law-abiding manner in Jersey belonged to the same race as the sadists in this camp.

He glanced at Harry, who looked like a ghost, and he fought down a rising sense of panic. If they were going to make it, they'd have to use every ounce of mental strength to keep their spirits up.

Pierre, one of the older Resistance fighters, was surveying him with a paternal expression.

'Listen, Churchill,' he said, '*Prends garde*. Watch yourself. What you did today was admirable, but this is not the place for heroics.'

'What do you mean?'

'You spoke up for your friend out there in the *appellplatz*. Very noble. But next time that will get you killed. The only way to survive in a place like this is to look after yourself. Only yourself. Remember that, *mon ami*.'

Tom nodded but didn't reply. His first instinct while Harry was being attacked was to avoid being noticed at all costs, to try and make himself invisible, to distance himself from what was happening. But he couldn't do it. It ran counter to everything that had been inculcated into him from childhood about honour, decency and British courage.

Tom gave a bitter laugh when he recalled that the person who had instilled all that into him was his father, who turned out to be the biggest coward of all. But although by speaking up he had risked injury, maybe even his life, his action gave him a sense of pride. At least on this occasion he hadn't let himself down.

Pierre was still looking at him and there was sympathy in his eyes. 'We all need an ideal to keep us going in here,' he said. 'We need to have faith in the future. My dream is that when this is over, I will help to rebuild France into the country I love and can be proud of. Do you have something you can cling to that will give you the strength to survive this hell?'

Tom considered this for a few moments and his eyes hardened. 'There is someone at home who betrayed me,' he said slowly. 'I can't wait to get my own back.'

Now it was Pierre's turn to be silent. He was obviously turning this over in his mind. 'I understand how you feel, *mon vieux*,' he said. 'That is natural. But revenge is the weapon of the weak, and I do not think you are weak. Forgiveness is the tool of the strong.'

Tom was still grappling with this when Pierre was distracted by a heated argument among his companions about communists in the Resistance.

'You cannot trust the Reds,' Luc was saying. 'They always look to Russia first. They didn't join us when the Germans occupied us because their hero Stalin had a pact with Hitler. It was only after Germany invaded Russia that they got Stalin's permission to fight the Nazis.'

Tom listened for a while but soon lost interest in their discussion. He turned his attention to Harry, who lay on the bunk, groaning with every movement.

He let out a long sigh. 'I don't know how much of this I can take, Tom.'

'You'll feel better tomorrow,' Tom said with a certainty he didn't feel. He looked at his friend's hollow cheeks and was suddenly overcome with remorse. 'I'm sorry I dragged you into this,' he said. 'You would have been happy to stay in St Helier if I hadn't egged you on to come with Frank and me.'

Harry tried to sit up but fell back on his bunk. 'Don't flatter yourself,' he said. 'I have a mind of my own and I decided to come. It's not your fault. How could you know that any of this would happen?'

Just then, their room senior, a Frenchman called Bruneau, rushed towards them, punched Harry in the face, and screamed, 'Who said you could talk, you English swine? I'm in charge here and you'd better do as I say. I'll make you English pay for abandoning us at Dunkirk and blowing up our fleet!'

With that, he pulled back his fist to land another blow on Harry's face but Tom and two of the French prisoners leaped forward, grabbed his arm and twisted it behind his back.

'Watch it, Bruneau,' one of them hissed. 'The war will be over soon, and you'll be the one who pays.'

'He's French!' Tom said in amazement when Bruneau had stormed out of the hut.

'He's a Nazi bootlicking rat, and we are ashamed of him,' Pierre said, and the others nodded. 'But you did abandon us at Dunkirk, and you did destroy our fleet!'

Tom's blood was up. 'I don't know anything about your fleet, but if Mr Churchill did it, I'm sure he had a good reason. As for Dunkirk, if our boatmen hadn't risked their lives to sail to Normandy and rescue some of your soldiers, all of them would have been killed on those beaches.'

'Let's drop it,' Luc intervened. 'This is something we'll never agree on, but now we are all in the same boat, *n'est-ce pas?*'

Still seething, Tom turned away to wipe the blood off Harry's face. He lay on his bunk, and it seemed as if he had barely closed his eyes when the deafening shrill of a whistle made him jump out of his bunk in panic. It was already four-thirty in the morning and Bruneau was back, dispensing blows in all directions and yelling that they were filthy swine and their hut was a pigsty.

'I thought we were at war with the Germans,' Harry whispered.

Outside, all hell broke loose. Accompanied by yells, screams and punches, they had to run the gauntlet of club-wielding SS men in order to reach the exercise yard for roll call, which was followed by exercises. The drill sergeant beat his leather drum with the enthusiasm of a percussionist in a symphony orchestra, and to complete the macabre scene, skeletal prisoners did back-breaking exercises in time to the drumbeat. It was hard to keep their wooden clogs on their feet, but Tom noticed that whenever a clog fell off, the *kapos* pounced on its unfortunate owner and punched him in the face.

That afternoon, as they talked to their fellow prisoners again, they discovered the answer to the question that had puzzled them ever since their capture. 'We are being detained under Hitler's *Nacht und Neben* decree,' explained Philippe, a young Luxembourg prisoner who had been caught distributing anti-Nazi leaflets.

'Night and Fog,' Tom translated for Harry, before asking, 'What decree is that?'

'It says that anyone accused of undermining German security can be cut off from the outside world, deported to Germany, and tried in a special court,' Philippe explained. 'This is Hitler's way of circumventing military courts and international agreements about the treatment of prisoners. That's why we haven't received any letters or parcels from home.'

They sat in silence trying to absorb what this meant. 'So we're regarded as political activists,' Harry said with a wry smile. 'I suppose that's a step up from being failed escapees.'

But Tom wasn't smiling. At last he understood why they had been denied all contact with their families from the very beginning. Philippe's explanation removed any vestige of hope he had entertained for their trial. Being charged with undermining Nazi security was far more serious than trying to escape, and the fact that they were imprisoned with genuine political dissidents didn't augur well.

'Night and Fog is a peculiar term for a repressive law,' Pierre commented.

There was a pause until Luc explained. 'It's a phrase from Goethe, the German poet, who used it to describe clandestine actions that are concealed in the darkness of night. So when you think about it, it's really quite apt.'

'We always knew the Germans were a cultured race,' Pierre said.

That evening, dinner consisted of thin soup that tasted like dishwater with tiny lumps of turnip floating in it, and a piece of black bread that tasted like sawdust. Tom, who had already lost so much weight that he'd had to find a length of rope to hold up his trousers, wondered how long he could survive on this starvation diet.

Harry held out his bread to Tom. 'You have it, I'm not hungry,' he said.

It was tempting but Tom forced himself to refuse. Harry was gaunt, and hardly any flesh covered his bones. 'You have to eat it,' he said.

Later, before falling asleep, Tom tried to comprehend their situation. After a week at this quarantine camp, they would be transferred to the main camp where, according to a Swiss *kapo* who was more approachable than the others, conditions were far worse.

'Here's some good advice,' the *kapo* had said. 'When you get there, always look busy. Never walk anywhere, but hurry as if you're on an important errand. Keep away from the *kapos* and the SS, and avoid the German doctor at all costs. He's a sadist and an alcoholic and they reckon he probably isn't a doctor at all. Try to see the French doctor instead.'

Tom was too much on edge to sleep even though he knew the daily chaos would erupt again in a few hours. To make things worse, he couldn't stop thinking about Milly and wondering if she was still with that Kraut. The idea of a Kraut's hands all over her body made his blood boil. His thoughts turned to his mother and he seethed even more. Did she ever feel guilty about turning him in? She was probably getting richer from all her black-market business and never gave him a thought. But she would have to think about him when he came back and made sure she got what she deserved. Then he recalled what Pierre had said about revenge, and decided that Pierre was wrong. Revenge would be sweet and that's what would keep him going.

Just before he fell asleep, he recalled an expression his mother had used whenever things went wrong. 'Never two without three,' she often said.

He used to dismiss it as an old wives' tale, but now the barb hooked into his mind and he couldn't dislodge it. First Frank had drowned and then he and Harry were captured. That made two. What would be the third?

CHAPTER TWENTY-FIVE

Dr Jackson

St Helier, April 1944

Whenever I listen to the BBC, I never hear any mention of the Channel Islands, and I can't help wondering whether anyone in the UK is even aware that we have been under German occupation for as long as most of the countries in Europe. That makes our situation even more frustrating, but there's nothing I can do about it.

All I can do is keep looking after my patients. Yesterday Mrs Blake called me in a panic – her little girl was having an asthma attack. I rushed over to St Saviour as fast as I could, terrified that I wouldn't get there in time. The poor child was wheezing and gasping, and the mother was beside herself, but after I had injected her with epinephrine, she began to settle down. Her grateful mother offered me a cup of acorn coffee, but I can't stand the stuff, and besides, I had to hurry back to my surgery.

It was a relief to see the child breathing normally again, but I worry about the future as our supplies of epinephrine are dwindling fast. What will happen next time Claire has an asthma attack?

The incidence of asthma seems to have increased in the past few years. Not surprising, really, given the level of stress we are under, but this is by no means a modern phenomenon. From what I remember of my medical studies, it was Hippocrates, the Greek physician, who first coined the word asthma to identify this distressing respiratory condition. It's humbling to realise that, back in the fifth century BC, he observed that climatic and environmental factors sometimes contribute to asthma.

A few hundred years later, in Roman times, Pliny noticed that the pollen of certain plants caused respiratory problems, and recommended the use of ephedra, which is actually the forerunner of ephedrine. The history of medicine is fascinating, and what I find intriguing is that in the twelfth century the Jewish scholar and physician Maimonides wrote a treatise on asthma in which he forbade nuts but recommended chicken soup!

I fantasised about an invention, an inhaler small enough to be portable, that asthmatics could carry around in case of an attack. Perhaps if a science-fiction writer ever describes such a thing in a novel, it will happen, for I firmly believe that whatever one human brain is capable of imagining, another brain is capable of inventing.

I can't vouch for chicken soup, but as things stand, ephedrine is the most effective treatment we have. Unfortunately, our medications come from France, so deliveries are unpredictable, and when they do arrive, the Germans grab most of them before they reach our hospitals. This is the case with insulin, which has been catastrophic for the diabetics who depend on it.

All this was churning in my mind as I drove back to my surgery, where several patients were already in the waiting room. Keeping people waiting makes me nervous, and I was apologising profusely when the door opened and Bob Blampied rushed in. From his expression I could see that something serious had happened.

Normally, I take my time with the patients, listening carefully to their symptoms to make sure I don't miss anything, even when they have come in just to share their problems, but on this occasion I was relieved that none of them were suffering from complicated ailments that required lengthy consultations.

As soon as the last one had left, I ushered Bob inside my consulting room and closed the door. He looked strained, and there was no trace of his usual good humour. I noticed that he was sitting on the edge of his chair, clasping and unclasping his hands.

'Those witches have done it now,' he blurted without any preamble.

It took me a few moments to realise he was referring to the women who had threatened to inform on Ethel Carter. I consoled myself with the thought that even if the German field police had searched her house, they wouldn't have found anything. Thank goodness we had warned her in time.

But Bob looked grim. 'They've taken her away,' he said.

I was shocked. 'Why on earth would they do that? I dropped in to see her the day after you moved Sasha to St Ouen, and she had removed every sign he'd ever been there. They couldn't possibly have found anything incriminating. What happened?'

Bob sighed. 'Yesterday I dropped in to see how she was, but she wasn't there. When I knocked next door, her neighbour looked upset. She said that she had dropped in to see Mrs Carter to borrow some flour when the German field police barged in and started searching the whole house – cupboards, drawers, shelves, everything. All this time, Mrs Carter was apparently quite calm. *I don't know why you're here, I've got nothing to hide,* she told the police, who just pushed past her taking no notice, and kept on searching.'

Unable to contain my impatience any longer, I burst in, 'But surely they didn't find anything?'

Bob sighed. 'Unfortunately they did. Under her bed, wrapped in a hand-crocheted quilt, they found a wireless. You can imagine how they pounced on that. But that's not the end of it,' he added glumly. 'In the attic, they found a rusty rifle.'

'But they must realise that an elderly widow wouldn't even know how to use a rifle.'

'You and I know that, Dr Jackson,' he replied. 'And according to her neighbour, that's what Mrs Carter kept telling them. She insisted she didn't even know it was there, that her husband must have put it there years ago, before the war. But they didn't take any notice of what she said.

'*And the wireless?* One of them sneered. *Maybe you didn't know about that either?* Then he called her an Englander liar.

'At that, Mrs Carter apparently lost her temper and let fly with a few choice expletives. She yelled at them to stop persecuting innocent people and making everyone's life a misery. *Just wait till your rotten Führer is defeated, then we'll show you who's been lying!* It's as if all her pent-up emotions over the past few years were flooding out of her mouth. Her neighbour was nudging her to keep quiet, but she wouldn't listen. They grabbed her arms, handcuffed her, and dragged her into their car, still shouting that they were murderers and would soon pay for their crimes.'

I was relieved she'd been caught with a rifle and a radio instead of an escaped slave labourer, which might have resulted in our entire network being exposed and the end of our efforts to help the fugitives.

Nevertheless, I was very worried about Mrs Carter. Possessing radios and firearms are serious offences. I know several people who have been sent to prison for having a secret wireless, and that's why I keep mine well hidden, and only listen through the earphones with the sound turned down whenever I tune in to the BBC News, in case a malicious neighbour with sharp ears is listening. A politician once said that truth was the first casualty of war, but in my opinion, it's loss of trust.

'I wonder what will happen to her,' I said.

Bob shook his head. 'All I know is that they've still got her in the police cell. Her neighbour said she wasn't allowed visitors, and they refused to answer her questions, so she doesn't know if she'll be charged.'

Recalling what happened to Tom Gaskell, I can't shake off a sense of dread. I only hope that her age will be a mitigating factor. And that she keeps her temper under control. As for the women that denounced her, I don't have a vocabulary colourful enough to express what I think about them. If they ever come to my surgery, I will refuse to see them, despite my Hippocratic oath.

It has now been several weeks since Mrs Carter's arrest, and I still don't know what has happened to her. In the meantime, Sasha seems to get on well with his new carers. We haven't told him about Mrs Carter's arrest for fear of distressing him. He's quite temperamental, as so many of those Russian and French prisoners seem to be, and for all our sakes, we need to keep him calm. As for Mrs Carter, all we can do is wait and hope, although I feel more apprehension than optimism.

I don't think my patients suspect that I am so stressed. As a doctor, I feel like a parent who has to appear self-assured and know all the answers. This is a role that I have practised over the years, as much to convince myself as others, and by now it has become second nature.

How can I expect patients to have enough confidence in me to confide their problems, and to trust me to diagnose and treat their diseases, if I seem weak and vulnerable?

The only person with whom I drop my mask is Aoife. She is my medicine and my healer, and at the end of another problem-filled day, I can't wait to spend a few hours with her.

So that evening, when I heard her car pull up outside my house, without waiting for her to ring the bell, I flung open the door and held her so tightly that she laughed and said I'd fair knocked the breath out of her.

It was that lovely time of day, neither day nor evening, when the light pouring from the sky had an opalescent sheen and flights of swallows winged across the garden. She had unpinned her hair, which she usually wore twisted into some sort of roll, and I loved to watch it flowing down her white back like a russet waterfall.

We were sitting side by side in contented silence, my arm around her shoulders. As a physician, I know that hearts don't swell with happiness, burst with pride, or change their dimensions with any other emotions, but I swear that at that moment I could feel mine expand to an almost unbearable degree of happiness. Nothing existed outside this room. I felt the serenity that the Buddhists describe during meditation. With all its imperfections, the world was perfect. Little did I suspect that my peace of mind was about to be shattered in a way I couldn't possibly have imagined.

I looked at her lovely face smiling up at me and knew that I would want to look at her for the rest of my life. Just then, a few lines of a love poem flashed across my mind, lines I wasn't even aware I had ever memorised.

'*If ever any beauty I desired and got,*
'twas but a dream of thee.'

She didn't speak, and when I looked down, I saw tears in her eyes. We sat in silence, with Donne's words garlanding the space around us.

Then Aoife spoke, and in a small, sad voice, she said, 'Hugh, there's something I have to tell you.'

My heart that only minutes before had swelled and expanded, now contracted into a cold fist. I didn't want to hear what she was about to say because I had a premonition that nothing would ever be the same again.

Even now, a week later, I'm still struggling with what she told me, and I hope that writing it down will help me to come to terms with it. I'll try to recall exactly what she said.

'You were probably puzzled, upset maybe, that I never wanted to talk about my life before we met,' she began in a tremulous voice.

It was unlike the firm voice I was accustomed to hearing, and it struck me that the woman speaking wasn't the capable, efficient matron I knew.

'I'm going to tell you this because I don't want to keep any secrets from you but this is very hard for me to say, so you'll have to let me finish.'

I nodded. My mouth was so dry that I doubt I would even have been capable of speaking.

'As you know, I was born in Ireland, in one of those picturesque little coastal towns surrounded by emerald fields.

'There were churches on every street, and pubs on every corner. The tourists loved our pubs, especially the jovial characters who entertained them singing and playing their fiddles. But I hated them because my da was one of those colourful pub characters, and he rolled home drunk every night. He spent all our money on whisky and when my mam complained, he knocked her around.'

She paused for a moment, and from the tightness in my chest, I realised I'd been holding my breath.

'The only thing he was good at was making children,' she continued. 'I was the oldest of seven, and with him spending all his time and money in the pub, Mam was worn out trying to make ends meet. That's where our local priest came in.'

Her voice, low and hesitant until now, assumed a hard edge. 'I was about twelve when Father O'Halloran started coming round to see how Mam was getting on. She thought the sun shone out of him, so when he started taking notice of me, and telling her what a clever girl I was, and what a beautiful singing voice I had, you'd have thought she'd won the lottery.

'When he suggested I should sing in the church choir, I was very proud, especially after he said he'd give me private lessons so I could catch up with the others. It was a great honour to be singled out by a priest, especially one as popular as Father O'Halloran.'

She turned away from me, and her tone became increasingly bitter. 'The first time he stroked my chest over my dress, I thought maybe it was accidental, or maybe I'd imagined it. But after he did it several more times, I knew it wasn't my imagination, not when I saw the way he looked at me. I didn't know what to do. I made excuses to stop coming to choir, but Mam got angry with me for letting Father down and ordered me to keep going. I didn't have the words to explain what he was doing, and I knew she wouldn't believe me. She would think I was making it up.

'So I had to go on seeing him and putting up with his wandering hands, which were soon wandering inside my pants. *You're my darlin' girl*, he used to murmur, with that revolting look on his face.'

I swallowed and reached forward to take her hand but she pulled it away, shook her head and folded her arms tightly, as if she was literally holding herself together.

'At first, I was flattered at being singled out by the priest for special attention. I didn't yet know what that special attention entailed. The day he pulled out his penis and told me to stroke it, I felt like vomiting. I threatened to tell Mam, but he said that would be a pity because she would lose her job at the presbytery and then where would we be?

'So I put up with his assaults, and sobbed all the way home. There was no-one I could tell, no-one who would believe me. I wondered if it was my fault somehow. *It's our little secret now, isn't it?* he would say when he'd finished ejaculating.

'But the day I came home doubled up in pain, with blood-stained underpants, I knew I had to tell my Mam what he'd done. She had to protect me, even if she lost her job.

'I'd just got through the door, when she ran towards me in tears. My little brother needed an urgent operation which she couldn't pay for, but the wonderful Father O'Halloran had come to the rescue and offered to pay for his surgery.'

Aoife turned and rested her large grey eyes on me for a few moments without speaking. Then she said slowly, 'Can you imagine what it feels like to be thirteen years old and know that you're trapped and can't escape? That you have to submit to a paedophile's lust because there's no-one in the whole world who can protect you?'

Her tears were falling and I wanted to take her in my arms to comfort her. I stretched out to take her hand again, and this time she didn't resist.

As she continued her story, I was quivering with apprehension. 'I was fifteen when my periods stopped. I didn't think anything of it at the time, but when my body began to change shape, I mentioned it to one of the nuns at school. She gave me a sharp look and asked, *What have you been up to? Have you committed a carnal sin?* Her reaction shocked me and at first I didn't understand what she meant, but later I realised what had happened to me. I panicked. I didn't know what to do or who to turn to. For a few months I did nothing at all, hoping it would just go away, but when I got bigger, and friends began to tease me about eating too many praties, I knew I'd have to tell someone.

'So I told my mam. She stepped away from me with a horrified look on her face, as if I'd murdered someone. *Who did this?* she demanded. I was relieved. Now I'd be able to tell her the whole story from the beginning. But when I told her it was Father O'Halloran, she screamed that I was a wicked girl, committing a sin, telling lies and blaming our priest for my shameful behaviour.

'That night, when my da came home, I heard her telling him. He took off his belt, grabbed me by the arm, dragged me into the living room, and started belting me. While my brothers and sisters watched from the doorway, he called me a whore for bringing disgrace on our family and said he never wanted to set eyes on me again.

'Until that moment, I had felt so depressed I wished I was dead, but when he said that, something inside me snapped. "You're a fine one to talk, coming home drunk every night and not supporting your own family," I shouted back. "I don't want to see you again either," and I ran out of the house.'

'Where did you go?' I whispered.

'That night I slept at my auntie's house. I could tell she didn't believe what I told her about Father O'Halloran, but she knew what my da was like, so she let me stay with her.

'You can't imagine what it was like living in that small town back then, pregnant at the age of fifteen, with everyone looking at you, whispering, and pointing. The worst part was that no-one believed me, not even my own parents, while Father O'Halloran was probably molesting other girls.

'Of course an abortion was unthinkable. It was regarded as murder and forbidden by a church which didn't seem to object to priests raping children.'

'So what happened?' I asked in a hoarse voice I hardly recognised as my own. It felt unreal, as if I was listening to a compelling story told by a stranger, not by the woman I loved. 'What did you do?'

'If I could have killed myself, I would have done it,' she said. 'I couldn't stay there but I had nowhere else to go. I had heard shocking stories about the cruel nuns who ran homes for unmarried mothers in Ireland, but there didn't seem to be any alternative until Auntie Kath found out about a convent in Jersey where pregnant girls did housework in return for their keep, and after the baby was born, the nuns would arrange for it to be adopted.'

Distracted by the sudden flapping of wings across the garden, she stopped talking and gazed through the window. Perhaps she needed to have a break from telling her painful story, but all my muscles were knotted, and I found it difficult to sit still while I waited for her to continue.

'So is that why you came here?' I asked, prodding her gently to return to her story.

She sighed, a very deep sigh that sounded as if it was dragged from the very depths of her being. 'That's why. At the age of fifteen, I travelled alone to St Helier. I'll never forget my first sight of L'Abbaye, where I was sentenced to live until my baby was born. It was a dark, forbidding place, but the nuns were the darkest of all.'

She shivered and blinked several times to hold back the tears. 'So many bitter, frustrated women free to take out their rage at the world on the poor orphans in their care. Sister Cecilia was an exception. She took care of me all through my pregnancy, and inspired me to become a nurse. So you see, one good thing came out of it.'

I could hardly bring myself to ask the question that was uppermost in my mind. 'And the baby?'

'They placed her in my arms for a few moments after she was born. Until then, I wasn't interested in the baby, and didn't even want to see her, but as soon as I looked at her, I fell in love. She looked like a delicate rose petal, with perfect tiny fingers and toes. I couldn't stop crying at the wonder of it, the miracle of her. And the pain of giving her up. While I sobbed, Sister Cecilia sat beside me stroking my hand, and assuring me that they would find a good home for her where she would be loved and cherished.'

Turning to face me now, her eyes full of tears, Aoife said quietly, 'Now you know. That was eighteen years ago, and I have never told anyone about it.'

My heart ached for Aoife. I wanted to protect her for the rest of her life so she would never feel such anguish again. I knew that having torn open the wound that she had concealed for so long, she would need to heal it, to resolve all the pain, rage and grief she had suppressed for most of her life. As I folded her in my arms and we watched the shadows fall across the garden, I recalled the poignant lyrics she had sung, and I wondered if they foretold our future.

CHAPTER TWENTY-SIX

Xanthe

St Helier, April 2019

It's the kind of spring morning that inspires poets, and Xanthe can almost taste its bright freshness on her tongue. The tide is ebbing, revealing an ever-widening stretch of wet sand. She is waiting for the sea to recede so she can walk across the causeway to Elizabeth Castle, but as soon as she catches sight of Bill McAllister striding along Royal Square, she abandons her plan and runs across the road to catch up with him.

From the broad smile on his freckled face, it seems he is pleased to see her.

'How are you enjoying your stay?' he asks. 'I've wrapped up my investigation, so I'll be heading back to Sussex tomorrow.'

It looks as if this will be her last chance to ask the question that has niggled at her ever since she read Hugh's last entry.

'Those human bones you told me about, the ones that were found at the back of that old convent, did you find out whose they were? Were they really children's bones?'

'I'm ready for a cup of tea. Why don't we sit down over there and I'll tell you all about it,' he suggests, pointing to the Regal Café on the corner.

A few minutes later they are sitting inside a café whose charmless interior belies its name. The waitress, in a black apron streaked with flour, clatters the cups and saucers as she sets them down, and Xanthe waits until she has disappeared into the curtained kitchen before speaking.

'I've been curious about it. It sounded like something from a horror movie.' She doesn't tell him that her interest in this place has been aroused by a true story she has read in a wartime journal.

He chuckles. 'So you'll be disappointed that those bones were the remains of monks who used to live there.'

'Monks? Wasn't this a convent?'

'I'm no' a history buff, but I believe it was originally a monastery and became a convent much later. There were horror stories about this place a couple of years ago. The tabloids had a field day speculating about murdered babies buried in secret and that's why I was sent here to investigate. It made news all over the world. Did you no' hear about it in Australia?'

She shakes her head. 'All I know is that it was once a home for unmarried girls. I heard that as soon as the babies were born, the nuns gave them to couples who wanted to adopt.'

He pours milk into his tea and takes a few sips before turning his gaze on her without giving away his thoughts. In the movies, it's the way detectives survey suspects to give them time to keep talking and incriminate themselves.

Putting down his cup, he leans forward. 'Tell me, do you have a personal interest in this place?'

Xanthe pauses before replying. 'I recently read a story about a girl who had a baby there in the 1920s, and had it adopted. Do you know anything about what was going on at the convent at that time?'

He looks thoughtful. 'The convent was closed down years ago and the nuns were probably relocated. I imagine that by then it wasn't regarded as such a disgrace for unmarried girls to keep their wee bairns. But there was gossip about abused orphans.'

'Really? Do you know anything about that?'

He scrolls through messages on his mobile before checking his watch. She notices that it's a solid old-fashioned one with a leather strap that she imagines once belonged to his father.

'As you're so interested in the place, would you like to see it? I could take you there now if you have time.'

As they drive towards L'Abbaye, Xanthe can hardly contain her excitement. She is about to see the place where Aoife had her baby, and she racks her brains to recall what Aoife had told Hugh about it. She remembered that the kindness of one of the nuns had inspired her to become a nurse.

They are driving north, past furrowed brown potato fields and miles of greenhouses where the sought-after Jersey tomatoes are cultivated. There are few cars on the road, and horseback riders in jodhpurs and helmets canter past on country lanes.

Closer to the coast, terns and kittiwakes screech as they fly around nests clinging to the rugged cliffs that plunge into foaming waters below.

Xanthe thinks back to the first time she saw this landscape and recalls her delight at the island's idyllic beauty, but driving towards L'Abbaye she wonders if she is about to glimpse its darkness.

From time to time Bill glances at her with concern, as if there's something on his mind. Finally he says, 'L'Abbaye is a strange place. A sensitive lassie like you might find it unsettling.'

He turns into a narrow lane lined with straight, dark poplars that almost touch the sky and cast long shadows on the path. The lane ends in a cul-de-sac and suddenly they are confronted by a gloomy building of dark stone with a large cross above the entrance.

Xanthe gets out of the car and walks towards it. It's just an abandoned building, she tells herself, but her heart is beating against her ribs and her legs are unsteady. She knows it's irrational, but an air of menace seems to emanate from its walls. Even the clump of daffodils growing on the small patch of grass to the left of the entrance looks contrived, as though it has been planted there to conceal its true nature.

Bill has been studying her in silence. 'They held an inquiry into this place back in the 1990s.'

'An inquiry? Why?'

He sits on a wooden bench beside the path, brushes aside some cobwebs, and motions for her to join him. 'I have to warn you, it's no' a pretty story,' he begins.

For the next half hour, she sits motionless as he describes the chilling testimony given by people who had suffered physical and sexual abuse as children at the hands of the nuns who ran this institution. At times she wants to block her ears, but she forces herself to listen to accounts of the cruelty these children were subjected to.

'So this was an orphanage as well as a home for unmarried mothers,' she says slowly.

'They used the pregnant girls as servants and cleaners for the orphanage, and they used the orphans as sex slaves. They knew the children wouldn't report the abuse, and even if they did, no-one would believe them, so they indulged their sexual fantasies with impunity.'

He looks at her white face and stops talking. 'This is upsetting you.'

She can't speak. Can't find the words to express her horror at the depths of human depravity masquerading as religious benevolence he has described.

'I had no idea. Was anyone charged?'

'By the time the victims gathered enough courage to come forward, several decades had passed, and most of the nuns they accused of abusing them were dead. Except for Sister Cecilia, who was in her nineties by then and claimed to have Alzheimer's. After protracted negotiations between the church authorities and the lawyers, the church ended up paying some compensation to the victims, but of course it came too late for those who had committed suicide or died from drug overdoses as a result of the trauma they'd suffered in there. I think the worst part was that they didn't live long enough to hear that the crimes had finally been acknowledged, so they never had the satisfaction of being validated.'

Xanthe's mind has stalled on something he said several minutes before. 'Did you say Sister Cecilia? Are you sure that was her name?'

Bill nods. 'The newspaper reports often mentioned her name because there was a lot of pressure from the victims' lawyers to question her, but she died a few months later. Why do you ask?'

'I was reading about a girl who had her baby there back in the 1920s, and I think that's the name of the nun she mentioned. But she said Sister Cecilia had been good to her. Do you think it's possible for a person to be cruel to some people, but compassionate to others?'

He looks down at his large freckled hands, and she senses that he is scrolling through a lifetime of cases, weighing up the proposition that good and evil can dwell inside the same person.

Because that's what she is really asking. Could Sister Cecilia, who showed Aoife so much compassion that she inspired her to become a nurse, be the same Sister Cecilia who abused the helpless orphans in her care? And if it is, what does it say about our human condition?

Xanthe gets up and walks slowly towards the entrance. She thinks of fifteen-year-old Aoife coming through these doors alone, and of the orphans who could not have imagined the misery that awaited them at the soft hands of the nuns who professed to be dedicated to their God.

Peering through a grimy window, she sees dusty timber floors, and imagines them being scrubbed and polished by girls with swollen bellies who were probably told they were doing penance for their carnal transgressions. As they mopped the soapy water swirling over the wooden floor, did they grieve at the thought of giving away the babies they would never recognise even when they passed them in the street?

Or were they impatient to be rid of this evidence of their shame? But as soon as they saw their babies for the first and last time, did it feel as if their own flesh was being ripped away? She is thinking of Aoife, who has now, for the first time, emerged from the shadows of Hugh's journal and assumed a life of her own. How ironic that being sent to this institution to hide her shameful pregnancy should have resulted in devoting her life to looking after pregnant women and their babies. Life seemed to lead us along strange paths to discover our strengths.

Xanthe opens a small side gate and follows a dirt path that leads to what was once a garden but is now overgrown with spindly grasses, thorny plants and straggly weeds. At the far end, a large patch of ground has been cordoned off with yellow tape. Spades, small brushes and trowels are piled in one corner, and she supposes they have been left here by the forensic scientists and anthropologists who had been excavating the remains.

The sky has been a flawless enamelled blue but now darkens and a wind gusts in from the sea. Xanthe pushes back the hair that has blown over her face.

She shivers, but it's not from the wind. It's something in the air that weighs her down like a heavy, damp blanket. She read once that the landscape is affected by the crimes committed on it, that events can pollute the soil below and the air above. The author of that article had maintained that in Polish forests, where deep pits were filled with the bodies of men, women and children machine-gunned or buried alive and sprinkled with quicklime, the earth covering them heaved for days, and for decades afterwards locals swore that the screams of the victims still hovered in the air, and their souls haunted passers-by.

Looking back at the dark building, Xanthe can almost hear the voices of the orphans who had been silenced for so many years. For the first time in several weeks, she thinks about the mysterious presence she sensed in Hugh's house after she moved in.

Lost in thought, she walks slowly back to the bench where Bill McAllister is staring into the distance. He sees her and starts, as if he too were immersed in a reverie.

'You look as if you've seen a ghost,' he says as she joins him. 'Are you okay?'

She sinks down beside him and nods.

'I've been thinking about your question, and I canna come up with a simple answer,' he says. 'As you can imagine, I've seen the worst of human nature in my time, but I have rarely met criminals who are totally evil. You're young, and young people tend to see things as black or white, but in my experience, most of us are a mixture of both.'

He turns to face her. 'I'm sure you have a reason for asking this, so I'm sorry I canna give you a satisfactory answer. I think of us as jigsaw puzzles with pieces missing or ill-matched. That's what makes it so difficult to sum people up.'

They are heading back to St Helier when her phone rings. It's Oliver.

'Hey sis. You never told me Jersey was such a wild place. You must be raging from morning till night and don't have a minute to call.'

Although her brother is joking, she feels a pang of guilt. It's hard to explain that she has been caught up in the dramas of the past.

'Are you okay, Xan?' Oliver says. Then he adds, 'And that lawyer of yours, is he still interesting?'

She is laughing now. 'He's more interesting than ever. You'd like him.'

'If he makes you happy, I'll like him. Anyway, you sound good. When are you coming home?'

'I think I'll stay an extra week, Ollie. I want to be here for their Liberation Day on 9 May.'

She makes the decision at just that moment, but as soon as she says it, she knows it will be the right time to leave.

'I thought you were already liberated,' he says.

She pulls a face. Oliver can never resist teasing her. 'And you? Everything okay?'

'Same old same old. Mum keeps asking if I have a girlfriend yet. I think she's worried it's going to be a boyfriend. Maybe I should go to Jersey and meet someone interesting.'

'Maybe you should,' she laughs, and promises to keep in touch.

'My brother,' she explains to Bill. 'He worries about me.'

The spires of St Helier appear in the distance and Bill asks, 'Have you ever read Hemingway?'

She shakes her head and wonders where this is heading.

'You should read *For Whom the Bell Tolls*. It's about the Spanish Civil War. That's where the hero asks his lover if the earth moved for her.'

Xanthe suppresses a smile. The last thing she expected to be discussing with him was romantic fiction.

'I was thinking about Hemingway when you asked me that question about human nature,' he says. 'Now there was a man you couldn't possibly sum up in a sentence. Fighter, writer, womaniser, drunkard, hero, philosopher, political activist, student of human nature.' Bill warms to his theme. 'He had a way of expressing things that you canna forget. He once wrote that life breaks us all, but afterwards we become stronger in the broken places.'

'Do you believe that?' she asks.

'I believe that over time life disappoints us in some ways but most of us find hope in the future. From what I've seen, some people stay broken but others heal.'

In the long silence that follows, Xanthe reflects on this. She was almost broken by her hospital experience, but she senses she is becoming stronger. And what about Aoife? She was broken by the trauma she suffered, but she used it to build a fulfilling new life. As for Hugh, she doesn't yet know how he coped with his lover's traumatic past.

Lost in her thoughts, she looks up and realises that they are already back in St Helier.

As she gets out of the car, Bill shakes her hand, looks into her eyes, and says, 'I believe you are one of the people who grow stronger. Don't forget to read Hemingway.'

That evening, nestled against Daniel on the lounge room sofa, contented to feel the warmth of his body, she describes her visit to L'Abbaye.

He fills their glasses, and the early evening light shining through the French windows makes the wine glow like liquid rubies.

Sipping the wine, Xanthe tells him about her surprising conversation with Bill Mc Allister about Hemingway.

Daniel chuckles. 'Hemingway said *Life's a bitch and then you die.*'

Xanthe bristles. 'Well, I prefer what he said about making love.'

He folds his arms tightly around her so she can feel his heart beating against hers, and murmurs. 'So let's go upstairs and see if we can make the earth move.'

CHAPTER TWENTY-SEVEN

Tom

Germany, July 1943

When Kapo Mintz warned them that the quarantine hut was a gentle introduction to the main camp, Tom assumed it was an empty threat. After all, what could possibly be worse than the brutal treatment they experienced throughout that week?

But as soon as they were transferred to the main camp, he realised Mintz hadn't been exaggerating. It was a Sunday, and to add to the degrading experience of having to parade naked in front of the doctor who made them expose every part of their bodies for his perverted inspection, the fence surrounding the yard was crowded with locals gawking at the spectacle inside the prison, almost salivating with enjoyment as if they were watching circus freaks.

Tom noticed that the self-satisfied matrons and the giggling teenage girls were in their Sunday best, and it was obvious that they had just come from church. The humiliation and hatred he felt was so intense he could feel it hardening his eyes and turning his face into stone.

He wanted to shout that he wasn't subhuman, he was just like them, but then it struck him that he wasn't anything like them. They had no human feeling and only deserved contempt. They were the ones who should be ashamed, not him.

The following day he was assigned to the coal-working group. He was told that the job of the KohlenKommando was to push the cart to the railway station, load it up with two tons of coal briquettes, haul it back to the camp, unload it, and then repeat the process three times each day.

Tom couldn't believe his ears. Having walked from the station to the camp when he arrived, he figured it was five miles away. How could they expect them to trudge thirty miles a day along a rough road, hauling a cart loaded with coal?

The wooden farm cart, which the French prisoners with their irrepressible wit had already christened The Chariot, had a long shaft to which horses would normally have been harnessed, but there were no horses in sight.

As they lined up beside the cart, Tom was horrified to see that the *kapo* in charge of their group was the brutal French Legionnaire Bruneau.

With his dark hair combed to one side and his toothbrush moustache, he reminded Tom of Hitler.

As soon as Bruneau saw Harry, his eyes lit up with a malicious gleam, and he hissed, 'Just wait. I'll teach you a lesson. I'll pay you filthy English swine back for destroying our fleet.'

Neither Tom nor Harry had any idea what he was ranting about, but there wasn't any point trying to explain that neither of them was personally responsible for attacking French ships.

The reason they hadn't seen any horses soon became apparent. Two of the prisoners were to become beasts of burden while a bored-looking middle-aged SS man sat on a small metal seat in the front, controlling the brake. The rest of the group were ordered to push the cart from the side and the back.

From the moment they set off, Bruneau yelled at them to pick up their pace. The route to the station was steep, and running on the gravel road made it hard to keep their clogs on.

To add to their gruelling task, the SS man decided to have some fun by letting go of the brake on downhill slopes, which forced them to run faster.

Within a few minutes, one of Harry's clogs flew off. Letting go of the cart, he ran back to retrieve it but before he could rejoin the group, Bruneau started bashing him with his cudgel, screaming, 'I'm going to kill you!'

When Tom looked around, he saw his friend lying curled on the road, trying to protect himself from the blows. Hearing his cries and Bruneau's screams, the SS man, probably grateful for the distraction, stopped the cart and got out, curious to see what was going on.

'He was trying to escape,' Bruneau said, still raining blows on Harry's back and shoulders. The SS man was already reaching for the Glock revolver in his holster when

Tom rushed up to him and shouted, 'Don't shoot! He wasn't trying to escape at all! He lost his clog and was running to pick it up.'

He said it in German. In his desperation, he forgot that he'd claimed he couldn't speak German but at that moment nothing mattered except saving Harry's life. 'If you don't believe me, ask the others,' Tom insisted. 'They'll back me up.'

The SS man glared at Tom. He scratched his head and looked from Tom to Bruneau and back again, trying to decide who was telling the truth.

Then with a shrug he put away his revolver and told Bruneau to get going and stop wasting time.

When they moved on again, Bruneau snarled at Harry, 'I haven't finished with you yet. I'll make you wish you'd never been born.' Then, turning to Tom he added, 'I'll get you too, you English troublemaker.'

Tom looked at Harry staggering behind the cart, and he boiled with rage. 'I'll get you first, you bastard,' he hissed in French to Bruneau. 'As soon as the war is over, your countrymen will find you and have you guillotined.'

Tom was shocked by his own defiance, but his words must have shocked Bruneau too, because without another word the *kapo* stomped away and took his malice out on other prisoners.

After loading up the cart with the briquettes, they were ready for the return trip. This time, Bruneau strode up to Tom and Harry, and, with an evil glint in his eyes, he ordered them to pull the cart on the way back.

Terrified of losing his clogs again, Harry took them off and ran barefoot. Tom could see that he was hobbling and in obvious pain. By the time they reached the camp, Harry's feet were torn and bleeding, and he could hardly walk.

One of the French prisoners gave him a piece of rope to strap on his clogs, but Bruneau kept bashing him for slacking.

When they reached the station for the last time that day, Harry could no longer walk. He crumpled up and slid onto the ground, half-conscious, and Tom persuaded the SS man on the brake to let him lie in the cart on top of the coal on the way back to the camp.

The journey back seemed interminable. Tom kept glancing anxiously at his friend's white face, which was contorted with pain while Bruneau kept swearing at them both. As soon as they were back at the camp, the other prisoners propped Harry against one of the cart wheels.

'Don't worry, you'll be fine,' Tom kept repeating because he didn't know what else to say.

While he was wiping the blood off Harry's face, a stinging blow to the back of his neck made him see stars. He wheeled around to see Kapo Mintz, who yelled, 'What the hell do you think you're doing?'

After Tom explained what had happened, Mintz turned to Bruneau. 'What's going on?' he asked.

'He's lying as usual,' Bruneau spat. 'He's covering for the slacker who was trying to escape.'

'The boy is telling the truth,' the SS man cut in. 'This one here –' he pointed at Bruneau, 'didn't stop bashing his friend all day for no reason that I could see.'

Without another word, Mintz dismissed Bruneau, who glared at Tom and muttered threats under his breath.

Turning to Tom and a couple of the French prisoners, Mintz told them to take Harry to the medical centre.

When Tom saw Harry's naked body, he gasped. His friend looked as if a building had fallen on top of him. He was covered in huge black and blue bruises, bleeding gashes and deep welts.

The German doctor waved his plump hand in a dismissive gesture when he heard what had happened to Harry.

'He's just a bloody malingerer,' he scoffed, and to prove his point, he punched Harry in the face, and kicked him in the ribs.

Once Tom would have taken comfort in the certainty that such cruelty could not go unpunished, but he no longer believed that. What was the point of trying to do the right thing and adhere to your principles, when the thugs of this world got away with such evil?

'You're supposed to help people, not beat them,' he shouted at the doctor who stared at him. Then with a shrug he beckoned to his French colleague.

'Clean up this English filth,' he said and strode away.

The French doctor gave Harry two days off work, while Tom continued toiling on the KohlenKommando, and wondered how long he'd last.

As soon as he returned from the afternoon shift the following day, his entire body aching and his legs almost giving way, he heard his number being called on the loudspeaker. On the way to the office, his heart was pounding. Now he was in for it. Bruneau must have reported him for threatening him the previous day.

Inside the office, Kapo Mintz was standing by the table, the club lying within reach. Tom thought the bulbous eyes in his red face looked more menacing than ever, and he held his breath and tried to steel himself for the blow he expected to come crashing down on his shoulders at any moment.

But leaving the cudgel where it was, Mintz walked towards the door and said curtly, 'Come with me.'

Still apprehensive, Tom followed the stocky camp director across the *appellplatz* until they reached the store and went inside. Mintz went straight to the shelf where boots were displayed, and after examining several pairs, he handed Tom a pair of brand-new leather boots.

'For your friend,' he said. At that moment, it seemed to Tom that the world had flipped on its axis and he had landed upside down.

After they left the store, Mintz turned to him. 'I want you to know that I'm not a bad person,' he said. 'Before the war, I was a carpenter. But I ran into a spot of trouble with the law, and they offered me this job instead of doing time. So I'm earning my way out of prison by working here and I have to follow their orders. Do you understand?'

Tom didn't think he did, but he nodded, too astonished to reply. He had just seen a side of Mintz that the terrifying *kapo* had concealed from everyone else. And for some reason, Mintz had glimpsed something in him that prompted him to show himself in a better light. It was flattering and confusing at the same time, and Tom didn't know what to make of this surprising new development.

When Tom gave Harry the boots that evening, his friend gave him a searching look and said, 'I hope you didn't do anything dishonest to get them.' The other prisoners were incredulous at this reaction, but knowing Harry, Tom wasn't surprised. It was only after he assured him that he'd obtained the boots honestly that Harry proceeded to try them on.

That night, lying on his bunk, Tom marvelled at his friend's strength of character. Despite everything he had suffered, his moral sense had remained intact. At school, his English teacher, Mr Ward, had tried to drum into them that a person's worth depended not on their skill on the football field or their speed in the swimming pool, but on their inner fortitude.

At the time, that didn't mean much to Tom, but he realised that Harry personified what Mr Ward had meant. The boots were a treasure, but Tom knew that if they had been stolen, Harry would have continued hobbling and staggering on his blistered, shredded feet rather than accept them.

That night, despite his exhaustion, Tom lay awake grappling with this issue. Surely survival was all that mattered here. When your life was at stake, surely it was permissible to bend your principles.

Then he mulled over Mintz's strange confession and wondered if he was an evil man with a spark of conscience, or a good person who had made a pact with the devil in order to survive. But when he glanced at Harry's serene expression, he knew that for his friend there would never be a compromise with evil. About himself, he wasn't so sure.

To his immense relief, at the end of the week the Kohlen-Kommando came to an end and Tom was assigned to work with a group in the forest to clear land for a road.

Tom's spirits rose at the prospect of working in the forest. He looked forward to filling his lungs with fresh air and breathing in the scent of the towering pines. But the tree roots he had to dig up were so deep, they seemed to reach into very centre of the earth. The labour, which was physically exhausting, was punctuated by blows from the *kapos* and the SS guards.

The day resounded with the noise of axes, hammers and the screams of those prisoners unlucky enough to attract the attention of the guards, who were itching to lash out.

There were civilian contractors working in the forest as well, and Tom noticed that they also enjoyed kicking the defenceless prisoners, and never offered to share the sandwiches whose mouth-watering smell tormented them.

Famished and exhausted, they couldn't wait to return to camp, but before they could have their midday bowl of watery soup, they had to run the gauntlet of SS guards, who attacked them with clubs on the way to the mess hall. Half an hour later they returned to the forest for more backbreaking work.

It took four men to lift one of the gigantic stumps onto a cart and pile it on top of the others. When the stumps were loaded up, they dragged the heavy carts over rough paths back to the camp. Tom hated being in the front, as the SS man, who was supposed to control the brake, persisted in playing his dangerous games and releasing the brake whenever the road sloped down.

Late one afternoon, as the cart was careering downhill, Emile, one of the French prisoners, tripped and fell. Before he could get up, the cart rolled over him and he was crushed under its weight.

They frantically tried to lift the cart off him, but by the time they managed to free him, he was dead. For days, Tom couldn't get Emile's screams out of his head.

Each evening, by the time the last shift finished and the savagery was over for the day, Tom couldn't wait for ten o'clock so he could finally collapse on his bunk, to sleep until the new day began at four-thirty next morning. His last waking thought was that he had managed to survive one more day.

He no longer thought about freedom or victory. These days his entire attention was focussed on trying to avoid being bashed. Sometimes as he lay on his bunk, knowing that in the twinkling of an eye another day of brutality and hunger would dawn, he wondered why he was trying so hard to survive. At those times, he remembered his promise that he would stay alive so he could tell Harry's parents what had happened. As he recalled that moment, he tried to shake off the unease he felt. Harry would return to tell his own story, he'd make sure of that.

He thought about the reason they were both in this predicament, and his mind hardened. It was all very well for Pierre to lecture him about the weakness of revenge, but that was all he had to keep him going. That and looking out for Harry.

From time to time, new prisoners arrived from France or Luxembourg, and they brought news of the war. It was going well for the Allies, they said. The Germans were being defeated and their cities were being bombed, but Tom drew little comfort from their optimism.

He felt as if he'd been at the camp forever and he had no idea how long he and Harry would be held there, or whether they'd be put on trial.

At bedtime, he listened to the stories of the Resistance men. It seemed that two things kept their spirits up. The hope of seeing their country freed from *les Boches,* and their determination to return home so they could deal with those who had betrayed them. The prospect of retribution motivated most of them as well, Tom realised.

He admired their spirit and their courage. Despite being tortured, none of them had revealed the names of their colleagues. One day Luc deliberately steered one of the coal carts into a ditch, sending the briquettes flying and shattering some of them. He received a savage beating for this act of sabotage but when he emerged staggering from his solitary cell, his face a mess and his teeth broken, he managed to give them a wry smile. 'It was worth it, *mes amis*,' he said.

Listening to Luc and his companions, it struck Tom that this war wasn't just a matter of military battles. The Nazis wanted to taint their souls and break their spirits, which was all they had left.

The weeks dragged into months. The seasons turned through a bitter winter into spring and the heat of summer. Tom calculated that it must be getting close to a year they had spent at Camp Reinsfeld. It felt like a lifetime.

Harry shuffled like an old man, and fear clawed at Tom's heart to see his friend's sunken eyes and shrunken frame. They were all emaciated and worn out, and he wondered if any of them would survive this inhuman treatment.

When he heard they were to be transported out of the camp the following day, his hopes rose. No-one knew where they were going, but Tom reckoned that any place would be better than this, even hell itself.

Before they climbed into the green police vans that had come to collect them, the Kommandant addressed them. 'I hope you appreciate the German training that you have received here, and that your attitude to Germany has changed.'

'It sure has,' Luc muttered when they climbed into the waiting trucks. 'I hate the bastards more than ever.'

The policemen escorting them were the same ones who had brought them there. Noticing their shocked expressions, Tom realised that they must look like walking skeletons, just like the prisoners they had encountered at the railway station on the day they arrived.

As the truck made its way up the hill, past the pine forest, Tom was relieved to see the gates of the camp receding. He nudged Harry.

'That's the last we'll see of that hellhole,' he whispered. His heart was beating with new hope and for the first time in months, he felt his mouth stretching into a grin. 'I reckon if we survived that, we can survive anything!'

Harry nodded. He started to say something when he was seized by a paroxysm of coughing that left him doubled over, struggling to catch his breath.

Tom looked at him and froze. The rag Harry held against his mouth was spotted with blood.

CHAPTER TWENTY-EIGHT

Dr Jackson

St Helier, August 1944

Aoife's traumatic story has obsessed me. I turn it over and over in my mind, like a Chinese puzzle that presents a different image on every side. Ever since confiding in me, she has become more withdrawn, and although I want to hold her in my arms and keep her safe for the rest of her life, I sense that she has retreated to some distant place beyond my reach.

My distress is compounded by a personal issue. Thinking about Aoife's child inevitably turns my thoughts to Jamie, the son I've never met. My little boy is four now, and hardly a day passes that I don't think about him. I long to hear his voice, to hold him and talk to him. What toys does he like? Is he quiet, playful or wilful? I imagine him as a lovable little tearaway, bright, energetic and full of mischief. I wonder what, if anything, Margaret has told him about me.

No matter how busy I am, my longing for him is a constant ache. The unfairness of it. Margaret continues to ignore my twenty-five-word messages, which is all the Red Cross allows us at the moment.

It was through the Red Cross that she recently sent me a photograph of Jamie on his birthday, her annual communication. I have framed it and placed it on my desk. As it wasn't accompanied by a single word, I sensed that in sending the photo she was gloating.

This is what you're missing because of your selfishness, it seemed to say. I wonder if she'll take this resentment to the grave.

In the photo, a bonny little boy with straight fair hair and a wide smile is delightedly cradling a toy train, a birthday present that was not from me. The pain I feel is visceral.

From what I've observed of human nature, most of us are not wired to sustain extreme emotions, either joy or sorrow, for lengthy periods, and in time we settle to an emotional equilibrium we can live with. The alternative is to adjust our emotions with narcotic drugs. I'm aware that some of my colleagues have resorted to this in the past, but it's an option I refuse to take. I would rather feel pain than become addicted.

By the time Bob Blampied appeared in my surgery this morning, I was functioning again, although at half strength. I looked up from the papers on my desk and was surprised to see this normally neat young man looking rather dishevelled.

From the way he panted and threw himself into a chair, I could see that he'd been rushing to get here. I soon found out why.

'Ethel Carter has been deported!' he gasped.

To say I was shocked is an understatement. Even though I knew she'd been arrested for possessing a radio and a rusty old rifle, I never imagined they would deport an elderly lady.

'Do you know where they've sent her?' I asked. I hoped it was France.

Bob's usually cheerful face looked glum. 'To Germany. They've taken her to some women's prison near Berlin. Called Ravensbrück or something like that.'

'A women's prison? So maybe it won't be too bad.'

But Bob's expression didn't convey optimism. 'I was told it's some sort of concentration camp and it's staffed by SS guards,' he said, and went on to explain that his informant was a German clerk who worked for the German administration.

'Did he say how long for?'

Bob shrugged. 'He didn't know, but he asked me if she was a strong woman. I don't think he was referring to physical strength.'

We sat in silence for a long time, letting the significance of that sink in. There was nothing to say. It was outrageous.

A dark mood settled over me as I contemplated her predicament. It would be an exaggeration to say I felt responsible for her plight, but I was keenly aware that if we hadn't placed Sasha with her, she would still be living in her cosy little house tending her rose bushes instead of being at the mercy of SS guards in some far-off German camp.

Finally I snapped out of it. There was no point in dwelling on negative thoughts. 'She might need warm clothes or some food,' I suggested. 'Can you find out from your chap if we can send her a parcel?'

Bob said he'd try. Then, glancing at his watch, he rose. A Polish slave labourer had escaped the previous evening, and Bob was on his way to drive him from the de Gruchy farmhouse to the Rosses in St Brelade.

'I'd better get going,' he said. 'Can't risk being on the road after curfew in case they stop me and find him in the car.'

He was already at the door when he turned and said, 'This chap is even more skeletal than the others. I've seen a lot of hungry prisoners, but this one devoured everything we put in front of him as if he hadn't eaten for a year. I think those Organisation Todt overseers must be eating the food allotted to the prisoners.'

After Bob left, I realised that the way the Germans have been raiding the farms and cutting our rations, their own food supply must have dwindled as well. That could be another sign that the war is going badly for them, but with the scarcity of food here in Jersey, we'll all be walking skeletons before it is over.

On Saturday morning I decided to get away from the house and my unsettling thoughts. A long ramble in the woods listening to the warbling of the birds, breathing in air sweetened by clovers, and strolling under spreading oaks and ancient beeches, is a salutary reminder of the wonders of nature and our small and insignificant part in it. But this time I heard few birdsongs. In light of what Bob had told me about the worsening plight of the prisoners, I wondered if some of them had been supplementing their diet with pigeons and wood grouse. Come to think of it, perhaps some of the locals had as well.

Not as refreshed after my ramble as I had hoped, I decided to go home via Royal Square and boost my spirits with a pint of Mary Ann at the Cock and Bottle. People were standing three-deep at the bar, and the outside tables were full. Apart from the unusual crowding, I noticed a frisson of excitement in the air. People were talking in animated voices the way they do when sharing salacious news.

Curious to find out what was going on, I looked around for a familiar face and saw Jack Lewis, the mechanic who always manages to fix my old Austin. He was at the bar and, seeing me, leaned in to say something to the barman. In a moment he was pushing his way through the crowd, weaving in between the tables, and almost spilling the frothing glasses he held as he made his way towards one of the outside tables where two of his workmates were waiting.

'Come and have a drink with us, Doc,' he said, setting the glasses on the table, and indicating that I should take one. I accepted on condition that the next round was on me.

After a few mouthfuls, I asked, 'What's going on today? What's all the excitement about?'

'Haven't you heard the news, Dr Jackson?' The speaker was Alan Drew, an electrician who had done some wiring at my home years ago.

I shook my head.

'Just wait till you hear this!' Jack burst in.

Alan sat forward, and his eyes were gleaming. 'You know that slag Milly Deveraux who's been going round with a Kraut?'

Although I'd never met Milly, I remembered young Tom talking about his sweetheart, but after he disappeared, I'd heard no more about her. Now it seemed she had taken up with a German soldier.

I felt a growing unease as the story unfolded.

The news that had stirred everyone up was that Milly's German soldier had deserted from the army. She had hidden him in the attic of the house where she lived with her widowed mother until a neighbour reported seeing a man at the attic window. The next day the Gestapo burst into the house and hauled the deserter off to jail.

No-one knew what would happen next, but Jack supposed that he would probably be shot. 'They shoot people for much less,' he commented.

Although I'd never met this soldier, I admired him for having the courage of his convictions. He had obviously decided to stop fighting for Hitler despite the risk of being caught and court-martialled.

As far as Milly was concerned, I was ambivalent. It was disappointing that she had fraternised with a German, and I could only imagine how distraught Tom would have been to lose his sweetheart, and to a German at that. But at the same time, in a grudging way, I admired her. It was brave of her to hide him, and I wondered what would happen to her now.

It's been several weeks since I last wrote in this journal, on account of several events that have taken place since I heard about Milly's German boyfriend.

The following Monday, there was standing room only in the waiting room, and each patient I saw presented with so many emotional and physical problems that I had to spend an inordinate amount of time with each one.

As a result, I was running late for my ward round at the hospital, and I heaved a sigh of relief when I'd finally seen the last patient. I was writing up my notes as fast as I could, impatient to see Aoife, when, to my chagrin, the door opened and in walked another patient.

I looked up. Standing in front of me was a comely young girl whose blonde prettiness reminded me of a white rose. Her hair was pulled back from her face and coiled in a sort of roll at the back of her neck, probably to make herself look older.

She didn't smile, and from her sad expression and distracted air, I saw that she was deeply troubled. My irritation at having to spend more time in the surgery was replaced by curiosity.

Before I could ask what was the matter, she burst into tears and heaved with sobs as she buried her face in her lace-edged handkerchief. I waited until she composed herself sufficiently to speak.

'I've come to see you because Tom always told me how understanding you were. He said he always found it easy to talk to you,' she said.

Two thoughts occurred to me simultaneously. The first was that the girl sitting in front of me was Milly. The second was a sense of guilt that I didn't deserve Tom's praise because the last time he came to see me, I had left the surgery on an urgent call, and neglected to find out what was on his mind. But it was futile to dwell on the past. I had to focus on the distraught girl in front of me.

'How can I help you?' I asked, although having heard that her deserter boyfriend had been arrested, I suspected there was nothing I could do.

She was blowing her nose and her shoulders were heaving again. 'I heard they're going to kill Konrad! I can't bear to think about it. I can't live without him. I don't know what to do. Please, please, can you help us?'

I know from experience how desperate love can make you feel, and my heart ached for the poor girl. I felt like putting my arms around her to comfort her, but all I could do was mouth useless phrases.

'I wish there was something I could do, but unfortunately there isn't,' I told her. 'I don't have any influence over the German administration or the military police, so they wouldn't listen to me or rescind their decision.'

Then I remembered Bob Blampied telling me that he had a contact inside the German headquarters, the fellow who had told him about Mrs Carter's deportation.

'As soon as the war is over, we want to get married.' She was sobbing. 'He hates Hitler and the army and never wants to go back to Germany. He wants to live here.'

I didn't bother pointing out that this attitude wouldn't endear him to his superiors. 'I'll try to find out what's happening to your Konrad,' I said.

'Please hurry,' she said. 'I don't know how long we've got.' Still sobbing, she thanked me and walked out, shoulders hunched over, the picture of misery.

As promised, I spoke to Bob, and the information he passed on several days later was grim, but not unexpected.

'They've got the young fellow in the police cell at the moment, but they all reckon he'll soon be shot,' Bob said.

I felt sorry for the soldier and for his heartbroken sweetheart, and didn't relish the prospect of having to tell her what I'd found out. But next morning there was a shocking development.

Sitting in front of me was a new patient, a middle-aged woman with protruding teeth and big glasses who introduced herself as Mrs Deveraux. Although she was clearly trying to keep herself under control, she was almost incoherent and I wondered why she had come to see me.

'Doctor, it's about my daughter, Milly. I know she came to see you yesterday. Oh God, this can't be true. It's inhuman, that's what it is.'

She bit her lip, trying not to break down. Taking a deep breath, she continued, 'Poor Milly. Oh dear God, something must be done.'

'Yes, I heard about her boyfriend,' I said gently. 'It really is terrible.'

I'd barely got that out when Mrs Deveraux became so agitated that I thought she might leap off her chair.

'You don't understand. That's not why I'm here,' she said. 'It's Milly. She told me to come and see you. Thinks you're the only one who might get her out of this terrible situation.'

I couldn't sort this out. 'Milly in a terrible situation?' I repeated. 'What happened to her?'

At this, the poor woman gave up her attempt to appear calm, and broke down, shaking her head and muttering, 'Oh God, please, don't let that happen.'

Puzzled, I waited. After a few minutes, she raised her head and blurted, 'They've arrested her, that's what happened! They grabbed her yesterday afternoon, put poor Milly in handcuffs, shoved her into one of their black cars, and that was the last I saw of her. I rushed around to the police station but they won't let me see her.'

Swallowing, she said, 'Dr Jackson, I've heard they plan to execute her together with Konrad. Do you understand? You have to do something to save her!' And she fixed me with an accusing stare, as if challenging me to refuse.

I was transfixed. Never did I expect to hear anything so appalling. My hands were shaking. Execute Milly? Surely they couldn't do that.

But of course they could, especially when their authority was flouted, especially now that the war was going badly for them. Like wounded feral animals, they now posed more danger than ever.

'If there was anything I could do, I would do it,' I began, but she cut me short.

'That's not good enough! Milly trusts you,' she repeated with that accusing look. 'I don't know who to turn to. You must know important people who might intervene. There's no time to waste. I'd move heaven and earth if I could, but all I can do is beg you to help. This is a matter of life and death. Her life. And that means my life too. You'll never forgive yourself if you don't do whatever you can.'

After she had left, her words resounded in my head, and I tried desperately to think of anyone who might influence the Germans. But as far as I knew, no-one, not even the Bailiff himself, had ever tried to intervene to rescue any of our locals, including Tom and Mrs Carter.

But as Mrs Devereaux said, this was a matter of life and death; a young girl's life was at stake.

Although I wasn't personally acquainted with Bailiff de Courcy, I remembered my father speaking very highly of him. They had met during army service back in the Great War, and Father had admired his rectitude, a word that had intrigued me when he said it, which was probably why I still remembered it. It was a tenuous connection, if you could even call it that, but Mrs Deveraux's desperate plea and Milly's plight impelled me to make use of it.

But the more I thought about the Bailiff's record where our citizens' safety was concerned, the more dubious I felt about enlisting his help. He had done nothing to protect our Jewish citizens from deportation, and from what I had heard, he and his administration had facilitated the Nazis' pernicious racial persecution by handing them a list of the Jews residing here.

But to be fair, I knew that the Bailiff had his hands full trying to navigate between Scylla and Charybdis – steering our leaky boat between his responsibilities to his citizens, and his need to cooperate with the occupiers.

When I explained to his secretary that the matter was urgent, she gave me an appointment for the following day.

Unfamiliar with the role of supplicant, I sat nervously in the Bailiff's waiting room, hoping to persuade him to intervene.

George de Courcy was a man with smooth silver hair, a commanding presence and an air of noblesse oblige that suited his official position. In an effort to forge a personal connection, I mentioned my father.

He nodded. 'I remember your father, a very fine man. And from the reports I hear about you, Dr Jackson, he must have been very proud of you,' he said in a booming voice. 'But do tell me, what brings you here? I gather it's a matter of some urgency.'

After I'd explained the situation, he sat back in his carved armchair and nodded. 'I have heard about that unfortunate case. It doesn't bear thinking about. But I'm afraid I cannot interfere when our people break German laws.'

I sat forward, mindful that every word I uttered must count. 'I do appreciate your difficult situation, and I'd like to explain that I'm asking you to intervene because of my compassion for this girl and her widowed mother,' I began.

'Milly Deveraux is a very young, unsophisticated girl who has acted on impulse, not realising that it might put her own life in danger. I think we're all aware how all-consuming and impetuous young love can be, so it's not difficult to imagine her desperation to protect her sweetheart. The Germans regard her action as criminal, but this is a girl with a blameless record, who threw caution to the wind because she was in love. She had no intention of breaking any laws.'

When I paused for breath, I saw that George de Courcy was giving me his whole attention, and that encouraged me to continue.

'I've heard that the war is going badly for the Germans. Without putting too fine a point on it, do you think it possible to hint to the Feldkommandant that killing this young girl would arouse enormous antagonism here at a time when they might prefer to keep the locals on-side?'

As I spoke, it occurred to me that interceding on Milly's behalf wouldn't do the Bailiff's reputation any harm either, but I refrained from saying that.

When I'd finished, he looked thoughtful.

'You'd make an excellent barrister, Dr Jackson. I'll see what I can do.'

As I left his office, I felt a lightness in my step for the first time in days. I hadn't been able to help Tom or Mrs Carter, and perhaps I wouldn't succeed in helping Milly either, but at least on this occasion, I had done my best.

A week later, on a drizzly, overcast morning, I watched as a large black truck made its way towards the cemetery at St Ouen. As it was passing a brick house with an attic, the passenger in the back looked up and tried to smile.

Standing at the attic window, tears streaming down her face, Milly waved a forlorn white lace handkerchief, and kept waving it long after the truck had disappeared from view.

CHAPTER TWENTY-NINE

Xanthe

St Helier, April 2019

Strolling through the woods on an April morning, Xanthe breathes in the sweetness of the new foliage and the earthy smell of the forest floor. Overhead, birds are warbling, and when she looks up, a flash of scarlet catches her eye. She stops, leans against the trunk of an oak tree, and watches robins flitting among the branches; she thinks about the assertive gargling of magpies, and the mocking laughter of kookaburras at home.

At the base of the tree, emerald clumps of moss are so vivid they almost seem alive, but in the patch of dappled grass past the oaks, the bluebells have wilted.

No wonder. April is drawing to a close, and she is shocked to realise that her holiday is almost over. She slides down to the soft ground and runs her hands over the spongy moss, contemplating the speed of time. It seems only a moment ago that she arrived, and time seemed to stretch ahead like an empty page waiting to be filled. But since that first day, time has gathered momentum, and the page has almost filled up. She wonders if perhaps this indicates a yet-to-be-discovered rule of physics, that time is able to stretch and accelerate.

She had expected that by now she would have resolved her dilemma and formed a plan for the future. But she hasn't resolved anything. Has hardly thought about it, really, having become too involved in the lives of strangers who lived here long ago.

What was that irritating feel-good quote that she had seen on a friend's Facebook page, about life happening while we are making other plans? But she hasn't moved on or made any plans. She's still stuck in the quagmire of her indecision.

Daniel has added to her uncertainty about the future. He ticks all the boxes, some she hadn't even thought of. Unlike her last boyfriend, who prided himself on being a sexual athlete, Daniel doesn't seem to need to prove anything. He has been focussed on giving her pleasure, with a tenderness that makes her feel she is dissolving into him. But sex is only part of the attraction. Every day she can hardly wait to see him, desperate to feel his strong arms enfolding her, and to share her thoughts and feelings.

It dawns on her that she can't bear to think of life without him. Snap out of it, she scolds herself. That's a romantic myth. You shouldn't need another person to feel complete. But the feeling persists. He is her other half, the part that has always been missing, and life without him seems only a half-life. A meal without salt, pepper or sugar, that you consumed merely to stay alive, not for any sensual pleasure. With him she has achieved that longed-for balance between control and surrender.

With a sigh she checks her Apple watch, pulls herself up from the ground, brushes the twigs and leaves from her jeans, and heads back to her car. She will sort it all out another time, but now she is going to meet Bob Blampied.

Something Hugh wrote in his journal has raised a question, and she hopes he'll be able to answer it.

Bob had suggested meeting on the Esplanade in front of the Grand Hotel, and Xanthe supposes they'll go inside and chat over a drink, but when he arrives, he proposes a stroll along the waterfront instead.

He's not wearing his peaked cap today and the sea breeze ruffles his hair, which is as fine and white as talc. Despite his age, he has a long, loping gait and she needs to walk fast to keep up with him.

Seagulls are wheeling and screeching overhead, and as she breathes in the salty smell of the sea, she marvels that only half an hour ago she was strolling in woodland and driving past rolling farmland, and now she is already on the coast. Within its miniature dimensions, this island seems to contain every landscape.

'Les Jardins de la Mer. Sea gardens,' Bob translates as they skirt an area of parkland by the shore. Pointing to a bronze statue in a fountain, he makes a grimace.

'See that? Two naked women swimming with a dolphin. Whatever next? I don't have anything against naked women or dolphins, you understand, but this shows the modern obsession with tearing down old buildings with character and replacing them with sterile spaces, pretentious artworks, and box-like structures.' As he speaks, he waves a disparaging arm in the direction of the buildings on the other side of the Esplanade. 'Thank goodness they've left the Grand alone.'

In between giving a commentary on what he considers deplorable contemporary architecture, Bob stops to chat to several passers-by eager to hear his views about a scandal involving a member of the local government.

Xanthe is impatient to move on but Bob, who is clearly something of a local institution, is in no hurry, and neither are the people who are listening avidly to his words.

As soon as they move on, she asks, 'What happened to that woman who looked after Sasha and was deported to Germany?' She speaks quickly before another acquaintance can monopolise his attention.

Bob stops walking. He turns towards her with a questioning look, and she realises that he is confused by the sudden change of subject.

'I'm sorry,' she begins but he is shaking his head.

'Not to worry. I'm with you now. Just had to adjust my old brain one hundred and eighty degrees to keep up with you. Let's sit over there in the park and I'll tell you what happened.'

They sit on a bench facing the fountain that he has just described as pretentious, and while she watches three children shrieking as they chase each other around the pool, he stares into the distance, as if retreating into the past.

'Mrs Carter was deported to a concentration camp north of Berlin. Ravensbrück, it was called,' he says after a while.

'Even after all this time, it still makes my blood boil. They accused her of being a spy. Said she listened to her illegal wireless and passed on information to other people.'

'Was that true?'

Bob shrugs. 'I doubt it. She would have known better than to let on that she had kept her wireless, but she had such an open, generous disposition that she probably didn't realise how vicious people could be.'

'I don't know anything about Ravensbrück,' Xanthe says.

'You don't hear much about it,' he says. 'I didn't know anything about it at the time, but I've since found out that it was a camp exclusively for female prisoners. Polish women, French women, Jewish women. Women from all over occupied Europe were interned there. They were supposed to be political prisoners, but I doubt if many of them were.'

'Was it as bad as the other camps we read about?'

'I don't know how you compare one hellhole with another. I think any camp in that frightful Nazi gulag would have been your worst nightmare. I read that conditions in Ravensbrück were terrible. Cruel female guards, gas chambers, and a sadistic camp doctor who experimented on the prisoners. After cutting them, he used to insert dirt or glass into the open wounds to see if they survived the infection.'

Xanthe shudders. 'A doctor did that?'

Bob studies her pale face. 'Yes, a doctor. And he wasn't the only one. There was a notorious one in Auschwitz. You have a lot to learn about human nature, my dear girl.'

She recalls what Daniel has told her about lawyers being complicit in the Nazi regime, but the thought that doctors, who had taken the Hippocratic oath, who were meant to heal the sick, had deliberately infected healthy people horrifies her. As a medico, she feels personally affronted by it.

With an effort, she returns to her question. 'So what happened to Mrs Carter in there?'

'Apparently she was very popular with the other inmates. She managed to keep everyone's spirits up and did whatever she could to help others.'

Xanthe is listening intently, eager to hear more, but at this point Bob hesitates, and she senses that he wants to delay telling her the rest of the story.

'Did she tell you about it when she came back after the war?' she prompts.

He sighs. 'Unfortunately she never returned. She died a few months before the war ended.'

'That's terrible. What did she die of?'

Bob swallows. 'They gassed her.'

Xanthe's hand covers her mouth. 'Oh no! Poor Mrs Carter. And all she did was look after an escaped slave labourer! But if she died in Ravensbrück, how did you know what happened to her?'

'A woman from Guernsey told me. She was deported to that camp at the same time as Mrs Carter, but she survived. Years later, I found out more about Mrs Carter when the German government released an archive of Nazi files they kept in Arolsen, and I requested her file. The amazing thing is that the bastards – excuse my French – kept meticulous records of their victims.' He is speaking faster now, warming to his theme. 'What I can't understand, is how morons these days can deny the Holocaust when the Germans themselves, even the Commandant of Auschwitz, left such detailed records of their crimes.'

They leave the park and continue strolling along the Esplanade in silence, reluctant to trivialise their discussion with small talk.

When they reach the Grand Hotel, Bob stops walking.

'Now, young lady, to dispel the dark shadow you've cast with your questions, shall we raise our spirits, so to speak, with a drink in the hotel bar?'

Ensconced in burgundy velvet armchairs by the large window facing the bay, they order their drinks from a waiter whose condescending manner irritates Xanthe. As soon as he walks away, Bob leans towards Xanthe and whispers with a wicked smile, 'The nobleman's valet is always a bigger snob than his master.'

When the waiter returns with a tumbler of Tobermory whisky for Bob and a fruit mocktail for her, it occurs to her that not so long ago, she would have jumped at the chance to down a Stoli or two, but she no longer feels the need to anaesthetise her feelings with alcohol.

Sipping his whisky, Bob studies her. 'You've been here for a few weeks now. Tell me, what do you think of our island?'

Her mocktail is decorated with pieces of pineapple and mango, and as she removes them carefully from the foil-edged skewers, she wonders how to sum up the impact that Jersey has had on her.

'It's a lot more varied and complex than I expected,' she says slowly. 'But I don't actually know what I expected. I didn't come with any preconceived ideas, and everything I've seen so far has amazed me.'

As an afterthought, she adds, 'I'm very grateful for the time you've spent with me, Bob. Thanks to you, I've seen such fascinating places and learned so much about Jersey's history.'

He drains his whisky and beams. 'It's been a real pleasure,' he says, inclining his head in a mock bow. 'At my age, every day is a precious gift. I can't afford to waste a single minute so I choose my activities – and my companions – very carefully.'

Then he adds, 'I've noticed that you find our past especially interesting. Am I right?'

She nods. 'I don't know why that is. I've never been interested in history before but ever since I got here, I've been fascinated by Jersey's past, especially during the Occupation.'

'If you'll forgive an old fogey spouting old-fashioned ideas, I often think the heart knows more than the mind realises.'

But Xanthe does know why she has become so fascinated with Jersey's past, and she is struggling with an urge to confide in Bob about Hugh's journal. She has become very fond of the old man and feels guilty keeping this secret from him. Besides, it would be an enormous relief to discuss the journal with him, but she holds back. Once taken, this step would be irrevocable, and she senses that until she has finished reading it, she can't risk disclosing its existence given the increasingly personal nature of the entries.

This was not merely a record of a doctor's life during the Occupation, a doctor Bob had known very well. It was an intimate account of events that involved not only Hugh Jackson, but people whose lives were interwoven with his.

As soon as she returns home, she picks up the journal and resumes reading. After a short time, she puts it down because her tears have blurred the words. Wiping her eyes, she looks straight ahead but she doesn't see anything in front of her. She sees Milly's tear-stained face pressed against her attic window as she waves a lace-edged handkerchief at a passing truck. She sees the pale face of the young man who looks up for a last sight of his sweetheart and tries to look brave as he is being driven to his execution. She feels that Milly is infusing all her love into that forlorn wave to give him the strength to face his fate.

It's as if Xanthe is part of that heartbreaking scene herself, and her tears keep flowing. Too upset to continue reading, she is pacing around the house, wondering what to do with herself until it's time to meet Daniel, when her phone rings.

'I've finished for the day,' Daniel says. 'I heard they have an interesting animal park near St Helier. Do you feel like going?'

As they drive north towards the Jersey zoo, Daniel reaches for her hand. 'I'm sorry I suggested going to the zoo,' he murmurs. 'What I really wanted was to go to bed and feel you against me.'

She smiles and squeezes his hand. 'We can do that later,' she says. Being with him has dissipated the sadness she felt earlier. 'So we're off to the zoo like little kids!' she says happily.

'Not just any zoo,' he says, and points to a sign. 'Durrell Wildlife Conservation.'

Xanthe cranes her neck for a better view and exclaims, 'Durrell! That must be Gerald Durrell, the naturalist. I read his book when I was in high school and loved it. *My Family and Other Animals.*'

At the ticket office, a large woman in a caftan printed with huge flowers explains that the aim of the zoo is to breed and protect endangered species from all over the world. She looks over their shoulders as they sign the visitors' book.

'Oh, you've come all the way from Australia! Have you heard of Jambo?'

They shake their heads, and she continues. 'Years ago a little boy fell into the gorilla pit, and a huge silverback stood guard over him until the keeper rescued him. Your papers must have reported it, they even wrote about it in America.' She sounds almost offended that they don't know anything about the zoo's gorilla hero.

The zoo is spacious and attractively landscaped with pools, stands of trees and flowering plants, and after wandering around, they sit in front of the gorilla enclosure in honour of Jambo.

'Daniel, how long do you think you'll stay here?' she asks.

'At the zoo you mean?' She is about to reply when she realises he is teasing her.

'Not quite sure,' he says. 'There are still some important documents I have to go through.' His dark blue eyes are searching her face. 'Why do you ask?'

She doesn't know how to reply. Should she come straight out with it and tell him that she can't bear the thought of going back home without him? Or play it cool and give some socially acceptable excuse that won't scare him off?

In the end, she does neither. 'I'm going to stay for Liberation Day and leave after that. The trouble is, I have no idea what I'm going to do when I get back, and not knowing is very stressful.'

In front of them, a small girl with her hair in bunches that stick out at right angles from her head is squealing with delight at the antics of the gorillas as she jumps against the railing to get a better view.

'They say you have to know which bridges to burn and which ones to cross,' Daniel observes.

'I've never thought about it like that,' she says. 'Can you do both?'

'What, you mean get halfway across your bridge and then set it on fire?' He's teasing again, but she is exploring a possibility she has never considered before.

The little girl's mother, who has obviously heard about the child who fell into the gorilla pit, rushes up to the railing and scoops up her daughter. 'Do you want to fall in there with the gorillas?' she shouts while the child kicks and flails her arms in protest.

'I suppose it depends on your flexibility and your vocation,' he says, serious now. 'I was disgusted with my grandfather's collusion during the war, and bored with the work in my legal firm, so I was ready to burn that bridge, but then I found a way of reconciling law with research, so I suppose you could say I did both.'

He waves his arm to indicate the zoo. 'Like Gerald Durrell. He was passionate about animals, so the logical step would have been to become a vet. But he wanted to use his love of animals to do something significant, so he created this to try and rescue them.'

Xanthe thinks back to her conversation with Bob Blampied about the Nazi doctors, and her horror at their perversion of her profession. Being a doctor and healing people was in her DNA.

She takes Daniel's hand. 'Good thing we came here today. You and Gerald Durrell have given me something to think about.'

They sit in silence watching the gorillas until Xanthe says, 'What do you think your research will achieve?'

Surprised by her question, Daniel pauses. 'It may not actually achieve anything, if you mean something concrete. I read somewhere that failure in any endeavour is inevitable but giving up is unforgiveable. So I'm prepared to fail, but I won't give up. If my research clarifies misconceptions and creates a more realistic picture of what happened here, then it will have achieved something worthwhile.'

'What misconceptions do you mean?'

'The conviction that the Jersey authorities did whatever they could to protect their Jews, when in fact their collusion and cooperation made it easy for the Nazis to deport their Jewish neighbours. Their collusion was typical of the behaviour that made the Holocaust possible. What happened to the Jews here was a microcosm of what happened to them in other occupied countries. So I'd like to scuttle the myth that the British were somehow superior to other countries, because after what happened here I'm convinced that had Britain been occupied, the Jews would have suffered the same treatment there as they did in the rest of Europe.'

'That's depressing, isn't it?'

'I think it shows that without strong moral leadership no nation is immune to a divisive racist agenda. The only places where it hasn't happened is where a leader with unshakeable moral values has been in charge. That was the case in Denmark, in Bulgaria, and to a smaller but equally impressive extent, in a corner of France.'

'But how will you know if your thesis has the desired effect? Changing attitudes takes a long time and it's pretty hard to quantify. For instance, can you see your relative Edward de Courcy changing his attitude?'

He shrugs. 'All I can do is put it out there and hope that the facts make people reassess what really happened.'

As soon as he pulls up outside her house, they jump out of the car, and in her haste to get inside Xanthe fumbles with the keys. Already on the stairs leading to the bedroom, he is unbuttoning his shirt and she pulls off her T-shirt. They fall onto the bed, and he is kissing her lips and stroking her hair when suddenly she sits up.

'That bridge between Sydney and Melbourne. Are we going to burn it or cross it?'

'What do you think?' he asks, and, laughing, he pulls her down onto the bed again.

CHAPTER THIRTY

Tom

Germany, September 1944

Lying on the bed in his clean, comfortable cell at Weissburg Prison, Tom marvelled that ever since he'd arrived, no-one had even tried to bash him. After the hell of Camp Reinsfeld, this felt like a holiday retreat. The first astonishing thing he noticed as soon as he stepped into the neat cobbled courtyard the previous day was that the guards weren't armed with cudgels or pick-axe shafts. In fact they didn't have any weapons at all, and they weren't yelling abuse.

The reason for this became clear when the camp superintendent addressed them. Oskar Schmidt was a broad-shouldered man with greying hair and a purposeful stride that suggested a military background.

'This is a law-abiding detention centre,' he said. 'In here, you will be treated decently and I have forbidden the guards to hit you.' Tom and Harry exchanged glances, incredulous that they'd no longer be at the mercy of Nazi sadists.

But after several days, the novelty of this benign environment began to wear off, and Tom felt restless. At Camp Reinsfeld his every waking thought had been focussed on avoiding blows. He had lived second by second, driven only by the need to survive one more day. But now that the threat of brutality had been removed, he began to take stock of his situation.

He had survived that horror camp. But for what? His mind roamed back to the world he had left behind, a world he longed for more each day with an ache that never let up. That ache was sharpened by the realisation that his homeland didn't care what happened to him. Little did they know, as he now did, that the Germans in Jersey were not the real Germans at all. They had fooled them by cloaking their vicious nature in polite manners.

But there was no point reviling the Jersey government when his own family had washed their hands of him. Even his father, who had always extolled the superiority of British courage, had done nothing to rescue him. Some hero Dad turned out to be, he thought, recalling the way he had colluded in his wife's illegal business and outrageous flirting with German officers. As for his mother, he had no illusions about her. He longed for the sweetness of revenge.

She had handed him over to the Germans without any qualms, and for all she knew or cared, he might be dead. Casting his mind back over his childhood, bitter memories succeeded each other like scenes on a movie reel. His mother had never been interested in him or his achievements unless they reflected well on her. She had never bothered to attend sports carnivals to watch him swim or run, and whenever he brought home sporting trophies, she shoved them into a cupboard, complaining that they'd only gather dust if left on the mantelpiece. The only time he remembered her praising him was when she boasted about his good German, and that was only to curry favour with her Kraut friends.

And there was Milly. Hers was a double betrayal. By consorting with a German she had not only betrayed him but their country as well.

He indulged in a daydream that made him smile. The war was over, the Germans defeated, and he had returned to Jersey. He was strolling along the Esplanade when Milly ran up to him, crying. She wanted him back because her Kraut boyfriend was in a British prisoner-of-war camp, and everyone had ostracised her for being a collaborator. But he pushed her away and told her it served her right for abandoning him and taking up with the enemy.

His French companions vowed they would shave the heads of women who had collaborated, but even in his fantasy of revenge, he couldn't bring himself to wish that for Milly. Or even for his mother.

Dwelling on past grievances and dreaming of revenge helped him forget that he didn't know what was happening in the outside world. Who was winning the war? His father had always said that Britain would never give in, and Mr Churchill said much the same, but Britain had never encountered Hitler.

The guards often taunted them, saying that German victory was imminent. 'You French are finished anyway, and we're getting the better of Britain and America all over

Europe,' they would gloat. 'Just wait, you'll see, the Führer will soon rule the world.'

Some of the French and Luxembourger prisoners who had recently been transferred to the prison told him that the Allies had been bombing German cities for some time. They mentioned Hamburg and Dresden, and whispered that the Russians were advancing from the east, but Tom found that hard to believe because the guards never mentioned it, and the war still dragged on.

Occasionally he heard the distant hum of aeroplane engines and recalled the terrible June day when German Dorniers had bombed St Helier. Four years had passed since then, but to Tom it seemed a lifetime ago.

If the planes he sometimes heard flying overhead were British Lancasters, he prayed their mission would be successful, but at the same time he was terrified in case they dropped their bombs on Weissburg Prison and killed the prisoners along with their guards.

As he mulled over the progress of the war, his gaze fell on the pile of small squares of German newspaper that the guard left beside his toilet pan every morning. Spreading them out on the floor, he tried to fit the squares together to see if he could form one complete article, but the pieces must have come from different papers and contained disconnected snippets.

Occasionally he came across a few lines that boasted of German victories, but if what the new prisoners had said was true, perhaps these newspaper articles were feeding readers lies and propaganda. As he continued to study the squares, he noticed that many of them contained black-edged notices announcing the deaths of German soldiers, and he was shocked to see that some of them were even younger than he was.

He started counting. His newspaper squares contained over a hundred names. The articles might be lying but the obituaries had to be genuine. And if so many of their soldiers were dying, perhaps the tide of war was turning against Germany after all.

Tom longed to discuss this with Harry and their French companions, but he was alone in his cell at night, and had to wait until the next day. Just then, from the cell across the corridor he heard a fit of coughing that terrified him. It was Harry, and he sounded as if he was coughing his lungs out. The optimism he'd felt a moment earlier vanished.

Harry's ribs protruded under his translucent skin, and his cheeks were hollow. When the prisoners jogged around the courtyard for their thirty minutes of exercise each morning, Harry could only manage to shuffle, hardly able to catch his breath. He insisted he was fine, just out of condition. Tom hoped that the improved conditions at Weissburg would soon put flesh on his bones and build him up.

He was looking for Harry in the exercise yard next morning to tell him about the obituaries in the German paper, when Luc, the joker among the French prisoners, ran up to him. For once he looked serious.

'Hey, Churchill, did you know they took your friend to the sick bay this morning?' he asked, still puffing from his jog around the perimeter of the yard.

Without waiting to hear any more, Tom rushed to see Dr Le Clerc, the French medic.

'I have admitted your friend to our hospital,' the doctor told him. 'He has a fever and is spitting blood. I suspect he has tuberculosis, but I will have him tested to make sure.'

Tom's heart was hammering. 'But he'll be all right, won't he?'

'We will know when we have the results,' the doctor said gently.

'Can I go and see him?'

Dr Le Clerc shook his head. 'I have placed him in the isolation ward.'

'But he'll be all right?'

The doctor's silence wasn't reassuring.

For the rest of the day, one thought kept going around in Tom's head: Harry had to get better. He had to. Everyone respected the French doctor, even the Germans in the town, who trusted him more than their own physicians. He'd soon fix Harry.

But despite his determined optimism, Tom knew that TB was highly contagious and had caused the death of many prisoners. 'But Harry will get better,' he kept telling himself as he paced around his cell.

As usual he was hungry. Although the food at Weissburg was more generous than that at Camp Reinsfeld, he hadn't put on any weight. Dr Le Clerc, who had noticed how thin he and Harry were, had told him that he'd asked for their rations to be increased.

That afternoon the prison superintendent called Tom into his office, which smelled strongly of tobacco. On the corner of his timber desk was a framed family photograph. Tom studied it with interest. A woman in what he supposed was a traditional German outfit, a sort of pinafore over an embroidered blouse with puffed sleeves, her hair in a thick plait on top of her head like a crown, had her arms around two pretty teenage girls who were similarly attired. They were all beaming into the camera. It had never occurred to Tom that the men in charge of these prisons had loving families they went home to at the end of the day.

Puffing on his pipe, Oskar Schmidt followed Tom's glance and waited for several moments before asking him to sit down.

'I have raised the matter of your rations with the local Gestapo, but I'm sorry to say that they categorically refused to increase them,' he said, and Tom wondered if he'd imagined a glimmer of concern in the superintendent's deep-set eyes.

Resting his pipe in the ashtray, he continued, 'I want you to know that I was a prisoner of war in 1918. The British treated me very well, so when I was appointed here, I decided to treat enemy prisoners the same way. I want you and your friend to survive so when you go back home, you'll be able to tell people that not all Germans were the same.'

Tom was so amazed that he forgot his disappointment about the rations. Schmidt's implied criticism of the Nazi regime was surprising, and Tom wondered if it hinted at the possibility of German defeat. Back in his cell, he went over every word of that conversation. So there were decent Germans who didn't abuse their power.

He wished he could tell Harry what Oskar Schmidt had said. That would cheer him up. And if he felt optimistic, his body would probably recover more quickly.

He couldn't stop thinking about his friend lying in the isolation ward, sick and alone. Tom trusted Dr Le Clerc to take care of him, but the doctor was run off his feet with so many patients to look after. How much time could he devote to Harry?

The more he thought about it, the more agitated he became. Harry was his only friend in the whole world, the only person he admired and trusted. He had never let him down and never would. Tom had to do something to help him.

Finally he figured out what to do. His plan involved deception and danger, but for Harry's sake he would risk it.

One week later, when he entered the isolation ward, he was shocked by Harry's appearance. Only ten days had passed since they'd last seen each other, but Harry's bones protruded like sharp rocks inside a bag of flimsy material. There were feverish spots on his sunken cheeks, and his eyes glittered with an unnatural brilliance.

His face lit up as soon as he saw Tom, and he tried to sit up but almost immediately he fell back against his pillow. His delight at seeing Tom quickly changed to dismay.

'You shouldn't be here, Tom,' he rasped. 'Don't you realise you're risking your life? We all have tuberculosis. Do you realise how contagious it is?'

Just then one of the patients began to cough and Harry looked at Tom meaningfully. 'You have to go. How come they let you come in?' Then he looked at Tom with concern. 'You're not ill, are you?'

Exhausted and out of breath, he started coughing, and placed a handkerchief over his mouth. When he took it away, Tom winced. It was spotted with blood.

'Don't worry about me,' he whispered, looking around to make sure no-one overheard. 'I'm not sick.'

'Thank God for that,' Harry said. Then he gave Tom a suspicious look. 'But I don't understand. If you're not ill, how come they let you in here?'

Tom placed a mask over his face and moved closer to Harry. For the next ten minutes he explained that he had feigned tuberculosis to deceive the doctor. 'I did it so I could stay close to you,' he said.

As Harry listened to Tom, his eyes widened and he looked more incredulous with every word. After Tom finished describing his subterfuge, Harry kept shaking his head in disbelief.

Finally he said, 'Are you saying you substituted the sputum of one of the infected prisoners for your own, so that when they tested it, they thought you were the one with TB?'

Tom nodded. He was proud that his scheme had worked. It was worth it to see Harry again. But instead of praising him, his friend looked horrified.

'But why did you do it, Tom? Why did you put yourself in such terrible danger?'

Tom hesitated. It would sound too soppy to confess that he missed him and couldn't bear to leave him to suffer alone, perhaps never to see him again.

Too soppy to admit that Harry was the best person he knew, and that after everything they'd been through together, he couldn't abandon him.

'Life was getting boring in here so I decided to get a bit of excitement. To play Russian roulette. Also, I heard that there was more food in your ward.'

But Harry didn't smile. 'You did the wrong thing, Tom,' he said, pausing between each word to catch his breath. 'Dr Le Clerc is a wonderful man. It was wrong to deceive him. And you shouldn't have put yourself in danger like this. Promise me that you'll go and see him and own up.'

His eyes, grown huge in his thin face, pierced Tom as if they were looking into his soul. He sensed that Harry was summoning every ounce of his remaining strength to induce him to live honourably and tell the truth.

Overwhelmed by conflicting emotions, his admiration for Harry's unwavering principles, his disappointment that his friend hadn't approved of the only unselfish thing he'd ever done, and his alarm at his condition, Tom couldn't speak. He uttered a croaking sound that might have started off as a false laugh but almost turned into a sob. He looked down and stared at his hands to avoid Harry's relentless gaze.

Suddenly he blurted, 'I only did it to keep you company.'

Harry's eyes brightened with tears. He swallowed and tried to speak but all he could do was nod.

'We'll have a lot to tell them when we get home, won't we,' Tom said, and forced a smile.

Harry shook his head. 'I won't make it, Tom. Remember you promised me once that you'd survive so you could tell my parents what happened to me? So get out of here before you get infected or you won't be able to keep your promise.'

Exhausted by speaking, he struggled to catch his breath, and the next coughing fit lasted longer than the one before.

'Don't talk tommyrot. You're going to get better,' Tom said, but Harry was gazing at him with an expression that he found unnerving.

He looked away. 'All right, I'll tell the doc what I did, but it means I won't be able to come and see you anymore.'

Harry managed a weak smile. 'That's good, Tom.' He pointed to some bread on the small table beside his bed.

'Take it,' he whispered. 'You're always hungry and I won't eat it.'

Tom started to reply, but something in Harry's eyes silenced him. Harry seemed to be looking at him from some faraway place, as if he was struggling to communicate something that he lacked the strength to express in words.

'Tom, I have a big favour to ask.' Harry's voice was so faint that Tom had to lean closer to hear him. 'Please don't leave me here.'

Tom thought he was referring to the isolation ward, until he added, 'One day, when the war is over, will you come back for me? I don't want to stay in Germany. I'd like to be buried in that old cemetery behind St Mark's, under the oak trees.'

Tom wanted to shout *Don't talk like that, you're not going to die!* He wanted to argue with Harry or say something comforting, but he was too numb to speak and remained silent. He couldn't bring himself to tell Harry the one thing his friend wanted to hear, that he would do what he asked. Saying it would mean facing something he couldn't bear to contemplate.

Harry's eyes lingered on Tom and in that glance Tom knew that no words were needed. Harry understood it all, the confusion, the guilt and the regret.

'I'm going to sleep now, Tom,' he whispered, and closed his eyes.

CHAPTER THIRTY-ONE

Dr Jackson

St Helier, October 1944

The tragic expression on Milly Deveraux's face that terrible morning was so deeply imprinted on my mind that for days afterwards I saw her before me, waving that pathetic little handkerchief as she pressed her face against the window for one final look at her sweetheart.

I must say I felt pleased that I'd played a part in saving her life; I believe it was as a result of my visit that the Bailiff had interceded with the Germans on her behalf.

Several weeks after the young German soldier's execution, I was sitting in my surgery after the last of my patients had gone, flipping through Mr Arundel's file. I was deep in thought, wondering whether to continue treating his angina at home or to have him admitted to hospital, when a peremptory knock on the door made me put the file aside and look up.

It was Milly Deveraux's mother. Assuming she had come to thank me, I started to say I was delighted to have played a small part in saving her daughter's life, when the look on her face stopped me in my tracks.

It was not an expression of gratitude. If a human could breathe fire and smoke, she came close to it. Her lips were tightly pressed together and her eyes were shooting thunderbolts in an intimidating mixture of agitation and rage. As there was no reason to assume I was the target, I asked her to sit down and tell me what was on her mind.

While waiting for her to speak, I noticed that she looked rather haggard, and her clothes hung loosely on her large frame, which isn't surprising given our desperate food shortage. The last time I saw her, she was plainly but neatly dressed, but this time I noticed that the buttons of her beige blouse were fastened in a lopsided fashion, the collar of her knitted brown cardigan was turned under, and her paisley scarf was crookedly tied under her chin. She had obviously dressed in great haste.

'It's Milly! She's up the duff!' she burst out.

At this point, I wondered if I'd misread Mrs Deveraux's expression. Perhaps she was upset rather than angry, but her next words dispelled that notion.

'Of course it's what they always say, isn't it, an apple doesn't fall far from the tree.'

Being a doctor, I'm used to remaining impassive while hearing startling confessions from my patients. Very little surprises me anymore, but on this occasion I found it difficult to conceal my perplexity. Only a few weeks ago she had sat in this same chair, distraught as any mother would be when her daughter had a death sentence hanging over her head, but this scathing comment was mystifying to say the least.

Uncertain how to react, I decided to approach her news in a matter-of-fact way, as I would any other confinement.

'Do you know how far gone she is?'

Mrs Deveraux gave me a look I can only describe as pitying. Rifling inside her large handbag she took out a pale blue handkerchief, took off her large spectacles, and polished them with such vigour that I thought the glass might spring out of the frames. After putting them back on, she continued looking at me without replying to my question.

I wondered how long we would continue looking at each other when she leaned forward and said in a conspiratorial whisper, 'You do understand that the situation is extremely delicate, doctor, don't you?'

Of course I did. I started to explain the options for unmarried mothers, but her derisive snort cut me short. It was accompanied by a look that spoke volumes about her opinion of me, and it wasn't flattering.

'The baby's father was German.' She said it slowly and loudly, the way many people speak to foreigners. 'Now do you see the problem, Dr Jackson?'

'I rather thought that might be the case,' I replied. The baby's paternity was so obvious that I couldn't for the life of me see why she was beating about the bush.

At this point, I think Mrs Deveraux decided that I was hopelessly dim, and she would have to spell it out for me. Tightening her lips, she said, 'You don't have children,

Dr Jackson, so it's probably difficult for you to understand the pain that they can cause.'

As she spoke, her eyes darted around the room. When they rested on the framed photograph of Jamie on my desk, she looked stricken.

'I'm sorry, Dr Jackson,' she stammered. 'I didn't realise …'

I waved away her apology but her remark stung me. It reminded me of my own painful situation, of having a child and being childless at the same time.

Losing concentration, I missed part of her next sentence, which I think was about Milly's ill-fated sweetheart.

'I curse the moment I let her bring that bloody Kraut into our home.' She spoke with such vehemence that I half expected to see sparks flying from her mouth.

'As for Milly,' she continued, 'I'm utterly disgusted. I always trusted her, I never expected her to behave like one of those floozies the Krauts brought over here from France. But what's done is done. I have to think of the future. Her reputation. You know how people talk about the women who consort with the Germans. Jerrybags, they call them, and there's talk of revenge when the war's over.'

Fuelled by indignation, the words tumbled from her mouth so fast that she ran out of breath and had to pause. She shook her head from side to side as if engaged in a silent argument, and her scarf slipped off her head, revealing brown hair streaked with grey.

With a long sigh she added, 'I suppose they'll regard Milly as a collaborator. I can't bear to think about it. I just didn't know where to turn. I need your help, Dr Jackson.'

At this point, she held my gaze with an expression of utter desperation. She stretched out her hand as if about to grip my arm, and for an instant I recalled the poem about the ancient mariner who grabbed his listener with a bony hand and hypnotised him with his tale of woe.

I felt as if a wave of emotion had spilled into my surgery and threatened to overwhelm us both. In an effort to extricate myself and calm her down, I said, 'This really is a very difficult situation, and I understand how you feel, but our worst fears are rarely realised, and things will probably work out much better than you expect. And you're bound to enjoy having a grandchild.'

At that, she winced and waved aside my weak attempt to induce her to accept this unfortunate situation. 'That's all very well for you to say, but just imagine what it will be like to have a German baby here, after the war. And what about that baby? How do you think people will react? It will be shunned. You must see that it's impossible.'

So that's what she was getting at.

'Are you suggesting that this pregnancy should be terminated?'

For the first time I saw gratitude on her face. The relief of finally being understood almost smoothed out the tense lines. 'Do you think that's possible?' she asked.

This placed me in a very awkward position and it took a few moments to decide how to respond. 'How does Milly feel about all this?' I asked. 'Is she as pessimistic about the future as you are?'

'I can't talk sense into her. She won't listen. Whenever I mention it, she bursts into tears and says they've taken Konrad away from her but they're not going to take his baby. But she's got her whole life ahead of her, Dr Jackson, and she's going to ruin it.'

'It is her life, though, isn't it?' I ventured, as gently as I could.

'Not just hers,' Mrs Deveraux retorted. 'Won't you talk to her?' she pleaded.

'I'm happy to talk to her any time, but you must realise all I can do is listen. Abortion is out of the question in this situation. It would be different in a case of life-threatening illness, rape or incest, which this clearly is not.'

Mrs Deveraux spread her large hands in a helpless gesture and sighed loudly. 'But she's just a child herself. She's only eighteen and she's quite naïve. She has no idea how cruel people can be. How can she possibly make the right decision?'

'The only alternative is to have the baby adopted, but from what you've told me, I doubt Milly would agree to that.'

'But if you could explain the problems she'll face, she might listen to you. Please talk to her.'

We were going round in circles. In the end, I agreed to talk to Milly, though I doubted if that would achieve anything. It was clear to me the young lady had already made up her mind, and I admired her for her devotion to her sweetheart and her determination to keep her child, although I agreed with her mother that she had no idea of all the problems she would face trying to bring up a child alone, especially in these circumstances.

Mrs Deveraux picked up her handbag and rose heavily to her feet, but just as she turned to leave, I remembered the enigmatic comment she made when she arrived.

'Would you mind telling me what you meant when you said the apple doesn't fall far from the tree?'

Red-faced, Mrs Deveraux started adjusting her scarf, which was sliding off her head again. 'I shouldn't have said that. I got all worked up.'

The quizzical look on my face probably made her sit down again. She shifted in her chair and studied her wedding ring before speaking. 'My late husband and I couldn't have children of our own. That was a bitter blow, but after a few years, we decided to adopt. We adopted Milly when she was a newborn baby.'

Her eyes filled with tears at the memory of the happy times past and her hopes for a future which now appeared so bleak.

'So when you made that comment,' I said slowly, 'were you referring to her natural parents?'

She was still looking down and twisting her wedding ring. 'To her mother. The almoner at the hospital told me that she gave the baby away because she was single, and I always thought of her as a woman with loose morals. So I meant like mother, like daughter, you know, both having a baby out of wedlock. It was a nasty thing to say and I am ashamed of saying it.'

She dabbed her eyes, and we sat in silence until she said, 'I suppose it's what they call poetic justice, isn't it, me thinking badly of the mother, and then Milly doing the same thing. But if Milly's mother hadn't got herself into trouble and given her up, then Herbert and I wouldn't have got Milly.'

I continued to sit there for a long time after she left, staring at Jamie's photo and contemplating the endless ways our choices turn our hopes and dreams upside down. It seemed we often met our fate on the road we'd taken to avoid it.

Although Mrs Deveraux was not a particularly likeable woman, I felt sorry for her. I felt even more sorry for Milly, who would have to endure not only the lifelong consequences of her illicit love affair, and the future sneers and gossip of the neighbours, but her mother's outspoken disapproval, at a time when she most needed her love and support.

I don't know how long I sat there, flipping the notes in Mr Arundel's file without taking in their contents. I was also thinking about Jamie and Mrs Deveraux's assumption that I didn't have any children.

For some time I had entertained the fantasy that Aoife and I might have children, but I doubt if that will ever happen now. Ever since she told me her secret, she has been withdrawn, as if it has created a barrier between us.

According to the Viennese psychiatrists, unless we confront past traumas, we have no chance of resolving the psychological damage they have caused, but to be honest, I wish she hadn't stirred this up because we were so happy before. But since then, she has been distant and distracted, and sometimes it feels as if she can hardly remember how close we used to be.

An unresolved situation always makes me restless and I'll have to confront her about it. I've been holding back to give her time to sort things out but I can't wait any longer. I have to find out whether we have a future together.

Having decided to bite the bullet, a few days later I invited her over for dinner. Initially she made an excuse, as I suspected she would. She claimed she was exhausted and overworked, which I didn't doubt for a moment.

Our situation here has deteriorated over the past month to such an extent that we wonder what will become of us unless urgent food supplies arrive. The Germans are stealing most of our rations, and supplies from France have dwindled.

I'm still comparatively well off but my pantry is almost bare. I still have several jars of preserved fruit, about a dozen bottles of Armagnac, four bottles of sherry, some dried rusks and a few precious jars of bottled chickens, but they won't keep me going for very long, especially with winter approaching.

The news on BBC radio in June that the Allies had invaded the north coast of France had made my spirits soar. It sounded as if the war would soon end. And then shortly after that, we heard that Paris had been liberated. Wonderful news, of course, and I don't want to sound like sour grapes, but it did seem rather unfair that a nation that had caved in without a fight should already have been liberated while we in the UK are still fighting and struggling to feed ourselves.

Anyway, to get back to Aoife, I think she sensed the urgency in my tone and agreed to come over.

No teenage lad on his first date was more nervous than I was as I waited for her to arrive. I wore the only pair of casual slacks that hadn't become threadbare, grey ones with turn-ups, but first I had to punch two extra holes in my leather belt, because like everything else in my wardrobe, the slacks had become loose. Over my white shirt I wore the Fair Isle sleeveless pullover she always admired.

Downstairs, to create a festive atmosphere, I covered the table with a fine lace tablecloth my mother had bought in Venice. Margaret had never used it because she was nervous of damaging it. I cut tea roses from my garden, lit a romantic candle, and, for a special treat, I opened one of my last jars of preserved chicken.

Everything was ready and I kept checking the time and paced around, unable to sit still. Finally I heard the bell and rushed to the door. I was about to embrace her, but instead of melting into my arms as she usually did, she seemed to shrink into herself, and I stepped back.

I poured us a sherry before dinner to help us relax.

'The table looks lovely,' she commented as I pulled out her chair. 'You've gone to a lot of trouble, Hugh.'

The words, like her tone, were perfunctory. It was what any guest would say, and her formal manner hurt me. It was as if she had forgotten who I was, that I loved her, and knew every inch of her body intimately. To settle my nerves, I poured myself another sherry but the presentiment was still there, like an ugly spider hovering over our heads.

Now that we were sitting at the table, I wasn't sure how to begin, without sounding petulant or demanding.

'Aoife, I want to ask you about something that's has been on my mind for quite some time,' I began, wishing I didn't sound so nervous.

She looked at me for a moment with those beautiful eyes, which that evening were the colour of twilight. Then she looked down and fiddled with the edge of the tablecloth, and I realised that she was as nervous as I was.

She let me finish without interrupting. Then she said quietly, 'You're quite right. I know I've changed but it's nothing you've said or done. It's me. I've been trying to sort out what to do.'

'Do you mean, like seeing a psychologist?'

She shook her head. 'Like going back to Ireland.'

I was floored. So many thoughts were crashing around in my head that I hardly knew how to reply.

'After all this time?' I asked. 'Who do you want to see there? What do you expect will happen?'

'He committed a crime and he can't get away with it,' she said. 'As far as I know, there isn't a statute of limitations on the sex abuse of children.'

I detected a dangerous splash of acid in her tone.

'But the priest who abused you mightn't be alive anymore. Or he might have been moved to another parish.'

'That doesn't matter. Wherever he is, he has to answer for what he did to me. And if not Father O'Halloran himself, then his bishop.'

I didn't mean to sound so negative, but I felt panic-stricken. I wanted to spare her the anguish I was certain she would suffer. I'd never heard of any woman accusing a priest of sex abuse, especially so long after the event, and I was convinced she was embarking on a hopeless mission. No-one would be brought to justice and she would be the only person to suffer in the process.

I reached across the table and took her hand. 'Aoife, I'm worried for you,' I said. 'I understand why you want to do this, and you have every right to try and make the church answer for what the priest did. But this happened so long ago. You'll be alone, fighting such a powerful organisation, and who will believe you? Who will back you up? It will be your word against his. And from what you told me, everyone loved and respected him.'

Her eyes flashed. 'Well, I thought you'd be more supportive,' she said. 'Did you forget what you said the night I told you? That you'd stand by me no matter what?'

I poured some water into her glass from my Waterford decanter, and she sipped it slowly, perhaps to give herself time to calm down.

Then she said, 'I don't know who will believe me, if they will believe me, or if anyone will back me up. But I have to do this. If I don't, I won't be able to live with myself. I can't be the only girl he abused. There must be others who have been too embarrassed or scared to come forward. Perhaps if I accuse him, they'll find the courage to speak up too. And if they don't, maybe in the future other girls will stand on my shoulders.'

I looked at her in dismay. She was about to embark on a painful journey that was bound to end in failure and despair. They would accuse her of trying to blacken the name of a respected priest, and no-one in that little town would have the courage to come forward.

I could see all this so clearly, and yet I was full of admiration for her, that she refused to be swayed by the price she might pay. I think if at that point she had agreed with me and given up, I would have been disappointed.

'As soon as the war is over, I'm going to resign my job at the hospital, and go to Ireland,' she said. 'I don't think it will be long now, do you? Even the Germans who come into the hospital look thin and depressed. In spite of the propaganda, they can see the writing on the wall.'

I envied her resolve. As for me, I had no idea what I would do when the war was finally over. As long as we were occupied, I didn't have any choice. But what would I do when we were free to leave and resume normal life? And what would I do without her?

As soon as dinner was over, we went upstairs and made love for the first time in over a month. Our lovemaking was slow, gentle, almost valedictory, as if the sadness we felt had permeated every fibre of our bodies, inhibiting the usual wildness of our passion.

It took me a very long time to fall asleep that night. The images in my head succeeded each other like photographs spilled from an album and lying disordered and disconnected on the floor.

Aoife, Milly, Konrad, Mrs Deveraux. I sensed that there was a link somewhere that might make sense of it all if only I could find it.

I must have fallen asleep because in my dream I was running frantically in a misty landscape, searching for something that kept slipping away from me and vanishing in the mist as soon as I was about to close my hand on it. Suddenly I was sitting bolt upright, my eyes wide open. My heart was pounding and every nerve in my body was tingling as if I'd received an electric shock.

There it was, the connection that had eluded me.

Milly and Aoife.

Could it possibly be true? I had to find out.

CHAPTER THIRTY-TWO

Xanthe

St Helier, May 2019

Xanthe places her empty coffee mug on the sill and watches motes of dust dancing on shafts of sunlight that slant through the open windows of her bedroom. It's still early, and the only person in the street is a woman who is dragging a toddler by the hand. The child hangs back to pat an ugly brown mongrel trotting behind them, and when his mother tries to pull him away, he stamps and screams. Glancing around to make sure there's no-one around, she smacks him hard enough for Xanthe to hear the thwack of her hand. He yells louder and she shouts, 'Stop that or you'll get another one.' They disappear around the corner, the child still screaming and the mother still shouting. Xanthe comes away from the window but looks back one more time. No matter how deserted a street seems to be, she thinks, someone is always watching.

The mother and child make her think of Milly. She wonders how she will cope as a single mother raising a German soldier's child in wartime. Then she laughs at herself. Hugh Jackson's vivid entries make her forget that this took place so long ago.

Hoping to find the answer, she picks up his journal and rereads the page she has left open. Once again, his last statement makes the hairs stand up on the back of her neck.

If his hunch is right, Milly is Aoife's daughter. Will he tell her, or remain silent? Having a secret like that gives you the power to transform or destroy someone's life, but it can affect your own as well. Damned if you do and damned if you don't. She knows that from experience. Years ago, she had agonised for a long time whether to tell her best friend Angie that she had seen her fiancé groping another girl. In the end she decided that Angie would want to know, that she should know. That she deserved to know. Angie was furious. Not with her philandering fiancé, who denied it, but with Xanthe.

'You're making it up to stir up trouble between me and Damien because you've always been jealous of us!' Angie almost spat the words at her. Their friendship never recovered. Perhaps honesty wasn't always the best policy.

Xanthe sighs. She picks up Hugh's journal again and flicks the pages, shocked to see that she has almost come to the end.

What will happen to his relationship with Aoife? How will he resolve the problem of his marriage? She is tempted to go straight to the end, as she often does when reading a detective story, but she curbs her curiosity. This true-life mystery should be unravelled page by page, just as he lived it. She owes him that much.

But her mind wanders. Liberation Day is not far off and only a few days of her holiday remain. Unable to concentrate, she closes the journal and goes to the window again. An old man in a blue windcheater is walking down the street pulling a shopping trolley behind him. It's one of the neighbours who glances up, sees her, and gives her a cheery wave. She waves back and comes away from the window.

She will miss St Helier, but she is looking forward to returning home. She has finally come to a decision and the future is no longer a canvas painted black. What will Daniel think about her plan?

But as she discovers when they meet, Daniel has plans of his own. She is sitting in a tan velvet armchair by the Palladian windows of the Grand Hotel when she sees him coming, and from his rapid stride and eager expression she can tell he's bursting with news. He is wearing a black Midnight Oil T-shirt and she smiles at this unexpected reminder of home. Life's paths were unfathomable. She thinks back to the day they met at Edward de Courcy's home, and how close they have become since then.

He gives her a perfunctory kiss, and his eyes don't linger on her face as they usually do. As soon as he sits down, he leans forward, his eyes bright with excitement.

'I'm going to Oxford.'

'To give a lecture?'

'To take up a post as history lecturer.'

'Congratulations.' It's an effort to say it while she struggles with conflicting emotions. Happiness for him but disappointment for herself. This has come from left field, and she is in turmoil. It's not what she expected – but what actually did she expect?

'So I suppose you'll be living there?' As soon as the words are out of her mouth, she regrets not filtering the resentment.

'Well, it might be rather difficult commuting between Melbourne and Oxford every day.'

He is being facetious of course, but she doesn't smile. She can't bear to think about the distance between them, which is already beginning to widen.

'When are you going?' she asks, trying to sound as if she doesn't care. And why should she? After all, nothing has been promised. Perhaps she had assumed they had a future together because they'd talked of crossing bridges. But they hadn't made a commitment. They were both free to do whatever they chose. So she shouldn't feel so let down.

But she does. Pissed off, in fact. She had no idea that while she was fantasising about their future, he had applied for a job in England. He had never mentioned it. She had assumed they'd both return to Australia and continue seeing each other. Only an hour's flight separated Sydney and Melbourne, far less time than it took to drive from one side of Sydney to the other. She had imagined how exciting it would be to fly to Melbourne, run into his arms and hear him whisper that he couldn't wait to take her to bed.

But none of this would happen.

He leans towards her, but she turns away and looks out of the window to avoid his gaze.

'I thought we might both go to Oxford, Xan,' he says. 'From what you've said, it doesn't sound as if you want to go on working at the hospital.'

So his plans did include her after all, but she still feels resentful.

'Well as it happens, I have plans too,' she says with a trace of defiance. 'I'm going back to Sydney. I plan to keep working in a teaching hospital, but I've figured out a way to help interns who are struggling to cope like I did. I've been thinking about what happened to me, and I know I'm not the only one who was almost crushed by the system, so maybe I can use my experience to help other interns.'

His eyes haven't left her face since she started talking and, confident that she has his entire attention, she speaks more passionately. 'I'm going to lobby the health department to set up a committee of inquiry to determine why so many interns have committed suicide, and what can be done to prevent it. Also, I want to create a dedicated space in teaching hospitals where interns can talk openly about their problems to counsellors without feeling like failures. Where they're not denigrated or threatened with being deregistered because they can't cope.'

'So you're going to become an activist!'

'I've been thinking about it lately. If a counselling service like that had existed, maybe Sumi wouldn't have killed herself. But she couldn't bring herself to tell her superiors or her colleagues how depressed she was in case they thought she was incompetent. Didn't even tell me. She thought she had to appear confident and in control all the time, but inside she was desperate. Like me.'

'So you've found your fire,' he says. 'That's terrific. That day we came across the guy injured on the road, I could tell you were cut out to be a doctor.' With a smile he adds, 'And not just on account of your name.'

She feels ambivalent about his reaction. Pleased that he supports her decision but upset that he doesn't seem to mind what it implies for their relationship. The more she thinks about it, the more upset she is. It's obvious he doesn't love her. His feeling for her is shallow, superficial, opportunistic and probably based on sex.

'It's good that you can move on so easily,' she says. She can't keep the sarcasm out of her tone.

He looks surprised. 'Are you talking about moving from Melbourne to Oxford?'

'I'm talking about us,' she snaps, and blinks rapidly but can't stop the tears starting to form. 'You don't seem to mind that we'll be living at opposite ends of the earth and will probably never see each other again.'

He seems taken aback by her vehemence. 'Of course I mind.' He reaches out and strokes her arm. 'That's why I was hoping you'd come to Oxford. I do want us to be together, but this is a fantastic opportunity for me and I have to take it. I don't think we want to hold each other back, do you? I hoped you'd come to Oxford with me, but your solution sounds perfect for you so that's what you have to do.'

As she bends forward to wipe her eyes, a strand of hair falls across her face. He reaches over, smooths it away from her forehead, and gently strokes her cheek.

She gives a mirthless laugh. 'And here I was, wondering if we'd manage to get between Sydney and Melbourne.'

He is holding her hands in both of his. 'It's not the end of the world and it's not forever. Anything can happen. You might come to the UK. I might hate Oxford. And who knows, I might be offered a position at the Sydney Law School.'

Xanthe sighs. 'So many ifs.'

'I know, but we have to keep moving forward. You wouldn't want me to give up this opportunity, and I don't want to stop you from pursuing yours. You once told me you'd come to Jersey because you were running away from a problem, but as it turns out, you were really running towards a solution. Well, you've found it, and it's brilliant. I'm sad for me but happy for you.'

She shrugs. 'I suppose that makes us both equally sad and happy.' She takes a deep breath to give herself the courage to ask, 'So when are you leaving?'

'The day after Liberation Day.'

She swallows. 'That's less than a week away.'

She wasn't going to say it, but then she did. 'I can't bear the thought of us parting. Of waking up without seeing you smiling at me, without you caressing me.'

'I always knew you only wanted me for my body,' he says, and suddenly they are both laughing, but when she looks up, she sees that his eyes are soft with love.

The waiter has been hovering around them for some time. 'We have freshly baked blueberry muffins this morning,' he suggests.

Xanthe asks for English breakfast tea, while Daniel orders a short black.

'I'll never forget the look on your face the day you took a sip of that flat white you ordered at the Royal Yacht Hotel,' he chuckles. 'I thought you were one of those entitled Sydney princesses we joke about in Melbourne.'

'And I thought you were one of those dry academic types we avoid in Sydney,' she retorts.

Daniel laughs. 'I probably am. I could tell you didn't like me.'

Xanthe stares into space, trying to retrace the mysterious steps that led from indifference to love. Was it destiny, or something more prosaic – the urgency of a deep-seated need to connect with someone in a strange place? The happiest interlude of her life is about to end, and suddenly she wants to curl up in a dark corner and weep.

Daniel gazes at her with concern. 'Are you okay?'

She looks up, startled by his question. Of course she is okay. She is stronger than that. She doesn't need to cling to a speeding train by her fingernails. Her own future is mapped out. The one she discovered while taking the path to avoid it.

She clears her throat. 'You're absolutely right,' she murmurs in a hoarse voice. 'We owe it to ourselves to make the most of the opportunities that come our way.'

They are walking towards the door when he stops, turns towards her and looks searchingly into her eyes.

'I love you very much,' he says.

She smiles up at him and they walk into the sunlight with their arms around each other.

Back home, sitting by the French windows that open onto the garden, she reflects on the bittersweetness of life, its lurches from dazzling heights to despairing depths.

Would she ever find a balance that might make some sense of it all and find a comfortable place for herself in the world?

A light breeze is swaying the oak branches, and she is mesmerised by the way each bough moves to its own rhythm. And yet each of those individual boughs contributes to the exquisite harmony of the whole, like a visual orchestra.

She doesn't know how long she has sat there, entranced by the swaying of the trees, when the insistent ringing of her mobile rouses her from her reverie.

It's her mother.

'You've been away for such a long time and I wanted to check when you're coming home,' she says. Xanthe knows her well enough to recognise the reproach behind the innocent words. 'Ollie has been updating us about your trip,' she is saying, 'but I wanted to hear your voice. What are you doing with yourself? Have you met some nice people?'

Xanthe hesitates. The previous day she would have told her about Daniel but now she doesn't know how to answer.

Without waiting for her reply, her mother changes the subject. 'By the way, I've been meaning to ask, did you find out anything about that relative of ours who came from Jersey?'

'No, but I didn't have much to go on, did I?' Xanthe retorts. 'I would have felt like an idiot asking if anyone knew anything about a woman called Nellie.'

There's a brief silence. 'Nellie? Who's Nellie?'

Now it's Xanthe's turn to be perplexed. 'You know, the woman you said was related to us.'

'You've got the names mixed up,' her mother is saying. 'Her name wasn't Nellie. It was Milly.'

Xanthe's heart pauses mid-beat. 'Are you sure?'

Her mother gives a short laugh. 'Of course I'm sure. She was my father's great-aunt or something like that. Now I think of it, he mentioned there was a scandal and she was ostracised by the family. You know what they were like in those days.'

'What kind of scandal?'

'Now you're asking me to dredge up something from the dim distant past. My father's been gone over twenty years now, and he never said much about her so all I remembered was her name. Hang on a minute while I rack my brains.'

Xanthe holds her breath.

'Okay, I think she took up with a German during the war and had his child. Not the smartest thing to do in wartime. So when did you say you were coming home?'

Xanthe can hear her heart thumping in her ears. She can't catch her breath. Her mother is saying something about Ollie's new girlfriend, but she can't concentrate. She promises to call back and hangs up.

She sits very still trying to make sense of what she has just heard. Was it possible that Milly, the girl whose tragic love story she has read about in Hugh's memoir, is her distant relative?

She tries to quieten the chaos in her mind while she unravels the story. So the woman she wasn't interested in tracing has been there in plain sight all along, in Hugh's journal. She was Aoife's daughter. Her mind does another somersault. So Aoife was also related to her. How was it that, without being aware of the connection, she has become so involved with their lives?

Forcing herself to focus, she retraces the steps that have led her to this improbable point. It began with a chance comment about a relative she had mistakenly thought of as Nellie. Even though she hadn't been interested in tracing Nellie, it was her mother's casual comment that had prompted her to take this journey.

If her mother hadn't mentioned her, if she hadn't travelled to Jersey and rented Hugh's house, if she hadn't found his diary, she would never have discovered this connection. If, if, if. So many chance events.

But was it really just a succession of random events and coincidences? Was it possible that something – something she didn't know she knew – had propelled her on this journey? She wasn't given to metaphysical speculation, and had always dismissed explanations that defied logic, but now, confronted with a situation she cannot explain in rational terms, she is forced to consider another possibility. Something beyond conscious thought. Something bigger.

Too excited to stay home, she jumps into her car, and as she drives she is gripping the steering wheel as if determined to hold on to something solid and real. She can almost feel the blood coursing through her body. Ten minutes later, she pulls up outside Daniel's apartment, and runs up the stairs two at a time.

She is outside his door when she hears music that seems to make the walls vibrate. Despite her impatience to talk to him, she is glued to the spot, transfixed by the choral singing she hears. Finally she rouses herself and presses the buzzer.

He opens the door with a look of delighted surprise. 'Wait, I'll just turn this off,' he says as she comes into the room.

'No, leave it on,' she says. 'What is it?'

'It's Beethoven's Ode to Joy.'

'It sounds triumphant,' she says.

He nods and they sit side by side on the settee. 'You're right. It's a triumph over Beethoven's deafness. He was totally deaf when he composed it, and when he conducted it at its first public performance, they had to turn him around to face the audience because he couldn't hear the applause.' Then he adds, 'I think it's also a triumph over human limitations.'

'I must have heard it before but I've never paid much attention,' she says slowly.

He puts his arms around her and kisses her tenderly. 'Sometimes it takes a long time to hear the music.'

The symphony ends and as she wipes away the tears, she recalls previous occasions when she has cried while they were together. There must be something about this man that creates a space for her to let go of her tightly held emotions.

He pulls her against him, and they sit in silence. He doesn't ask why she has come to see him.

Then she tells him. About Milly and Aoife, and her connection to them.

'Even while I'm telling you, I can't believe it.' she says. 'I keep thinking I'll wake up and discover I dreamed it all.

'I feel stunned, confused and elated all at once. I suppose it will take time for me to process it all. But I can't stop wondering how it all came about.'

He shakes his head. 'It's extraordinary,' he says. He is looking at her in silence, and then says, 'Maybe you'll never know the answer.'

Suddenly she recalls the silent presence she sensed in the bedroom. She never discovered what caused it, or why she had experienced the same phenomenon as Hugh. In the end, she had given up trying to find a rational explanation for something that didn't appear to have one.

'You're probably right. I can't figure out why any of this happened and maybe I never will,' she muses. 'I don't know if this sounds crazy, but I'm wondering if it has anything to do with Jung's theory about the collective unconscious. I'm wondering if something I didn't consciously know or understand pushed me to follow the path that led me to this point.

'Because how come all those coincidences happened as soon as I got here? How come I got so involved with the lives of total strangers who lived here seventy years ago when I didn't know I was connected to them? This isn't just mysterious. It's overwhelming.' She turns to Daniel. 'Am I making any sense?'

'You're still searching for an answer when maybe there isn't one. Maybe that's how the early astronomers felt when they came across stars and planets for the first time and realised they were part of something whose magnitude defied understanding.'

'Well this definitely defies my understanding,' she murmurs and nestles into him.

He holds her close. 'You could always regard it as a gift from the universe.'

He looks into her eyes and she knows she has finally heard the music.

CHAPTER THIRTY-THREE

Tom

Breslau, December 1944

As the train sped from Weissburg prison towards Breslau, Tom pressed his face against the window of his armoured cell wagon, shocked at the contrast between the countryside of forests and meadows, and the ruined townships in between. Streets reduced to rubble, buildings shattered, scenes of apocalyptic destruction. Here and there, shadowy figures picked their way among the splintered timber and broken bricks, heads down, searching for anything left inside their bombed-out homes.

People dragged battered suitcases along the highways, some lugged bulging knapsacks and pushed wheelbarrows heaped with bedding, others hauled unwieldy bundles or carried children and bird cages; all refugees escaping their bombed-out homes in search of safety and shelter.

Next to Tom in the cramped train compartment, Luc was also staring at the smashed villages they passed.

'Just look at that!' he said. 'The Soviets must be close. It can't be long now. Maybe the war will end before they can put us on trial.'

Shocked by the desolation around them, Tom had temporarily forgotten why he was on the train. His trial date had finally been set, and together with his French, Dutch and Luxemburger fellow prisoners, he was being transferred from Weissburg to Breslau for trial.

He had always assumed that he and Harry would face the court together, but now it hit him that they would never again share good times or the bad times, that he would have to face the court, and the rest of his life, without his closest friend. He hadn't wept for Harry before, but now, overwhelmed by the loss, he blinked several times to hold back the tears. Harry wouldn't want him to be sad. He could almost hear his friend urging him to buck up and keep a stiff upper lip.

After being informed of their approaching court date, he and the other inmates had been speculating about their future. Unnerving rumours circulated that some prisoners had been sentenced to death by guillotine.

Ever since he saw a movie about Mary Queen of Scots at the Forum in St Helier, Tom had been haunted by the image of the executioner raising his axe above the queen, then holding up her severed head, dripping with blood, before a cheering crowd. The possibility that this might now happen to him made him shudder.

'Hey Churchill, cheer up,' Luc said. 'Did you know that they save money on the coffins for guillotined prisoners? They make them a head shorter.'

His macabre joke aroused laughter from the others, but Tom couldn't even smile. Surely they wouldn't condemn him to such a hideous death.

He turned to Luc. 'The prisoners they sentenced to death,' he began. 'I suppose they must have committed really serious crimes?'

Luc snorted. *'Tu rigoles, n'est-ce pas?* You must be joking. They were arrested under that Night and Fog law like us.'

That's when Tom realised that neither his age, his nationality nor the relatively minor nature of his crime would mitigate his sentence. Prisoners charged with offences under that draconian decree were treated far more harshly than others, no matter what crime they'd committed. And as far as the authorities were concerned, trying to escape was a serious crime.

Finally the train ground to a halt at a dilapidated station whose name Tom didn't recognise. They were ordered to alight, and after being counted several times, they were marched to a prison. Tom's filthy cell was home to millions of bedbugs that jumped on him as soon as he lay down on the straw pallet.

Sleep was impossible, and he spent the night scratching and watching the beams of searchlights intersecting across the dark sky. He heard the shriek of air raid sirens followed by the boom of distant explosions. Bombs were falling on Germany.

If Luc was right and the Russians were coming closer, perhaps he would be released soon. But when he finally fell into a restless sleep, he dreamed he was kneeling before an executioner's block. Just as the axe was about to fall, he sat up, trembling and covered in cold sweat. As he wiped the perspiration off his neck, he hoped the dream wasn't prophetic.

The following day they got back on the train, which brought them to the Silesian city of Breslau. As they passed the market square, Tom gazed admiringly at the intricately painted facades of the ancient buildings, and he felt more hopeful. Perhaps they would dismiss the charges against him.

But that hope was dashed inside the jail, where he heard that some of the prisoners had already been sentenced to death. They were spending their last days chained in their cells without food, as the jailers didn't see the point of wasting supplies on them.

Tom's glance continually strayed to the yard below his cell where the hideous contraption stood, its sharply angled blade poised to drop onto the naked necks of condemned prisoners.

But neither the menacing sight of the guillotine, nor fear for their own fates, seemed to dampen the spirits of his French comrades, who spent the time discussing their favourite foods, arguing about the best wines, and boasting about the attributes of their girlfriends. Tom, whose eyes kept returning to the guillotine, envied their ability to block out fear.

Sometimes, to cheer him up, they told him that some comrades had received light sentences. That meant five to ten years' imprisonment in the nearby camp of Gross-Rosen, which was guarded by the SS. As Tom had already experienced the savagery of the SS and had heard chilling stories about the cruelty inside that camp, it wasn't a comforting option. Death by one stroke might be preferable to death by slow degrees.

Waiting for his day in court, he paced up and down in his cell. Although he dreaded the trial, it would be a relief to end the uncertainty.

Finally the suspense was over. Six days after arriving in Breslau, he was escorted into a gloomy courtroom whose small windows let in very little light. From the way people on the public benches turned and whispered when he was brought in, he realised his case had attracted local interest.

As the guard led him to the prisoner's dock, his knees shook so violently that he could hardly stand up, and a tennis ball was pounding inside his chest. The door behind the judges' bench opened, and in walked three judges in black robes carrying thick dossiers and black leather briefcases.

Anxiously he scanned their faces, but they took their seats without looking at him. Their expressions gave nothing away, and the swastikas embroidered on the shoulders of their robes made him nervous.

He wondered whether, when they became lawyers, they had ever thought they would have to enforce a law like the repressive Night and Fog decree, and whether any of them ever felt qualms about it. But looking at their businesslike demeanour, and the concentration with which they examined their files, he doubted it.

The oldest judge in the centre, who was bald and had a bulging forehead and large fleshy ears, leaned towards him and spoke in a quiet voice that commanded attention. 'Do you need an interpreter?'

Surprised, Tom nodded. 'I'd like an English one,' he replied in German. Emboldened by the question, he decided to push his luck. 'And I'd like to be represented by an English-speaking lawyer.'

This seemed to cause some consternation among the judges, who conferred for several minutes, until the one with the bony face and prominent nose took off his glasses and fixed Tom with an unblinking stare.

'A defence lawyer is not necessary,' he said, and pointed to the bulging file in front of him. 'We are already in possession of all the relevant facts in your case. As for an English-speaking interpreter, we weren't informed you were British, so we don't have one available. But you seem to speak German quite well, young man. Do you think you can understand enough to continue the trial?'

Tom hadn't expected his request would be taken seriously. He had asked for an interpreter merely to emphasise the fact that he was British and unafraid. The judge's response encouraged him to explain that although he had learned German in Jersey, his command of the language might not be adequate for legal terms but he would do his best.

As he spoke, Tom watched the judge on the left, who had a clipped black moustache and hair cut very short and parted in the middle. He extracted a document from his file and passed it to the senior judge, who spoke in an almost inaudible voice.

'There are five serious charges against you,' he began, and Tom almost stopped breathing as he listed them.

'Espionage, attempting to escape from Jersey in order to assist Britain wage war against Germany, illegal possession of a boat in which you escaped, possessing an illegal maritime chart used during the escape, and being an enemy of the German Reich.'

He looked straight at Tom. 'How do you plead?'

Tom was so overwhelmed that he struggled to construct a coherent answer. To add to his turmoil, the judge with the moustache looked up from his dossier and addressed him in a pompous tone. 'You should be aware that the last charge, being an enemy of the Reich, can carry the death sentence.'

Tom's mouth was so dry that when he tried to swallow, it felt as if his throat was lined with sandpaper. So much hinged on his reply. But maybe they had already made their decision and the whole trial was a charade intended to give the appearance of justice. Probably nothing he said in his own defence would make any difference.

While they waited for him to speak, he remembered the advice he'd been given by his fellow inmates. *Deny everything. Admit nothing.* Then he heard Harry saying, *'Keep on fighting, don't give in.'*

He pulled his shoulders back and looked at the judges with a level gaze.

'Not guilty to all charges,' he stated in a voice that resounded though the courtroom.

The judge who had been examining the documents inclined his head towards him attentively and nodded. Assuming this signified approval, Tom began to relax but a moment later his composure was shattered. The judge was holding up his photo album.

'How can you say you're not guilty of spying when your album contains photos of German troops, military installations, aircraft and fortifications?'

Tom felt as though a ton of bricks had just knocked him over. He had been hoping that his album had disappeared somewhere between St Helier and Germany. While trying to figure out how to reply, he asked to see it, to play for time. His hands shook as he turned the incriminating pages.

'It is your album, is it not?' the judge on the right demanded, taking off his glasses. 'Please do not waste the court's time.'

Tom cleared his throat. 'It is my album, but if you look carefully at the photos, you'll see that they can't possibly be proof of espionage. You see my father was the official German photographer in Jersey, and these are the photos the German soldiers took, and brought them to my father to print.'

The bald judge seemed to be considering this before asking, 'So why did you take them with you on the boat?'

Tom took a deep breath. Trying to sound bewildered and sincere, he said, 'I really don't know how it got there, sir. I certainly didn't bring it. I had no reason to. It must have been one of my companions, maybe as a souvenir of Jersey. But if you regard the photos as proof of spying, then you should charge every German soldier who took them with espionage.'

He knew he was playing to the gallery, because nods and chuckles greeted this statement until the judge banged his gavel and warned the public that this wasn't a Berlin cabaret, and if they didn't maintain decorum, he'd eject them from the courtroom.

After conferring about Tom's answers, the judges moved on to another charge.

'You left Jersey to join the British army to wage war on Germany, didn't you?' the senior judge asked.

This time Tom's indignation was genuine. 'Certainly not. As you know, I was only sixteen at the time, and the British army doesn't accept boys that young.'

Then he added, 'Anyway, leaving Jersey wasn't my idea. My friends were older than me, and they talked me into it. I only decided to join them so I could study in England, because we don't have a university in the Channel Islands. So my only crime is that I allowed myself to be influenced by others.'

He hoped they were convinced, but he felt bad. Once again he had betrayed not only his friends, but his principles as well. He could hear Harry's voice accusing him of lying. But surely even Harry would understand that lying in this situation was not only excusable, but essential. His life was at stake, and no matter what he said, he couldn't hurt Harry or Frank now.

The judge with the bony face took off his glasses and leaned forward. 'How do you explain the fact that you were in possession of an illegal boat?' he asked.

'It wasn't illegal,' Tom retorted, relieved to be able to tell the truth at last. 'I had it registered and I had a fishing permit. Food was so scarce we had to supplement our rations with fish.'

The judge pursed his lips and looked at the wrinkled document in his hand as if it had an unpleasant odour. 'So perhaps you can tell the court why you had a hand-drawn maritime chart showing the route from Jersey to England?'

Tom felt his knees buckling. He had to think fast. Just in time, he remembered the Gestapo officers in France saying that the map had been found on Frank's body.

'I swear I've never seen this before, sir,' he said. 'I have no idea whose it is or why my friends had it. I don't know the first thing about navigation so I wouldn't have had a clue how to use it to get to England.'

His reply seemed to satisfy them, and after noting his answer, the senior judge asked, 'How can you deny being an enemy of the Reich when you tried to escape?'

At least this accusation was easy to refute. 'You can't possibly accuse me of being an enemy of the Reich. I was always friendly with the Germans, as was my whole family. You only have to ask the officers of the Water Police who were stationed at the Pomme d'Or and they'll tell you. I often ran errands for them. My father was the official photographer, my parents had social evenings for German officers every week at our house, and my mother's cooperation with the German administration was well known.'

If there was any justice on earth, the skies should have crashed down on his head at this point. He marvelled that those words hadn't choked him, that he had actually sunk so low that he had used his mother's behaviour and his father's compliance to save himself. His parents had become his toehold on the slippery slope of survival to which he was desperately clinging.

The judge seemed to be considering his reply.

'Do you have anything else to say in your defence?'

'All I can say is that I'm not guilty of any of the charges against me,' Tom began. 'I never meant to harm Germany in any way. The only thing I'm guilty of is allowing myself to be influenced by others. As you know, I've already suffered for that. I've spent nearly two years in your camps and prisons, and one of my friends died of TB in one of them.'

He paused for effect before adding, 'I want to ask you – do I look like a spy?'

The judge suppressed a smile. 'You certainly did not need a lawyer, young man. Your German is excellent, and the court appreciates the respectful way you conducted yourself. But you must realise that the charges against you are punishable by death. Now we will go and deliberate on your case.'

Trembling with apprehension, Tom watched them place their dossiers in their briefcases and rise from the bench without another glance in his direction. As they left the courtroom, their black robes billowing in the breeze of the open door reminded Tom of flights of crows over the potato fields of St Helier.

He couldn't stop shaking. It was impossible to gauge their thoughts from their impenetrable expressions. At times he had sensed they were sympathetic. But did they believe him when he pleaded ignorance about the album and the maritime chart? Had he said too little or too much? And what would their verdict be?

When the judges returned an hour later, Tom gripped the edge of the prisoner's dock and tried not to think about the guillotine. The senior judge spoke so quietly that he had to strain to hear every word. 'Thomas Stanley Gaskell, we find you guilty of all charges, which are punishable by death.'

Tom swayed and only the confined space of the dock prevented him from falling. The judge was still speaking. 'But as you are young, and your guilt is mostly by association, we have decided to be merciful and commute the mandatory death sentence to eight years hard labour.'

Tom groaned. Eight years hard labour at Gross-Rosen. They thought they were being merciful but he was convinced that death by guillotine would be preferable to eight years in the power of the SS sadists.

The judge continued. 'But because we are impressed by your manners and your attitude, we have taken into account the time you have already served, and have decided to hand down the minimum sentence. Four years in prison.'

Tom left the court in a daze. He knew he had just been given a reprieve. He would not be decapitated, and perhaps he'd survive four years in an ordinary prison, but he felt too numb to rejoice.

He knew he had just given the performance of his life. It had paid off, but when he recalled having lied, betrayed his friends, and made use of his parents' collusion, it felt like a hollow victory.

That night, when he lay in his cell going over the trial, a line he had learned in scripture classes came into his mind. *For what shall it profit a man, if he shall gain the whole world, and lose his own soul?* He had gained the world – the world that his life represented – but had he bargained away his soul in return?

For hours he tossed on the thin straw mattress in his cell. If only he could beg Frank's and Harry's forgiveness. Exhausted, he closed his eyes. He dreamed he was back in St Helier. He knew he should visit Harry but he was too ashamed to face him and then remembered that his friend was dead. But just then Harry appeared. So he's alive after all, Tom thought, overwhelmed with joy. He knew there was something he wanted to say to Harry but as he tried to remember what it was, Harry gave him that wonderful smile, clapped him on the shoulder, and said, *Good on you Tom!*

When Tom woke up, he could still feel the warmth of Harry's hand on his shoulder.

CHAPTER THIRTY-FOUR

Dr Jackson

St Helier, January 1945

They say it's darkest before dawn, but this dawn is a long time coming. Our hope that the war would soon end was raised sky high after the Allied landing in Normandy in June. Surely it would only be a matter of weeks before we too would be freed.

But alas, we are still waiting. Months have passed, and the situation drags on with no hope of rescue on the horizon, leaving us dispirited, demoralised and embittered. When will British troops liberate us? Have they and the rest of the world forgotten us? Sometimes I think that having no hope is better than having hope that is continually dashed.

Disappointment is just one of the problems we face. A more pressing problem is lack of food. Ever since the Normandy landing, no food supplies have arrived from

France and our situation is becoming desperate. We seem to be in a state of siege, worse than anything we've experienced over the past four years.

Some food deliveries have arrived on Red Cross ships, but those relief vessels are few and far between, and for the past few weeks we've had no flour at all, which is disastrous, especially as the potatoes we have to make do with are mostly rotten. I still have some of the provisions I squirreled away at the start of the Occupation, but they won't last much longer.

As you'd expect, this situation has affected not only morale but also our health. Everyone looks gaunt and strained, and with the lack of nutritious food, people have become more susceptible to infections, so I am run off my feet trying to look after my debilitated patients with the inadequate medications at my disposal. Exhausted and anxious, I haven't had the energy to write up my journal for the past few months.

August passed and September, with no end to our misery in sight. By October, our golden autumn was over. The trees had shed their leaves, and we had shed weight. There was little to celebrate at Christmastime. Now it's 1945, but no-one is in the mood to celebrate the start of the new year while the war continues to drag on. The temperature has dropped, and the grey winter skies mirror our state of mind.

To make things worse, wood is unobtainable, so heating our homes is becoming impossible. I still have some logs in my woodpile, but they won't last the whole winter and I go to bed almost as soon as I get home, to preserve the few I have left.

What with the famine conditions, power shortages and the scarcity of wood for fuel, people are cold as well as hungry. On top of that, we feel helpless and frustrated at being so close to the finishing line, which seems to retreat as we approach.

It isn't much consolation that the German soldiers here are in a bad state as well. Their rations have also been severely reduced, and we often see them wandering around the rocks on the coast, heads down, searching for limpets to supplement their meagre diet. Some of them have been caught stealing food from the residents, for which they are severely punished by their superiors, who have probably stashed away some provisions for themselves, judging by their robust appearance.

I've noticed that the soldiers no longer look immaculate. They've lost their arrogant 'supermen' expression. In fact, from their chastened demeanour, it's obvious that, like us, they are fed up with this war.

They've finally realised that the tales of Nazi victories they've been fed are lies and propaganda. They can see that their bloody Führer will soon be defeated, so they are likely to become prisoners of war. Which is probably why they've been going out of their way lately to be friendly and helpful.

I've gone into all this detail to describe our hardships during what I hope are the final months of the war because I'm aware that once the war ends, people will focus on the liberation, so I hope my record will go some way towards ensuring that future generations don't forget the prolonged suffering that preceded it.

Perhaps because we are worn out, cold and hungry, these last months have seemed longer and more difficult than the preceding ones. I feel that an important part of my job is to keep my patients' spirits up, because I have observed that one's state of mind affects one's health, and in the absence of necessary medications, all I have to offer them is hope and encouragement. But I am no Churchill, and as time goes on, I am finding it increasingly difficult to be positive.

I must admit that this isn't entirely due to the continued uncertainty we live in and the physical hardships we suffer. It is partly, and possibly largely, due to the emotional cancer that has invaded my life.

And this is really why I have been too dispirited to record anything for the past few months. Knowing that Aoife has decided to leave for Ireland as soon as the war is over has cast a black cloud over my life that grows heavier and darker with every passing day, so I find myself in a paradoxical situation. While I long for the end of the war, at the same time I dread it. So instead of savouring every hour that Aoife and I still have together, I find it difficult to stop dwelling on the future that looms ahead without her.

I keep hoping against hope that I'll be able to talk her out of it. So time and time again we go over the same fruitless discussion where I urge her not to expose herself to certain failure by confronting the might of the Catholic church, and she reiterates that she feels compelled to do it, regardless of the outcome.

I've never heard of anyone accusing a priest of rape. Who would believe her? Even in the unlikely event that it leads to an investigation, it would just be her word against his. And who could she produce as a witness? Her estranged parents wouldn't help. She couldn't prove it was the priest, and if he is still alive, he would deny it.

She maintains that this is not just to get justice for herself, but for the other girls who might take courage from her actions and realise that they do not have to remain helpless victims, that they can speak up against their abusers. I think she's being quixotic, but she is unshakeable,

One evening, after we had gone over the same argument, and sat in tense silence on the couch, I recalled the plaintive Irish song she had once sung. I remembered the strange feeling I had experienced, as if someone had walked over my grave.

'When you sang that song, did you already know you were going to leave, that we would part?' I asked her. 'Was I the one who was too young and foolish to understand?'

She looked surprised. 'Of course not.'

'So what made you sing that particular song about lost love?' I persisted. 'You must know other songs, but something made you choose that one.'

Aoife considered my question and then, in her lovely lilting voice she said, 'I don't really know why. Yeats's poem came into my mind at that moment, and that's all there is to it, so.'

She could see I wasn't satisfied with her answer and, to diffuse the tension between us, she said lightly, 'Perhaps it's the little people that put it into my mind.'

The weak light from the standard lamp cast a glow over her pale face and made gold highlights dance on her hair whenever she moved. Gazing at her, I ached for the loss that was about to befall me. She was sitting beside me, but already I was grieving her absence.

Then very slowly, she said, 'Do you think it's possible that, deep inside, I knew something I didn't know I knew?'

I know that many people, particularly those who are trained in scientific subjects, tend to dismiss such ideas as fanciful if not downright foolish, but I have always kept my mind open to things not explicable by logic alone. Like the mysterious presence I felt before I went to sleep, which vanished as soon as I turned on the light. Was the room haunted by the troubled soul of the previous occupant? Was it the physical manifestation of my own anxiety? Or was it fate knocking at my door? In the end I had to concede that I couldn't explain it and perhaps I never would.

Our conversation had shifted from poetry to leprechauns and metaphysics, but I was too preoccupied with her return to Ireland to concentrate on anything else.

How would she manage alone in a town where she would be shunned and vilified? I couldn't bear to think of her going through such a devastating experience, her reputation dragged through the mud. Or of me living here alone, without her.

But Aoife had a question of her own.

'Have you thought about your marriage?'

That startled me. Because of our long separation, Margaret's silence, and my feelings for Aoife, I no longer considered myself married, but her question forced me to confront the fact that no matter how long Margaret and I had been separated, legally we were still married.

And Jamie. The bond that linked me to him had never weakened, but I had come to consider him a separate entity, overlooking the painful fact that he was inextricably yoked to my relationship with his mother.

I had never given up hope that when the war was over, we would finally meet and be together, but I had never considered what legal negotiations that might involve, or how acrimonious they might turn out to be.

Aoife's question brought me down to earth. For us to be married, I'd have to divorce Margaret. But on what grounds? I couldn't claim she had deserted me. Or been unfaithful. According to the law, I was the unfaithful one. But also she could quite correctly claim that I'd failed to support her and the child financially during the Occupation. Maybe she would claim desertion? So perhaps she might agree to divorce me. But what if, from sheer spite, she refused? And if we did divorce, how would that impact my ability to see Jamie? Would she try to stop him from seeing me? Would he even want to see me? After all, he doesn't know me and she has probably turned him against me. For all I know, she has never told him about my letters, so he would think of me with resentment if he ever thinks about me at all. And where would we live after the war? Would she return to Jersey or stay in England with her family?

The light flickered and went out, and we sat in the dark while outside the light of the moon cast long shadows on the lawn. Aoife shivered, and I threw a log on the fire. I drew her so close that I could feel her heart beating under the navy Guernsey that I'd wrapped her in to keep warm. Entwined, we continued to sit in silence as the turmoil in my mind intensified.

For once, I had no answers. The irony of it didn't escape me. Other people turned to me for help with their crises, but I couldn't solve my own. In fact I had no idea what to do.

As we sat there, in unhappy silence, I was tormented by a dangerous topic I longed to share with her but didn't dare to raise. I was at a loss to know whether I even had the right to speak of it, or whether doing so might unbalance the delicate equilibrium that she had created in her life.

Ever since I began to suspect the identity of Aoife's child, I haven't been able to stop wondering if I was right. Perhaps I'd jumped to the wrong conclusion. I had to know the truth. So yesterday I decided to check it out once and for all. At the Jersey Archive office, I asked to see documents pertaining to L'Abbaye. It had ceased operating as a home for unwed mothers some years ago, though the nuns were still in residence and continued to look after a small number of orphans.

My fingers shook as I leafed through the birth entries for 1925. And there it was in black and white: Aoife O'Connor, aged sixteen, gave birth to a baby girl who was adopted by Flora and Harold Deveraux.

I had imagined that ascertaining the truth would put my mind at rest, but instead it created a dilemma that almost tore me apart. I was now in possession of crucial information that Aoife herself didn't know. Although I sensed it might be wiser to remain silent, I wondered how Aoife would feel if she discovered at some later date that I not only knew who her daughter was, but that I had met her. Surely she'd be furious that I'd withheld information of such profound significance in her life.

Ever since confiding in me about her baby, she had never expressed any longing to see her daughter; never said she dreamed of contacting the child she had given away, or shown any curiosity about her life. I wondered if she wanted to spare herself the anguish of confronting her loss, or perhaps avoid rejection, in case her child refused to meet her.

Either way, it was a personal issue and I sensed it would it be insensitive of me to raise it.

And yet.

We should listen to our instincts. Mine told me that revealing this secret could lead to disaster. That it wasn't mine to divulge. It was hers to deal with as she chose.

I was perched on the razor-sharp edge of an upturned sword, knowing that any movement I made – or failed to make – could cause us both injury from which we might never recover. And yet, knowing what I know, how could I remain silent? I struggled between courage and cowardice.

I cleared my throat. Several times. I drew her closer.

She looked at me questioningly. 'Are you all right, my darling?'

I took a very deep breath. I had to proceed very carefully. 'A woman came in to see me today and said she had a baby when she was single, and had given it up for adoption,' I began. 'Some years later she got married but she never told her husband about the baby she had before they met. She never talked about that child or tried to find out anything about it. She said she had decided to start a new life and put the past behind her.'

I paused and then asked, 'What do you think about that?'

Aoife pulled away and gave me a hard look. 'And what would make you want to ask me that?'

That should have warned me to make some excuse and drop the subject but having embarked on it, I felt it would be cowardly to back away.

'It made me think about you and wonder if you ever think about your child. It would be natural to think about her, especially now that you're going to Ireland, wouldn't it?'

'Well you seem to know all about it, so you tell me what's natural and what isn't.'

I could feel her shrinking away from me, and even in the dark I could see her eyes flashing with anger. I'd wedged myself into an uncomfortable corner, and it was too late to extricate myself.

She was staring straight ahead, avoiding my eyes. It was some time before she spoke, and when she did, her tone chilled the air around us.

'When I told you what happened, I broke a silence that had lasted twenty years. I broke it because I love you and I didn't want to keep a secret from you.'

I stretched out my hand but she pulled hers away and turned to look straight at me.

'I thought you would understand how painful this subject was, and that you would respect that. But since you seem to need more information, here it is, and I hope this will be the last time we have to talk about it.'

Her tone made me wince. She had never spoken to me so coldly before, and I wished I had listened to the warning voice in my head while there was still time.

'I have made a good life for myself here. Bringing babies into the world and seeing the mothers' elation at producing life's greatest miracle is a privilege I am grateful for. You ask if I ever think about my own child. Of course I do. It's an ache that never goes away. She is a part of me but I'm not part of her life and probably never will be. I hope she is healthy and happy wherever she is, and that the people who adopted her are good to her. But I will never make inquiries about her whereabouts because that wouldn't be fair. I made my decision to give her up, and I don't want to create conflict in her life, especially if she doesn't know she's been adopted. But if the day ever comes when she tries to find me, I'll be waiting with open arms.'

She slipped out of my embrace, stood up, took off my Guernsey sweater and placed it on the couch. 'I think I'll be going now,' she said, and left.

I sat in front of the dying embers for a long time, too shaken to move. Cowardice has its price, but so does courage.

I tried to visualise life here without her and I knew that it would be like living in a winter without end, never seeing the sun's light or feeling its warmth.

The solution startled me with its clarity. This didn't have to be the end. I didn't have to stay here alone. I didn't have to live without her; there was nothing to keep me in Jersey.

CHAPTER THIRTY-FIVE

Tom

Germany, February 1945

On a winter's morning cold enough to freeze the nose off his face, Tom and his cellmates stood shivering in the courtyard of the prison where he was serving his four-year sentence. They were issued with a chunk of black bread and a piece of sausage, but no-one told them where they were going.

Tom looked around at the others, who shrugged or shook their heads. Another journey to an unknown destination. As they set off, he overheard their police escorts saying they had to hurry as the Red Army was on their heels. Tom was elated. He could already sense liberation floating above him like a balloon of hope.

Ever since his trial three months before, he had been languishing in a cold, filthy prison cell, wondering how long he could survive on the watery turnip soup the surly guards doled out twice a day. And if starvation didn't kill him, tuberculosis probably would.

Now, as they marched out of the prison gate, his pulse quickened at the prospect of the approaching Soviets. Just then, he heard the drone of aeroplanes and looked up.

Above them, a squadron of fighter planes with red stars on their wings sliced through the pale sky and he had to restrain himself from waving and cheering.

But a moment later he heard the crisp stuttering of machine guns followed by the thud of explosions and realised that what promised deliverance also threatened death. Russian bombs and machine guns wouldn't distinguish between Germans and their prisoners. They might blow him up before they rescued him.

These thoughts weighed on his mind while they trudged along the endless road. Tom's face smarted from sleet that stung like needles and he could no longer feel his hands and feet.

For hours he stumbled along the road in the fading winter light, yearning for a hot drink and a warm bed. Just as he was wondering how long it would be before frostbite set in, their nervous escorts pushed them into an empty barn for the night.

It was still dark next morning when they set off, and Tom braced himself for another freezing day.

'Step on it or the Russians will catch up with us,' their police escorts warned.

'If only,' sighed Tom's cellmate Pascal.

It was agony to keep walking on swollen feet, their clogs little protection against the icy ground, but something on the lonely road in front of them distracted Tom from his misery.

From a distance, it looked as if lumpy bundles of dirty rags had been scattered all over the road, but when they came closer, he realised he was looking at corpses. *'Mon dieu,'* Pascal kept saying. *'Mon dieu.'*

Tom pressed his numb hands over his mouth as he stared at the ghastly scene before them. In the contorted faces of the dead, unseeing eyes were sunk deep into their sockets, and mouths gaped open as if caught mid-scream. Everything that was human and individual had been stripped from these skeletal bodies covered in skin that resembled old parchment. Without understanding why, Tom forced himself to keep looking, as if it was his duty to commit this gruesome sight to memory.

Pascal pointed to the striped uniforms and wooden clogs. 'Probably Jews from a concentration camp,' he said. 'The SS must have evacuated the camp when the Russians were on their doorstep and then shot them when they were too weak to keep up.'

'What makes you think they're Jews?'

Pascal's dark eyes flashed with anger. 'Because all over Europe the Krauts rounded them up and deported them to concentration camps. Probably killed most of them in there. That's what happened to the Jews I knew in Paris. They were loaded onto cattle trucks that went east and never returned.'

He paused when he saw Tom's astonished expression. 'You have no idea what went on, do you? What about the island you come from? Weren't there any Jews there?'

Tom tried to think back. He remembered Mrs Goldman, who had sold him some piano music when he didn't have enough money to pay for it, and who had looked so worried the last time he saw her. There were also some Jewish people his parents knew in St Saviour, but it all seemed so long ago.

'There were some,' he said slowly, 'but I don't know what happened to them. I suppose our States would have protected them from the Nazis.'

'In France that *salaud* Pétain collaborated with the Germans, and in the occupied zone French collaborators turned the Jews over to the Gestapo,' Pascal said.

He turned his piercing gaze on Tom, who was frowning as he tried to follow French politics.

'You know what keeps me going?' Pascal went on. 'I can't wait to get home and expose those Nazi arse-lickers. I'll make sure they get what's coming to them.'

Tom nodded. That was something he understood. Revenge was the fuel that had propelled him to survive as well. Revenge on his mother. And Milly too. But it seemed petty to focus on his personal vendetta in a world where, according to Pascal, millions had been slaughtered.

He looked back at the corpses on the road. 'We have to remember this,' he muttered. As they trudged on, he hardly noticed his throbbing hands and shivering body. Muscles could lose their elasticity, joints could swell, flesh could rot and bones could snap, but he thought of Harry and sensed the existence of something intangible that was stronger than the body's fragile frame.

Despite all his suffering, Harry had died with grace, while Tom continued to cling to life with a desperation that almost embarrassed him. Was it shameful to claw at life at all costs?

They spent that night in an open field and marched on the following day. Their food was gone, and they lived on mouthfuls of snow, walking like automatons, dragging one swollen foot after the other, unsure if they were alive or dead.

'If the Russians are so close, where are they?' Tom rasped through swollen lips.

Pascal sighed. 'They must have missed us.'

On the third day of their march, with all hope of rescue gone, Tom felt he had come to the end of his endurance. They had been staggering for several hours when they came to a prison. As they walked through the gate, Tom felt like a parched wanderer in the desert who had found an oasis. Prison meant sleeping inside a cell instead of endless walking through sleet and frost, frozen to the bone. It meant having a hot drink for the first time in three days.

But his relief didn't last long. For the next few weeks, shivering inside his cold cell, he listened in vain for Russian bombardments that might presage the end of the war, but instead of coming closer, they seemed to recede. By some evil twist of fate, the Russians had bypassed them. He would die in this prison near the German–Polish border. He would never be liberated.

March passed, and April, and Tom was slumped in his cell staring at the wall when he was startled by a guard who ordered him to go and see Johannes Webber, the prison warden. Tom was apprehensive. It was probably bad news.

Inside his small office, the warden looked at Tom and there was a strange expression on his usually impassive face.

'I called you in here because you speak German, and I have something important to say,' he began in a sepulchral voice. 'The war is over. Germany is *kaput*. The Red Army has surrounded Berlin, and our brave Führer is dead. I heard he died at the head of his troops defending the Fatherland.'

Tom heard the words but it took a while to take them in. He waited.

'Because we have been defeated, I have decided to set you all free,' Johannes Webber was saying. 'Please tell the others. Tomorrow I will open the prison gate and you can leave. But I advise you to keep away from the Soviets and the SS.'

When Tom finally found his voice, it sounded thin and uncertain. 'What is the date today, sir?'

'May 8, 1945,' the warden sighed, and passed a weary hand over his eyes. 'I don't suppose either of us will ever forget it.'

Back in his cell, Tom discussed this startling information with the others. Like him, they were dubious and subdued. Could this really be true?

They had visualised being liberated by a brigade of triumphant Russians who would burst into the prison like the revolutionary forces storming the Bastille, tearing down swastikas and portraits of Hitler and arresting all the Germans. They had imagined an atmosphere of jubilation and euphoria, with Soviet soldiers exulting at defeating the enemy.

The warden's depressed announcement came as an anticlimax.

It didn't seem real until the next morning as they watched the warden unbolt the heavy iron gate. The prisoners started streaming through, jostling each other in their haste to get away before the warden changed his mind, but Tom couldn't move. Perhaps it was a trick after all, and SS were lurking nearby armed with clubs and pistols, waiting to murder them. But when the gate was fully open, the warden shook his hand, wished him luck, and walked slowly inside, his head bowed and his shoulders slumped.

Tom ventured through the gate on unsteady legs. He kept telling himself he was actually free, free after two years that had felt like a lifetime, yet the longed-for word sounded empty. What did it really mean? Where should he go?

He looked around for his French and Luxembourger comrades. They might know how to get to the Allies. But he couldn't see any of them and realised that while he'd been standing there, paralysed, they must have gone. After all the hardships they had suffered together, all the support they had given each other, they hadn't waited for him.

Standing outside the prison gates, he felt like a child whose mother had forgotten to pick him up after school. Abandoned and alone. There was no-one in charge, no-one he could ask for advice. No-one to tell him where to go or what to do. For two years he had dreamed of freedom, and now that it had finally come, it felt too sudden and bewildering.

He straightened his shoulders. He had to stand on his own two feet and find a way to reach the Allies by himself. Flagging down a German army truck, he asked the driver the way.

'There are Polish troops in the next town,' the man said. 'You'll be safer with them than with the Reds.'

While the driver was speaking, Tom noticed that he'd torn the Nazi insignia off his jacket. No wonder he was scared of the Russians, but being British, Tom knew he had nothing to fear from his allies.

It was a clear May morning, and, feeling more confident, Tom headed towards the town. Occasionally he rested against the mottled trunk of a birch tree to listen to a sound he hadn't heard for a long time: birds chirping in branches covered in pale green leaves. There was a freshness in the air, a feeling of renewal, and strengthened by the beauty around him, he walked on with a spring in his step.

By evening, tired and hungry, he reached a neat little village where every immaculate house had scarlet geraniums in window boxes. He wanted to ask someone where to get some food, but there was no-one in the street.

He looked up and saw movement behind the upstairs window of a house across the road. A stout woman in a kerchief was peering through the net curtain.

But when he knocked on the door, no-one answered. He had almost given up when the door opened a fraction and the woman gave him a suspicious look.

'I'm British, I was a prisoner and they've just released me,' he explained.

The woman nodded, and opened the door just wide enough to let him in, and quickly closed it behind him. In her kitchen, Frau Strauss explained that the Russians had descended on the village several days before and she was afraid they'd soon return.

'They are depraved beasts,' she said. 'They raped every woman they could find. Not even old women were safe.

I ran and hid in the forest with my daughter. Luckily they didn't find us. When they weren't raping they were looting and shooting. They shot people they accused of being spies or fascists.'

Tom found this hard to believe. Throughout his imprisonment, he and his fellow inmates had regarded the Russians as heroes, but from what the truck driver and this woman said, they sounded lawless and dangerous. Yet they had fought with the Allies against the Nazis. It was too confusing and he was too exhausted to figure it out.

Next morning, while he was devouring the eggs Frau Strauss put in front of him, he glanced out of the window and saw a Russian officer in a brown leather jacket sitting astride a motorcycle in the empty street. Unlike the villagers, he had no reason to fear the Russians.

Running outside, he started telling the officer who he was, but before he could ask him how to get back home, the Russian took out his pistol and with a peremptory gesture motioned for him to get on the motorcycle. They roared off at breakneck speed with Tom gripping the seat.

After a hair-raising ride that lasted about half an hour, they stopped at a Russian encampment. Inside a large tent, an officer in a belted khaki jacket with epaulettes sat with his black-booted legs stretched out under a roughly hewn oak table.

He regarded Tom with a disdainful expression and cut short his explanations.

'*Dokumienty*,' he barked. 'Papers.'

Uncertain which language to use, from habit Tom started speaking in German. 'I don't have any papers. I'm English and I was a prisoner'.

The officer dismissed his explanations with an impatient gesture. 'You talk German,' he said. 'You not British. You German.'

Tom's heart was knocking against his ribs. 'I'm not,' he said in English. 'I'm from Jersey.' He gestured at his ragged prison uniform. 'I've been in Nazi jails.'

Giving him a disbelieving look, the officer spoke to two offsiders who addressed him as Captain Rostov. They all looked at Tom with suspicious eyes. It was obvious they had no idea where Jersey was.

'Jersey in the Channel Islands,' Tom said.

That didn't help. 'You German spy,' Captain Rostov shouted and the finality in his voice made Tom's blood run cold. During his trial, German judges had charged him with being a British spy. And now that he was free, the Russians, who were supposed to be his allies, were accusing him of being a German spy. But he didn't have the luxury of dwelling on the surreal nature of the situation. From what Frau Strauss had said, that accusation could have him shot.

'So where you learn German?' the captain demanded. When Tom insisted that he learned it at school, the Russian shouted, 'Nyet! Not school. You collaborate with Nazis in prison. You spy.'

Furious, Tom yelled back, 'That's a lie. You're supposed to be our allies but you're no better than the Gestapo!'

At this, the captain leaped up from his desk and pointed his pistol at him. He was restrained by his lieutenant, the motorcycle rider in the leather jacket.

In desperation, Tom played his last card. Stripping off all his clothes with feverish hands, he displayed his emaciated body to the startled Russians. 'German prison,' he kept repeating.

The captain stopped yelling, and they all stared at Tom. Motioning for him to get dressed, the captain sent an orderly to the field kitchen to fetch some food.

The greasy soup with pieces of beetroot and cabbage floating in it made Tom nauseous, but as he spooned it into his mouth, he congratulated himself on finally convincing the officers that he wasn't a spy.

As he ate, it struck him that without an ID, he'd be in danger whenever he encountered Russian officers, who seemed paranoid about espionage.

'Could you please issue me with a document so I can prove I'm a British prisoner of war just released from a German prison?' he asked.

Tearing a scrap of headed paper from a notepad, Captain Rostov scrawled something and handed it to him.

'Go back to village and stay. I move unit there tomorrow and talk to you again,' he said.

Clutching his document, Tom climbed onto the lieutenant's motorcycle and they roared down country roads until they reached the village. Tom was about to dismount when the lieutenant spoke to him in German.

'If I were you, I wouldn't hang around. Captain Rostov doesn't believe a word you said. He thinks your German is too good for an Englishman and he'll probably have you tried for espionage. If you're lucky, you'll end up in Siberia.'

Tom couldn't believe his ears. He'd been fooled, and without the lieutenant's warning, he might have ended up in a Soviet labour camp or dead. He had never imagined that the freedom he had longed for could be so fraught with danger.

He had to get away from there as soon as possible. As soon as he dismounted from the motorcycle, he started walking towards the town where Polish troops were stationed.

He hadn't walked very far when a farmer in a horse-drawn cart loaded with turnips offered to take him there. As they bumped along on a road streaming with refugees, cars, trucks and buses, all heading east, Tom examined the paper Captain Rostov had given him. It didn't look official, and for all he knew, it might describe him as a spy who should be detained. He would have to avoid Russian checkpoints and stop speaking German.

In the small Silesian town of Legnica, he found the Polish military office. Hearing his story, the officers slapped him on the back, produced a bottle of vodka, and toasted Britain and Churchill. As they had never heard of Jersey, he drew them a map which inspired another toast, one to the Channel Islands. They explained that to reach England he would have to travel to Cottbus by train, and gave him a railway pass.

Once inside the train compartment, dressed in the civilian clothes the Polish officers had given him, Tom breathed out. He was finally on his way home. But as soon as he stepped outside the railway station at Cottbus, he saw Russian soldiers in the street and ducked into the doorway of a tailor's shop.

While pretending to study the jacket in the window he overheard the tailor and his customer talking about a prisoner exchange point in the neighbouring town.

Avoiding the main highways that were choked with Russian army trucks going one way, and German buses and cars heading in the opposite direction, Tom walked for most of the day on side roads until he reached the town.

The exchange point was the bridge over the river. Crouching in the bushes to avoid being seen, Tom tried to figure out what was going on. The Russian authorities were located at one end of the bridge and the Americans at the other. The problem was that to reach the American side, he would have to get past the Russian checkpoint, which was set up in front of the official Russian tent.

Observing the exchange procedure, Tom saw American trucks on the other side of the river disgorging Soviet prisoners of war who marched in formation across the bridge. They stood at attention while the Soviet military band played a stirring tune that Tom assumed was their national anthem. While this was playing, the Russian and American guards on either side of the bridge presented arms. This procedure was repeated when British and American soldiers were exchanged.

Tom assessed his chances of getting across. They weren't good. He didn't want to risk showing the Russians a slip of paper that might incriminate him. If only he could get past the tent …

Before he had formulated a plan, he was on his feet, sprinting the way he used to race during school athletic carnivals, with only one thing on his mind, the finishing line. Somewhere behind him he heard Russian voices yelling for him to stop but he quickened his pace. A shot rang out but he kept running. Only a few more yards to the bridge. Only a couple of feet. He waved Captain Rostov's scribbles at the startled sentry, mumbled a few words in what he thought was Russian and didn't stop until he fell into the arms of the British sentry at the other end, and gasped, 'I'm Tom Gaskell from Jersey.'

'Bloody hell, he's one of ours!' were the last words he heard before he collapsed on the ground.

CHAPTER THIRTY-SIX

Tom

St Helier, June 1945

The crowd jostling for a vantage point in Royal Square swept Tom along with it. Surrounded by a sea of red, white and blue flags, he was so tightly wedged against people waving Union Jacks that if he'd needed to blow his nose, he wouldn't have been able to raise his arm.

Suddenly a mighty roar rose from the crowd. People surged forward, shouting themselves hoarse, and men threw their hats in the air. A woman's penetrating voice rang out singing the national anthem with such fervour that people joined in, their eyes welling with emotion.

Craning forward, Tom caught a glimpse of the couple who had inspired this flood of patriotism. A thin man in a navy uniform acknowledged the crowd's enthusiasm with a formal wave, while his beaming wife appeared to relish the adulation of the crowd. Dressed in a hat that reminded Tom of a flying saucer, with a fluffy fur stole around her plump shoulders, the Queen looked disappointingly average. Quite motherly.

That certainly wasn't the way he would describe his own mother, and the prospect of finally coming face to face with Alma twisted his intestines into knots.

He had arrived in St Helier that morning, rage in his heart and revenge on his mind. It was a month since liberation. It had taken more than a month to make his tortuous way from the Polish–German border, through villages, past Russian checkpoints, to England, and finally to Jersey. For a fleeting moment, he fantasised that the celebratory atmosphere in town was to welcome him. But of course no-one knew he had come home.

While people around him sang 'God Save the King', he brooded about his journey home. Victory confused him. How come their allies had turned into enemies? He looked at the people cheering and waving and his blood boiled. They had already forgotten that the British government had washed its hypocritical hands of the Channel Islands and left them to the tender mercies of the Germans.

Alone among the thousands lining the road, he wasn't cheering or waving a Union Jack. He had never imagined that coming home would be such a let-down. For over two years, he had longed for the moment when he would set foot in his homeland again. But now that the moment had arrived, he felt numb and bewildered. Freedom seemed to have sneaked up on him before he was ready.

It was as if the essence of Tom Gaskell, the person he had once been, had been sucked out and spat out over the course of the war, leaving a hollow husk. As though he'd been left standing on the platform after the train had pulled out of the station. He was almost nineteen, but he felt older than Methuselah.

He saw it all clearly now. What he had really longed for was release from captivity, not a return to a place where he had such bitter memories, parents he didn't respect and a government he despised. Where he would have to face the parents of friends who had died, deaths for which he felt responsible; the mother who had betrayed him to the Germans, and the father who had become her accomplice. Where his sweetheart Milly had dumped him for a Kraut.

Looking up, he saw the Union Jack fluttering from the top of Fort Regent again. Five years before, seeing the loathsome swastika with its obscene black spider looming over the island, he had been ashamed of their surrender. Now he surveyed the Union Jack with quiet satisfaction but not the elation he had once expected.

When he looked around the crowd, he saw a few familiar faces, some neighbours from Gloucester Road, and the parents of some school friends, but they looked past him as though he were a stranger. He was disappointed until it struck him that they didn't recognise him because he no longer resembled the schoolboy they had last seen.

After the royal couple and their entourage had moved out of sight, the crowd began to disperse, leaving in their wake the sound of excited chatter and a road littered with paper flags, but Tom stood still, uncertain where to go.

He walked aimlessly through the town until he found himself at the Esplanade. He sank onto a bench and closed his eyes. He heard Frank's exuberant voice shouting *I'll race you! Last one buys ice creams!* and saw them both pedalling full pelt down the hill towards the Italian's ice-cream cart. And there was Milly, looking adoringly at her Kraut boyfriend who had just bought her an ice-cream cone. That was the last time he'd seen her but he still felt the ache of his shattered dreams. He sighed. What had led him to a place with so many painful memories?

He wondered if he'd ever find the courage to face Frank's parents. And Harry's parents. Would they ever forgive him? How could they when he couldn't forgive himself? And yet Harry had never blamed him, not even at the end, and perhaps that made it so unbearable. It struck him, sitting there staring unseeingly at the ground, that Harry had faced his death with greater equanimity than he himself was now facing his own life. Harry had died without rancour, regret or reproach. With grace. Perhaps it was easier to die than to continue living.

He didn't know how long he sat there, lost in thought. Then he sprang up. He had a score to settle. The prospect of revenge had kept him going in German camps and prisons, and it energised him now. Finally, there would be a reckoning.

He would tell his mother what he thought of her and expose her collaboration with the enemy. She was the architect of all his misery, his capture, the years of mistreatment and near-starvation, and the death of his friend.

Fired up, he started walking towards his old home. As he crossed Royal Square past the Cock and Bottle, he saw men crowding around the bar in a holiday mood, laughing as though they hadn't a care in the world.

It was as though a magic wand had erased the past five years. As though the Occupation had never existed and he alone had just woken from a nightmare no-one else had experienced.

Perhaps that's how life was. As soon as a crisis ended, people moved on, determined not to look back, as if their memories were toxic wells that had to be lidded and clamped shut before the poison contaminated their lives. But he would never forget.

His footsteps slowed when he reached the familiar corner of Gloucester Road. He stood outside his home, shocked to see it unchanged. Even the lace curtains and the crimson dahlias outside the bay window looked the same. It was like looking at a scene frozen in time.

Taking a deep breath, he raised his arm to press the key-shaped buzzer. But at that precise moment, the door opened and his father was standing there, staring at him as if trying to convince himself that what he saw was real and not a figment of his imagination.

Eventually he spoke in a hoarse whisper. 'Tom! It's really you. You're home at last, son!'

For the first time in his life, Tom saw tears in his father's eyes. There were deep lines in his cheeks and his clothes hung on him like ill-fitting hand-me-downs. Tom's impulse was to step into his father's outstretched arms, to forget everything, and to surrender to the nostalgia of childhood memories and the relief of being held, safe at last. Of finally being home. But then he remembered and stood back, stiff and accusing.

'Come in, come in, you must be exhausted. I don't know what I'm thinking, keeping you standing out here like this,'

his father was saying. 'It's just such a shock. You turning up like this out of the blue. I can't believe you're here. We were at our wits' end wondering what had happened to you.'

Tom looked around the sitting room that had once been filled with boxes, bottles and cartons of his mother's smuggled goods. The last time he'd stood in that room, his mother was dancing with one of the Kraut officers to raucous jazz music on the gramophone, while his father served glasses of schnapps to her German cronies.

'All Mum had to do was ask her friends at the Water Police where I was,' Tom retorted. He looked around. 'Where is she?'

Stanley's haggard face seemed to crumple. 'She's gone, Tom. She left me!'

'Gone where?'

His father sighed. 'Don't know. Haven't had a word from her. She always said she fancied living in France. Maybe that's where she's gone. As soon as the war ended, she packed her bags and went. Never said a word to me.'

Tom struggled to grasp the situation. No wonder she had fled Jersey. The good times were over and she had escaped retribution, but she had also cheated him of the revenge he'd dreamed of for so long.

His father was gazing at him as though he couldn't get his fill. 'I can't stop looking at you to make sure you're really here,' he said.

Tom studied his father. 'What I want to know is why you didn't stop her from betraying me to the Krauts.'

Stanley Gaskell looked down at his hands and sighed loudly. 'Do you really want to go over that terrible night right now? There's not a day I don't think about it. Let's just sit and talk, son. Tell me what happened to you. Tell me everything. We didn't even know if you were alive. But first let me make you a cup of tea.'

While his father bustled about in the kitchen, Tom sat on the edge of his chair, tapping his foot on the patterned Axminster carpet as his eyes darted around the room.

He hadn't anticipated how painful this encounter would be, how conflicted he would feel seeing his father again. How difficult it would be to balance his anger and contempt with the unexpected surge of emotion he felt when he looked at his father's worn face.

Stanley was back with the teapot. After pouring the tea with hands that shook, he sat back with an expectant expression, but Tom remained silent.

Even if he'd been capable of giving an account of his harrowing years of captivity, he wasn't willing to do it. Maybe he never would.

Uncomfortable with the silence that stretched between them, Stanley said, 'You must have gone through a tough time over there, but things haven't been easy for us here either. We didn't have any deliveries from the mainland for several weeks ...'

He was about to continue but when he saw the look on Tom's face, he stopped talking.

Tom struggled to suppress the sarcastic comment that rose to his lips. Instead, he repeated his question.

'Why didn't you stop her? You must have known what would happen if the Krauts caught me.'

Stanley avoided his eyes. 'You know what your mother's like once she makes up her mind about something. I couldn't talk her out of it.'

Tom decided to ask the question that had tormented him for the past three years.

'How come she knew where we were? We didn't tell anyone.'

'Your friend's father, George Arundel, told us.'

Tom stared at him. How could Harry's father have known about their plan?

'He came round that evening to see us,' his father was saying. 'In a panic, he was. Harry hadn't come home, and he was terrified because he suspected Harry was planning to escape and thought we might know something about it, seeing you two were such good friends.'

Tom was shaking his head. None of this made any sense.

'As soon as George Arundel left, your mother said she wouldn't put it past you to concoct some crazy plan, and we had to tell the Water Police straightaway, before you got away. She said if you escaped we'd be accused of helping you, and we'd probably be arrested.'

'Trust her to think about herself,' Tom said.

Stanley shifted in his chair and cleared his throat. 'When your mother came home that night, she told me the Water Police officers had promised to give you a good telling off and bring you back. She couldn't have known that the military police would turn up and arrest you.'

'But you didn't try to stop her.'

'I told her not to go, but she wouldn't listen.'

'You've never stood up to her,' Tom burst out. 'You let her carry on an illegal smuggling business that made her the talk of the town. You watched her carrying on with those officers, I saw you. You even served them drinks while they were buzzing around her like bees around a honey pot. And you used to lecture me about British courage and honour! You were one of the reasons I was desperate to get away, because I was so disgusted with you.'

He ran out of breath and stopped, astonished at his own audacity. He hadn't intended to say any of this but it had just poured out of him, as if a dam wall had burst and the mud that had accumulated over the past five years had gushed out. He was surprised at the power it gave him. Their roles had become reversed and this time he was the one in control.

Slumped in the armchair, his father dropped his head. He looked beaten, and Tom felt almost sorry for him.

'Tom, don't be so hard on her,' Stanley began. 'I do think that in her own way, she was trying to protect you.'

Tom didn't wait to hear any more. He said a curt goodbye and walked out, slamming the door behind him.

Half an hour later, he was standing in front of Harry's house. He took a deep breath and tried to summon the courage to face his friend's parents. Mrs Arundel opened the door. For a moment she looked at him blankly, and then she threw her arms around him and sobbed loud gulping sobs. While they stood there, Mr Arundel appeared.

'Why it's Tom!' he exclaimed. 'Come in, come in, my boy.'

Tom sat down, wondering how to begin. This was worse than he had imagined. Their eyes were glued to his face and the only sound in the room was Mrs Arundel's sobbing. There was no colour in their faces and no light in their eyes, as if the marrow had been sucked out of their bones.

Mr Arundel was shaking his head. 'It's a terrible thing when a son dies before his father. It's unnatural, like a river flowing backwards.'

Tom was clasping and unclasping his hands. 'I don't know what to say. I'm so sorry about everything,' he began. 'It should have been Harry that came back, not me. It was all my fault.'

The silence that followed seemed interminable. With a sigh, Mr Arundel put his arm around his shoulders. 'Don't blame yourself, son,' he said. 'You weren't to know what would happen. If anyone is to blame, I am.'

Tom looked up, astonished.

'If I hadn't gone round to your parents' place that night, you probably wouldn't have been caught.'

'But how did you know where we were? We didn't tell anyone.'

Mr Arundel sighed again. 'Harry had said he was going fishing with you and the other lad, but I had a strange feeling about it. A presentiment, you might call it. You see, a few days before, when Mrs Arundel was doing a spring clean, she found a map under Harry's mattress and showed me. I didn't think about it at the time and told her to put it back, but when he didn't come home that night I looked for it. It was gone. That made me suspicious. It wasn't like him to be secretive, you see. So when I thought back, I realised it was a navigation chart and it showed a route from Green Bay to England and that's when I got very worried.'

Tom remembered the discussion the three of them had had about where to hide Captain Beaumont's chart. He hadn't wanted it at home in case his mother's sharp eyes found it, and Frank shared a room with his nosy little brother, so that only left Harry. 'It'll be safe at my place,' he'd said. 'No-one will look under my mattress.'

So that's how they had known. 'But what made you go to see my parents?'

George Arundel exchanged glances with his wife before replying.

'We knew your mother had friends in the Water Police, and if anyone could persuade them to look for you boys and bring you back, she could. Of course none of us envisaged that the military police would arrest you. I will never forgive myself.'

'Harry wouldn't want you to feel like that,' Tom said, struggling to steady his voice. 'He was brave to the end. He died of TB and was buried in the cemetery at Weissburg. He wanted to be buried in St Mark's cemetery, and I promised to bring his body back to Jersey one day.'

The lump in Tom's throat was so huge that he couldn't say another word. The only sound in the room was Mrs Arundel's heartbroken sobbing. Mr Arundel held his head in his hands and, too distressed to stay there any longer, Tom rose and let himself out. He didn't think either of them had noticed that he'd left.

Relieved to be outside, he wandered around until he reached a small park on a hill overlooking the coast. Exhausted, he sank down on the grass. So many emotions in such a short time. Relief, sorrow, regret. So much to process. The sun shining through the oak trees varnished the leaves with light and revealed flashes of scarlet as robins hopped from branch to branch. On the ground, bright-eyed squirrels darted among flowerbeds of petunias, asters and snapdragons. In the distance, the foaming waves frilled at the base of Elizabeth Castle, which seemed to float in the water. Further along the coast, just out of sight, was the treacherous bay from which they had launched their disastrous escape.

He closed his eyes, felt the sun on his face and breathed in the green scent of grass and the subtle perfume of the flowers, and listened to the mesmerising buzz of bees.

He felt his muscles softening. He had almost forgotten how blue and innocent the sky was, forgotten the pleasure of living without terror. He wondered how long it would take him to get into the rhythm of life in peacetime.

He thought about Harry, but this time it was without guilt. He felt he had been absolved by Mr Arundel. Perhaps forgiveness was the key after all.

On a hot Sunday afternoon in August, Tom watched people strolling past his bench on the Esplanade. Children tugged their parents' arms to lead them to the ice-cream vendor, couples held hands, and friends chatted. Tom wondered how these people had spent the war years and what secrets were concealed behind their smiles. Perhaps, like him, they were trying to put the past behind them.

Like Mr Blampied, his boss at the insurance company where he was working as a clerk. From what people had intimated, it sounded as if Mr Blampied had been something of a wartime hero, but when Tom had broached the subject, he had laughed and said that he'd done nothing special, that they'd all had their fair share of excitement one way and another.

Reflecting on the war years, Tom thought about his mother, who had cheated him of his revenge, and he recalled the words of his fellow prisoner Pierre: *Revenge is the weapon of the weak.*

Tom hadn't believed him then, probably because he'd been powerless at the time. In fact, it had been the desire for revenge that had sustained him in the camps. But now, recalling the atmosphere of jubilation during the royal visit, and watching the happy crowd around him, he envied their ability to enjoy life.

If only he could let go of his anger. He knew that even if his mother was still here, she would refuse to take responsibility for her betrayal, and no-one in authority would want to delve into wartime grievances. He could envisage years of fruitless accusations that wouldn't lead anywhere, and would only embitter him more.

Perhaps what his father had said was true, that she hadn't expected him to be arrested, but he didn't think he would ever forgive her. His thoughts turned to Harry, as they often did whenever he grappled with a moral conundrum.

Harry had accepted a tragic situation that he was powerless to change, and for the first time it struck Tom that acceptance required more strength than vengeance. That perhaps the best revenge was letting go of the past, moving forward, and making the most of your life.

After a week spent inside the insurance office poring over ledgers and files, it was good to feel the sun on his face and fill his lungs with fresh air. He was thinking of going to the Grand Hotel for a lager when something caught his eye.

At the other end of the Esplanade, a young woman in a faded blue gingham dress with a white peter pan collar was pushing a small perambulator. He sat forward. There was something familiar about that dress and the silvery blonde hair that waved down to her shoulders.

She was still some distance away when she bent over to give the baby a rattle, straightened up, and their eyes met.

It was Milly.

A hammer inside his chest was threatening to smash his ribs. He had never experienced such turmoil, such a rush of conflicting emotions all at once. Shock, anger, anxiety, rancour and bitterness, but also wild excitement.

He remembered that dress. She had worn it the day they had gone to the cinema at the Forum. At that moment, his resolve to leave the past behind evaporated. He would tell her what he thought of her. Or, better still, pretend he didn't know her.

But there she was, standing right in front of him, looking at him with a wistful expression.

'Tom? I'm so glad to see you.'

'Really?' His voice was a splinter of ice. 'You weren't glad to see me last time we met.'

She sat down beside him on the bench and when she turned her lovely face towards him, he saw the sadness in her eyes.

Just then the baby began to whimper and she lifted it from the carriage and bounced it on her knee. His eyes slid to her ring finger. It was bare.

'Don't be angry with me, Tom,' she said. 'That was over two years ago and we've all been through so much since then.'

'Have we? Tell me what terrible things you've been through with your Kraut boyfriend protecting you while I've been in prison camps all over Germany.'

He had meant to sound cool and distant and not to indulge in self-pity, but seeing her had whipped up his anger.

She continued sitting there, sad but silent, rocking the baby. He stole another look at her ring finger and curiosity got the better of him.

'So what happened to your Kraut? I suppose he's in a prisoner-of-war camp?' He tried to sound casual but knew he sounded vindictive.

She swallowed and looked straight ahead without answering. Then in a voice that was so soft that he had to sit forward to hear her, she told him about Konrad's desertion from the army and his arrest and execution.

Tears slid down her cheeks as she described the last time she saw him from her window as he was being driven to his execution on the back of a German army truck, with his coffin beside him.

As she spoke, Tom could visualise that terrible scene. He couldn't think of anything to say that wouldn't sound trite and superficial.

'They sentenced me to death as well, but I was reprieved,' she said after a long pause. 'Dr Jackson spoke to the Bailiff and he persuaded the Germans to release me.'

'At least the Bailiff interceded for someone,' Tom said. He couldn't keep the bitterness out of his tone.

She was looking down at her hands. 'It was really thanks to Dr Jackson. But at that point I didn't care if I lived or died. Then I discovered I did have a reason to go on living. I was pregnant.'

Part of him wanted to say it served her right, but he stifled his malicious thought. All he wanted to do was pull her towards him, place his arms around her and comfort her. The bench suddenly felt so hard that he couldn't sit still, he didn't know what to do with his arms and the words caught in his throat.

'So you've had a baby to look after all by yourself. A German's baby, too. That can't be easy.'

The baby was gurgling and Milly wrapped the pink bunny rug more firmly around it before putting it back in the baby carriage, which she rocked gently with one hand.

'You do whatever you have to. My mum wanted me to have her adopted but I couldn't give her away. The neighbours whisper and glare whenever they see me, as if I'm some sort of criminal, but I suppose they'll get over it eventually.' Then she added, 'Did you know I was adopted?'

He shook his head.

'Having a baby made me realise how hard it must have been for my real mother to give me away. I've decided that when things settle down, I'm going to try and find her. There's a place called L'Abbaye where they used to look after unmarried mothers. They might still have records of babies given up for adoption. I just hope that when I find her, she'll want to meet me.'

Tom was looking at her as if seeing her for the first time. How strong she was. It seemed that life tested everyone, one way or another, and not only in times of war. His war had ended, but the responsibility she had taken on would never end.

He edged closer and tentatively took her hand. He had forgotten how small, how soft it was. Even that light touch aroused an involuntary frisson, like a slight electric current, and he glanced at her to see if she felt it as well.

She didn't speak or return his gaze. Perhaps she was offended. He'd probably been insensitive and should have held back. He wondered what to say, but the baby started crying and Milly got up and smoothed down her dress.

'I'd better get back,' she said.

Then she smiled at him, the dimpled smile that had captivated him when he first saw her. 'I'm really glad you came back, Tom.'

As he watched her walk away, pushing the perambulator, the thought of the two of them making their way alone in a hostile world choked him up.

At that charged moment he knew that his heart had cracked open and let them both in.

CHAPTER THIRTY-SEVEN

Xanthe

St Helier, Liberation Day, May 2019

All around her, the air vibrates with whistling, and a flash of olive and tangerine cuts across the sky. Lorikeets! A moment later, she hears the cackling laugh of kookaburras.

Xanthe wakes up, startled. The bird sounds in her dream belong to Sydney but when she turns in bed, she sees Daniel lying beside her. She is still in Jersey. But not for long. She sighs and turns over. Ever since deciding to use her own experiences to help other interns, she has been on a high, but now that it's almost time to put her plan into action, she is assailed by doubts.

She sighs again, louder this time, and Daniel stirs.

'Are you okay?' he mumbles, half asleep. He reaches for her but she avoids his outstretched arm, sits up, hugs her knees, and stares moodily into space.

'I'm apprehensive about going home. I was so excited about agitating for an inquiry and setting up a counselling service for interns, but now I've got cold feet,' she says. 'I'm a doctor. What do I know about advocacy?'

Wide awake now, he pulls her in and puts his arm around her.

'It's a great idea, Xan. Don't be put off just because it's something you've never done before. You know what they say, when you let go of what you are, you might discover what you can be.'

Her eyes widen and suddenly she is laughing. She's laughing so much that her stomach hurts and she is wheezing while he is looking at her, clearly perplexed.

'I'm sorry, but that just cracked me up. Where on earth did you hear that? It sounds like one of those pseudo-philosophical messages they print on greeting cards.'

She stops in case he is offended but he is surveying her with an indulgent smile.

'That pseudo-philosopher was Lao-tse, who wrote it about two thousand years ago, and I actually think there's a lot of truth in it. Anyway, it cheered you up no end.'

That's one of the things she loves about him, that he doesn't take things personally. His ego doesn't intrude. She loves that he sees her in a way no-one has ever seen her before, the way she has always longed to be seen, without judgement, criticism or expectations. She has always slotted into the expectations of others or fallen short of their approval. She was the daughter expected to follow her family tradition, the student expected to excel in exams, the intern expected to know all the answers, the lover expected to fulfil her partners' erotic fantasies. But to Daniel she is Xanthe, and that is enough for him.

He holds her against him, caressing her with long, slow strokes, and aroused by his touch, the heat of his naked body, and the unmistakeable intensity of his gaze, she feels a quiver between her legs.

She is pulling off her T-shirt when she notices the time on the alarm clock and leaps out of bed with a shout of dismay.

'Shit! He'll be here soon!'

It's Liberation Day, and Bob Blampied is due to pick them up for the commemoration ceremony. 'This is St Helier's big day,' he'd said. 'Every man and his dog will be there.'

Twenty minutes later they rush outside. Daniel is still buttoning his white Oxford shirt, and she is fumbling with a rubber band to draw her hair into a ponytail. Bob is already waiting in his Triumph and although a strong breeze is blowing on this bright May morning, tossing the boughs on the oak and chestnut trees, he has the hood down as usual.

Instead of his peaked cap, blue jeans and maroon cardigan, he is wearing a white shirt, red and white striped tie, and a well-worn grey suit, and she realises that for him this is not just a holiday. It's a meaningful occasion.

He waves them inside the car and guns the engine even before they've fastened their seatbelts. As they speed along the streets of St Helier, she notices the festive atmosphere in town. Windows are festooned with bunting, banners and flags, and the roads are crammed with people heading for the town centre.

Bob parks the car in a side street and they join the throng filling the roadway. In Liberation Square, a huge Union

Jack is hanging over the balcony of the Pomme d'Or, with smaller flags draped along the railing.

Nudging her arm, Bob points to the flag. 'That takes me back to the scene in 1945 as if it was yesterday. The HMS *Beagle* had just docked in the harbour and two naval officers came ashore and hoisted the Union Jack first on top of the harbourmaster's building, and then here, because the Pomme d'Or was the headquarters of the German Water Police. You can't imagine how thrilling it was to see our rightful flag there again after five long years.'

As they take their seats on the white chairs that have been set up in the centre of the square, a woman with wispy grey hair and a tartan shawl next to Xanthe leans towards her.

'I was two years old when the Tommies landed that day,' she says and her wrinkled face lights up at the memory. 'My dad picked me up and placed me in a Tommy's arms. It didn't half give the poor lad a shock! My dad said it was a historic moment and I should never forget it. And I haven't. I come here every year. Wouldn't miss it for quids.'

In the distance, a military band is playing rousing marches. Then the music stops, people fall silent, and all eyes turn to the far end of the square where a solemn procession is advancing towards the Pomme d'Or.

Leading the parade is an official bearing the Royal Mace. 'The Mace symbolises our connection with the Crown,' Bob whispers. 'The officials behind it are the States members and our judges, the Jurats.'

Xanthe cranes forward. Walking at the head of the officials, wearing a scarlet robe trimmed with ermine and hung with medals, is Edward de Courcy. He enters the Pomme d'Or and reappears a few moments later on the hotel's balcony.

The choir conductor, a young woman in a high-necked white blouse under a navy blazer, raises her baton and schoolchildren in burgundy uniforms rise and start singing patriotic songs. Then everyone joins in what sounds like an anthem. Xanthe can't catch the Jèrriais words but she senses their heartfelt intensity.

In a voice hoarse with emotion, Bob says, 'That's called "My Beautiful Jersey".'

A hush falls over the crowd as the Bailiff picks up the microphone and begins to address the crowd. Xanthe hopes his speech won't be too long and boring.

'We have gathered here on this special day, as we do every year on May 9, to commemorate the courage and endurance of those who lived through the Occupation, five dark years that tested everyone's strength to the limit and should never be forgotten,' he begins.

'We are fortunate that still among us are some men and women who lived through those years. By sharing their memories with us, they ensure that younger generations won't forget the hardship and oppression the people of Jersey suffered during the war. At this point I'd like to pay a special tribute to those who, at enormous risk to their own lives, sheltered slave labourers who escaped from horrific conditions.'

His searching glance rests on Bob, who is looking down at his large hands. Xanthe knows that he is embarrassed by praise for his wartime activities.

'We are fortunate to live in freedom on this blessed island,' the Bailiff continues. 'This is a day for celebration, not recrimination. But I would be derelict in my obligation to the entire community, and indeed to history, if I were to ignore one group of residents who sadly did not receive the protection they deserved.'

Xanthe sits up. The atmosphere is palpitating with tension as people turn to their neighbours and a murmur runs through the crowd. She looks questioningly at Daniel, who raises his eyebrows and whispers, 'I wonder where he's going with that.'

His question is answered a moment later. 'During the Occupation, our Jewish neighbours were identified, registered, and dispossessed of their businesses, their belongings, their homes and their liberty,' the Bailiff says. 'They lived in constant fear. Some were unable to endure the terror and killed themselves. Others were deported to German concentration camps where they were killed.

'For many years, we have taken the easy way out and blamed the Germans. After all, they were the occupiers, the perpetrators. But perhaps the time has come to look history squarely in the eye and confront an uncomfortable truth.'

The Bailiff pauses, looks around, and continues. 'It has been easy to justify inaction on the grounds of scale. After all, there were so few of them. Why would anyone stick their necks out and antagonise the occupier on behalf of such a small group? But when did the size of an oppressed group ever provide a morally cogent reason for not only abandoning them to their fate, but for facilitating that process?

'We know that the lawyers and Jersey officials were just obeying the law when they passed the names of their Jewish clients to the Germans, together with a list of their assets. We all know what Charles Dickens said about the law, but in this case the law wasn't just an ass. It was evil, immoral and racist, and sadly, our officials complied with it unquestioningly.'

His tone, which had been quiet and measured, has grown louder, and his words ring out over the square with the force of a prophet addressing his people.

Xanthe is squeezing Daniel's hand so hard that hers has become numb. All around her, people seem frozen. No-one moves or makes a sound. From their expressions, she sees that most of them are stunned and incredulous. As she is. This is not what they had come to hear and they are indignant but spellbound at the same time.

'Can you believe this?' she whispers. Without replying, Daniel squeezes back.

'In life, we learn from failure, not success,' the Bailiff says. 'And from what took place here, we can see what happens when an evil law, unchallenged, becomes normality. But, you might ask, what could they have done? Perhaps not much. But they could have hesitated, challenged, objected, delayed, or even refused to hand over lists of their Jewish neighbours. It might not have affected the outcome, but it would have been a stand for morality.'

He pauses, looks around the crowd, and his eyes rest briefly on Daniel. 'I'd like to conclude by making an apology to the Jersey Jewish community and the descendants of those who suffered or perished during the Occupation, on account of our government's failure to protect them.'

As soon as the Bailiff ends his address, Daniel is on his feet, clapping loudly. So are Xanthe and Bob. A scattering of applause resounds in the square, but there is an angry undercurrent, and heated discussions and arguments break out.

'Well I never,' the man in front of Bob is saying to his neighbour. 'My parents lived through the Occupation and they always said how people helped each other. Of course there were Jerrybags and an informer or two, but they never mentioned no Jews. So why make all this fuss now?'

The breeze has intensified, and the flags make a sharp slapping sound. The elderly woman beside Xanthe pulls her tartan shawl closer around her bony shoulders.

'Well, we've never had a Liberation Day address like that one,' she says, her eyes bright at the prospect of controversy. 'He's really put the cat among the pigeons now!'

'What do you think about what he said?' Xanthe asks.

'Well, when you've lived as long as I have, dearie, you know that people are capable of everything, good and bad. Myths are all very well, but it's important to let the truth come out, isn't it? One of my neighbours hid a Jewish woman in his attic and got some award from Jerusalem, I think it was, but most people just closed their eyes to what was happening. Reckoned later they didn't know anything about it.'

Xanthe turns to Bob, who is smoothing down his windswept white hair. He looks euphoric. 'I never thought he had it in him. He has started a conversation we've never had before.'

Xanthe is still squeezing Daniel's hand. 'I think you've just had your thesis validated in public. Did you have any idea he'd come up with this?'

'Not the slightest. The last thing I heard him say on the subject was *You weren't here.*'

As they walk away from the square, Bob stops to talk to a tall man with iron grey hair who is standing at the back of the crowd.

As Xanthe watches from a distance, she recognises his intense expression, and the unforgiving cast of his craggy features. It's the man she saw in the hotel bar soon after she arrived in St Helier, who refused to talk to a reporter and stomped out.

'I thought it was time,' she hears him saying.

Bob shakes his hand, nods, and rejoins her and Daniel.

'That was Tom Gaskell,' he says. 'He's been living overseas, but came back this year to visit the graves of two friends in St Mark's cemetery. After the war he married a local lass who'd had a baby with a German soldier.'

Xanthe can hardly contain her excitement. She turns to look at Tom who has already disappeared in the crowd. So he was the man she had read about in Hugh's journal, who had tried to escape from Jersey as a boy. And after the war, he had been big-hearted enough to marry one of the girls who had danced with the enemy who happened to be related to her ... It was too much to take in.

She turns to Bob. 'Do you know what happened to his wife?'

But before he can reply, a couple stop to ask him what he thinks about the Bailiff's speech, and not wanting to intrude on their conversation, Xanthe and Daniel walk on, past carousels, jumping castles, and stalls selling pasties, Jersey hotpot and scones. When they reach a quiet street, she stops and looks at Daniel.

'I can't believe everything that's happened. You and I came to this place to connect with distant relatives – I wasn't even that interested in finding mine – and I discovered all these amazing connections. And we've found each other.'

He is smiling. 'The wonderful, unfathomable connectedness of life.'

'Another gift from the universe?'

In reply he throws his arms around her and they stand locked together, oblivious to the crowd, the noise and the activity all around them. She looks up and as he gazes into her eyes she feels he is looking straight into her soul.

CHAPTER THIRTY-EIGHT

Xanthe

St Helier, Evening, Liberation Day, May 2019

The day is drawing to a close, and standing by the French windows Xanthe is mesmerised by the setting sun, which paints the sky in swirls of rose and apricot. It's her last evening in St Helier, and she should pack but she can't settle down and wanders from room to room, as if trying to imprint every detail of this house on her memory.

Upstairs, in the bedroom, her gaze falls on Hugh's journal. 'Shit!' she says aloud. She hasn't decided what to do with it. When she started reading it, she planned to donate it to the Jersey Historical Association, but its increasingly intimate details made her hesitate. She picks up the journal and wonders what Hugh would want to do. Perhaps she should just replace it at the back of the chimney where she found it.

Her thoughts turn to Daniel and she fights the despair that threatens to overwhelm her. She sinks onto the bed and closes her eyes, but the future looms ahead like a black question mark. When she looks out of the window again, the sun has almost set and against the darkening sky, the boughs of the oak and chestnut trees are tossing violently in the wind like an unsettling Van Gogh landscape.

The doorbell rings, and as she runs downstairs, her heart is pounding. Perhaps it's Daniel after all, even though they had agreed not to prolong their painful goodbyes.

The smile is still on her face when she opens the door. But standing there is a young man she has never seen before, and she can't conceal her disappointment.

'I'm sorry to disturb you, perhaps this isn't a good time,' he says. 'Can I come back in the morning?'

'I won't be here tomorrow. What did you want to see me about?'

'Actually, it was the house I wanted to see.'

'Are you going to rent it?'

He shakes his head. 'I should introduce myself. I'm Anthony Jackson. This house once belonged to my grandfather Hugh Jackson.'

Xanthe stares at him. When she snaps out of her trance, she can't stop talking.

'Do come in, feel free to look around. It's rather untidy because I'm leaving in the morning. Would you like to sit down? Can I make you a cup of tea? Or something stronger, perhaps? I think there's vodka in the cabinet. Do you know anything about this house?'

Gazing at this tall young man in blue jeans, check shirt and navy sneakers, she tries to grasp the fact that he is the grandson of the man whose intimate thoughts she has read and to whom she feels so connected.

'Tea would be great, if that's okay,' he says. With his direct gaze and engaging manner, it feels as if she is looking at Hugh Jackson as a young man. She ushers him into the sitting room and goes into the kitchen to collect her thoughts. Her hands shake so much that she spills the sugar and the mugs clatter.

When she comes back with the tea, he is standing in front of the French windows gazing at the garden.

'Did you know your grandfather?'

'Unfortunately not. I don't know much about him really. According to my father, there was a rift in the family just before he was born and he and my grandmother didn't have any contact with him. Sad, isn't it?'

She nods, and studies him, wondering what she should tell. And what she shouldn't. Knowing so much more about his family than he does gives her power that she must temper with tact.

'So how did you know he lived here?'

He has flopped into an armchair, and with his legs stretched out, he looks as if he is at home, which of course he is.

'When my father died, the probate listed a house in Ireland, and this one. I'm passionate about history – I'm actually reading history at Oxford – so I thought I'd come and look around, to connect with my ancestor and see where he – and the family – originated.'

She listens, struck by the similarity of their quest. 'Do you know what became of him?' she asks.

'While my grandmother was alive, she never mentioned him except to say that he had abandoned her and my father and had never contacted them.'

Xanthe seethes at the injustice of that. He should know the truth, but not from her, not now.

'And afterwards? Did your father ever meet him?'

Anthony takes another sip of tea and places his mug on the side table. 'I think my grandfather tried to get in touch with him. He was living in Ireland with some woman but I don't know her name. He sent letters to my father with some landscapes he'd painted. I still have them. He was quite talented.'

Xanthe sits forward, anxious not to miss a word. This is a part of Hugh's life she knows nothing about.

'Did your father reply?'

'Not while my grandmother was alive, but by the time he wrote back, it was too late. Shortly afterwards my father got a letter from a solicitor in Dublin to let him know that his father had died, leaving everything to him. Including this house. My father had it renovated before he died. That was two years ago.'

'So your grandfather didn't abandon him after all,' Xanthe can't resist saying.

Anthony nods. 'I suppose not. I think they would have got on very well. My father was a doctor too.' He turns to Xanthe. 'What about you? How did you come to be staying here?'

She shrugs. 'Pure chance. That's if you believe in chance. I used to, but now I'm not so sure.'

He nods. 'That's what I think as well. Too many things happen just at the right moment for it to be accidental.'

If only you knew, she thinks.

'I'd better head off,' he says. 'I've enjoyed talking to you. If you're ever in Oxford, look me up.'

He is almost at the door when she says, 'Wait a minute. There's something I'd like to give you.'

She runs upstairs and a moment later, she hands him a thick notebook. 'I found this behind the chimney in the bedroom. Your grandfather must have put it there. I'm sure he'd want you to have it.'

He gives her a hug, and she watches him walk away with his real inheritance, his grandfather's journal.

She stands at the French windows. In the garden, moonlight silvers the leaves of the trees and dapples the ground beneath. Her gaze is drawn to the sky, which darkens, but as she watches, the wind blows the clouds apart, creating a narrow opening through which the crescent moon lights up the sky. The world is dark and bright at the same time.

Something makes her turn, and she feels Hugh's spirit in the room. Her thoughts turn to the unexpected connections she has made, and the surprising gifts she has received; the secrets the dead have whispered, and the bonds the living have revealed, and she knows now that it is all part of the bittersweet poetry of life.

AUTHOR'S NOTE

My fascination with Jersey began back in 1987. I'd heard about Jersey's cows, potatoes and tomatoes, but that's all I knew about this island in the English Channel. I was doing a great deal of travel writing at the time, and travelled there in search of something new. I didn't suspect that what I would discover would send my imagination into overdrive and ultimately result in this novel.

As I drove along sunny country lanes that delighted me with their blossoming hedgerows and granite manor houses, I stopped to admire one that was even more impressive than the others. While I was standing there, gawking, the owner came out and introduced himself. Chance – if that's what it was – had led me to Philip de Carteret, a member of the oldest and most prominent family on the island. A friendly and hospitable man, he invited me inside and had me spellbound with his family history. It turned out that his illustrious ancestors had arrived in Jersey with William the Conqueror, and over the centuries, the de Carterets had taken part in every battle and war ever since, from the Crusades to the English Civil War.

But it was on the following day, during a visit to the Jersey War Tunnels, that I became fascinated by Jersey's wartime past. As soon as I entered these long narrow tunnels, the eerie sound of spades and pickaxes striking on granite made the hairs on the back of my neck stand up. A sign explained that these sound effects replicated the sounds made by slave labourers who gouged out the tunnels using those implements during the Occupation. As I approached the entrance, I heard bombs exploding.

Slave labourers? Bombs exploding? Here, on this speck in the English Channel? As I entered the museum, I was astonished to discover that Jersey had been occupied throughout the entire war, and that the Channel Islands were the only part of the United Kingdom that had been occupied. The displays included German orders threatening severe penalties for owning wireless sets, wartime memorabilia, oral histories, and letters written by locals accusing their neighbours of possessing illegal amounts of coal. As I read those letters, I reflected on the universal power of envy and greed, and the way in which war brought out the best and worst in people. A notice issued by the German administration inviting the locals to attend a dance aroused my curiosity. So there were local girls who danced with the enemy. It occurred to me that this tiny island was really a microcosm of life. And that's when the idea of writing a novel set in Jersey began to form in my mind.

But, as they say, life is what happens when you're making other plans. In the intervening years, I wrote five other books, but my enthusiasm for writing this novel never waned.

Four years ago, I travelled to Jersey again, this time with my partner Bert. And on this visit fortune smiled on me once more. I couldn't believe my luck that our guide Bob Le Sueur, an engaging and enthusiastic ninety year old, had lived in Jersey throughout the entire Occupation. An entertaining raconteur with a beautifully modulated voice, he told amazing stories about wartime Jersey. Bob had risked his life to shelter escaped slave labourers, and his enthralling stories revived my determination to write this novel.

The time had come to start writing, but first I had to research the period of the Occupation. While browsing the internet, I came across the harrowing memoir of Peter Hassall, who had written an extraordinarily detailed and honest account of his life on Jersey as a teenager, and of his traumatic experiences in German camps. His courage throughout his ordeal inspired me, and I couldn't get him out of my mind. My character Tom Gaskell is partly based on Peter Hassall's experiences, but I have fictionalised some aspects of his story and invented others, such as his love affair with Milly.

Another unforgettable memoir was *A Doctor's Occupation* by John Lewis. As I read it, I couldn't stop marvelling at this resourceful, humane and highly principled medico who put responsibility for his patients above his personal interests, and who organised a network to help escaped slave labourers. Although I have drawn on some of his experiences and dilemmas for my character Dr Hugh Jackson, I have taken a novelist's liberty to fictionalise many incidents and relationships. John Lewis wasn't involved in the Mass Observation Project, which I have used as a vehicle for his story, but this project did exist. It was initiated by the British government inviting ordinary people to record their experiences, and resulted in many perceptive accounts of life during wartime. What's more, Dr Lewis was happily reunited with his wife after the war, and the character of Aoife and the relationship between her and Hugh Jackson is totally fictitious.

Although I have used parts of Philip de Carteret's remarkable family history when I introduced Edward de Courcy, Edward is a totally fictitious character.

ACKNOWLEDGEMENTS

First of all, I'd like to express my indebtedness to Peter Hassall for his extraordinary memoir, *Night and Fog*, which brought to life the experiences of a courageous teenage boy caught up in a web of duplicity and violence during the Occupation of Jersey. Inspired by Peter's story, I based my character Tom Gaskell on him, as a tribute to his courage and strength of character.

I am also deeply indebted to Dr John Lewis for his wartime memoir *A Doctor's Occupation*, which painted such a vivid picture of a doctor's professional dilemmas and personal conflicts during the Occupation. When torn between love and duty, he chose his responsibility to his patients above all else. So when I decided to make a Jersey doctor one of the protagonists of my novel, Dr Lewis became my model for Hugh Jackson.

I was very fortunate in having Bob le Sueur as my guide in Jersey. A larger-than-life personality and compelling raconteur who had spent the war years in Jersey, Bob generously shared his enthralling wartime stories with me. My character Bob Blampied shares his delightful personality and many of his experiences.

I am grateful to the Jersey Historical Society who sent me oral histories of residents who had lived through the Occupation and whose stories have illuminated that period of history. Thank you to Michael Ginns for sharing his interesting story.

Finally I'd like to thank Philip de Carteret, who lit the spark so long ago when he invited me into his home and told me about his ancestors.

In Australia, I'd like to thank the outstanding team at Harlequin/HarperCollins, especially Jo Mackay, who embraced this story so enthusiastically. I appreciate Annabel Blay's awesome coordinating ability, her patience and kindness. Thanks too to Kate James, whose keen eye picked up inconsistencies and extraneous commas.

I'm extremely lucky to have Linda Funnell as my editor. It's a blessing for an author to have an editor who enters into the spirit of a manuscript and really gets it, and it's been a joy to work with her. I'm delighted by her insight and sensitivity, and awed by her meticulous attention to detail, and the light touch with which she suggests modifications and elucidations to the text. Any mistakes are my own.

Selwa Anthony has been my literary agent for over twenty years and I admire her dedication and professionalism as well as her judgement. She is always receptive to my ideas, and tireless in her support and encouragement.

It's always difficult to envisage the finished novel when it consists of half-formed ideas and vague plots, but Dasia Black has always helped me see the bigger picture and comprehend the significance of the story that has enthralled me.

Finally, my gratitude to Bert, my life partner and first reader. I appreciate the way you put down whatever you're doing to read each chapter I've written. This is always such a sensitive part of the process, but your comments always encourage me. But most of all, I am more grateful than I can say, for your support, understanding, and love.

READING LIST

A Doctor's Occupation, John Lewis. Hodder & Stoughton (1983)
Nella Last's War: A Mother's Diary, Nella Last. Sphere (1983)
Night and Fog, Peter Hassall. (Unpublished)
The Day the Nazis Came, Stephen R. Matthews. John Blake (2016)
The German Occupation of Jersey, L.P. Sinel. Corgi (1969)
Jews in the Channel Islands during the German Occupation 1940–1945, Frederick E. Cohen. Jersey Heritage Trust (2000)
The Jews of the Channel Islands and the Rule of Law 1940–1945, David Fraser. Sussex Academic Press (2000)
This is Going to Hurt: Secret Diaries of a Junior Doctor, Adam Kay. Picador (2017)
Your Life in My Hands: A Junior Doctor's Story, Rachel Clarke. Bonnier (2017)
Going Under, Sonia Henry. Allen & Unwin (2020)
A Model Occupation: The Channel Island Under German Rule, 1940–1945, Madeleine Bunting. Pimlico (2004)
The Organisation Todt and the Fortress Engineers in the Channel Islands (Archive Book No.8), Michael Ginns. Channel Islands Occupation Society (1994)

Jersey: Occupation Remembered, Sonia Hillsdon. The History Press (1986)
The British Channel Islands Under German Occupation 1940–1945, Paul Sanders. Jersey Heritage Trust (2005)

The Man from Belsen, BBC program about Harold Osmond le Druillenec
Occupation, 18-part series on BBC Radio Jersey, consisting of oral histories told by those who lived through it, produced by Beth Lloyd, and available on cassette

talk about it

Let's talk about books.

Join the conversation:

facebook.com/harlequinaustralia

@harlequinaus

@harlequinaus

harpercollins.com.au/hq

If you love reading and want to know about our authors and titles, then let's talk about it.